ASSASSINS

MIKE BOND

ALSO BY
MIKE BOND

Holy War

The Last Savanna

House of Jaguar

Saving Paradise

Killing Maine

Tibetan Cross

CRITICS' PRAISE FOR MIKE BOND

"The master of the existential thriller." – *BBC*

"One of America's best thriller writers." – *Culture Buzz*

"One of the 21ˢᵗ Century's most exciting authors… spellbinding readers with a writing style that pits hard-boiled, force of nature-like characters against politically adept, staccato-paced plots." – *Washington Times*

"Bond never loses the reader's attention… working that fatalistic margin where life and death are one and the existential reality leaves one caring only to survive." – *Sunday Oregonian*

"One of the best thriller writers, in the same league as Gerald Seymour and Frederick Forsyth." – *NetGalley Reviews*

"Mike Bond is not only an acclaimed novelist… His intellect and creativity dance together on the pages, braiding fiction into deeper truths about ourselves, our nature, our government, our history and our future." – *Where Truth Meets Fiction*

"Bond touches on the vast and eerie depths that lie under the thin crust of civilization and the base instinct within man to survive." – *Nottingham Observer (UK)*

"Mike Bond's books are a national treasure." – Art Zuckerman, *WVOX*

Bond uses his gift for fiction to teach us hard truths about religion, human nature, and warfare." – *Masterful Book Reviews*

"Bond's specialty in producing thrillers that editorialize human weakness and bring to light pressing world problems." – *Yahoo Reviews*

"A highly distinctive writer." – *Liverpool Daily Post (UK)*

"Each character is gradually laid bare so that there is no good or bad, nothing written judgmentally. It is as if Mike Bond is saying, this is the story, it is as it is, these are the people, nothing more, nothing less." – *Great Book Escapes*

Holy War

"One of the best reads of 2014... A fast-paced, beautifully written, heart-breaking thriller." – *NetGalley Reviews*

"Mike Bond does it again – A gripping tale of passion, hostage-taking and war, set against a war-ravaged Beirut." – *Evening News (UK)*

"The suspense-laden novel has a never-ending sense of impending doom... The dual protagonists are laudable, not just for the missions they've undertaken, but for their emotional investments as well. But the book's most remarkable character is Rosa... She represents the story's cogent theme of peace achieved through hostile means... An unyielding tension leaves a lasting impression." – *Kirkus*

"A profound tale of war, written with grace and understanding by a novelist who thoroughly knows the subject... Literally impossible to stop reading..." – *British Armed Forces Broadcasting*

"This is a terrific book that does not favor any side in this messed up Holy War, but shows the futility fighting something which can never be won... The smells, taste, noise, dust, and fear are communicated so clearly... a brutal and honest account that sets out to describe the war in the Middle East without leading the reader in any direction, giving each side a history of their own." – *Great Book Escapes*

"A supercharged thriller set in the hell hole that was Beirut... Evokes the human tragedy behind headlines of killing, maiming, terrorism and political chicanery. A story to chill and haunt you." – *Peterborough Evening Telegraph (UK)*

"A rough, vivid window into the brutal reality of modern conflict... If you are looking to get a driver's seat look at the landscape of modern conflict, holy wars, and the Middle East then this is the perfect book to do so." – *Masterful Book Reviews*

"Intense, chilling and unforgettable." – *Suncoast Reader's Reviews*

"Eye-opening, terrifying and realistic, Mike Bond writes from the heart... I promise you, if you read *Holy War*, you will come away changed." – *Tometender Reviews*

"A pacy and convincing thriller with a deeper than usual understanding about his subject and a sure feel for his characters." – *Daily Examiner (UK)*

"A marvelous book – impossible to put down. A sense of being where few people have survived." – *London Broadcasting*

"This is a true saga that concentrates on a religious war where various factions fight for their own beliefs. Included in the thrills are terrorists, hostages, and enemies fighting in a place that simply cannot find peace... It will also provide a look into how peace can be achieved, how the innocents of the world can survive, and the passion that ignites just as fast as the exploding of a bomb." – *Suspense Magazine*

"A tangled web and an entertaining one. Action-filled thriller." – *Manchester Evening News (UK)*

"Short sharp sentences that grip from the start... A tale of fear, hatred, revenge, and desire, flicking between bloody Beirut and the lesser battles of London and Paris." – *Evening Herald (UK)*

"A novel about the horrors of war... a very authentic look at the situation which was Beirut." – *South Wales Evening Post (UK)*

"A stunning novel of love and loss, good and evil, of real people who live in our hearts after the last page is done... Unusual and profound." – *Greater London Radio*

The Last Savanna

FIRST PRIZE, 2016, *Los Angeles Book Festival:* "One of the best books yet on Africa, a stunning tale of love and loss amid a magnificent wilderness and its myriad animals, and a deadly manhunt through savage jungles, steep mountains and fierce deserts as an SAS commando tries to save the elephants, the woman he loves and the soul of Africa itself."

"Tragic and beautiful, sentimental and ruthless, *The Last Savanna* is a vast and wonderful book." – *NetGalley Reviews*

"One of the most realistic portrayals of Africa yet... expertly captures the ravenous, chaotic and frustrating battles raging across the continent... and paints a vivid picture of life in the savanna. Dynamic, heart-breaking and timely to current events, Bond's latest book is a must-read." – *Yahoo Reviews*

"Exciting, action-packed... A nightmarish vision of Africa." – *Manchester Evening News (UK)*

"The novel is sheer intensity, depicting the immense, arid land and never-ending scenes of people trekking across it... The villains are so strongly developed... but it's the volatile nature of nature itself that gives the story its greatest distinction... Will make readers sweat with its relentless pace." – *Kirkus*

"A powerful love story set in the savage jungles and deserts of East Africa." – *Daily Examiner (UK)*

"An intense and emotional story about the African wilderness... masterfully done... so many characters and themes that come into this, it's amazing... *The Last Savanna* is intense, beautiful and completely captures the powerful emotion in this story." – *RealityLapse Reviews*

"A manhunt through crocodile-infested jungle, sun-scorched savannah, and impenetrable mountains as a former SAS man tries to save the life of the woman he loves but cannot have." – *Evening Telegraph (UK)*

"A fast-paced action novel set in Kenya, Ethiopia and Somalia... an intense and personal portrayal of the beauty and violence of Africa, from the brutal slaughter of iconic wildlife species, the stunning wildness of the landscape, and the growth of terrorism." – *Out There Monthly*

"Pulsating with the sights, sounds, and dangers of wild Africa, its varied languages and peoples, the harsh warfare of the northern deserts and the hunger of denied love." – *Newton Chronicle (UK)*

"A gripping thriller." – *Liverpool Daily Post (UK)*

"You could feel the action, adventure, and thrill. The action, animals, characters were all real, the fact that the challenges faced by Africa is highlighted in the story made it more interesting to follow. Bringing us between nature and greed, men been pushed to devour nature because of their lost love. The book made me realize adventure could be found in almost everything in life." – *BookFreez*

"The imagery was so powerful and built emotions so intense that I had to stop reading a few times to regain my composure." – *African Publishers' Network*

"An unforgettable odyssey into the wilderness, mysteries, and perils of Africa... A book to be cherished and remembered." – *Greater London Radio*

"The central figure is not human; it is the barren, terrifying landscape of Northern Kenya and the deadly creatures who inhabit it." – *Daily Telegraph (UK)*

"An entrancing, terrifying vision of Africa. A story that not only thrills but informs... Impossible to set aside or forget." – *BBC*

"*The Last Savanna* is shot through with images of the natural world at its most fearsome and most merciful. With his weapons, man is a conqueror – without them he is a fugitive in an alien land... A thoroughly enjoyable read that comes highly recommended." – *Nottingham Observer (UK)*

"The opening of the book alone is so beautifully written that it was hard not to fall instantly into the story. It definitely feels like you are right there in Africa... the kind of book where just about anyone can enjoy it because it encompasses so much and is placed in such a beautiful and yet dangerous setting." – *Exploring All Genres*

"*The Last Savanna* is an unflinching look at the beauty and violence of Africa, the horror of the slaughter of the great beasts, the delicate balance of tribal life, the growth of terrorism and the timeless landscape. Its insights into how elephant poaching and drug sales are used to fund Islamic terrorist activities by Al Qaeda offshoots like Al-Shabaab are shockingly relevant and little known." – *Insatiable Readers*

"Each of the characters, both man and beast is both the hunter and the hunted, literally and figuratively, and the tension in the novel begins in the first pages and clutches the reader in its grasp until the end... The violence is unsheathed and unforgiving, and the trek across the savanna escalates into a feeling of near-insanity, the characters confusing reality with their inner demons, clarity and madness only a breath apart, hope dancing just out of reach on the horizon. Bond expertly draws in the reader, using the brutal beauty of Africa to show the blurry line between humanity and the animal world, letting the readers question for themselves which is the most savage. Readers will find similarities to the emotional tension and themes in William Golding's *The Lord of the Flies*, and *The Last Savanna sheds light on the dark corners of Africa — and mankind.*" – *Angela Amman Reviews*

"*The Last Savanna* is an unflinching look at the beauty and violence of Africa, the horror of the slaughter of the great beasts, the delicate balance of tribal life, the growth of terrorism and the timeless landscape." – *Book Binge*

"There were many parts that set this book apart from other books about Africa, but most notably the characters and beautiful writing... The plot was strong before the love element was introduced, but after that I found myself having a difficult time putting the book down... Although the plot and characters are strong throughout the book, I thought that the strongest point for this book would be the writing. There were numerous times throughout the book where I paused in my reading and thought to myself, "Wow, that was a really beautiful sentence". And while the sentences were beautiful on their own, together they painted a wondrous picture of Africa and a beautiful wilderness... I think it's worth mentioning that the start of this book is really strong and unique. – *Book Reviews*

"From the opening page maintains an exhilarating pace until the closing line... A highly entertaining and gripping read." – *East African Wild Life Society*

House of Jaguar

"A riveting thriller of murder, politics, and lies." – *London Broadcasting*

"Tough and tense thriller." – *Manchester Evening News (UK)*

"A high-octane story rife with action, from U.S. streets to Guatemalan jungles... Bond's kinetic novel abounds with intense scenes... The characters are fully limned... Not surprisingly, the novel ends with a shock, one that might have a few readers gasping." – *Kirkus*

"A thoroughly amazing book... And a terrifying depiction of one man's battle against the CIA and Latin American death squads." – *BBC*

"There are not enough words to describe how outstanding and entertaining this book is. Intriguing, exciting, captivating, sexy... absolutely incredible... a great thriller." – *NetGalley*

"Vicious thriller of drugs and revolution in the wilds of Guatemala, with the adventurer hero, aided by a woman doctor, facing a crooked CIA agent. The climax is among the most horrifying I have ever read." – *Liverpool Daily Post (UK)*

"A riveting story where even the good guys are bad guys, set in the politically corrupt and drug infested world of present-day Central America." – *Middlesborough Evening Gazette (UK)*

"Based upon Bond's own experiences in Guatemala... With detailed descriptions of actual jungle battles and manhunts, vanishing rain forests and the ferocity of guerrilla war, *House of Jaguar* also reveals the CIA's role in both death squads and drug running, twin scourges of Central America." – *Newton Chronicle (UK)*

"Bond grips the reader from the very first page. An ideal thriller for the beach, but be prepared to be there when the sun goes down." – *Herald Express (UK)*

Saving Paradise
(Pono Hawkins Book 1)

"An action-packed, must read novel... taking readers behind the alluring façade of Hawaii's pristine beaches and tourist traps into a festering underworld of murder, intrigue and corruption... *Saving Paradise* is a powerful editorial against the cancerous trends of crony capitalism and corrupt governance." – *Washington Times*

"A complex, entertaining... lusciously convoluted story." – *Kirkus*

"*Saving Paradise* will change you... It will call into question what little you really know, what people want you to believe you know and then hit you with a deep wave of dangerous truths... *Saving Paradise* is a thrill ride to read and pulls you in and out of plots until you don't know who to trust or what to do any more than the character. You trust no one, you keep going, hoping not to get caught before figuring out what is happening." – *Where Truth Meets Fiction*

"*Saving Paradise* is an absolutely fabulous book... a wonderful book." – *Art Zuckerman, WVOX*

"*Saving Paradise* is a rousing crime thriller – but it is so much more. Pono Hawkins is a dedicated environmentalist, a native of Hawaii who very much loves the islands but regrets what they have become. Pono is a thinker, a man who sees a bigger picture than most, and Mike Bond deftly (and painlessly) uses the character to instruct the reader in Hawaiian history from an insider's point-of-view. *Saving Paradise* is a highly atmospheric thriller focusing on a side of Hawaiian life that tourists seldom see." – *Book Chase*

"An absolute page-turner" – *Ecotopia Radio*

"An unusual thriller and a must-read." – *Fresh Fiction*

"He's a tough guy, a cynic who describes the problems of the world as a bottomless pit, but can't stop trying to solve them. He's Pono Hawkins, the hero of Mike Bond's new Hawaii-based thriller, *Saving Paradise*... an intersection of fiction and real life."

– *Hawaii Public Radio*

"Mike Bond's *Saving Paradise* is a complex murder mystery about political and corporate greed and corruption... Bond's vivid descriptions of Hawaii bring *Saving Paradise* vibrantly to life. The plot is unique and the environmental aspect of the storyline is thought-provoking and informative. The story's twists and turns will keep you guessing the killer's identity right up until the very end." – *Book Reviews and More*

"From start to finish, I never put it down." – *Bucket List Publications*

"*Saving Paradise* is one heck of a crime novel/thriller and highly recommended!" – *Crystal Book Reviews*

"You're going to love the plot of this book." – *KFVE TV*

"A very well written, fast-paced and exciting thriller." – *Mystery Maven Reviews*

Bond "incorporate(s) a lot of the reality of wind turbines and wind energy hype and fantasy into *Saving Paradise* along with a very spectacular character, former Special Forces veteran Pono Hawkins..." – Chris DeBello, *Issues and Ideas, WNNJ-FM*

"A fast-paced thrill ride... The descriptions of Hawaii are beautiful and detailed." – *Romancebookworm's Reviews*

"A wonderful book that everyone should read." – *Clear Channel Radio*

Killing Maine
(Pono Hawkins Book 2)

FIRST PRIZE, 2016, *New England Book Festival*: "A gripping tale of murders, manhunts and other crimes set amidst today's dirty politics and corporate graft, an unforgettable hero facing enormous dangers as he tries to save a friend, protect the women he loves, and defend a beautiful, endangered place."

"Another stellar ride from Bond; checking out Pono's first

adventure isn't a prerequisite, but this will make readers want to." – *Kirkus*

"The suspense, mystery, and intrigue will keep you on the edge of your seat." – *Goodreads*

"The action is exciting, and a surprise awaits over each new page... Bond is clearly one of the master authors for thrillers of this century." – *NetGalley Reviews*

"A work of compelling fiction... Very highly recommended." – *Midwest Book Review*

"Bond tackles many important social and environmental issues in a fast-paced, politically charged plot with a passionate main character. *Killing Maine* is a twisting mystery with enough suspicious characters and red herrings to keep you guessing. It's also a dire warning about the power of big industry and a commentary on our modern ecological responsibilities. A great read for the socially and environmentally conscious mystery lover." – *Honolulu Star-Advertiser*

"*Killing Maine* is quite a ride for those who love good crime thrillers. But, too, like its predecessor, it is much more than just another rousing crime thriller. This is another of Mike Bond's environmental eye-openers that will leave readers a lot wiser about alternative energy plans, state and federal politics, and the huge profits that are being stolen from the pockets of American taxpayers by the scam artists who often surround an industry like this one. I can't recommend this one strongly enough." – *Book Chase*

"Mike Bond has produced another nail-bitter... "*Killing Maine* just sucks in the reader and makes it difficult to put the book down until the very last page... A winner of a thriller." – *Mystery Maven*

"In this multi-complex novel... Friendship, loyalty, love, revenge and greed are just some of the issues brought to light in this novel. Author Mike Bond scores some high points and shoots straight to the top of the rating list!" – *Just Reviews*

"There's more than plenty of high-paced action and thrills... Read it and root for those who would "save Maine" from the devastating effects of what was originally publicized as an energy source that would tip the scales to energy independence. Nicely paced and plotted... As an aside it just might compel readers to look into its underlying issue as well!" – *Crystal Book Reviews*

Tibetan Cross

"A thriller that everyone should go out and buy right away. The writing is wonderful throughout, and Bond never loses the reader's attention. This is less a thriller, at times, than essay, with Bond working that fatalistic margin where life and death are one and the existential reality leaves one caring only to survive." – *Sunday Oregonian*

"A tautly written study of one man's descent into living hell... Strong and forceful, its sharply written prose, combined with a straightforward plot, builds a mood of near claustrophobic intensity." – *Spokane Chronicle*

"Grips the reader from the very first chapter until the climactic ending." – *UPI*

"Bond's deft thriller will reinforce your worst fears about the CIA and the Bomb... A taut, tense tale of pursuit through exotic and unsavory locales." – *Publishers Weekly*

"One of the most exciting in recent fiction... an astonishing thriller that speaks profoundly about the venality of governments and the nobility of man." – *San Francisco Examiner*

"It *is* a thriller... Incredible, but also believable." – *Associated Press*

"Another fantastic thriller from Mike Bond. He is a lyric writer whose prose is beautiful and provocative. His descriptions strike to the heart and evoke strong emotions. I could not put the book down once I started reading... Gripping, enthralling and imaginative... It is not for the faint of heart, but includes a great love story." – *NetGalley Reviews*

"Murderous intensity... A tense and graphically written story." – *Richmond Times-Dispatch*

"Excruciatingly fast-paced... It was impossible to catch my breath. Each time I thought I found a stopping point, my eyes would glance at the next line and drag me deeper into the story. I felt as though I was on a violent roller coaster, gripping the rail and praying that I would not go flying out of my seat. It was painful but awesome." – *Bitten By Books*

"The most jaundiced adventure fan will be held by *Tibetan Cross*... It's a superb volume with enough action for anyone, a well-told story that deserves the increasing attention it's getting." – *Sacramento Bee*

"Intense and unforgettable from the opening chapter... thought-provoking and very well written." – *Fort Lauderdale News*

"Grips the reader from the opening chapter and never lets go." – *Miami Herald*

A "chilling story of escape and pursuit." – *Tacoma News-Tribune*

"This novel is touted as a thriller – and that is what it is... The settings are exotic, minutely described, filled with colorful characters." – *Pittsburgh Post-Gazette*

"Almost impossible to put down... Relentless. As only reality can have a certain ring to it, so does this book. It is naked and brutal and mind boggling in its scope. It is a living example of not being able to hide, ever... The hardest-toned book I've ever read. And the most frightening glimpse of mankind I've seen. This is a 10 if ever there was one." – *I Love a Mystery*

ASSASSINS

MIKE BOND

MANDEVILLA PRESS
Weston, CT 06883

LIBRARY OF CONGRESS CATALOGING-IN-PUBLICATION DATA

Bond, Mike

Assassins: a novel/Mike Bond

p. cm.

ISBN 978-1-62704-035-8

1. Islamic Terrorism – Fiction. 2. ISIS – Fiction. 3. CIA – Fiction. 4. Afghanistan War – Fiction. 5. Iraq War – Fiction. 6. Syrian War – Fiction. 7. Paris – Fiction. I. Title

10 9 8 7 6 5 4 3 2 1

Author photo by Peggy Bond
Cover design: Asha Hossain Design, Inc.
Printed in the United States of America
www.MikeBondBooks.com

And ye shall know the truth and the truth shall make you free.
– New Testament, John 8:32, inscribed on the wall,
CIA Headquarters, Langley

One who knows neither the enemy
nor himself will invariably be defeated.
– Sun Tzu

You can go your own way.
– Fleetwood Mac

In memoriam

Paul Lewis Stimpson
First Lieutenant
United States Army

An Evening in Paris

November 2015

I T WAS WARM for mid-November. They sat on the terrace of a little restaurant. Anyplace in France, she said, how wonderful the food, the delicious wine, the gentle harmony of others there for love, food, friendship, ideas, freedom, the joys of life.

They had been through the wars together, fallen in love amid the hail of bullets and thud of explosions in cities drenched with blood. Knowing, as the cliché put it, any moment could be their last.

It gave an intensity to love, that this person dearer to you than life itself could be extinguished at any instant. Someone you cherished so completely, composed of neurons, cells, muscles, bone, tissue and memories, could be blown apart, riddled with bullets, any second.

"I love you so much," she said. "But I think I love you even more in Paris."

"France does that to us all. What was it Hemingway said –"

"Paris is a moveable feast."

"Yes, and we will happily feast, in whatever life brings us."

"As you've said, to follow the path with heart?"

"Yes." He caressed the back of her hand. "For us, the wars are over."

"For us the wars will never be over. You know that."

He looked out on the quiet street. "Let's take time out. Then we decide."

"Decide what?"

"Whether we keep fighting or run for cover." He smiled at the thought. Not once in all these years had he ever run for cover. Nor had she.

"Your buddy Owen said that people like us, once we're in, we can never get out."

"Look where it got him. You want that?" Again he checked the street. It was automatic, this watchfulness. On the edge of consciousness.

He scanned the passing pedestrians – happy couples hand in hand, an old man with a wispy beard, a little girl walking a black poodle, an ancient limping Chinese woman, a kid on a skateboard.

But it worried him, this *something*; he wished he'd brought a sidearm, but Home Office didn't want you carrying one here. And everything seemed so peaceful. He sipped his wine, the raw ancient roots of Provence...

A black Seat slowed as it came down the street. A grinning face full of hatred, an AK barrel aiming at them out its window, a blasting muzzle as he leaped across the table knocking her to the sidewalk and covered her with his body amid the hideous twanging hammer of bullets and smashing glass and screams and clatter of chairs and tables crashing and the howl of the Kalashnikov and awful whap of bullets into flesh as people tumbled crying.

It couldn't be, this horror, he'd left it all behind.

I

Afghanistan

Death Mountains

March 1982

HE GRABBED FOR THE RIPCORD but it wasn't there. Icy night howled past, clouds and black peaks racing up. Spinning out of control he yanked again at the ripcord but it was his rifle sling. He snatched for the spare chute but it wasn't there. *I packed it,* he told himself. *I had to.*

Falling out of the dream he felt a surge of joy it wasn't real, that he was safe in his bunk. Then waking more, he realized he was in a thundering tunnel, huge engines shaking the floor, the aluminum bench vibrating beneath him. *The plane.*

"Jack!" The Jump Master in a silvery space suit shook him. "Going up to drop height! Twenty minutes to the Afghan border." The Jump Master bent over the three others and gave them a thumbs up: *The mission is on.*

He took a deep, chilled breath. The engine roar loudened as the two Pratt & Whitneys on each wing clawed up through thinning air. He bent his arm, awkward in the insulated jump suit, to check his altimeter. *8,600 feet.*

"You're falling at two hundred miles an hour," Colonel Ackerman had reminded them last week in Sin City, "at sixty below zero. Guys die if they wait one extra instant to deploy their chute. Always remember, *Maintain Altitude Awareness.*"

Tonight anything could happen over the Hindu Kush. MiGs, high winds, tangled chutes, enemy waiting on the ground. Hindu Kush – *Death Mountains*. He thought of his father's last Huey into Ia Drang twenty years before, the green hills below the chopper's open doors, the rankness of jungle, guns and fear. Do you know when you're about to die?

Glancing around the rumbling fuselage he was stunned at how lovely and significant everything was: a canvas strip dangling from a bench, the rough fabric of his jump boot, a rifle's worn stock, the yellow bulb dancing on the ceiling, the avgas-tainted air. Next to him Owen McPhee stood up, awkward and bearlike in his Extended Cold Weather suit, smiled at Jack and shrugged: *Never thought we'd get to do it.*

"They might still abort," Jack yelled over the engine noise.

McPhee grinned: *Stop worrying.*

Jack turned to Loxley and Gustafson. "Time to get ready, girls."

Bent over his rucksack, Sean Loxley gave him the finger. Beyond him Neil Gustafson glanced up, his broad face serious. "I was fearing," he called, "we'd get scrubbed."

Jack tugged his kit bag from under the bench to final-check its contents: two goatskin bags of grenades and AK cartridges, a padded wool Afghani jacket, long wool shirt and trousers, a blackened pot of rice and dried goat meat, two Paki plastic soda bottles of water, a woven willow backpack, a Soviet Special Forces Spetsnaz watch. He slid on his parachute, nestled the canopy releases into his shoulders, secured all the straps and turned to help Loxley. "If these chutes don't open," Loxley yelled, "we'll never have to do this again."

At first Jack had been put off by Loxley's California surfer cool, his gregarious grin and jokes about Home Office and military politics. But Loxley had always backed it up, always put his buddies first. And he made them laugh; even tough-faced sarcastic McPhee with his small hard mouth, tight on the balls of his feet as a welterweight, couldn't keep from grinning. "You dumb hippie," he'd growl, trying not to laugh.

The Jump Master raised both arms sideways, bent his elbows and touched his fingertips to his helmet. Jack nodded and slid his padded leather helmet over his head, tucked the goggles up on its brim, settled the Makarov pistol on his thigh. Now the JM raised his right hand, thumb to his cheek, and swung the hand over his nose. Jack took a last breath from the plane's oxygen supply and slipped on his radio unit and mask, gave the JM a thumb up to say his own oxygen was working.

22,500 feet.

"To avoid Soviet and Paki radar," Colonel Ackerman had said, "it has to be a Blind Drop."

"No marching bands?" Loxley had snickered. "No girls waving panties?"

"We've calculated your Release Point based on your DZ," Ackerman said. "And where we think the wind'll be."

"In the Hindu Kush," Loxley added, "I can't imagine wind will be a problem."

"Shut up, Sean," Ackerman said. "And there'll be no external resupply. No exfil. We've devised an Evasion and Escape but you may want to change that on the ground."

"You're making it sound like we're not really welcome."

"Remember up there, *Maintain Altitude Awareness*."

"That's right, girls. Know when you're high..."

Ackerman glared at him. "If this mission were to exist, its purpose would be to build an Afghani guerrilla movement against the Soviets, not tied to the Pakis but on your own. By themselves the Afghanis can't beat the Soviets. But with our help – *your* help – we might just reverse the Soviet conquest of Asia and get the bastards back for Vietnam. But we don't intend to start World War Three or fuck up our relations with ISI. So once you drop out of that plane we can't help you."

Slender and rugged with a black moustache and graying curly hair, Levi Ackerman had lost his right forearm in the same Ia Drang battle that killed Jack's father. Ever since then Levi had watched over Jack, got him into West Point, then after that fell apart and Jack had finished at University of Maine, Levi got him into the military ops division of Home Office – "I want you near me, kid," he'd said. Would Levi now send him to die?

In the thundering airless fuselage the JM swung up his left hand and tapped the wrist with two fingers of his right, opened and closed his palms twice: the Twenty-Minute Warning.

34,000.

"When I was a kid," Loxley said, "my Grandma use to make Afghans–"

"Your Grandma," McPhee yelled, "was a chimpanzee –"

Jack plugged in his backpack oxygen and checked his AIROX on/off valve.

"Whatever you do, guys," Ackerman had added, "don't get separated from Jack. He's your squad leader, knows the lingo, the country. Lose Jack you die."

The Red Light over the rear ramp flicked on. Courage isn't the absence of fear, their weapons trainer, Captain Perkins, used to say in Sin City, but action despite it.

They could still abort. The JM would give the abort signal if an Unsafe Condition existed either in the aircraft, outside it, or on the DZ. As if the whole damn mission weren't insanely unsafe.

Haloed in the Red Light the JM gave the Ten-Minute Warning. Eight times his hands closed and opened: Wind speed 80 knots.

Way too fast. They'd have to abort. But the JM swung his arm outward, the command to check their automatic ripcord releases. Jack slid his combat pack harness up under his parachute, its seventy-pounds added to the chute's forty-five making him stagger backward. He checked that the sling of his AKMS rifle was fully extended and taped at the end, that the tapes on the muzzle, front sight, magazine, and ejector port were tight and not unfurled except where he'd folded over the ends for a quick release.

"*Strela?*" Jack called. McPhee lifted up a long heavy tube wrapped in sheepskin and lashed it vertically on one side of Jack's combat pack. Jack helped Loxley and McPhee lash two more *Strela* tubes to their packs. Jack secured his rifle muzzle-down over his left shoulder, the curved magazine to the rear so it nestled against the side of the chute and wouldn't tangle in the lines.

With a fat gloved thumb he pushed the altimeter light. *39,750.* The JM gave the Two-Minute Command. Jack tightened his straps, checked everyone's oxygen pressure gauge, patted their shoulders. *Be safe*, he told each silently.

His breath was wet and hot inside the mask; his beard itched. His goggles fogged, the Red Light danced. Buzzing filled his ears, his stomach was an aching hole. The plane shivered, the ramp cracked open, began to drop. Air sucked past. Beyond was black. A styrofoam cup scuttled down the fuselage and blasted out the ramp. The JM gave the Salute

Command: *Move to the Rear.*

Jack switched on his bailout oxygen and disconnected from the plane's oxygen console. This was what happened when you got executed, you numbly stood up and let them put a bullet through you.

The JM gave the thumbs up Stand By Command and Jack gave it back. He thought of his father in the chopper, his father's Golden Rule: "Do what you say, and say what you do." Keep your word, and speak the truth. So when you die you've lived the way you should.

The Green Light flashed on. The JM swung his arm toward the hole and Owen McPhee dropped into the darkness. A second later Neil Gustafson. Then Sean Loxley.

Jack halted on the ramp. *You're going to die. That's all.* The JM swung down his arm. Jack arched his back and dove into the night.

Tao of War

H E SLAMMED into the plane's wake, spinning wildly, stars flashing past, flung out his arms into the Stable Free Fall Position but the off-balanced *Strela* made him spin faster. Tumbling in a dizzy spiral he was icing up, had to *Maintain Altitude Awareness*, couldn't see his altimeter. Cold bit through his gloves into his fingers and into his elbows and knees where the jumpsuit was tight.

You drop a thousand feet every five seconds. How long had he fallen? He hunched to balance the pack but that made him spin worse. He shoved the chute left to offset the *Strela* and combat pack; the tumbling slowed, the huge white-black Hindu Kush rushing up. Grabbing his left wrist he pushed the altimeter button. *29,000*: he'd dropped ten thousand already. But in a few seconds, at 25,000, he could deploy the chute.

Safe now. Thicker air hissed past, the black ridges and white cliffs of the Death Mountains rising fast. To the east, behind him now, Chitral Valley and Pakistan. To the west the snowy peaks, barren slopes and desert valleys of Afghanistan.

27,500. He couldn't see the red chemlites on the others' suits. But no one had broken silence. *So they're fine too. We made it.* He felt a warm happiness, the fear receding.

26,500. He reached for the main ripcord handle.

25,250. He pulled the ripcord; the pilot chute yanked out the main bag and he lurched into a wide down-pulling arc. Tugging the steering toggles he swung in a circle but still couldn't see chemlites, only frozen Bandakur mountain rising toward him, the snow-thick valleys eight thousand feet below, dim lights to the east that could be the village of Sang Lech. He lined up to fly northwest across Bandakur so he'd hit the DZ on the mountain's western flank. The stars above the black dome of his chute were thick as milk. The great peaks climbed past him, entombed in ice. He sucked in oxygen, felt peace.

A huge force smashed into him collapsing his chute; he somersaulted tangled in another chute, somebody spinning on its lines. "Cutaway!" he screamed. They looped around again, caught in the lines. Jack wrenched an arm free but that spun him the other way, the tangled chutes swung him down and the other man up then the stars were below him so for an instant he thought he was falling into space. He yanked the chute releases and dropped away from the tangled chutes, accelerating in free fall till with a great *whoof* the reserve chute jerked him up and the tangled chutes whistled past, the man wrapped in them. "Cutaway!" Jack screamed into his radio. "This is Tracker. *Cutaway!*"

"This is Domino," McPhee said. "What's your situation?"

"Tracker this is Silver," Loxley said. "I can't see you. Over."

"Come in, Whiskey!" Jack yelled at Gustafson. "If you're caught, cut away the main chute and deploy reserve. *Maintain Altitude Awareness.* Cut *away!*"

His hands had frozen. "Whiskey!" he screamed, "what's your situation?"

He switched off his oxygen. Below was a tiny chemlite. "Whiskey," McPhee radioed Gustafson. "Do you read me?"

Rocky ridges coming up fast. If Gustafson hadn't deployed his reserve he'd have hit by now. A fierce wind was blowing snow off the peaks; they had to land into it. Short of the DZ, way short. Maybe in the boulders. *Bend your knees. Roll with the fall.* He snapped off his chemlite.

"Whiskey," McPhee radioed. "Do you read me?"

Bend your knees. Loosen shoulders. Adjust rifle so it doesn't smash ribs on impact. The ground raced up. He dropped the combat pack and *Strela.* The mountain slammed into him; he tumbled backward his head smashing boulders. He leaped up and scrambled downhill unbuckling the chute harness and stamping on the chute, dragged it together and knelt on it.

A steep stony slope, wind screaming, shaly rock clattering down. He snatched off his helmet and clutched his head, blood hot between his fingers, the pain unbearable. He untaped his rifle, checked the safety. "Tracker here," he whispered, gripping his skull to hold in the agony. He feared his skull was broken, the way the blood poured out. "Touchdown. Over."

"Silver here," Loxley answered. "TD. Over."

"Domino here," McPhee said raggedly. "TD. Over."

"Whiskey!" Jack called. Silence, hissing of wind in the radio. "Stow your chutes in your packs and link up," he told them. "Look for my chemlite. Over."

"Domino here," McPhee said. "Come to me. Over."

"I want us uphill." Jack gritted his teeth. "Get up here."

"Hurt," McPhee grunted. "Not going anywhere."

The blood running out Jack's nose had frozen in his moustache. Clutching his skull he steadily descended the slope, each step jolting new agony into his head. When he reached McPhee, Loxley was already there. "Goddamn rocks," McPhee groaned. "Goddamn leg."

Clamping a light in his teeth Loxley eased off McPhee's boot. "Tibia and fibula both broken."

Behind the wind Jack heard a faint rumble through swirling snow. *How could a helicopter be up here at night?* "Wrap it," he snapped. "Chopper!"

"Can't see us in this," Loxley yelled into the wind. "What happened?"

"Gus hit me from above," Jack yelled back, making the pain worse. "About eighteen. We tangled. I cut away at the top."

"He streamed," McPhee said, as if stating the worst might prevent it. He gripped his radio. "Whiskey! Do you read me?"

"Stop sending!" Jack said. "We'll get the Russians on us." He stuffed all their jump gear under a boulder and jammed it with snow. Now except for their *Spetsnaz* watches, Russian field glasses, AKs, pistols, and *Strelas*, everything they had was Afghani. "Leave the channel open. In fifteen minutes try again."

"Gus is our medic," Loxley yelled. "Owen's got a broken leg. If we abort, try for Pakistan –"

"Abortion's for girls," McPhee snarled. "We find Gus."

Jack thought of Gus falling tangled in his chutes, icy rock racing up. "If his reserve didn't open his body's way behind us and there's nothing we can do. If it opened he's somewhere on this ridge."

The radio buzzed, stuttered. "That's him!" McPhee said. "Whiskey!" he coaxed. "Come in Whiskey..."

The radio was silent. *One man gone, another injured.* Jack's head pounded like a jackhammer. He'd failed, the mission screwed before it even started. He broke away the chunks of frozen blood clogging his nose and mouth, slung McPhee's rifle over his own, and pulled McPhee up.

"You asshole," McPhee hissed, "you're bleeding."

"Bit my tongue when I landed," Jack spit a dark streak on the snow. "No big deal."

Loxley shouldered McPhee's combat pack, stumbling under the weight, stood and looped the *Strela* tube over his other shoulder. "Where to, Boss?"

"We find a place to stow Owen," Jack said. "Then we find Gus. Before the Russians do."

WITH McPHEE HOBBLING between them they climbed Bandakur's south ridge through howling snow that froze in their beards and drove icicles through their coats. Every fifteen minutes they tried the radio but there was no sound from Gus.

It was worse than Jack could have imagined; they might not live, let alone complete the mission. Pakistan seemed the only choice. *If* they could get McPhee back across the Kush without being caught by the Soviets or Pakis. He saw Ackerman's taut angry face. *You didn't do what we trained you for.*

"It's not to put you in shape that we drive you so hard," Ackerman had told them in Sin City, speaking of the five a.m. runs with full packs, the crawling on hands and toes under machine gun fire, the rappelling down cliffs and buildings. "You men were already hard as steel when you came here."

"Not McPhee," Loxley snickered, "he's never been hard at all."

Ackerman ignored him. "It's so you *know* you can do them. Once you've done them, even in training, you'll *know* in Afghanistan you can endure almost anything..."

"And you're going to learn everything you can about ordnance," Captain Perkins added. "From Makarovs to SA-

7s, about setting ambushes and nailing a guy in the head at eight hundred yards. How to set Claymores and dig pit traps, how to get the jugular when you cut a throat, how to recognize Soviet infantry units and tell a T-72 tank from the later T-72S, and the RPG-7 from the RPG-16. And *no*, RPG does *not* stand for 'rocket-propelled grenade'. It's Russian for rocket anti-tank grenade launcher – *Reactiviniyi Protivotankovyi Granatomet*, and I want you girls to know how to spell that."

"We've been agitating these damn Afghanis for years," Ackerman said, "fed them fanatic Islamic stuff till we finally got a fundamentalist government going in Kabul and the Soviets *had* to come in, for their whole soft Muslim underbelly – Tajikistan, Uzbekistan, and Kazakhstan, *and all that oil* – was at risk. Now," he'd added, "We're going to do to them in Afghanistan what they did to us in Vietnam. We're going to bleed them dry."

Now the peaks blocking the stars and the sheer icy canyons filled Jack with a vast, desolate despair. It was a perfect place to bleed and die.

"The Special Forces man is the essence," Ackerman said, "of the Art of War. He's not *where* he appears to be, nor *what* he appears to be. He strikes where and when the enemy's not ready. He inflicts great harm with few resources because *he* is the Tao of War."

"The SF man," said Perkins, "makes losing part of the enemy's fate."

Jack smiled, shook his head. "That is *such* bullshit."

"Someday, if you're good enough," Levi Ackerman had answered, "it won't be."

Now within two months they had to report to Ackerman in Rawalpindi. Even if Gus was dead, they might still be able to reach Jack's old village, Edeni, where people would care for McPhee. Then Jack could find his former enemy Wahid al-Din, now a famous warlord fighting the Soviets. They could still start a third front uniting the Afghani opposition...

He took a breath, bit back the agony in his head, spit a clot of blood snatched by the wind. "Edeni," he yelled. "Even if we can't find Gus we're going to Edeni."

Morphine

WAHID AL-DIN followed his squad of fourteen mujihadeen in darkness from their cave in the hills below Bandakur down the defile of the Varduj River toward the Soviet encampment outside Sang Lech.

The men moved quietly, just a hiss of footfalls on the hard-packed trail, the rustle of worn leather and padded coats, the clink of a rifle buckle where a tape had worn through.

After midnight they reached the River valley and the narrow road from Khoran to Ishasshim on the Pakistani border. At the ruins of a bombed farmhouse they dashed across the road and turned north through an overgrown apple orchard then untended fields of oats and barley, stepping single-file behind a man who knew the way between the land mines.

In a few places where farmers had tried to harvest crops there were pits where mines had exploded. It irritated Wahid that the farmers were such fools – only poppies were worth lives, the lives of orphans sent out to pick the ripened husks.

Mines had no significance except you avoided some areas or tried to entice the enemy into them. Eventually the crops would come back. That, like everything else, was God's decision. *For the grain that ye sow, do ye cause it to spring forth, or do I?*

He thought of the Soviet soldiers sleeping in their tents along the River outside Sang Lech, their officers billeted in the farms on the edge of town. In a few minutes these farmers would lose their eternal lives, for hadn't they consorted with the enemies of Islam? *They shall have garments of fire fitted on them, and boiling water poured on their heads and their bowels rent asunder, and also their skins, and they shall be beaten with maces of iron.* They'd read the Koran. They couldn't say they didn't know.

Bitter wind moaned down from the white cliffs of Bandakur. The River was high and icy. He wanted to fire from here at the Soviet tents on the other bank and then run, but his men had too few bullets. Nine of his seventeen men had old bolt-action .303 Enfields and a handful of cartridges. The rest had Soviet AK-47s but only a hundred twenty-four rounds of 7.62 mm cartridges total, barely half a 30-round magazine each. No, they had to move closer, kill fast and take what arms they could before surviving Soviets could reach their tanks and open up with their machine guns.

Wahid waved his men down the gravelly bank into the fast-moving water. *I was nothing*, he reminded himself, *until this war*. Now he might control the Panjshir when the Soviets left. *I must be careful not to die before then.*

The River rocks were cold and slippery, but moving carefully behind his men he did not founder. He reached the far bank two hundred yards from the nearest Soviet tents, his men moving forward through the willows.

He let them go ahead – he was needed back here in case anything went wrong. Someone yelled and he dove into the grass. Gunfire rang out, the Soviets shouting. A grenade exploded and his heart congealed. A bullet snapped past his ear and he squirmed lower into the grass clawing the dirt.

A man scrambled from the first tent. Wahid sprayed rounds at him, afraid he might miss and the man would kill him. Amid the horrid thunder of guns, voices in Russian and Kazakh, Wahid crawled forward to grab the man's pistol and the man fired, the bullet searing Wahid's side. Moaning he bellied back through the willows toward the River.

Tanks rumbled, rifles chattered, machine guns snarled, flares flashed shadows and bullets whacked past. He fell down the cutbank losing his rifle. Fearing to cross the open water he ran splashing downriver till the rumble of guns and tanks faded behind him.

The Russian's bullet had burnt a crease along his waist. It stung terribly but there was no blood. *Morphine. Back at the cave there was morphine.*

At a bend in the River he crawled across, soaking his coat that froze as he climbed the canyon above the trail. Below in the starlight he saw the dark shapes of his men cross the River and jog up the trail. Eleven – only six lost, though several seemed wounded. He would wait then come up behind them saying *You left me behind to fight alone.*

Far away a *whack-whack-whack* nearing fast. Three helicopters thundered around the mountain; their white-red flares caught out his men like puppets on a string, their machine guns stitching them to earth. So faraway, a game really, how they fell.

Wahid squirmed tighter into the rocks. The helicopters drifted down and settled among his men, monstrous wasps in the flares' flickering gleam. Now and again the wind carried up to him the bang of a pistol as the Soviets finished off a wounded man. Then like sated vultures the helicopters flew away.

Shaking with fear and cold he huddled there a long time then descended timidly and searched the dead till he found a new AK and trotted back up the trail toward the cave. At the cave he could get morphine. To kill this awful pain. Then he'd tell everyone how his men had deserted him and were annihilated by the helicopters because they'd run from battle.

There had to be a way to kill the helicopters.

Or he would fail and never control the Panjshir.

How could God want that?

IN THE KABUL CLINIC of Médecins Sans Frontières, Sophie Dassault knelt beside a shepherd boy with lovely eyes and a gray pinched face, his golden hair sweaty with agony, both legs and one arm gone, shards of metal jutting from his belly and chest. Why was it always children who stepped on mines? And not the men who planted them?

A voice called her, Didier the nurse. "Man named Ahmad for you, Doctor."

"Tell him wait." She touched the boy's face. "*Au revoir, mon cher tout petit Prince –*"

The boy's eyes caught hers and she saw he knew no miracle would save him. It didn't matter she spoke French for now he understood all language, knew like the Little Prince that words are the source of all misunderstandings. She tightened the tourniquet around his one arm, held up the syringe with its five milligrams of morphine, flicked it to clear it of air that could cause an embolism, tried to find a vein, waited just a second for the strength to do it and pushed the plunger home.

"Wait a little, just under a star," she whispered, words she'd heard so often as a little girl, "If a child comes, if he laughs, if he has golden hair..." She recapped the needle and softly tousled his hair, thinking *his last human touch*, held his hand as if he were her only son, felt the pulse soften as his breathing slowed and stilled, waited for the pulse to stop.

"He's yours," she said to the crippled old man who with his retarded nephew was responsible for dragging corpses from their cots and carrying them to Kabul's graveyard of wrecked cars where an artillery shell had made a hole big enough to shove in the bodies. She stepped out of the tent's stench of kerosene, hydrogen peroxide, bile, and blood, and looked up at the stars. "If You existed, and I could get my hands on You, I'd kill You!"

She seemed to float from the ground and looking down saw herself in her dirty gown, long-limbed and thin, with her tangled auburn hair and long face. Didier called her again. "This man Ahmad says it's urgent."

When she'd come from Paris she'd told herself this would happen, the horrible torturing wounds and senseless deaths, the endless nights of no sleep, fatigue and despair. "You got what you asked for," she muttered to herself, stepped into the tent, in its dim lantern light a slender unshaven man in a long white shirt, a weary face and thinning hair, a man young just a few years ago. "What do you want?" she said in Pashto.

"Please come. I have sick children."

She thought of the boy she had just killed. "Who doesn't?"

"There are many –"

Her body ached so with exhaustion she wanted to fall down in the mud and die. "What's wrong?"

"They keep going, they can't stop, it comes out of them like water. We have two hundred. It's an orphanage. Some thirty, maybe, have this sickness."

"I don't have enough medicine, just a few doses..."

"It's not too far – Shari Kuhna, behind the old mosque."

"I'm a westerner, a woman... I can get killed just being there –"

"We all can, Doctor."

She took her medical bag and stumbled after him. Shrapnel was falling with a random ticking sound. Shells were hitting toward Hazara and Bagnal in the north, bright red and yellow flowers, their shock waves slapping her face. With its telltale whooshing chatter a PK machine gun opened up, a few rifles returning fire, and the sharp crescendo of cracks she had come to know were grenades from a Plamya launcher.

"Why are you here?" he said.

When she didn't answer he said, "I was a teacher. In Edeni, a village in the Kush."

"Never heard of it."

"No one has. But now my brother Wahid's a famous warlord – Eagle of the Hindu Kush. Soon Edeni also will be famous," he added sarcastically.

"Assassins," she gasped. "You're all assassins."

He picked up speed. "Here is the dangerous part. Hurry!" They ran down an alley to a cratered boulevard and along a line of deserted sidewalk stalls. Something came up behind them, footsteps. Ahmad grabbed her hand. "Faster!"

A light flashed on, shapes surrounding them. "What *have* we here?" a deep voice.

"A foreign woman?" another said. Men with guns, *mujihadeen.*

"You bastard," Sophie hissed at Ahmad. "You set me up."

A hand whacked her mouth. "Cover your head, slut!" Someone yanked her kerchief over her eyes and shoved her into the street. She fell banging her knee, tried to stand but he pushed her down. "Here?" one said. A snick of rifle bolt.

A muzzle jabbed the back of her head. "No!" she begged.

"She's not Russian!" Ahmad screamed. "She's a doctor! Saving our children!"

A 155 hit with a great fiery whack knocking them down. Ahmad snatched her arm and they ran through clouds of dust and crashing stones, beams, and roof tiles, the air wailing with bullets. Ahead the street caught fire, red flashes of exploding ammo and gasoline. Two machine guns were firing to the right, rifles everywhere. They dodged through markets blasted by explosions, shrapnel glowing like coals. The Salaam Hotel had been hit, the front wall gone, empty rooms staring through the smoke, a bed standing sideways in the street like a tethered mule.

The orphanage was a low building with shuttered windows and three candlelit rooms where children lay on straw and burlap sacks. Holding her breath against the stink she stepped around piles of mucused bloody feces. "I have only twelve doses," she said. "We pick the sickest ones. But not those who'll die anyway."

One by one she treated them, scanning their feverish eyes, her cool hand on hot foreheads. "Feed them rice and lots of boiled water. Be sure to boil the water. Most of them will live." She stood, fighting the pain in her knee where she'd been knocked down. "Now let's look at the other kids..."

Daylight began to slink through the shuttered windows. From distant streets came a hubbub of voices, women calling children, storekeepers announcing their wares, sounds of cars and animals... It seemed unreal that after such a night of carnage and terror anyone still lived. "I'll go back with you," Ahmad said.

"No, it's safe now." She could tasted blood in her mouth where she'd been slapped. "With the veil I'm fine."

She limped the rubbled streets through the beautiful bright morning. A loudspeaker crackled with a muezzin's call to morning prayer. A deep despair filled her. Again she wondered why she'd come: had her life in Paris been so bad?

Why be a doctor? What in all this insanity was worth saving? She thought of the boy she had killed, and again of St. Exupéry: the parable of Mozart assassinated. Would that angelic boy have grown up just another religion-maddened killer? How could he not? She fell to her knees tugging aside her veil and vomited on the street. A man walking by kicked her. She raised herself dizzily, refastened her veil and continued on her way.

Tracks

"IT'S GUS!" McPhee pointed at the footprint in the crusted snow.

Jack knelt beside it, fighting hope. An Afghani boot, large. "Could be a shepherd, anyone."

"It's *his* size. Tracking toward the DZ."

The rising sun was a dim yellow orb in the snow blowing north from the peaks. The wind cut like acid, making his head throb. The pain was so awful he feared it would kill him, wanted desperately to take codeine but couldn't risk the numbness. "We need to stow you somewhere," he said to McPhee. "So Seán and I can look for Gus."

"I want a suite with a bar and Jacuzzi. And three hookers. It's in my contract."

"You couldn't even get it up with one," Loxley grunted.

"Chopper!" Jack yelled, shoving McPhee behind a boulder as a black gunship screamed over the ridge and down the far side.

"Coming back," Loxley said.

"No," Jack said. "That's trucks." He ran to the ridgetop. In the valley below three halftracks with red stars on the roofs and twin machine guns were coming up a dirt road. Grabbing McPhee Jack ran for a gully, knocking down rocks that clattered into the valley. The halftracks growled nearer. There was no place to hide, just rocks in sight of the chopper or the halftracks that had stopped two hundred feet below. Soldiers jumped from them and deployed along the road.

"Chopper!" Jack snapped, "northeast." The soldiers were coming up the road. The chopper roared back over and dropped out of sight.

One halftrack driver stood smoking in his open door. In Jack's sights he had a boyish familiar mouth, sandy hair poking from under a gray fatigue cap. Shielding his eyes with one hand he stared up at them. "Oh shit." McPhee tucked his rifle into his cheek.

A hawk drifted over, low and broad-winged. The boy tossed his cigarette, jumped down and watched it slip over the ridge. "Regular ornithologist," Loxley said.

"Let's waste him," McPhee said. "All three drivers."

"Can't," Jack said, "that patrol'll have us –"

"Here they come anyway." The Soviets crossed the road in patrol formation and started up the ridge, short dark-faced Kazakhs in burly coats and flat gray hats. "Too many," Loxley whispered. "Can't get them all."

"Coming up both sides of this gully –"

"Let's hit them now," McPhee said.

"Rest of them'll get us."

The chopper flitted back over, an alien bird guarding its brood. A deep voice called and the soldiers turned parallel to the slope, one passing below Jack with his fuzzy hat low over his brow, eyes on the ground. The officer called again and the soldiers quartered back down to the road, stamping snow off their boots as they climbed into the tracks.

"How the Hell," Loxley said, "didn't they *see* us?"

"Didn't expect us to be here," Jack said. The halftracks gurgled to life and snarled back down the road. Jack noticed he was clenching his rifle, tried to relax his fingers but they were frozen to the stock. The last halftrack halted in a puff of smoke. With a ragged *ya-ya-ya* the starter turned over but the engine wouldn't catch. One by one the soldiers jumped out of the back, one glancing uphill.

"Here we go again," Loxley said.

"The other two are around the turn," McPhee said. "Let's take this one out. *Now.*"

"No!" Jack hissed. "It'll bring the chopper back."

"What's that!" Loxley said. "In the back?"

A reddened body lay on the track's deck beside a pack and tangled parachute. "We don't have to look for Gus anymore," Loxley said quietly.

The soldiers push-started the halftrack and climbed on, standing on the muddy bloody form that had been Gus. "Our cover's blown," McPhee said. "They'll be all over this mountain."

"We're moving out fast." Jack eyed the sky. "Snow's coming."

Everything before now seemed unreal: the C-130 from Sin City to Guam, the mess hall and bunks the night before, the last bottle of tequila, screwing the last Filipino girl on the beach, riding the last soft phosphorent roll of surf to the shallows, Gus singing off-key to the Eagles and Pink Floyd –

The Russian boy on the track had seemed like Jack's friend Cole Svenson, made him think of Cole's grin as he pulled in a trout and almost fell out of the canoe, or the night he and Cole had gotten stoned with Susie and Barb in the woods where two centuries ago Jack's ancestors had farmed, and now it was forest again, old rock walls snaking between the trees.

Cole a Marine now in Beirut. Keeping the ragheads from killing each other.

ALL DAY THEY CLIMBED the mountain into a blizzard that burned their lungs like fire. After dark they laid up for a half hour in the rocks. Jack checked his watch: *21:20 hours. 11,740 feet.* 41 below zero. The glow of the watch blinded him. His fingers were freezing though he kept sticking them in his crotch to warm them. "Another twenty hours maybe, to get there."

"This guy in Edeni –" McPhee chewed his icy mustache. "Wahid al-Din –"

"– better be easy to find."

Edeni. Warm fires, warm stone huts, warm smiles. Something to stop this head from hurting. Food. Safe. Jack shouldered his and McPhee's willow backpacks and goat bags, slung the *Strela* tubes alongside them, and picked up his rifle. He spit another mouthful of blood, pulled up McPhee and started up the mountain.

DUSK WAS DYING on the high black cliffs of the Little Kowkcheh River as they neared Edeni. Climbing the riverside path toward the village Jack switched to point, Loxley with McPhee a hundred feet behind. "If there's something I don't like," Jack said, "I'll wave you back."

But what could change in three years in Edeni? They might even ask him to start teaching again. His blood brother Ahmad, genial and harassed, glasses sliding down his nose. Ahmad's mother singing Tajik folk songs as she crouched over the fire cooking goat stew and barley. She who tried to be the mother she'd thought Jack'd lost, because no mother would let her son come to this bedeviled country. Her evil son Wahid finger-combing his beard, the Koran like a bulletproof amulet clutched to his chest.

The night he and Ahmad had cut their palms and clasped bloody hands saying the tribal oath, "Now you are my brother." Wahid in the background smiling through his hatred.

Jack's old students, their ready jokes and laughter. The snake in his desk drawer, the mouse in his tea, the burrs under his saddle the first time he'd ridden *buzkashi*. When Jack had asked a class, "How can I share nine goats among three brothers?" a boy had laughed, "I'd keep seven, and give one to each of my brothers."

Home Office had sent him to Afghanistan with a Peace Corps cover before the Soviets invaded because he spoke Russian, had learned it with French and Spanish at U of Maine. He was quick with languages and had learned Pashto easily, and they wanted "viable Intel on the evolving situation". Though he'd been thrown out of West Point he still owed four years and this was one way to do them. Soon he had come to love the village and teaching and his kids, and now he was coming home with one buddy dead and another smashed up.

The time he'd shown the kids a *Time* magazine photo of Manhattan's night skyline, the two new Towers gleaming, and a sour-tempered boy named Suley quoted the Koran about the cities God destroyed because their inhabitants lived in too much ease and plenty.

The Koran. Wahid's contemptuous glare, endlessly finger-combing his beard and spitting proverbs. "How is it," Jack once asked Ahmad, "that you and your brother are so unlike?"

"He was from a different father who was killed by the Uzbeks for stealing sheep. My father died fighting Pitav men who tried to take our horses, so we both knew sorrow. But he can never see joy in life. Most people when they see a happy person it makes them happy too. But Wahid when he sees a happy person says *Just wait, some day you'll be miserable as me.*" Ahmad shrugged. "Maybe why he loves the Koran."

"Either unhappy people are drawn to religion," Jack said, "or religion makes people unhappy – I'm not sure which."

"Islam means *I submit*," Ahmad answered. "But how can we submit to God's will in a world with so much pain and evil? Are pain and evil what God wants?"

The trail into Edeni had changed, no tracks of horses, goats, or men. Rifle off safety, Jack eased round the last bluff.

Bare blackened timbers pointed up from snow-covered shattered walls. His hut was gone, and Ahmad's mother's. He crouched watching, saw no movement, took up a position in the ruins of his hut against the pile of flat stones that had once been its roof.

After a while he waved the others up. "Now what?" McPhee said.

"We kill them all."

"They look to be already dead."

"The Russians. We kill them till the last one in Afghanistan is dead."

"No problem," Loxley said. "There's only a few million."

Jack checked the perimeter of the dead village. *I should have killed the blond kid at the halftracks. I should've killed them all.*

Every Russian in Afghanistan.

Now I will.

Necessary Evil

WHEN THE PRIEST'S brown Dodge had pulled up the drive one warm November afternoon eighteen years ago Jack's mother had screamed and clasped her hands to her face. Fearing he'd done something wrong Jack ran into the barn and climbed up among the sweet-smelling prickery bales. But she'd soon walked tall and tear-streaked into the barn to call him down and tell him his father had died in a faraway place she called Viet Nam.

He could still smell the spicy hay, still hear the song on the radio that warm November afternoon, *To dance beneath the diamond skies with one hand waving free.*

Wind from the Kowkcheh canyon walls blew ice down his neck. "These ruins," he said, "were my neighbor's house. Those walls, that's where I taught school."

"Let it go, Jack," McPhee said.

"There was a huge old tree shaded the whole place..."

Loxley slid a chunk of wood into the flames. "To think *you* were their teacher! No wonder this country's so screwed."

"Everyone lived on nothing and worked like mules. Half their kids died before they were five. But they were happier than the young Americans the Peace Corps sent to teach them how to live."

"The guys have multiple wives," Loxley said. "Of course they're happier."

McPhee eased himself up against the broken wall. "Are you *nuts?*"

"The idea," Jack said, "was stir up the Muslims, send in all these Korans, fund the *mullahs* and bomb-throwers. Pay the Soviets back for Nam. But this..."

McPhee cut goat meat on his rifle stock. "Everybody knows war sucks." He chewed a piece, working the toughness back and forth in his teeth. "Except the politicians who start them. Who won't get hurt in them."

Jack leaned aside to spit blood. Sometimes he feared the pain might crush his brain, spread in waves down his spine. "It's a bad concussion," McPhee said, "bleeding like that."

"It's getting better."

"Stop lying, asshole."

Jack glanced at McPhee's leg. "Three weeks till you can walk."

"So where's my hookers and tequila?" McPhee brushed snow off his shoulders. "My damn Jacuzzi?"

"We should abort," Loxley said, "get this numbnut's ass to Pakistan."

"We're not supposed to go there," Jack said. "Or be *here*, for that matter."

"Military intelligence," McPhee sighed, "is an oxymoron."

"Remember the night driving to Vegas," Loxley said, "and Gus asked is an oxymoron a dumb steer? And you said no, it's a bum steer, and he said no, that's a hobo driving..."

"I keep seeing him," McPhee said. "But he's not here."

Jack stepped outside to dig in the snow for more wood, tugged a long hard piece from the drifts but it was a skinny arm and hand with curled frozen fingers. He dropped it and wiped his hand but the greasy frozen flesh stuck to his palm. He kept looking for wood, rubbing his hand on his pants.

New tracks crossed the snow. *Loxley, out hunting wood like me.* The tracks skirted the last burnt houses and vanished. Fear snaked up his back. He crouched to make a smaller target, blew on his hand trying to loosen his fingers, reached for the Makarov.

"Touch that gun," a voice from the ruins said in Pashto, "and you die."

"I'm not Russian."

"You're a foreigner. I'll shoot you just for that."

"My friends are in the hills. They'll kill you."

"You have two friends. One of them's wounded. Both are in that hut over there. I can kill them both from here. You're injured too, aren't you?"

Jack felt fury that he'd duped himself into feeling safe. "I was a teacher here. I've come back to help my friends."

"What friends?"

"Ahmad al-Din."

"Brother of Wahid?"

"It's cold. Come to the fire and talk."

The man was short and wiry, in his fifties, named Sayed, icicles in his short black beard, dressed in a knit hat and sheepwool coat, with a worn and polished Enfield that he kept close. As he tore through the goat meat Jack gave him he said he'd come to Edeni to bury his cousin, but when he'd seen their fire decided to wait till morning and kill them. "I thought you were Russian," he said. "You weren't speaking Pashto."

"Only I speak Pashto," Jack said.

Sayed nodded his chin at McPhee and Loxley, meaning *what about them?*

"They also come to help my friends."

Sayed smiled. "Everyone's helpful these days."

"Where can I find Wahid?"

"My uncle might know. He lives an hour upriver."

"We'd be grateful, Sayed, if in the morning you could show us."

"And your friend there, with the broken leg?"

"We'll walk slowly, and help him."

"It's foolish to help the injured. If God wants him out of the way, why interfere?"

SOPHIE CUT AWAY the woman's veil where it had hardened with blood to her face. The woman snatched her hand. "No!"

"I have to cut it to fix your face."

"Mule. Mule kick very much. Not take away the veil."

"And broke your arms, too? How did it kick the back of your head?" Sophie ducked into the tent where Jean-Luc, a flashlight in his teeth, was operating on a farmer who had stepped on a mine. "I need another morphine," she said.

Jean-Luc put down his scalpel and the flashlight and wiped sweat from his brow with the back of his arm. "Who for?"

"That woman's been beaten. Won't let me take off the veil. It'll infect."

"Damn it, Sophie! Every one you give to takes it from someone else."

"You think I don't know?" She took one of the last vials outside and injected the woman. After a few moments the woman quieted and Sophie pulled the veil from her skin. Both cheekbones were broken, top front teeth gone, one eye swollen shut. "Tell me," she whispered, "who did this to you?"

"Mule kick. Mule kick very bad."

Sophie covered the woman with a blue UN tarp and left her half asleep on the stretcher. Soon she'd come down from the morphine and there'd be no more to give her and the pain would drive her crazy. And in the morning there'd be new wounded coming in from the bombing of Charikar.

She took a bucket to the well but it only brought up mud. Staying on the path that had been cleared of mines she went to the stream and came back with a half-bucket of foul liquid, but the gasoline stove wouldn't light. She searched among the gas cans but they were all empty. She cast around for wood chips or camel dung for a fire but they were gone too. She lay on the ground beside the woman's stretcher and wrapped herself in her robes. To hell with Jean-Luc. To hell with all men. Either they beat women or destroyed the world. Or both.

Unlike this woman she could leave any time. Another PIA flight to France, another job in a Paris emergency room. But what good was experience treating napalm burns and land mines there? What good would Paris *be*, after this?

SAYED'S UNCLE lived with three sons and their families in a stone compound above the Little Kowkcheh. Cherry trees grew in the courtyard and junipers along the walls. An old man with a knife scar down his face, he sat by the fire holding his baby granddaughter.

"Infidels!" He spat; it hissed in the fire. "Each time they come we kill them. Long ago the Persians. Then the Greek Alexander. Genghis Khan. Tamerlane of Samarkand. The English pale-skinned like you – three times they came, three times defeated... Now these Russians spill our blood and we theirs." The baby whimpered, he stroked her head.

"Vengeance is a joy divine, the Koran says," Jack answered.

"Vengeance is poisoned meat you feed your enemies. But you must then eat yourself."

"I'd like to leave my friend here – he of the broken leg. Till he's better."

"You have to pay. If the Russians come we leave him."

Next morning one of his sons led Jack and Loxley up the cliff past frozen waterfalls and across an icy log over a crashing tributary of the Little Kowkcheh to a hanging valley where junipers grew along a cliff. "I ain't doing this again," Loxley said. "I do *not* intend to die falling."

Hidden by a fallen rock slab a Russian Army blanket covered a cave mouth. They crawled down a long tunnel into a smoky cavern stinking of spoiled mutton, sheepskins, sweat, clove tobacco and gun oil. In the gloom men crouched round two fires drinking tea and cleaning weapons; others lay sleeping on a rocky platform. Wahid stared up at Jack, surprise then anger contorting his features. "What evil jinni brings *you* here?"

"When I left, before the Russians came, I said I'd return."

"But why?" Firelight deepened the cobra-shaped scar on Wahid's right cheek. He had grown angular and thin, Jack noticed; gray snaked through his tangled hair and beard.

"What happened to Edeni?"

Wahid half-smiled. "The Russians can't defeat us, so they kill our families."

"Ahmad?"

"Run to Kabul. War's too rough for him."

"Your mother?"

Wahid swung his head, meaning *Don't ask.*

"My students?"

"Their deaths were a necessary evil. To give us strength."

Jack stared into the fire seeing their faces. Yesterday he

thought he had all his children. Now he had none. He wanted to clasp his aching head, lie down forever. "We bring you weapons. And the promise of more."

"When you left Edeni you were a teacher. Now you're a soldier, promising guns?"

A man brought *chai*, the cup warming Jack's hands. "More than guns."

"A few infidels from across the ocean, you're going to kill a million Russians?"

"No. We're here to help *you* kill them."

"No. You want the Russians tied up in Afghanistan forever. We've been fighting them while you Americans have been drinking liquor and consorting with your women. We can kill them, blow up their tanks and trucks. But not helicopters. Because of the helicopters we can't hide, can't travel except at night. We're easy to track in winter. In the last battle I was the only one who survived, and even then I was wounded."

"To destroy Russian helicopters you need missiles. From us infidels."

"So I've heard. *Strelas*, the Russians call them…"

"It means *Arrow*. It's also called SA-7. We've brought you two, and a launcher."

"You come here, after *three* years, with *two* missiles, and expect to be welcomed?"

"The hungry man shouldn't complain how he's fed –"

"We don't need infidels to kill infidels."

With his Russian combat knife Jack cut a loose thread from his sleeve. "Any time the Russians want they'll chopper you to pieces."

"Yes," a gap-toothed man said. "We should try these *Strelas*."

"That's true, Aktoub," another added. "I'm tired of hiding from the helicopters."

Wahid smiled. "I was only angry because two missiles is not enough. Of course you should try them – next time the Russians come up Kowkcheh canyon."

Aktoub nodded. "In a week perhaps they come. We can try them then."

"Bring the Algerian named Husseini and the other new Arabs," Wahid said. "Let them taste blood."

"In a week, then." Jack sheathed his knife. "If the *Strelas* work we might find more. With two hundred camels of *Strelas* maybe you could win this war."

Ghost Bait

DAWN BLOODIED the peaks above the Kowk-cheh canyon. An early spring wind hissed through last year's dead grass, bringing the rushing sound of the river up from the canyon far below. A hawk circled overhead and dove fast digging its talons into the grass, then flapped slowly upward, a brown rabbit jerking in its claws.

"See how well we're hidden," Hassan Husseini said in French. "If the hawk can't see us surely the Russians can't."

Jack scanned the rocky, bouldered slope below where Loxley and Wahid's other *mujihadeen* hid in their spider holes, glanced down at the dirt road snaking along the edge of the cliffs beneath them. "The hawk saw us. She just didn't care."

"*He*," Husseini said. "It is the male that hunts."

Jack tried to ignore the dull throb in his brain. "*She*. The male is brighter-colored. And they both hunt."

He tried to recapture his thoughts. Perhaps due to the danger, they flitted quickly from one memory to another. He had been thinking of his dream last night where all his students were still alive and were singing and playing and happy. Then seeing the hawk had made him think of the fields and forests of home, why Susie didn't love him, if anyone would ever love him. Would he have been different, more lovable, if his father had lived?

He rubbed his chin on the breech of his AKMS. For months in Sin City and now in this month in Afghanistan his beard had grown, but still it itched. "Pull your muzzle in under the overhang," he said to Husseini, "so it doesn't reflect, and a MiG sees it."

"MiG? I see no MiG."

"There'll be one. And he'll pick you out just like the hawk did that rabbit. And you'll squeal, too, when you die."

"In a bad mood today? Miss your television, easy women, going to the mall?"

From almost beyond hearing came a far rumble. He felt a stab of fear, a weird frailty, an uprushing in his throat. "The Russian tanks!" Husseini shivered. "They're coming!"

"They're climbing to the pass. It'll be twenty-two minutes before they're here. *If* they don't take the other road."

"*Inshallah.*"

"Forget God's will. Just do what *I* tell you."

Husseini pretended Jack wasn't there. Pouting like a girl. But push him too hard and he'll shoot you in the back and call it another victory for Allah. You couldn't trust the Afghanis – many who'd rather bury a knife in a friend than a Russian. But even more you couldn't trust these holy warriors Home Office was bringing in from Egypt, Saudi, Yemen and other Muslim countries. Even the Afghanis said *Never let an Arab walk behind you.*

Particularly Algerians like Husseini, although they spoke French. The France you loved they hated. All of them finding their way to Hell for a shot at Paradise.

If the tanks didn't come then everything would be fine. In three weeks they had to report to Ackerman in Pakistan;

maybe there'd be no need to return here. But if the tanks came there would be a firefight and he might die, Loxley too, when otherwise they would have lived. His stomach fluttered; sweat slid down his arms; he feared Husseini might see.

"You shouldn't smile," Husseini said. "I am doing this for a spiritual reason. I am not a mercenary like you."

Jack sighed. "Aren't there any atheist Muslims?"

"It is against Sharia. To be a Muslim is to know that the Koran is the exact perfect word of God. A Muslim who does not believe the Koran must be killed."

"If the Koran is perfect it has no mistakes? Then who's right – Sunni or Shiite?"

"That came later –"

Jack felt an itch to needle him. "The Koran says the world is flat. Yet you came in an airplane around it."

"God brought me –"

"Sura Twenty-two says one of God's days is a thousand of ours, but Sura Seventy says fifty thousand... The Second Sura says God created the earth then the heavens, but the Seventy-ninth says the opposite. If one's wrong, how can the Koran be perfect?"

"Do not challenge God. Or you will burn in Hell forever." Husseini shrugged. "Actually, as an infidel you will anyway."

The vapor trails of two MiGs cleared the peaks, pink in early sun, the planes silver pinpoints before them. Jack checked his watch. "Eighteen minutes," he called to Loxley.

"Eighteen minutes," Loxley answered.

"And why," Jack turned to Husseini, "does the Tenth Sura say God guides us to the truth, yet the Fourteenth says God leads astray whom he pleases? How can we know if we're guided to the truth or led astray?"

The tanks made a steady grumble now, mixed with the

jagged whine of APCs. How many troops in those APCs – a hundred? How were twenty-one *mujihadeen*, plus five new Arab "warriors of God" like Husseini, and him and Loxley, going to stop well-trained Soviet troops with tanks and APCs? And if choppers came?

If the *Strelas* had been damaged in the jump? They sometimes misfired anyway – what then? His wrist was trembling; he reminded himself of what had happened to Edeni.

Once long ago you went to war with a stone, a knife, a club. You faced the man you fought. You didn't die from a speeding chunk of lead you never knew was coming. Then came the thrown rock, the spear, the arrow. Death you can't see coming. Now this.

Husseini was rubbing his thumb on his AK sling, a little scratching noise. *Scared too.*

If the tanks came this way and the MiGs could make the cut down the canyon, he and the others would be blown apart. He imagined his body in bloody chunks; it made his gut lurch. But Wahid's men had said the MiGs couldn't make the cut.

If he died here no one would ever know where or how.

God guides us to the truth, yet God leads astray whom he pleases. *Fools.*

If you're never afraid, Captain Perkins had said back in Sin City, *we don't want you.*

He checked his *Spetsnaz* watch, wondered what had happened to the Soviet Special Forces commando who once had worn it. "Eleven minutes."

Think what they did to Edeni. Get them for that.

IN THE LEAD T-55 TANK Captain Leo Gregoriev was also thinking of death. How it came when you least expected – you were bending to tie a shoe and stepped on a mine, or taking a leak beside your tank like Kostlev and a sniper spread your brains across the turret for crows to feed on. "Throttle back!" he yelled at the driver. "Number Two can't keep up."

"It's not him, Sir. He's slowing for those damned sardine cans behind him."

They bothered him, those APCs, the men packed into them. He shoved up the tank's hatch and dawn poured in lovely after the oily stench inside, the wind sharp in his lungs. It made you so alive to breathe this air, see these mountains. Even in Afghanistan, dung heap of human misery and cunning.

"Which way at the top, Sir?" the driver called.

Ahead the dirt track widened as it eased up the slope to the pass. He stopped the tank and stepped down. *Only danger and love make you alive.* Was that why he was here?

Gravel crunched under his boots and hissed away on the wind. Among the rocks so many places a sniper could hide. The thought made his chest feel hollow, afraid. *You're the one who asked to be here.* The battle of modern civilization against backward fanaticism, science and reason versus superstition and hatred. *Is that why?*

A half-fallen cairn cast a rumpled shadow where the road forked. One fork bent east toward the headwaters of the Mashhad River. The other cut right and dropped round a cliff toward the Kowkcheh canyon.

His body ached to climb inside the safety of the tank. Instead he walked a few meters down the right fork, saw another section far below notched across walls of stone. Vertical canyons below it, above it cliffs and wide avalanche fans of tawny rock.

His men called the Afghanis *duki* – ghosts. We're ghost bait, the men said. You go on patrol to draw fire so the Air Force can come down and hit them. But by the time the MiGs arrive the *duki* are gone.

That's why they call them ghosts.

On the left fork there'd be no *duki* on the saddle, but they could be down in the valleys above the Mashhad River. But on the right fork, toward Kowkcheh canyon, where would they hide in the steep rock and still have good fields of fire?

Either way could be *duki*. Which way did *they* think he'd go? *Imagine you're a superstitious peasant and you hate everyone who comes here. How would you think?*

Would they think he'd go left because the first part was less dangerous? Or that he'd first think that but therefore go right?

If the patrol's purpose was to entice the *duki* to shoot at you then you should take the fork where they might do so. Where *they* felt safer. Or thought you were more exposed. Far above two MiGs sketched rosy trails across the brightening sky making him feel safer.

With his seniority and combat time he could be in Moscow, vodka bars and luscious willing girls, working his way up the promotion ladder. He hitched his jacket and kicked a rock off the cliff. "We're going right," he called climbing onto his tank. "Spread the word."

The tank lurched forward, slowed where the road squeezed round the cliff. The sky narrowed, darkened. The canyon was like this war: *the deeper you go the worse it gets.*

With a shock he realized Number Two had pulled within ten meters. "Speed up!" he yelled down. He couldn't hear the driver over the clanking treads and roaring engine. He bent down into the open turret.

"No traction, Sir," the driver called. "Road's getting bad."

Behind his tank came the second T-55 then the line of sardine cans and a last tank. He felt better when the two first tanks and the first APCs had passed the rock face, the road slanting sharply down, on the right a four-foot high shoulder, on the left abyss.

The tank slowed to nudge its way round a nose of rock. Ahead there was no road, nothing but straight cliff where the road had been. And far below the river.

"Back up! Come in, Rabbit!" he yelled into the radio.

"Rabbit here!" came from the last tank. "We're taking fire, Sir."

"Turn upslope till you can fire the fifties over the shoulder!" He snatched the airlink radio. "Othello this is Truelove!"

Through the tank's armor came the whack of bullets, the ear-cracking shudder of a grenade. "Come in Othello!" he radioed to the MiGs high above, "Truelove here!" The tank lurched back, whammed into the tank behind it, snapping his neck.

"Othello here." The pilot's voice was tinny, indistinct. "I hear you, Truelove."

"We're being hit! Get down here!"

"On our way."

"They're up the canyon above the road. They've cut it in front of us. You can't hit them from above, you have to drop on them from the west."

"Can't from the west, Truelove. No approach."

"You have to! Drop them high."

"We might hit you –"

"*Do it*! Otherwise we're fucked. Call the choppers!"

"Hinds on their way."

"You've *got* to hit that slope."

"Coming down. Keep your kids indoors."

Leo yanked an AK from the clips on the turret wall and unsnapped the hatch, tugged on a radio helmet and leaped out into the roar of machine guns, thudding grenades, the horrid *whap* of an RPG into steel, the scream of tank engines. The first APC had turned and its rear treads hung over the edge. "Tell APC One don't back up," he yelled into the radio.

The road edge behind APC One buckled. He squirmed under it and hammered on the rear door. "Tell APC One open up!" he radioed. Bullets howled past his head. The first MiG roared in, sheered for the bend and screamed for altitude, the air cracked and split apart, the earth writhing with the blast of bombs. The APC settled lower, on his chest.

Its door opened. "Thought you were *duki*!" a soldier shouted. Again the earth and sky compressed as the second MiG came down. Its bombs shuddered the canyon and the APC lurched as the road fell away.

"Get out!" Leo screamed. "Get out! *Get out!*" Soldiers scrambled past him, one falling as a bullet hit him. The APC tipped up and spun over the cliff, the agonized face of the last soldier framed in its door.

He dragged the one who'd been hit to the shoulder, bullets spitting along the road. The others had taken up positions firing over the shoulder. "Call APC Two," he yelled. "I want their Fifty firing straight up the canyon, not to the left."

A thud exploded his head and he realized he was dead, felt a fleeting touch of earth beneath his back, heard a howl in his ears wondering *how can I think if I'm dead*. A kid with a bloody face dragged him to the shoulder. "Medic!" the kid yelled. "Medic!"

I'm at peace, Leo Gregoriev thought. *I'm at peace in this world.*

WHEN THE FIRST MiG screamed into the canyon its napalm pod seemed first tiny then huge, crashing high overhead, flame spouting up the cliffs searing Jack's face.

The second MiG banked into the canyon and there was nowhere to hide; it would blow them to shreds. "Shoot ahead of it!" he screamed. One man fired an RPG that darted upward, missed the MiG and fell end over end into the void. The MiG howled for altitude, its bombs hammering the cliffs. Boulders bounded over them, missed the APCs and dove into the canyon.

The first MiG came back, wingtips nearly scraping the cliffs, the pilot's courage astonishing him. Its tracers ripped the slope but it couldn't get low enough – Wahid's men had chosen this place too well, and his terror switched to fierce exaltation.

"Stop hiding!" he yelled at Husseini. "Nail that burning APC!"

Husseini screamed something. In Jack's ears a huge roar, Husseini's lips moving but making no sound. "The MiGs come back!" Husseini wailed.

Jack snatched Husseini's gun. On the road below an officer was dragging a wounded man toward the safety of the shoulder. Jack squeezed off a round, and the officer dropped, headshot. Another Russian grabbed him and dragged him to the shoulder. "Aim carefully!" Jack yelled, shoved the AK at Husseini. "*For Allah!*"

Husseini sprayed bullets. "There. I *got* one. A medic."

The back of Jack's hand caught fire. He shook off the chunk of hot metal and ran across the slope to two Afghanis whose machine gun had stopped firing. One lay wide-eyed against the cliff, a red hole in his forehead. "It's jammed," the other yelled.

Jack shoved him aside and flipped the gun over. The cartridge belt entered at an angle; he tugged but it wouldn't come lose. "He pulled the belt backwards," the Afghani said, "when he was hit. So it's jammed."

Jack yanked at the PK's cartridge belt but it would not

come free. Bullets drummed off the rock. "We're pulling back," he called. "Take it with you."

The Afghani nodded at the body. "I take him."

"He's dead!"

"He's my brother."

Jack ran back along the slope, bullets sucking at his head. "*Go! Go!*" They ran after him, one with his dead brother over his shoulder, another lugging the PK, through a notch between the cliffs up a steep ridge and along a goat trail to a bend where they'd dug spider holes the day before overlooking the road a mile above the ambush. He dashed from man to man checking that each one's magazine was full and he was hidden from both road and sky.

"Now we'll see," Husseini panted, "if infidels can predict the future."

"They're coming!" an Afghani called.

Choppers coming, the flutter of heavy rotors. *If there's more than two... Crazy to survive the MiGs then die from choppers.* "Aktoub!" he called. "Bring the RPG!"

Aktoub ran up with the RPG. "But you have this *Strela*!" he gasped.

The first chopper came up the valley four hundred feet above the road. Again Jack felt horror and fear. The Mi-24 was armored; even machine gun bullets bounced off it. He slid his SA-7 into the launching tube.

"It won't work!" Husseini moaned. "And we'll be dead."

A second Mi-24 dropped into the valley, sere and deadly.

"You take the first," Jack called to Loxley, trying to keep his voice steady. "Me the second." With a whine Jack's SA-7 locked on and launched with a peaceable *whuff* as the missile cleared the launching tube. The rocket motor ignited and the white trails of both missiles accelerated toward the fast-approaching choppers.

With a great white-black blast the missiles hit the choppers. The first Mi-24 broke apart, tail section spinning upward, the cockpit continuing on as if determined to reach its goal. A man tumbled grabbing at air and bounced along the ground. The other chopper drifted onto its side, its rotor exploding like daisy petals, settled into a steep dive and blew apart as it hit the road. "They worked!" Jack yelled at Husseini. "They worked!"

A third chopper swung down the valley.

"Now we're truly dead," Husseini screamed.

"Fire at the rotor!" Jack called, knowing it was useless. He leaped from his hole and grabbed the RPG from Aktoub but the chopper swung away, climbing fast, and he realized it was spooked by the SA-7s, didn't know they had no more.

"Pull back!" he called, counting the men as he and Loxley ran after them into the morass of cliffs and hanging valleys where even choppers couldn't find them.

Gasping for breath he glanced back at the cliffs and the twin pillars of black smoke rising into the blue sky.

Again he saw the man fall from the chopper, saw it crash and explode, the Soviet troop carriers, the soldiers pinned down and dying along the road.

For three years he'd been trained to kill. Now he had.

He imagined those soldiers' families back in Moscow or Kiev or somewhere, getting their telegrams.

It doesn't bother me at all, he told himself.

First blood.

Opium

"**W**HEN THAT BULLET hit your helmet," the field doctor told Leo, "it punched a lot of metal and plastic into your skull. We need to chopper you to Kabul, find a surgeon to dig it out."

Alive. Leo felt giddy exuberance. "Fine with me."

"But we don't have a brain surgeon in Kabul. And with all this crap in your head we can't fly you to Moscow. Only reason you feel good is you're high on morphine."

"Afghani opium no doubt." He wanted to laugh; ecstasy surged through him. *Alive.* He had tried to be brave, risked death but had lived anyway. The road ahead was bright and joyous. Why do people fight when they have this mysterious gift, this magic joy, of life?

Even this field clinic piled with bloody bandages, this morose doctor with nicotined fingers and dead eyes, the stainless steel coffins stacked up the wall – all seemed imbued with sacred immanence. "I can't keep anything in my head... What happened?"

"I'm told it was a great victory. Many *ghosts* dead, weapons deserted..."

"How many dead?"

"Central Command didn't say."

"How many our dead?"

"Twelve that I've seen. And ten wounded, plus three criticals already flown out."

His exuberance died. "And matériel?"

"They say one APC –"

"I saw three," he now remembered. "Two burning and one went off the ledge."

"– and..." the doctor glanced out the window, "two Hinds."

Leo snatched the doctor's arm. "A disaster, wasn't it?" The road ahead was no longer joyous; it was narrow and steep and ended in the middle of a cliff.

He thought of the boys now still alive whose bodies soon would be inside these silver coffins flying in the Black Tulips back to Russia. "We're killing and dying for nothing."

"That's war." The doctor held out a cigarette pack. "Have a Yava."

Leo waved it away. "I'm giving up smoking."

AT DUSK Jack and Loxley descended the canyon of the Little Kowkcheh and crossed the River above Edeni. Loxley turned upstream toward Sayed's uncle's farm to check on McPhee, and Jack climbed the path into the mountains to Wahid's base.

He ducked under the Russian Army blanket into the smoky fetid cave. The men cooking a sheep by the fire moved to make him a place. Wahid lay on sheepskins with his head against a Russian blanket roll. "Now you have faith in *Strelas*?" Jack said.

"Whatever good a man does comes from God – you know that."

"Then we'll take our *Strelas* elsewhere. To Hekmatyar, perhaps?"

"He's nearby I hear. But you have no more *Strelas*."

With his combat knife Jack sliced off a chunk of mutton. "More *Strelas* can be bought in Pakistan, for they are also made in China. But how to get them over the Hindu Kush?"

"Why not across the same mountains the opium goes out? One camel carries a hundred fifty kilos of opium. How much weighs one *Strela*?"

"Eleven kilos for the launcher, nine for each missile."

"So seven to a camel..."

"You need more missiles than launchers."

Wahid sat back, finger-combing his beard, watching Jack down his long nose. "And these *Strelas*, who pays?"

"I'm not here to give them. Just to help you find them."

"So why do other Americans working with Pakistan give guns to Hekmatyar?"

"Perhaps *he* will be Eagle of the Hindu Kush? He has more of Afghanistan than you."

"The Pakistanis own him." Wahid unclipped his bayonet and cut a chunk of mutton. "No one owns me."

Jack glanced at the rings of a burning branch in the fire, imagined the tree that had clung to the mountain for so many years. "Probably no one wants to."

Wahid grinned. "For having killed so many Russians you are not happy?"

Jack glanced at a man in the corner sharpening a knife on a stone, another playing a flute, those dozing round the fire or sleeping on willow mats. "I don't need to kill to be happy."

"You're a coward then." Wahid chewed the mutton off the end of his bayonet, blood dribbling into his beard. "These *Strelas*, when America buys them –"

"America has no part in this. *You* buy them. That's what I'm telling you."

"I am a philanthropist? I do this for pleasure?"

"You do this to kill Russians."

"You are fucking the wrong dog, my friend –"

"I leave that to you. And I'm not your friend."

"Your blood brother is my brother –"

"You are not my brother."

"You love Hekmatyar? He's a whore's cunt. A hundred fifty-four mules and camels of opium I sent last year over the Kush to Pakistan. Hekmatyar didn't even send seventy."

"I don't give a shit about opium –"

"Since Pakistan won't share their American weapons with me as they do with Hekmatyar, you think they'll trade Chinese *Strelas* for my opium?"

"My job was bring those two *Strelas*. To see if you could use them."

"And so I did." Wahid waved a hand at the cave entrance. "I have ten camels leaving for Pakistan next month. So go with them, bring back as many missiles as you can?"

"I thought you didn't need *infidel* weapons."

"The Koran says to use infidels any time we want, your souls don't matter... So, ten camels of Strelas, perhaps, are worth one camel of opium?"

Jack stood, slung his rifle. "I'll talk to my infidel friends." He stepped through the Army blanket into frozen night and turned down the trail toward Sayed's uncle's farm. A step hissed the snow behind him and he spun round aiming his gun.

"You mustn't fear me," Aktoub said.

"I fear everything. That's how one stays alive in this place."

"Please, *Jyek*, do not bear him ill will. He's proud."

"A commander should love his men more than himself."

Aktoub raised his hands, a gesture of helplessness. "We thank Allah for your help."

Jack felt a rush of affection. "Thank the American people." He turned and started down the mountain, walking fast and steadily, for in the falling snow he needn't fear Soviet patrols, would leave no tracks. The cold thin air tasted wonderful after the putrid cave.

In the ambush he'd been so *alive*, aware in slow motion, seeing everything – the white Cyrillic letters on an APC's gray door, a green fatigue cap tumbling, a man's surprised face as he was hit, a spent round spinning in the dust, the chopper's spiraling death.

Impossible that he was alive and the men he'd killed were dead.

If he'd stayed with Susie they'd have kids now. He'd be coming home at night from some job, fixing up the house on weekends. But she'd fucked another guy and got knocked up and now what they'd had they didn't have any more.

If Home Office wanted him and Loxley and McPhee to start this Third Force, one not run through Islamabad or by the Saudis, then Wahid was right: how would the *mujihadeen* pay for it except with opium? Had Home Office known all along and never said?

What would his father think of trading opium for guns? Didn't we do that in Nam, tons and tons of opium and hash flown out by the CIA's Air America, keeping Americans high while our bombs obliterated Indochina?

Ahead on the trail a dark spot coming. Jack dove into the boulders aiming at it. If it was a patrol they'd see his tracks. If it was just a few Russians maybe he could get them all. But the Russians never patrolled with just a few. *Asshole*, he swore silently at himself. *You're going to die.*

The dark spot grew, a man coming fast. Afghani maybe. On whose side?

Shoot him before he gets you.

A tall man, rifle slung, jogging uphill through the deep powder. Jack tightened his finger on the trigger. "Who are you?" he yelled in Pashto.

The man stopped, raised his hands. "I seek Wahid," he said, in bad Pashto.

"You asshole!" Jack yelled. "I almost shot you!"

"Jack, hurry," Loxley said. "We've got to go down!"

"You missed dinner. *Chez* Wahid."

"McPhee's not there. At Sayed's uncle's."

"Not *there*?"

"Gone." Hands on knees Loxley caught his breath. "Fuckin place. Empty."

City of the Blind

LEO DREAMED of running along a street in Ekaterinburg rolling a willow hoop with a stick, the childish joy in such a simple game. Now, awakening, the elation slid away and he looked up into a young woman's face, beautiful but drawn, her green surgeon's mask pulled up over glistening auburn hair.

"*Xorosho?*" she asked. A strange accent.

"Yes, good," he answered. "Fantastic. Who are you?"

"She doesn't speak Russian," an orderly said. "She just operated on your skull."

"Where's *our* doctors?"

"Our hospital got hit."

Leo shook his head in frustration and the woman spoke angrily. He'd understood what she'd said, he realized slowly. "*Vous êtes française?*"

Her eyes widened. "You speak French?"

He tried to remember why. "I was an attaché. Paris. Why are *you* here?"

"I'm in Doctors Without Borders – the French medical group. Why are *you* here?"

"Soldiers do what they're told."

"Who told you to come destroy Afghanistan?"

"The heart has its reasons," he started to say, making a joke of Pascal, but her eyes hardened and he stopped. "I don't know," he said, and drifted away.

JACK AND LOXLEY RAN along the tracks of Sayed's uncle and his family and one larger unevenly treading boot that might be McPhee's. After descending the Little Kowkcheh toward Edeni the tracks split, the women and old man continuing downriver and the three men – perhaps the brothers – and McPhee climbing the switchbacks above the Panjshir River.

Jack brushed snow from his hair, pulled a chunk of bread from his pack and gave half to Loxley. First he'd lost Gus and now maybe McPhee. What was he doing wrong? How many men had his father lost at Ia Drang before he died? What does it feel like, seeing your men go down? Fury and despair.

The snow fell harder. "Now we'll lose their trail," Loxley said matter-of-factly.

Jack ate some snow. "Maybe they'll keep climbing. Above the clouds there'll be no new snow."

The snow eased; stars slid past gaps in the clouds. The tracks led up an icefall on one side of a steep scarp. Chunks of snow came scooting down from Loxley's feet into Jack's face. *How did McPhee make this?* Jack kept thinking. *Maybe it isn't him.*

They reached a ridge between two ice-clad peaks, the scarp below them now. Dawn clouds filled the east. "We can't get caught up here!" Jack yelled over the wind. He pointed up at the pyramid of black rock and ice above them. "That's Bandakur. The other side of those mountains was our DZ."

"Month ago." Loxley took a breath. "Another life."

As they followed the trail down the tracks grew fresher. From a rocky spur they saw down into the Panjshir Valley, a huge canyon of red and brown rock soaring up into glaciers and vertical peaks. Far below the River sparkled in its black bed like a new-skinned snake.

Beyond was Pakistan. Strange that they could cross that and in days be in Peshawar, take a plane home. He sat on the rock spur. There was a howl like the wind, growing louder.

"Plane!" He shoved Loxley into the rocks as the MiG screamed down at them with guns blazing and the world exploded.

"EVERYTHING'S OKAY on your X-rays," Sophie said.

Leo held his head steady. Every time he moved it the damned thing hurt like hell. "I suppose I have to thank you."

"It's my job. If I had the choice I'd let you all die."

"In that field clinic, when I realized I was alive, that I had a new life..."

"Sometimes that happens when you're wounded. We normally don't realize how close death always is."

"Before this I was just a tank commander. Now I don't see the point." It irritated him how difficult it was to understand what he wanted to say, how the drugs made him mumble.

"Your young men who come in here all shot up. Nineteen years old, a pretty girl at home and now they have no legs, no testicles, or they're blind. Ask *them*."

A rat scampered along the wall and hid behind a gurney, its tail sticking out like a gray string. "So you think Afghanistan would be better as a feudal theocracy?" he said sharply. "People killing people because they wear the wrong kind of veil?"

"So you're killing them so they don't kill each other? Is that it?"

"To hell with all that. As soon as I'm better will you have dinner with me?"

"With *you?*"

"What, you have a husband or something? To hell with him too."

"I don't have a husband. Or something." Her green eyes hardened. "Why would I spend time with a killer? You realize what you're doing to Afghanistan?"

This was his new life, he told himself, he didn't have to reasonable. "We'll go to the officers' mess, or the Hotel International –"

"I just took twenty-six pieces of metal and plastic out of your skull."

"My father's lived forty years with slivers of *Panzerfaust* in him."

She turned to check a monitor behind him. "So get him down here and we'll operate on him too."

New sun through a bandanna stretched across the window warmed his face. He started to stand. "Don't do that!" she snapped but the damn room spun around and the edge of the bed came up and smacked him in the face.

She had him by the arm; he stood. "Got to do what you feel. Life's too short."

She sat him on the edge of the bed. "And you, back in Moscow –"

"Leningrad. Once was called St. Petersburg but we don't mention that."

"– you don't, back there, have a wife or 'something'?"

"I wouldn't ask you if I did."

She was gone. Yet he could imagine her clearly as if he'd always known her: a runner's tall lithe form – when could she have time to run in all this insanity? Strong cheekbones and a wide mouth over large white teeth, long honey-auburn hair – the beauty of someone who doesn't know how lovely she is.

He couldn't breathe, dizzy. His head throbbed; blood was trickling down inside the bandages. *Valley of the Moon,* the words came to him but he did not know why.

JACK COULDN'T understand what had happened, then remembered. "Where's the MiG?"

"Left us for dead." Loxley said. "I *told* you we shouldn't get caught up here."

"Asshole," Jack laughed, dizzy with joy at evading death. "*I* was the one said that."

The world was silent but for the hiss of falling snow. Jack glanced at the sky: no snow was falling. "My ears." His voice bounced around inside his head like a ping-pong ball.

"Me too," Loxley batted an ear with the heel of his hand. "Gonna need a hearing aid. Like my Grandma. Suppose that's covered in our retirement?"

"Yeah, just like Owen's twenty-four hour hookers and Jacuzzi."

Loxley pulled him up. "So let's go find him."

They jogged along the tracks down toward the Panjshir River and southward toward the Soviet base at Parian. "They're gonna sell him to the Russians," Loxley said.

Jack thought of Sayed's uncle and his three sons who had led him to Wahid. If you couldn't trust the people from one valley to the next, how could you unite them?

"If the Soviets get him – whole thing – will unravel." Lose another man and he was a failure as an officer. As a man. The words echoed in his head, a metronome pacing him as he ran, *Lose another man... Failure as a man... Lose another man...*

The snow thinned and soon the tracks picked up a mule

trail that was wider and easier to run on. "He's dragging one foot," Loxley said, "going slow as he can."

"He goes too slow they'll shoot him." Jack saw the three brothers shooting Owen and that made him run faster, holding the AK in his right hand, gripping one strap of his willow basket pack against his shoulder with his left.

LEO SAT IN MORNING sun in the hospital ward, a book on his lap, watching his fellow wounded soldiers. The one-legged hobbling on crutches, the wheel-chaired somberly rolling, another going round in circles by himself. A few with wrapped heads sitting quietly, some with bandages over their eyes. One on a bench kept chuckling as he snatched with his left hand at a right arm that was no longer there.

Heroes of the Soviet Union. For this wound he'd get a – what medal was it they gave to those stupid enough to step in the way of a bullet? And he was a lucky one.

"Still alive?" the doctor said, her French alien amidst the din of Russian. "I did too good a job –"

"I've been watching these wounded men. And trying to understand why, in the vast chaos of life, did they end up here to be killed or ruined for life?"

"It disgusts me, healing people so they can kill again."

"Me too. I don't understand why we fight... this damn wound has ruined me... But why are *you* here?"

"Too many injured Afghani women – the male doctors here won't touch them."

"Damn it, that's why *I'm* here – to help change this place!"

"Evil always starts with good intentions."

"A waste of time, talking with you." He turned away, furious yet not wanting her to leave, surprised to find himself reach out and take her hand. "You look exhausted..."

She yanked it away. "Been here all night."

"Doctors Without Borders – I thought you pulled back to the refugee camps in Pakistan?"

"I had a choice, stay or go."

"So you *stay*?"

"Like I said, I'm the only one to treat the women." Her face was half-turned toward the sun; he could see the tendons in her neck, the steady pulse in her throat, the smooth luster of her skin, her small full breasts and the long indent of her waist. He imagined her naked, his mouth dry. Yet how defenseless she was, soft skin and long limbs and lovely lips. Wasn't it better to be in a tank with seven inches of steel around you? But then the *duki* hit you with an RPG that drives through the steel and fills the inside with flame, so nothing's left of you but charred teeth.

"*Now* what are you thinking?" she said.

"The Big Bang."

"Big Bang?"

"This physicist in Moscow, he thinks the universe began with the collision of two particles, two neutrinos maybe. But of course the question –"

"Where did the two neutrinos come from?"

"Do you know *City of the Blind,* by the Afghani poet Sana'i? When an elephant arrives, all the blind people touch a different part of it trying to understand what it is." He picked up the book, translating slowly,

"*Those who touched the ear said an elephant is thick and flat as a carpet*

Those who touched his trunk said it is a terrifying shape like a pipe

Those who touched its foot said it is long and straight as a column

Each one, discovering a part, formed the wrong idea,

And not understanding the elephant as a whole, re-
mained in blindness
  This is how people think of God
  And why the reason goes astray."

"You believe that?"

"Like them, I believe only what I can feel for myself."

A bell was ringing. She stood. "Incoming."

He flinched. "It's not your problem."

"My problem *is* injured people. People hurt by soldiers like you –"

"I don't want to argue with you, damn it. Before you came I was thinking of Rumi –

Before death's swordsman charges,
Call for the scarlet wine
You are not gold, O careless fool!
To be buried and dug up again."

She moved to the door. "So what's the point?"

"The point is you should have dinner with me. We'll drink wine, like Rumi says. Because once we're dead we'll never drink wine again."

IN BRIGHT sun Sophie crossed Al Minaya, humming under her breath so none of the passing men would hit her for speaking aloud.

"What a lovely day!" she exclaimed to the old crone at the desk as she closed the door of the woman's shelter behind her.

The woman glanced at Sophie over her spectacles. "You were out all night."

"Extra wounded." Why, Sophie wondered, am I explaining myself to this rancorous prude? These women who become what their men see in them...

In the hall she went to the sink and turned on the faucet. It spat air, then nothing. What a fool she was to think there'd be water. She took water from a pail on the woodstove and washed her hands in the sink and with an old toothbrush from her pocket scrubbed under her nails. Galaya the new girl came into the kitchen with another pail of water. "I put aside some rice for you last night," Galaya said. "Sorry there's no lamb. The other women ate it all."

Sophie restrained the ditzy urge to hug her. "They need it more than I do."

Galaya smiled then caught herself and hid her face. Sophie took the bowl of rice to her room. "Having a good day?" she said to the crucifix over the bed. She did not feel sleepy. She sat at her desk eating the rice and studying her Russian lesson book. *Сегодня ясное небо,* she wrote, *и птицы летают высоко*: The sky is clear today, and the birds are flying high.

Rue the Day

THROUGH HIS SOVIET field glasses Jack scanned the stone farmhouse hunched in the lee of wind-stripped trees in the valley below. Two mules huddled against a wall, tails between their legs. Smoke pointed like an arrow northward; a bright spot of green was a Soviet tarp pinned by stones to the roof and crackling in the wind.

"He's got to be here." He checked the setting sun.

"They're not mounting watch," Loxley said. "Think they own the place."

"We got two grenades left. If he comes out to piss, we take the guy with him and toss the grenades inside?"

"One guy on each side of the door."

"Or one guy in front, the other in back."

"I don't want you shooting me by accident, asshole."

"What if he don't have to piss?"

"Owen? All he ever does. Remember Vegas, him pissing in that fountain?"

Jack settled into the rocks. *The beauty of sleep.* "I'll wake you in half an hour. Then I'll sleep half an hour. Then we move in."

"Imagine, those fuckers in there... Talkin shit. Eatin Mohammed up sideways. Don't even know, dumb fuckers. They're about to die."

AHMAD CLIMBED a tank barrier of charred cars and splintered telephone poles, dragging his sack of food behind him. In the old days Kabul had been warmer, but now with so many buildings knocked down and no trees standing, nothing stopped the cold wind. In the old days of the king, before the Muslim uprising, when there'd been food for everyone, a multiparty assembly, a constitution, girls in miniskirts, rock'n roll on the radio, cafés and movies...

Now by day he prowled Kabul's bludgeoned streets for food – beet tops, rancid potatoes, spoiled feed from slaughterhouse pens, discarded Soviet rations, old cans from bombed-out basements. At night, exhausted and hungry, he carried what food he'd found or stolen back to the orphanage where a hundred seventy children – the number changed depending on who died, what new ones came – waited with bleak eyes and swollen bellies. It wasn't an orphanage, really, just Ahmad and an ancient woman named Safír whose husband was dead and whose home this house had once been.

When he could he sent kids across the Pakistan border to the UN camps, but this was dangerous and expensive. And more and more new ones kept coming – in Afghanistan there was no lack of orphans.

Today he'd found five candles in a blasted teashop. This was a dilemma. It would be wonderful to have them when Safír amputated a gangrened or mine-shattered limb – this she did with a little curved saw her husband had used to prune fruit trees in what had been the garden. But if she used the candles he could not trade them for food, for a sack of maggoty grain from the United Nations, or even a box of powdered milk robbed from the Soviet "Peace Through Friendship" warehouse.

A rustle behind him made him spin round: nothing. Rats, or a starving dog, or just this Kush wind from the north. When death comes they say sometimes you hear it coming.

A smashed Soviet armored car lurked in an alley. It might have rations, even vodka, God willing, that he could trade for medicine or use to anesthetize a child or sterilize a wound. Why say "God willing"? Anyone who'd lived through this would never believe in God.

He put down his bag, inside it the day's find of barley swept up from a shop floor, a chocolate bar from under a bed in a deserted Soviet bivouac, seven good cabbages, a pigeon not long dead, the five candles. The armored car's seats were carbonized and bent by an explosion; it looked like the interior of an oven. But in the back, that silver glow – a canteen, maybe? Gingerly he squirmed through the shattered windshield.

No, it was just a canister of some kind – teargas maybe, broken and useless for trading. He heard a noise outside, a skidding sound – *his bag*! He dove out the windshield and sprinted after a kid dragging the bag down the street. The kid caught an ankle in barbed wire and fell spilling cabbages and candles. Ahmad grabbed him. "You little bastard!"

"I'm *not* a bastard," the kid answered, barely breathless.

Ahmad suppressed a laugh. This country with its insane proprieties, to be dying of hunger yet worry what someone calls you. "What are you, then?"

"My mother and father are dead. But I'm not a bastard."

Ahmad pulled him closer. "I know you! From Edeni. It can't be – Suley?"

The kid would not face him. "It's me!" Ahmad shook him. "Your teacher!"

Suley had grown into a gaunt fierce boy, perhaps thirteen, so skinny and dirty it was hard to tell. Grasping his wrist Ahmad tried to gather the cabbages back into the bag but they kept rolling downhill. He swore when he saw that two candles had broken.

Suley snatched at Ahmad's hand to pry it from his wrist. The kid's fingers were like steel. Ahmad grabbed his hair. "You're coming to our orphanage. There's other kids your age. And food, when guys like you don't steal it."

"You'll rue the day," the boy tried to yank free, "you found me."

"KNIFE –" Jack rubbed his hands, trying to warm them.

"Check." Loxley was shivering too.

"Full magazine mounted, two spares."

"Check."

"One grenade each."

"Check."

"20:03:15."

Loxley looked at his *Spetsnaz* watch. "Check."

"20:18 we're on both sides of the door, behind the wall. Anybody comes out is gonna be night-blind, we can move in behind them soon as the door's closed."

Night had fallen, bitter cold. Rocks stung Jack's hands as he crawled toward the door. To his left he could not see Loxley. Even when they had taken up positions he could barely make him out on the far side of the door. From inside a steady rumble of voices.

A voice moved toward the door. Wood squeaked on the mud floor as the door dragged open, then closed. An Afghani came out, relieved himself, burped and went inside. Odors of wood smoke and cooked barley lingered.

After a few minutes two voices came toward the door. A dark shape moved out into the night, then another, a third.

The door shut.

"Here I am," a voice said in English. *McPhee.* "Out here with two assholes, one on each side, both with guns..."

"Shut up," a voice said in Pashto.

". . . and a bunch of people inside, one guy with a gun, the rest civilians..."

"Shut *up!*" the voice said again, a thunk of a rifle butt against flesh. After a moment, spattering sounds on the frozen ground. "Let's go in," another voice said in Pashto. "Catch your death out here."

Jack and Loxley closed in behind them. Jack yanked back one man's head and drove the combat knife into his throat. The man gurgled, dropped to his knees, tried to shake him off. "Owen!" Jack whispered. "It's us!" He pulled the man back up to keep his rifle from hitting the ground.

"Where the fuck you been!" McPhee whispered.

"Grab their guns. Can you walk?"

They left the two bodies behind a boulder, circled back to the mule track and ran down it toward the Panjshir Valley. After a few minutes they pulled up.

"That was brilliant, telling us who they were," Jack panted. "How many." He wiped blood from his hands with snow, thinking that with each new death the killing bothered him less. "We have to run all night or these guys'll catch us. There's a trail along the west side of the valley, about a thousand feet above it. We take that toward the Soviet outpost at Parian, then swing back up toward the Little Kowkcheh."

"Parian's where *they* were taking me, sell me to the Russians."

"They won't expect us to go that way."

McPhee took a breath. "What happened with the ambush?"

"We took out two Hinds," Loxley said. "Blew them

right out of the sky."

"Who'd we lose?"

"One guy. We also got three APCs and a bunch of soldiers."

"Jesus, Ackerman was right. If we can interdict the Russian air war with our missiles, the Afghanis might beat them on the ground. It could change the whole fuckin war."

Jack shifted the two rifles on his shoulder. "Wahid wants more missiles. In two weeks we report to Ackerman in Pakistan, so we take one of Wahid's camel trains over the Kush to Pakistan and maybe bring back more *Strelas*. We'll leave you in Rawalpindi till your ankle's healed."

"The fuck you will. This's *my* mission too. It's gonna be a whole new war."

LEO PACED the hospital garden where mortar-shattered fruit trees lay under a fresh dusting of snow. An orange sun was creeping over the Hindu Kush. To the east trucks or oil tanks were burning; from the north came a deepening thunder as MiG 28's took off from Bagram. Somewhere a child was giggling.

He beckoned an army orderly, a young woman with a wide Ukrainian face. "Where's the French doctor?"

"She's in the critical ward doing her rounds."

"She has no business there!" He ran up the stairs three at a time and stomped into the ward. There she was, bent over a heavily bandaged soldier, a young doctor beside her. "Who said you could come in here?"

She held a finger to her lips. "Wait a few minutes, till I'm done."

Who was *she* giving orders? He stood in the entry, slippers sticking in fresh blood.

"You don't even speak Russian!" he snapped when she came through the double doors. "How can you treat soldiers when you don't understand them?"

"Doctor Sushlev speaks French better than you. I'm working with him. Doctor Denisov said I could."

Denisov was the hospital commandant. *I've been ambushed*, Leo realized. But a battle wasn't a war. "For how long?"

She looked at him oddly. "Let's go outside."

He walked back and forth while she sat on a bench, hands in her lap, the sun on her face. "Things are going badly for us," he said. "So I worry about security."

"If the Afghanis didn't have you for enemies they'd just keep killing each other."

"Religion's man's oldest plague, isn't it?" He pulled a pack of Yavas from his breast pocket and lit one. "If these fundamentalists take over Afghanistan they'll undermine Tajikistan, Uzbekistan. Our empire falls apart. A civilized world falls apart."

She cocked her head. "You shouldn't smoke those."

He took the cigarette from his mouth. "You interfere in everything, don't you?"

"Empires always fall apart. You're a soldier – you know that."

"I'm just here because they sent me."

"You always do what you're told? You'll make some woman a fine husband."

Again he felt outflanked. "Or would you?" she smiled.

He flicked the cigarette away. "So if we leave?"

"You're bringing peace? *Peace through war* – the new slogan of international socialism?"

He ached to take out another cigarette but didn't. "So we leave, what then?"

"I'm only a doctor, Captain. I go where pain is and try to lessen it."

"How's that different from being a soldier?" Why did he

keep explaining himself to her?

She pulled herself up on the bench. "Please, Captain, sit beside me. As we've seen, life's very short."

He sat stiffly. Why did he always do what she said? "Soon as I'm out of here I'm going back to the Panjshir. So it's good you have this other guy who speaks French."

"I'm learning Russian: *Ya govaryu ochen pa-russki.* See?"

"That's a good accent –"

"You're gone how long?"

"Couple weeks."

"Is it dangerous?" She turned away. "That's a stupid question."

He took her long fingers in his hand. "Speaking of dangerous – you should go back to Paris."

"I never do what I don't want." She turned over his hand. "How rough your skin is." She squeezed his fingernail. "See, you need more vitamins. What's this black?"

"Engine oil. All tank men get that – becomes part of your skin."

She said nothing, then, "It's not just saving the women that I stay for. It's the mystery of life – I'm closer to it here."

He looked out at the smoky Kabul morning, half-hearing the chatter of helicopters in the distance, the keening of jets, a rumble of APCs heading north on Karaya Boulevard. "I got bored with dull mornings in Leningrad, training exercises without purpose, social dinners with Army brass... At least here I'm doing something."

"We're symbiotic, aren't we, Captain? You kill people, I heal them."

"Did it ever occur to you that some men become soldiers to try to lessen killing, not increase it?"

"That's like making people sick to heal them –"

"Isn't that inoculation? How we develop immunities,

my dear."

"You know it's not the same."

"I try to understand where we're going," he said after a while. "Why we do what we do. War's how humans progress. Even space travel uses the technologies of war – all based on Nazi V2 rockets." He took out another cigarette but didn't light it. "Humans are a teeming mass devouring and destroying everything. The only excuse is," and he looked away, trying to understand his thought, "is if we expand to other worlds. When I think of humans on this earth I think of maggots on a corpse. How they pick it clean. Then they turn into flies and fly to the next one."

"You've been badly injured. You should go home. You don't have to fight any more."

"Then what?"

"Will you be in Kabul," she said suddenly, "when you return from the Panjshir?" She seemed softer, nearly afraid, as if he'd say no.

"When I thought I was dead, you were *there*, speaking to me. You brought me back." He kissed her, gently then hard, tasted her tongue and gums and teeth, feeling her electric angularity, the power of her body. A bell rang and she jumped up and ran back inside. He wandered the garden feeling useless and angry, thought of the poem by Attar of Nishapur, killed when an old man by the invading Mongols,

If you love her do not ask about existence and non-existence...

Don't talk about the beginning and do not ask about the end.

But I hardly know her, he reminded himself.

II

Pakistan

Bandit

April 1983

"I'D WALK A MILE for a camel," Loxley sang off-key as they followed Wahid's camels up the stony trail through the mountains toward Pakistan.

"In the true religion," Hassan Husseini said, trotting to catch up, "the camel is seen as an example of God's wisdom. *De la sagesse de Dieu.*"

"Yes." Jack watched the rear of the camel before him rise and fall with each step of its elongated, double-jointed rear legs. "It surely is."

"The Koran tells how the prophet Salih gave the people of Thamud a she-camel as a gift from God, but they killed the camel and so God brought down an earthquake upon them."

Jack stepped around a steaming manure pile. "Served them right."

"It's good to hear that even among infidels there is respect for camels."

They came to a stream with a cluster of mud houses with shell-holed walls and charred beams, a shattered granary where crows flew away cawing. Wind had scattered barley the crows were eating. Wahid's men began to gather up the barley and feed it to the camels.

Jack scouted the ruins hoping for a chicken to kill. A growl stopped him. He peered into the gloom of a shed. "Loxley!" he called. "Bring a light."

Loxley came stepping around places that looked mined. "It's a dog."

"I can see that."

The dog backed away from the light, straining at a chain, yellow eyes wild. "Somebody's mined him," Loxley said. "Go any closer and you'll blow yourself to kingdom come."

Jack knelt, extended a hand. "Here, puppy." The dog bared huge teeth.

"If that's a puppy I'm a fuckin dromedary."

McPhee limped over watching the ground for trigger wires. "That's a beautiful dog."

"I guaran-fuckin-tee you," Loxley said, "the front of this shed's mined."

"Yeah," McPhee agreed. "Guaranteed."

"Dog don't like it," Loxley said. "He knows."

McPhee unshouldered his rifle. "Best to put him down."

"No." Jack raised his hand. "I'm going around the back, see if I can free him that way."

"You're gonna step on something and get your testicles all mixed up with your eyeballs."

Jack unsnapped his bayonet and moved along the shed, probing the earth with its tip. The wall of the shed stank of burnt mud and dung. He heard the dog panting inside. He moved around the back, still probing. His bayonet clicked on something solid. He backed away, stepping in exactly the same places. "Found one!" he called.

"Goddammit get out of there!" McPhee yelled.

"Moving around the side. Going to get him this way." Jack dug out a brick with his bayonet, widened a hole at the bottom, reached inside and grabbed the dog's leather collar.

The dog came out quickly, trying to pull away. He was huge and wolflike, black with a white blaze on his chest. As Jack tugged him closer the dog snarled and nipped his hand, so gently Jack did not let go. "Hey, puppy," Jack said. "Stop that."

"Russian shepherd," McPhee said. "The Afghanis tied him in there, hoping some Russian'd come along and try to free him, get blown away."

"What's that written on his collar?" Loxley said.

Jack looked down at the words in Cyrillic: Бандит. "Bandit." The dog cocked his head. "Same in Russian as English." He tied a camel halter to the dog's collar and took him down to the stream where he lay down and drank.

The Afghanis were spreading prayer rugs beside the camels. Bandit growled at them, his back fur raised. Jack gave him a bowl of rice and mutton.

"In the Koran," Husseini said," dogs are false messengers. Enemies of God."

"In the Koran," Jack said, "everything's an enemy of God."

When the dog had finished eating he sat on his haunches beside Jack watching Husseini and the *mujihadeen*, his tall pointed ears cocked forward, as Jack finger-combed his fur tugging out burrs and tangles. *Bandit's what the Russians call Afghanis*, he remembered, wondered who Bandit's master had been – a Russian officer perhaps – and what had happened to him.

With the camel halter tied to Bandit's collar he wandered down the trail. Soon the dog no longer shied away from him, and when Jack sat cross-legged on a boulder still warm from the sun Bandit sat next to him, nuzzled his arm and then reached up and licked his face. "Hey Big Ears," Jack laughed, "stop that."

He untied the halter from his collar. Bandit put a great paw on Jack's knee and looked into his face. For an instant Jack felt fear – this huge dog with his inch-long canines could rip his neck open in a second – but the look in Bandit's golden-brown eyes was warm and thankful – *I know what you did for me.*

He held the dog's paw in his hand, feeling the supple tendons and rough pads, the hard claws. "I once lost a friend like you," he said, feeling not at all weird talking to a strange dog in the wilds of the Hindu Kush. "I've never had a lot of friends... maybe I'm too hard to know, don't like attachments..."

The kindness in the dog's lustrous eyes with their strong black pupils seemed to accept everything Jack said, made talk unnecessary. He ran his fingers through the fur of Bandit's neck, undid the leather collar and massaged the thick muscles. "You're free," he smiled. "If you want to be with me, I want to be with you."

THAT NIGHT they led the camels over the ridge into Pakistan and down the Darband valley and in the morning tied them in a pine grove near a dirt road. Aktoub and another of Wahid's men walked down the road toward a distant village and came back in a Toyota pickup mounted with a machine gun.

"I want you out first," Jack told McPhee. "Go to our Embassy in Islamabad, the military section. Tell them you've come from Cleveland looking for a job. That's code to send you to Ackerman, who will be somewhere in Rawalpindi. The Pakis have the Embassy wired, so watch what you say. Soon as you see Ackerman, have them take care of that leg."

McPhee left in the Toyota pickup and returned two days later wearing clean civilian clothes, bringing cold roast beef, apples, and three cans of dog food. "You girls look like shit," he commented.

"And you smell like a Texas whore," Loxley said.

"That's shampoo, darling. First shower in months. You girls could sure use one."

"What about Gus?" Jack said, killing the mood.

"Nothing from the Soviets – don't know what they thought..." McPhee stared at the Afghanis, the hills. "Ackerman says we're fucking heroes. That we can turn this war around."

Jack shook his head. "It isn't worth Gus."

"Bastards at Islamic Jihad just bombed our Beirut Embassy. Sixty dead and hundreds wounded."

"*What?*" Loxley yelled. "What they hit *us* for?"

"Don't like Americans, apparently... Had an extra truck of Semtex."

Jack glanced at the Arabs squatting with the Afghanis in a close circle by the camels. "And we're breeding these assholes?"

"Tell it to Ackerman," McPhee said. "He's in the back of New Asia Paradise Heavy Tools Import-Export. I'll tell you how to get there –"

At dusk Jack and Loxley reached Rawalpindi. The racket of motorbikes and clatter of trucks and buses spewing diesel exhaust, the canned *mullah* loudspeakers wailing, the sewage in chunks and rivulets in the gutters, the thronging scrawny men in rags and headwraps, the women in *yashmaks* and slippers tiptoeing through the muck, the odors of death and decay, the constant din and filthy air, and the crushing presence of far too many impoverished people driven together by hunger, despair, and Islam's fanatic renunciation – all made him desperate to regain the empty vast mountains with their knife-edge air and blue-white vistas. If Rawalpindi was life, then fuck it the Hindu Kush was better.

New Asia Paradise Heavy Tools was a warehouse in a back lot in an industrial area where the long-distance trucks left for Karachi and Lahore. Stacks of steel pipe, coils of heavy plaited wire, rolls of sheet metal, and bundles of PVC pipe wrapped in white plastic were piled to the ceiling. In the back were offices, and a stairway up to a closed steel door.

"Took you long enough," Levi Ackerman said. "I been here, what, five days?"

"Probably good for you, Sir," Jack said. "Got you out of Sin City."

Ackerman glanced at Bandit. "That's a beautiful dog. He kill people?"

"Maybe."

Ackerman tugged a pencil from behind his left ear and spun it on his fingertips. "Your Dad would be proud of you."

Jack flinched. "Yes, Sir."

"We get Wahid enough missiles maybe he can retake the Panjshir." Ackerman tilted back his chair, dropped forward. "Thanks to what you've done, the stakes have gone up a notch. We've got a new Home Office guy flying in, Timothy Cormac. To look at the bigger picture. Strategy guy, not military." Ackerman shrugged. "You want to grow your career, get close to him."

Jack bent to scratch Bandit behind the ears. "I told Wahid we're independents, don't have a Home Office pipeline to give him SA-7s. So he's paying with opium. Did you know?"

Ackerman tipped back again, making Jack fear he'd go over. "We've been through all this. What Home Office does with the Pakis –"

"You mean the weapons for Hekmatyar –"

"– is not our business. *Our* business is *you guys* building a third force to counter the Soviets without the Pakis *or* Saudis. Or Hekmatyar, or this new guy Massoud –"

"The one who signed the truce with the Russians?"

Ackerman rubbed the stump of his missing forearm. Jack wondered did it still hurt, after all these years? Does all pain endure like that, long after you think it will be gone?

"If that Goddamn truce spreads it'll kill our whole deal," Ackerman said. "We *need* the Soviets tied down in Afghanistan. So we need this Massoud dealt with."

"We help Wahid get his SA-7s, but he has to kill Massoud?"

"I didn't *say* that," Ackerman said. "They going to win, these *mujihadeen* of yours?"

"Depends how many weapons we give them."

"And if they do?"

"The insane ones like Wahid and Hekmatyar will take control. When the Soviets leave they'll go for each other's throats."

"We're sending ten more *holy warriors* back with you. From Saudi, Yemen, and Algeria. Ask *them* about the Beirut Embassy bombing, see what you learn."

"I don't want them."

"Jack, this war has to *seem* a pan-Islamic thing: Muslims versus Soviets. So we import holy warriors from wherever. Good pay, learn how to kill, maybe die for Allah."

"Like I said, we shouldn't be training these assholes –"

"You let Home Office worry about that." Ackerman stood looking out the office window. "Tomorrow we'll decide how many SA-7s and launchers you need." Ackerman opened a side drawer of the desk and reached inside to sharpen his pencil with an electric sharpener. "On the ad-

MIKE BOND

min side, you want any changes in survivor notification and
benefits, that kind of thing?"

"Just my mother, like before."

"A few house rules for while you're here. We're private citizens, not representatives of any government. Carry
your sidearm at all times but keep it concealed. Always let
Sergeant Malkowich know where you're going and when
you'll be back. There's a pussy shop down the street but I'm
told the ones in Ketta Jalaya are better –"

"Levi, where are *we* in all this?"

"Nowhere. *We* don't exist."

"We're trading opium for guns. We're drug dealers."

"That's not how your Dad would see it. We're taking
down the world's dirtiest empire. The one that killed *him*...
We're freeing a billion people from Communism –"

"To give them what? Heroin?"

"Think of it as a necessary evil." One-handed, Ackerman took out more pencils and began to sharpen them one
by one. "Because, as this new guy Timothy will explain tomorrow, you're the one who has to run it."

Can't Get No

THE CAFÉ DEAFENED her with the din of soldiers' laughter and the Rolling Stones out of a JVC tape deck, the air acrid with cigarette smoke and the floor sticky with spilt vodka and Georgian champagne. Her head was spinning with the vodka and noise and the way Leo kept twirling her around and handing her off from one friend to the next. "Life may be short!" he laughed, "but it's joyous."

"Stop!" she yelled. "I'm getting too dizzy."

"You're the only girl here," he twirled her again. "You have to dance with everyone!"

"I have, I *have*," she giggled as he spun her off to another officer.

"*Ne xorosho govaryu pa-russki*," she said to the gray-haired man, who held her carefully at arms' length as if she might explode. *I don't good speak Russian.*

"That's fine, my dear," he said in perfect French, "Your friend Leo's not the only civilized one here... He shouldn't monopolize you."

They went round again, the room seeming to go slower

than they did. "He's not!" She rushed to defend him. "He wants me to dance with *every*one –"

"And you only want to dance with him."

She smiled, warming to him. "Of course."

He tucked back a strand of her hair over her shoulder, a grandfatherly gesture. "And I'm sure *he* only wants to dance with you."

"It's hard for all these men, being out here, so far from home."

"And you too, so far from France…"

She felt she could confide in him. *It's just the vodka*, she told herself. "Afghanistan ruins everything – you hate it, but it leaves you nothing to go home to."

"You'll get over this place, my dear." He squeezed her arm. "We all will."

She turned away. *Except those who die.*

Leo handed her champagne that spilled down her wrist. "You like General Volnev?"

"You had me dance with a *general*?" She downed the champagne and kissed him, his moustache soft and exciting, making her ache for him. "What if I'd said something *bad*?"

"As a teenager he fought the Germans all the way from the Volga to Berlin. There's nothing you could imagine he hasn't seen." He clasped his big thick hands behind her neck, holding her sweaty hair away from her skin, and kissed her hard, and she felt her body go soft against him.

"We can't do this," she shivered. "In front of these poor guys."

His fingers rose up her spine, each hand gripping half the width of her back. "We can leave now."

"We've got nowhere to go… I don't want to go home. I want to be with you."

He took her hand. "Have you ever seen the inside of a Vosporonetz?"

They went out of the cigarette smoke and laughter into the night. "Spring is here," he said, his arm round her waist. "Even Afghanistan is beautiful in springtime."

"You shouldn't be drinking so much. You're not completely healed."

"Stop being my doctor."

She reached her arm round his hard back. "What's a *Vospro*-whatsis?"

"Here it is. A wonder of Soviet engineering –"

"It's a little tank?"

"An armored car." The rear door squealed as he opened it.

She slipped fingers between his shirt buttons. "You want me to go in *there?*"

"You are beautiful and I love you." *If you love her, don't ask about existence and non-existence...* "There's nowhere in Kabul – I can't take you to my quarters, where can we go?"

"We can find our own little house." She bent to step into the armored car. "Even Kabul has houses." Inside smelled of grease and sweat. She squeezed into a stiff bucket seat banging her knee. "Ouch!" she said. "*Damn!*"

He climbed in beside her shoving her over. "Move!"

"I am, I *am*."

He kissed her, a steel medal against her breast. "I'm a little drunk," she said. "You're taking advantage of me."

"I'm a little drunk and *you're* taking advantage of me!"

"Yes," she mumbled through his kiss. "You should be in the barracks studying Lenin."

He kissed her harder, faster, his hand circling her waist, his arm tickling her nipple and making her bite his lips, her tongue hard against his as she moved her mouth up and down against his and her breast up and down his arm and her body up and down against him and already he had her

skirt up around her thighs and the cool air felt good between them and his hand filling the space…

"Ow, damn!" she yelped. "My eye!"

"That's a gun mount. Sorry!"

"Here!" she slipped a long thigh around him. "We're
going to have to do it this way." She squirmed sideways.
"Quick come inside me! *Damn*! What's this?"

He groped for it in the dark. "Machine gun cartridge –"

"What if it goes off?"

He slid her to him. "Already fired."

"Hurry! Hurry!"

"The seat," he grunted. "Ouch."

"Oh God," she pulled herself against him. "Just come in
me fast."

She kept opening to him as if she'd been made for him, a
tightly perfect fit. "I've wanted you so long," he said, driving
deeper. "So much –"

"And I've wanted you so much. Oh God you feel good…"

"Let's do this all the time. Can you come soon –"

"I'm coming Oh God I love you."

"I love you too. I love you. Thank God we're finally saying this. I love you so…"

THE CANDLE on the floor of the girl's hut guttered in
the wind through cracks in the rush wall. Rawalpindi's like
Kabul, Jack thought. Too hot in the day, too cold at night.

"Why do you carry that gun?" She was short and slender, a mole on the side of her nose and another on her neck,
her hair full and silky and black as coal.

"How old are you?" he answered.

"Twenty."

"No you're not. Sixteen, maybe."

When she smiled her teeth were bright against her dark
lips. Making love she'd been exciting, and the months with-

out a woman had been a wave that drowned his senses. But now he wanted to be anywhere but here, disgusted with himself and repulsed by her small upturned breasts and their large umber nipples, her odors of sex and curry. The cotton sheet on the mattress felt dirty; he wondered how many other men had stained it. "Where are you from?"

"Ghazni. When the Russian helicopters killed my family I escaped to the camps in Pakistan. But there was no food. I had to work." She shrugged. "There was this."

"Someday maybe you can go back to Afghanistan."

"We had a house with a garden. A stone-walled garden."

"Maybe it's still there –"

"For my tenth birthday I got blue jeans – can you imagine? And I had a radio, it was pink... I could listen to Elvis..." She looked at Bandit. "I even had a puppy. One night he didn't come home."

"When I was a boy one night my dog didn't come home. A guy had poisoned him."

She bit her lip, said nothing, then, "You have a wife in America?"

"If I did I wouldn't be with you."

"So while you're in Rawalpindi I can keep your house and cook your food and take care of you every night."

This made him smile and no longer mind the smells and dirt and meaningless of it. "I'm just here a few days."

"You can stay all night. I won't ask more money. Didn't I do good for you?"

He slid on his shirt. "You did fine."

She watched him buckle the Makarov into its holster under his left armpit. "What's it like," she said, "to kill a man?"

"What's it like to sleep with a man?"

"Everybody knows you Americans are sending many guns and bombs across the Khyber Pass to kill Russians.

You are killing lots of them?"

"How many men have you slept with?"

Her smile sparkled in the candlelight. "See, you're just like me – we both have secrets. We *would* be good together."

The wind down from Karakoram had driven the stench of diesel, sewers and charcoal smoke out of Rawalpindi. Bandit at his side, Jack walked the empty streets. Once the dog dashed ahead; there was a squeal in the darkness and he returned and dropped a rat in front of Jack. The rat convulsed and lay still, a female with full nipples.

"You shouldn't do that." Jack thought of the baby rats starving, waiting for their mother who would never come home. "Don't kill except to defend yourself. Or eat."

Khief

"WE MUST KILL this Massoud guy," Timothy Cormac said. He glanced around the New Asia warehouse like a king brought down to live with peasants.

Jack stared into Timothy's bluish eyes. "Because of his truce?"

Timothy sucked at a tooth. "Tell Wahid make it happen."

"Massoud controls most of the Panjshir. If he could convince the other warlords to make peace... wouldn't Afghanistan be better off than in endless war with the Soviets?"

"Your mission's to help them *ruin* the Soviets. Not kiss their ass." In his late thirties, Timothy already looked older: thinning sandy hair, purple bags under the eyes, a smoker's yellow teeth, the opulent belly and saggy cheeks from too many Beltway dinners. What had Ackerman said? *He's on the way up.*

"A lot of folks in Home Office," Timothy added, "still aren't on board with your mission."

"What exactly don't they like?"

"Too much exposure. If the Russians find out... State's

very concerned."

"Christ, Timothy!" Levi Ackerman said. "You told fucking *State*?"

"Not I. But other people in Home Office keep the lines open."

Jack sensed that Timothy would tell anybody anything if it was an angle that might help him. "Did you know Gustafson?"

"Gustafson – he's with the Swedish Foreign Office, no?"

"He fell thirty thousand feet into a mountain. As part of this mission."

"No need to get huffy." Timothy thrust a pale hand across the table to pat Jack's wrist. "I hear your Dad was First Cav in Nam? Mine was the Marines. Korea."

"Really? What were *you*?"

"Jack!" Ackerman snapped. "For Chrissake."

"Hey," Timothy smiled but his eyes didn't, "there's more than one way to serve our country."

"That's what the folks say who drive Cadillacs and don't pay taxes."

"Jack!" Ackerman snarled.

"Sorry. I've been out killing people. Had a friend die. Tends to piss one off."

"Don't like your job?" Timothy smiled yellow teeth. "Leave any time you like."

"I like the job. It's just some of the people I have to deal with."

"Like me," Loxley said. "I'm a pain in the ass."

Jack watched Timothy knead pale pulpy hands. "So you're *on board*," Jack said, "with our dealing heroin for missiles?"

"Anyone using heroin deserves what he gets. But I don't do details." Timothy dropped flaccid fingers over Ackerman's sinewy wrist. "That's my friend Levi's job."

"And all this is C.O.D.?" Jack said.

"Wahid's men send the stuff," Ackerman said. "Same as ever, from Chitral over to Gilgit into China. We send the hardware back with you, over the Hindu Kush."

"You knew about this all along," Jack said. "Didn't you?"

"*Listen* to Levi," Timothy said. "It's compartmentalized. You do your job, we do ours."

Bandit growled. "That's a nasty dog," Timothy said.

"He's got a great sense about people."

"You've had two months in Afghanistan: I'll give you three more. Levi will decide on the missiles and launchers. But I want *results*. Not just a couple of Russian helicopters – Christ, bad weather could do that! And get Wahid to solve this Massoud thing." Timothy's tongue moved back and forth under his lips.

Sticky teeth, Jack thought. He stood. "You're welcome, any time you want, to join us up in the hills, shitting blood and ducking bullets. A fine time can be had by all –"

"If and when I see you," Timothy smirked, "it's on my terms."

LATE THE LAST NIGHT Jack knocked on the girl's door. There was no answer and he walked with Bandit a while and came back just as a gray-haired man with a cane was leaving.

"I thought you weren't coming back," she said.

"Who was that, just here?"

"He's a teacher. His wife's crippled. He comes once a month. All he can afford." She slipped out of her cotton robe and stood naked before him, a little bronze statue.

"I don't want to," Jack said, thinking with disgust of the old teacher.

"You're a funny man." She knelt in the corner, by the

bed, brought out a small leather bag and an ornamental brass pipe with a lapis lazuli bowl. "Give me your knife."

Without thinking he slipped his combat knife out of the ankle sheath and handed it to her. Outside the door Bandit growled once, softly. "You have someone coming?" Jack said.

"It's just rats."

She put a chunk of *khief* on the table, cut a slice with his knife and put it in the bowl. "I don't smoke that," he started to say, then thought *What harm can it do?* Maybe if he got high he'd want to screw her. *Why isn't she cold*, he wondered, *naked like that.*

"I wish I could go with you," she said.

He smiled, suddenly liking her. "In a way I do too. In another life."

She kissed him. "The Assassins, they smoked this, before they went to kill."

"No, the name comes from Hassan-i-Sabah. The Old Man of the Mountain."

"No, they smoked this to make them fearless." She lit the pipe holding it sideways so he could suck the flame down into the bowl, smiling at him over the bowl in which the *khief* glowed like an amber sun. It was strong, tasted like the opium and horse manure mixture he had smelled so many times when the Afghanis smoked before riding *buzkashi.*

"The new opium from Afghanistan..." She inhaled deeply, ". . . and the hashish of Chitral. You American *business-men* are very good for opium business too."

It came fast to his head, the room warm and the candlelight golden. There was a far-off thud of a drum, slow and steady, that he realized was his heart. He took off his clothes, careful to keep the gun and knife under them next to his head. She lay down beside him and his skin caught fire at her touch. He could feel the cells in her body like his own; inside her was part of himself, her cries like some voice within him that had too long been silent.

She went outside to pee in the ditch. Bandit stood in the door giving Jack an irritated look. She came back in and took a wooden bowl from a table by the door. "The last bitterberries from the Indus valley."

They tasted like her, pungent and tart. Thoughts cascaded through his mind. There was no barrier between her body and his and he wondered *can I think her thoughts too?*

They made love again and again, her silken skin and lithe arching body merging with his, and he understood that making love was exactly that, and that sex was life and nothing less, its purpose and end.

Finally he lay still, breathing softly, the intricate weave of thatch in the ceiling a metaphor for all he'd ever known, the lovely half-moon of her fingernail and each cell of her body a separate world.

Why am I fighting? he wondered. Each time I kill I die too. Is *that* what I want?

There were no boundaries between her and him, between them and this simple room, this teeming filthy city, this world. He thought of Wahid, of a Longfellow saying he'd long ago learned in school, that those who seem most evil have just suffered the most pain.

He'd quit Home Office. After this trip back into Afghanistan with the new *Strelas* he'd return to the States and start a new life. Reach out to people instead of hardening himself against them. *Life isn't war...*

Bandit was whining, the candle flickering like the last star in a dying universe, cracks of purple dawn slipping through the window. He scrambled into his clothes and ran back to New Asia Paradise. "Jesus Christ, Jack!" Ackerman screamed.

"Sorry, Sir. Three months of fucking to catch up on."

"You're *fucking* lucky I don't shoot you! You and Loxley were supposed to leave six hours ago! You have to meet McPhee in Darband at eleven hundred! What's got into you?"

Jack glanced at Loxley, who looked away. "Don't know, Sir."

"If you don't get to Darband on time you won't get over the pass by dark." Ackerman walked away, came back, rubbing the back of his head in fury. "We have diversions set up to keep the Russians away from that goddamn pass. And you won't even *be* there!"

"We'll hurry, Sir."

"The ten new *mujihadeen* will be in a second truck."

"What do we do with them, Sir?"

"Train them, goddammit! Make sure *they* don't bomb us." One-handed, Ackerman shook him. "I want you to watch over these missiles like they're your fucking *babies*. There's Paki guards in the cars ahead and behind you, and two more in the back of your truck. But if something fucks up, *you're* the guy I come after."

AT 16:00 they passed through Chitral, and reached the pine grove at dusk. "Where the *fuck* you guys been?" McPhee yelled.

Jack nodded at the Arabs standing in a nervous silent circle. "Home Office sent us ten new *fedayeen*."

"What are we supposed to do with ten more fucking A-rabs?"

"And twenty launchers and a hundred ninety-seven SA-7s."

It started raining as they lashed the launchers and missiles to the camels' packsaddles and roped them down under Russian tarps. The rain and wind and the kerosene lanterns made the camels nervous and they stamped their hooves and bit at the men. Bandit stood under a pine watching and shaking rain off his fur.

Before they reached the pass into Afghanistan the rain had turned to blizzard. The camels bellowed and tried to turn back and kicked at the men when they poked them with bayonets to keep them going. Jack's gloves froze to his rifle; rain had frozen his Pakistani coat and he couldn't stop shivering no matter how fast he climbed.

Loxley grabbed Jack's shoulder and yelled into his face. "Gotta bivvie up."

"We'll fucking die! With this wind chill it's fifty below." Jack yanked at the lead camel looking for the trail in the blinding snow, but each time he opened his eyes the snow sliced into them. Then in the darkness he made out a trail. Thank you God, he thought. I promise I'll believe in You, just make *this* the trail.

It *was*. A deep wide furrow in the snow, drifted over but still visible. He could just make out the first of Wahid's men behind him leading the second camel. Ahead a rock rose from the snow – a cairn. Joy surged through him. *Going to make it.*

The cairn was soft and warm. Not a rock. Fresh camel dung. They'd come in a circle. Tracking themselves.

Bandit sat on his haunches looking quizzically at Jack. His ears and the bridge of his nose were white. *Why are you going round in circles?* he seemed to ask. *Can't you smell the trail? For goodness sakes it's right in front of you. We were here only a week ago – can't you remember?*

"Show us the trail, Bandit," Jack tried to say, but his lips had frozen.

Bandit shook off snow, raised a rear foot and scratched at his ear, sniffed the camel dung, lifted a leg and peed on it, scuffed snow over it and trotted into the night.

Jack dragged the camel along behind Bandit. When the dog got too far ahead he sat in the snow waiting. Jack looked back, barely seeing the next man and camel behind him.

They were going down. With each step the camel slid forward on Jack's heels. Bandit came back barking and wagging his tail.

The wind knocked Jack over, cracking his knee on a rock under the snow. He tried to rub the knee but could not feel his hands, saw one glove was missing, his hand cold as a metal claw. He fumbled the rope into the other hand and stuck the numb hand inside his pants.

In minutes the snow had risen to their waists. The camels stumbled and skidded, faltering under the weight of the missiles. Even Bandit grew afraid, plowing ahead, begging them *Hurry, hurry.*

The wind raged against a headwall beside them. He remembered this place: the trail two feet wide notched into the cliff, loose rock under the slippery snow, at his left elbow a straight drop to rocks a half mile below. Climbing this section a week ago the camels had been frightened.

When he looked there was no one behind.

He shoved back on the halter but the camel ran him down and skidded him off the edge, his body dangling by the halter wrapped around his wrist. He snatched at the rock with numb hands, but it was sheer, no grip. The camel jumped back, slamming him against the cliff. The rope had frozen round his wrist; he couldn't free it. The camel swung him over the edge and back again, his rifle banging his ribs.

His fingers were helpless against the ice-hard rope. He bit at an end but the camel jerked back and tore it from his teeth. He was blinded by snow, his hat gone. Wind screamed in his ears. The camel backed up, dragging him onto the trail. She pawed a front hoof at the snow, lowered her head to his. Unexpectedly she nuzzled him, her triangular mouth warm hairy and lip-thick against his face. "You saved me," he told her. "Good girl." He rose and she followed him, head bobbing up and down at his elbow. Bandit came back barking: *I've followed the trail down. It's easy.*

The trail leveled. Ahead were huts, a great bowl of rock sheltered from the wind. The camel knelt with a groan and he started to unsaddle her. "We're saved!" he told her.

Someone whacked his shoulder. McPhee. "Loxley!" McPhee screamed. "He fell!"

Jack leaped up. "Where?"

"Over the edge. You and your camel kept on going and his fell over!"

Jack ran back up the mountain screaming "Sean! Sean!" He knelt on the narrow trail where gouged snow showed someone had fallen, tried to climb down the cliff in the darkness but it was vertical and icy. He started to fall, scrambled back.

His face had frozen. He went back down the trail to the huts and unsaddled his camel. Aktoub came with a plastic cup and milked her as she stood shivering in bowl of rock, and handed the cup to Jack. "It is a very tall cliff," Aktoub yelled over the wind. "Even in summer we can't reach the bottom."

McPhee had built a fire of camel dung and window frames from one of the huts. He did not speak.

Nothing's more important than your buddy's life.

Bandit came, licked Jack's hand and curled up by his feet. *I'll make it up to him,* Jack told himself. *Whatever it takes, I'll be stronger, harder.*

More deadly than before.

Coals

BY APRIL THE KABUL HILLS shimmered with new grass. On the low south-facing slopes the snow had gone except in canyons the sun could not reach. With the warmer weather, *mujihadeen* offensives were picking up, and the roar of MiGs taking off from Bagram and the thud of distant artillery grew constant as the rumble of a sea.

Sophie had put apple blossoms in a bowl on the table of the little house they'd found near the Hospital. "I didn't pick them," she said. "The wind knocked them down."

Leo hung his coat on the nail by the door. "I worry about you alone here. When I go back to the Panjshir you should move in with the old women –"

"Isn't that what the Crusaders did – sent their women to live with nuns?"

"Things are getting worse –"

"I see how many wounded come in every day."

"Yesterday a shell hit the Haji Yaqub mosque."

"Do Muslims get Heaven credits if they die in a mosque? Like dying in battle?"

He fumbled for his Yavas, remembered he'd stopped smoking. "Fuck them."

"I'm so tired of their needs and fanaticism. It's like shooting yourself in the foot and then saying, 'It's your fault, fix me or I'll kill you.'"

He unwrapped the newspaper around the mule steak he'd bought at Jade Welayal Bazaar. "You know what today is?"

"The twenty-fifth, isn't it? Or the twenty-fourth?"

"You don't remember?"

"Stop teasing me!"

"Our anniversary – the night we went to the café –"

"You're right – one month!"

He put rice a pan and poured water over it. "See, already you've forgotten."

"How could I? The sweat and cigarette smoke, the canned beef from Dushanbe –"

"Any normal woman would've jumped at that." He took two bottles from his rucksack. "The best Georgian champagne."

"My God! How did you find it?"

"The *Chizikhs* won't miss it..."

"What is *Chizikhs*?"

"Rear echelon bigwigs." He lit the kerosene stove and put the rice on to boil, and in the street found some boughs and planks and made a fire in the courtyard. They sat with their backs against the west wall of the house, drinking the first bottle of champagne as the sun sank behind the Paghman hills and the fire burned down to coals and he put the mule steak over the fire on a window screen from a blasted house.

"I saw Ahmad today," she said. "He needs more food for the children... He told me his brother's a *mujihadeen* leader in the Panjshir – some Eagle of the Hindu Kush."

Leo scratched his back against the coarse wall. "Wahid al-Din. The one who suddenly has missiles."

"He wants you to meet his brother, try to arrange a peace."

He slid his palm up her thigh. "In this place there's no word for peace."

"Stop *that*! He met Galaya, the girl who used to help me at the clinic. He seems quite taken with her."

"Nothing like war to make people horny."

"It's easy to be happy, isn't it? All you need is somebody to love and food and a place to sleep. Why isn't everybody happy? Then we wouldn't have wars..."

"That night at the café a month ago – really now, what did you think about being there, with this dirty old tank commander, his lecherous friends –"

"I only cared about you."

"I was sure you didn't like me."

"Already I was in love with you."

"Suppose someday we'll be like my folks – old and chubby and wrinkled and a little forgetful and still always calling each other '*Lyubemets*' – that means 'Darling'?"

"*I'll* never be chubby." She squeezed his hand. "Your fire's dying out – hadn't you better go fix it?"

"That's when it cooks the best. After the flames are out, and all that's left is coals."

"YOU'RE THE ONE making making all these orphans," Ahmad said. "Your opium from the Panjshir – you have more money than I can dream of – can't you give just a little?"

Wahid put down the stone with which he was sharpening his bayonet. "You've come all the way from Kabul to beg?"

Ahmad glanced round the circle of grim men. "It's for

children, Wahid –"

"Send the boys to *madrasah* to learn proper Islamic ways. The girls don't matter."

"Massoud's agreed to a peace – why won't you?"

"He won't live out the year." Wahid smiled at the men around him. "True?"

"True," they murmured.

"If all the clans could make peace with each other, we could negotiate with the Soviets... They've lost thousands of soldiers. They'd like to find a way out."

"They make the same mistake the English did a hundred years ago: not closing the passes into Pakistan. And not understanding that we're not afraid to die."

"Because we have nothing to live for." Ahmad felt exhausted and dispirited. "The Americans who bring you arms and *mujihadeen* – they're infidels too –"

"True. Even this Jyek who was your friend in Edeni, it's he who brings the *Strelas*."

"*He*'s here? *Jyek*? Where?"

"Gone to Pakistan with the other Americans to get more missiles. He's very good at killing Russians, by the way, these Communists who now seem to be your friends."

How could this be? Ahmad wondered. He thought of the night in Edeni when he and Jack had clasped bloodied hands – *I will always defend my blood brother*, they had sworn, *with my own blood*. Had Jack come back to avenge Afghanistan? "If I meet some Soviet officers," Ahmad said, "through a doctor I know, would you talk with them?"

"What would I gain," Wahid chuckled, "from peace?"

"You have so much influence with the northern clans – not for nothing they call you Eagle of the Hindu Kush... Use this power to unite us and you'll be our leader."

Wahid snapped the bayonet onto his AKMS. "There'll be a *shura* council in a week. Perhaps I might discuss with the other chiefs what we could gain by talking peace."

"And the children in the orphanage, can't you give something?"

Wahid shook his head. "God takes care of children as He wishes. Money is for guns." He smiled. "And missiles, when we can get them."

AT 40th ARMY HQ Leo took the stairs to General Volnev's office two at a time but that made his head pound. He slowed, surprised to feel winded at the top. Damn cigarettes – she was right to make him stop.

He watched the cigarette pinched into a notch of the General's ashtray, could almost taste its slender ascending veil of smoke. *Smoking's like war, we hate it but can't stop doing it.* "If we can expand this truce beyond Massoud –"

"All it's done is start a civil war between him and the other warlords." Volnev drained a plastic coffee cup. "The moment we're gone..."

"This Ahmad seems real. And his brother's a big *mujihadeen*. If I can learn what they want..."

"Doesn't matter what they want, Gregoriev. It's what they *need*."

Like everyone else, Leo thought, what they *need* is peace to raise their children. Be with the one they love. Enough to eat. "Everyone wants peace, Sir."

Volnev sucked at his cigarette, waved away smoke. "These bastards *want* war. War and more war. They don't love their women, they love *war*."

Leo waited. "I try to understand the Afghanis, but..."

"We can't. They're not *like* us. *We* send rockets into space, unravel the secrets of the human mind, create superb engineering, raise our daughters to be brain surgeons. *They* step in the same medieval camel shit they've always walked in, huddle in mud hovels, hide their daughters in head rags and beat them if they show their face." Volnev paced, waving his empty cup. "Sixty years ago we *were* like them – theocratic superstitious peasants in straw huts, leading our nags around parsimonious fields rented from *nobles* who thought because they had twenty words of French and wiped their ass with paper they were better than us!"

He snuffed out his cigarette. "Look what *we've* done in sixty years – twice defeated the world's most evil war machine, created the world's highest educational standards – out of *our* superstitious theocratic peasants, mind you! Ah shit!" Volnev tossed his cup onto his desk, spattering the papers scattered across it. "All the good men we've lost!"

"Maybe it's time *we* stop. Sir."

Bent forward with both palms on his desk Volnev stared at him. "We thought everyone could be brought into one modern world." He laughed. "But they're *infected* with Islam – this theocracy of theirs. We're pissing in the wind."

"It's the leaders who want war... The crazy mullahs and tribal chieftains."

"Isn't that *la condition humaine?*"

"I'd like to give it a shot, Sir."

"You've had a serious head wound. And you've got that lovely French doctor... Somebody's got to make babies in this world instead of killing. I'm going to send you home."

"We Russians aren't supposed to die a natural death, as Gogol says. And I can't leave my men, no more than you can."

Volnev snatched the coffee cup from his desk, refilled it from the jug on the teletype table. "Fine," he sighed, "Meet them halfway. Then maybe we can take our dead and go home."

Stronger than Stone

O UT OF THE DUSK came the muezzin's wail for
evening prayer. In the distance small arms were firing, then the steady thump of D-30 howitzers, each
a *jinni* sucking life from the world.

Ahmad slipped past the silent children and out the back
of the orphanage. At night Kabul so terrifying. Couldn't see
where mines might be, or who might be hunting him in the
darkness.

Leo was waiting with a translator in the teashop near
Soviet HQ where they'd met before. "It's dangerous here,"
Ahmad said.

Leo rose to shake his hand. "Where isn't?"

Ahmad could not help but smile at this grizzled, coarse
big-fisted man from far away. Easy to see why the French
doctor loved him. "Thank you for the rice last week."

"We're sending more tomorrow. What does Wahid say?"

"The Americans are sending even the teachers who were
here before, to fight you."

"Teachers? Tell me."

"One who was my friend... If only you and he could

meet..." Ahmad broke off. "Speaking of food –"

"He's with your brother, this American?"

Ahmad did not like this translator. Unshaven, in a Soviet army tunic, with an Uzbeki accent. Like the bandits
who had killed his father. "If you meet Wahid what will you
say?"

"That we'd like to see Afghanistan united. Putting its
energy into schools, health care, infrastructure."

"If you want to make a deal with my brother don't mention unification."

"Why not?"

"He'd lose influence. He wants power, not peace. Like
Hekmatyar, all these Lords of War – isn't that what you call
them?"

"Warlords, yes."

Ahmad started to drink his tea, stopped. You never
knew what was poisoned anymore. "If they had to choose
between a healthy Afghanistan under foreign influence, or a
bombed-out slaughterhouse under *their* rule..."

Leo said nothing, nodded. "So what do I offer him?"

"A piece of somebody else's territory. That's how to ex-
cite him."

Leo grinned. "Whose?"

"More of the Panjshir."

"Take it from Massoud?"

"Because Massoud's made a truce with you. Then go to
Massoud, offer him Wahid's territory in Badakhshan. That's
how things are done in Afghanistan."

"There's a Russian proverb about giving the same horse
to two men. Instead of sharing it they cut it in half."

"Wahid offers to meet in Kowkcheh Valley, where the
Varduj River comes in."

"That valley's too narrow. Parian – where the tar road
stops?"

"The Valley of the Moon? It's narrow there too."

"Tell him a week from today. At noon." Leo stood. "We'll be in a convoy, with air cover. Defensive only."

Ahmad snuck home through the dark and broken streets. Food tomorrow. Why was he possessed by such sorrow and dread? Because of this war, he decided. It kills all hope. Not this Gregoriev, though. He seemed the type to look into the jaws of Hell and not lose courage.

"SO YOU LIKED it in Kabul," Wahid said.

Suley snuck another lamb rib from the pot. "There was lots to steal. Not like Edeni."

"Eat up," Wahid smiled. "With us there's always plenty."

"In the orphanage there was nothing. Rice swept from a floor. Weeds from the road."

"Ahmad comes begging for money. For the orphanage he says. I give him all I can."

"He must have kept it for himself. I was the one who brought food. Finally I left and went to the Koran school."

"And in the *madrasah* what have you learned?"

"*To kill the infidels wherever we find them.*"

"Very good –"

"Once I found a grenade. Some Russians were singing and drinking wine in a café. I threw it in and ran away." Suley snatched another rib. "Even on the houses across the street there was blood."

"Well done!"

"Once I saw three of Hekmatyar's men take a woman into a cellar. Her hands were tied behind her and they pushed up her clothes and did things to her. One man left his rifle against the wall... I went quietly down the stairs. I feared they would kill me, but they were like goats at a female. I had never shot a rifle before. My hands were shaking. It is loud. It is hard to hold the barrel straight when it is firing."

"Do you remember the infidel teacher? From your school in Edeni?"

"He scorned me."

"He's in the mountains now with other Americans. They say they want to help –"

"*O true believers, take not the Jews or Christians for your friends.*"

"You have learned your Koran well." Wahid pulled him close. "The Russians are speaking of peace. We must seem to welcome this yet prevent it. To keep them and the Americans killing each other."

SUMMER WAS NEAR but nights stayed cold. Sophie sat cross-legged on the bed, wearing Leo's green wool socks. He came in and dropped his combat boots in the corner. She snatched her Russian-French dictionary. "Болван! No, wait – that's not it! Бойня! Бокал!"

He stretched out on the bed beside her. "You need more lessons."

"I was calling you an oaf!"

"Oaf? What is that?"

"The kind of person who drops his muddy boots on the bedroom floor."

"Ah... Болван – 'Bolvan' – that is a woodenhead, a dolt. Very good. But you also called me 'Bokal' – that is a wine glass."

"That's not quite your shape."

"And also 'Boinya' – that means massacre. A slaughter." He tugged off her socks. "*These* are property of the Soviet Army."

"I requisitioned them. As part of the Peace Through Friendship program." She burrowed her toes under his back. "What did he say, General Volnev?"

"He doesn't like Malraux."

"So what did he *say*? Stop teasing me!"

"That when this peace mission's over I'm reassigned to Brussels. Because of my head wound. That's the best he can do."

"The best he can do? Oh my God!" The air had wings, had risen from the back of her neck and left her free, as if it were possible again to want, to dare. "Darling I never hoped!"

"Ah you French." He pulled her into his warm arms. "You're *all* like Malraux."

"You should have foraged more champagne – to celebrate our leaving."

"First we'll go to Moscow. To meet my parents. Then we'll go to the Caspian. There's a lovely headland covered in pines, a white village where we can get married. My friend Dmitri will come from Poland, your parents from France... Then in Brussels I'll come home in my major's uniform and you'll come back from the hospital and we'll drink wine and laugh about how silly is the human race."

"Major's uniform?"

"I forgot. Volnev's made me a major."

She grabbed his hands. "Darling that's marvelous!"

"Funny how I spent years working for it and now it doesn't matter."

"It's wonderful. *Please* admit you're happy! I feel so good for you."

He slipped his hand under her shirt. "Yes, you *do* feel good."

"Be serious! Anyway, there's something wrong with your Brussels picture... Maybe I won't be coming home from working at the hospital. Maybe I'll stay home."

"Home?" The thought astounded him. "You're a doctor ."

She slid up his undershirt, kissing his chest. "Even doctors have babies..."

Joy filled him. Could you wish for things that really matter, and receive them? It was fine to believe in joy, but did it really happen? He thought of the famous poem they'd memorized in school about the Nazi siege of Leningrad,

We have battled our way out of that long darkness,
And fought through barrages of fire.
You used to say, "We have turned to stone,"
No,
We're stronger than stone,
We are alive.

All his life he had fought for the good, never expecting it to touch him. As if he were outside life somehow, made of stone. Now Sophie had changed everything: to be alive was to make love, make life, to pass on this joyous mystery. Was it perhaps true, what Dostoyevsky's Father Zossima had said, that we *are* made for happiness, and he who is completely happy can say to himself, *I've carried out God's sacred will on earth?*

Had he too battled out of the long darkness, was he stronger than stone?

But why did it take war to make us alive?

Sunflower

DUST CLOUDS HOWLED down the Panjshir Valley, buffeting the APCs and driving grit through the firing ports. How, Leo wondered, do people *live* up here?

The engines howled with the climb as the road rose toward Kalat pass. Snow clouds wreathed the Anjoman crests; wind through the open front hatch made his eyes water and froze the tears to his cheeks.

Wahid must've talked to the weatherman, Leo decided, found out it was going to be stormy. If Massoud had agreed to a truce, would Wahid?

"Back home I'd still be in bed," Kolya said. He was nineteen maybe, with blond hair and blue eyes, and he drove this APC that he'd named Sunflower with a nonchalant grace.

"Good you're in the Army," Leo said. "Keeps you from that kind of lazy behavior."

"Lazy? You should see my girl."

You should see mine, Leo thought. *You kids don't know anything.*

"I can't imagine any girl would fancy waking up beside

you," the gunner told Kolya.

"Snowing," Kolya changed the subject. "Now the road'll be slippery on the pass."

Leo glanced out. They had driven right into it, a wall of tiny hard-driven flakes. The engine yowled as Kolya geared down. "Can't see a thing!" he yelled.

"Just stay in the middle –"

"What about mines?"

"They cleared this road last week."

"That don't mean shit," the gunner said.

It was warm inside the APC, and Leo forced himself to keep his head out, to take turns watching with the gunner through the snow. Looking back over the gun mount he could see only the first APC behind him, a ghost. "Hold that music down," he said to Kolya.

"It's AC/DC," Kolya said. "*If you want blood...*" he sang in Russianized English.

"We'll go far as Kalat," Leo called out. It was unfair, this late storm. In the valley the fruit trees had already started blooming. "If the snow keeps up we turn back there."

The road worsened, as did the storm, the snow straight into their faces. Over the howl of the wind and the roar of engines he heard the river frothing and booming down the canyon beside them.

"*If you want blood,*" Kolya was singing, "*you got it –*"

"*Blood on the streets,*" the gunner answered.

"*Blood on the rock –*" Kolya added.

"*Blood in the gutter,*" the gunner sang.

"*Every last drop,*" Kolya sang back, and to Leo it was bad medicine, but these were young guys, heedless. Thought they would live forever.

The road curved to the right and down across the River, the APC's wheels slithering as it fought its way up the other side. A gray shape in the gloom ahead became a burnt-out

119

tank, half on its side in the ditch.

Ruined buildings edged the road, naked trees. Clouds seethed overhead. "This sucks," Kolya shouted.

"Watch the goddamn road!" Leo yelled.

Snow had blown through the front slot and was piling up around Leo's feet. "Why can't we fight wars in Tahiti?" the gunner said.

With a roar the world turned black then white as the APC's dashboard leaped up and smashed his forehead, and he was on the floor with an arm under the brake pedal and voices yelling and a whine in the back of his head and someone tugged his arm free and he pulled himself out of the hatch and fell face first in the snow.

"Good," the gunner said. "We're out of it."

Leo sat up. The snow was warm as a down blanket. "Goddamn mines," he said. "Goddamn *duki*." He checked that the soldiers had taken up defensive positions around the APCs. There was nothing to see but snow, nothing to shoot at.

The APC caught fire and for an instant Leo wanted to stay near it. The soldiers in the second APC made room for him, the gunner, and Kolya, jamming together on the floor between the rifle butts and boots and ammunition boxes. Kolya had wrapped a scarf across his bleeding nose. "She was my favorite," he said. "Sunflower."

"What the fuck is Sunflower?"

"My APC."

"It was just a mine," Leo said. "Random, nothing to do with us."

The wretched bedraggled town of Kalat came and went, then Anjoman.

If Massoud had agreed to a truce, why not Wahid?

FROM HIS ROCK NICHE above the deserted village

Jack watched the APCs take form out of the white. At first he thought he imagined them, then they were barely darker than the snow, then squat ugly arachnids coming fast.

The terror returned, the nearness of death. *Come*, he urged the APCs, *Come closer*, at the same time wanting them to go. Closer they came, bigger and bigger, metal edges and thick steel, wheels crushing snow, gun barrel stingers of death.

His body felt naked, exposed. *They* had steel sides and he had only this spider hole in the scree. He glanced across at Bandit, who sat apart in a snow hole because he would not be near Husseini. *Am I going to get you killed too?*

The snowfall was thinning and he could see the raveled slope below them and the rooftops of the village where his *mujihadeen* hid, even the ridge across the road where McPhee and Aktoub waited in their rock holes.

Here it was just him and Bandit and Husseini the Algerian. And an SA-7 and three missiles. If choppers came they had to bring them down. But not him or McPhee – this time the *Strelas* would be fired by *mujihadeen*. "Technology transfer," McPhee had grinned with the coolness he affected before battle. "First world helping the third into the modern age."

"They're going to see us!" Husseini whispered in French. "We should pull back!"

"You don't care about our men below?"

"God will protect them!"

The lead APC hesitated at the first houses, a huge mantis before a spider's web. Its cannon traversed, barked flame. A building convulsed in a white-red flash somersaulting chunks high into the air and down on the street and on the roofs of other houses.

Jack swore at himself for not training his *mujihadeen* well enough. Some asshole had shown himself – an inch of cloth, the momentary glisten of a barrel.

The APC backed off, cannon swiveling, the others backing up behind it. "They're running away," Husseini said. "Cowards!"

"I'll kill him," Jack said. "Whoever showed himself."

The lead APC revved and lurched forward, picked its way over the rubble past all the houses and accelerated into the clear, stopped a hundred meters further down the road and swung its cannon back toward the village.

"They see us!" Husseini moaned.

"Shut up."

On the other side of the village the other APCs edged closer. The second geared down and raced through. It halted thirty meters past the first.

One by one the other APCs passed through the village, linked up thirty meters apart and vanished. The growl of their engines faded over the ridge.

"One at a time like that," Husseini said, "how could we get them?"

"Once they find no one's waiting to meet them in Skazar they'll come running back."

From the south, above the clouds, came the *whuh whuh whuh* of helicopters.

Jack imagined the gunships bristling with death, a rocket blowing him into the little chunks of flesh that were often all that remained of a man. He wanted to go down and check on his men but that would leave tracks in the snow. "Anybody hit?" he called.

"All is well, praise God," Aktoub shouted up. "They shot at nothing."

Before *we* came, Jack thought, you would've fired back. Consumed by images of manhood and courage, hungry for the life you imagine comes after. It's us who've taught you to be soldiers, not God.

"They're coming back," Husseini said. "Fast."

"I hear nothing."

"That's because you grew up with cars and television. They kill the hearing."

The first APC resolved out of the white, then one by one the others. When the lead APC was nearly through the village Aktoub detonated the mine in the middle of the road, the one Jack had wrapped the night before in extra nitro. The APC seemed to take flight then collapsed on itself, pieces settling to earth like feathers of a bird hit by a shotgun.

The others behind it braked hard. As the last skidded sideways the *mujihadeen* at the end of the village detonated the mine beneath it and it spun awkwardly on its tail and crashed backward into the huts. With a wham of RPGs the *mujihadeen* hidden on the near side of the road opened up. The soldiers inside the trapped APCs scrambled out and took cover behind them.

A chopper screamed over, invisible in the snow, and Jack had a moment's astonished fear of a pilot who would fly so low in blinding conditions in the doomed attempt to save his comrades. "Fire!" he screamed, and Husseini's *Strela* hit it showering chunks of metal through the storm.

The soldiers pinned behind the APCs were returning fire now, green tracers flashing through the snowstorm. The *mujihadeen* on the near side had stopped firing. As the soldiers began to regroup behind their vehicles the *mujihadeen* on the far side opened up, the bullets cutting them down like toy figures knocked over by a child's hand, and there was nowhere for them to go, nothing to do but die.

Jack ran down the hill through the knee-deep snow. "Pull out! Before the storm clears!" A second chopper roared over, trying to see them through downblasting snow.

"We got him." Aktoub bent to wipe bloody hands on the snow. "Their major."

"Praise God," Husseini grinned through crooked teeth.

"*We* got him, Goddammit!" Jack yelled.

"How many times I've told you?" Husseini yelled back. "*Whatever good befalleth thee, O man, it is from God. And whatever evil befalleth thee, it is from thyself!*"

The major lay in bloody snow, gripping his belly in massive bloody hands. He had a thick moustache and pockmarked face. "Who are you?" Jack said in Russian.

The man glared up at him. "Death to you and all your children, may they never have children."

Husseini nudged his rifle muzzle against the man's cheek. "I shall shoot him?"

"No!" Jack knelt to look at the major's wound.

Something shoved against Jack's shoulder. Suley. "Get up the hill," Jack snapped.

"He's the one who destroyed Edeni." Suley choked back a breath. "He stood my parents against the apple tree and shot them."

Jack saw Ahmad's mother and the school children being shot down by this man.

"What's he saying?" the Russian gasped.

"That you destroyed his village."

"I fight *duki*. Not civilians."

Husseini edged closer, racked his AK. The Russian pointed to his heart.

"No!" Jack screamed.

Husseini shot Leo in the head.

Bridge over a Stream

THE ONLY SANE THING, Ahmad told himself, was get out.

Kabul was Hell, eternal suffering and endless death. The orphans were an inundating sea, more each week, many of them partial humans only, missing limbs and eyes and genitals and minds. Widow Safír had been killed by an errant shell that had also killed twenty-one kids and maimed forty-two of which eleven had died, but now the orphanage had over three hundred and every day there was less food.

If he left, most or all of them would die. If he stayed wouldn't they die anyway?

A veiled girl in a purple *yashmak* came in without knocking and stood before him with her head bowed. "I was a teacher," she said. "Then the religious police killed the teachers so I became a nurse. Now they're killing nurses. I thought I might ask if there is work here."

"There's much work but nothing to eat."

"I can find food. I can cook. I worked in the clinic, can heal sick children."

"Take your veil off, child. And look at me."

She pulled it back. "Already you know me." She was not a child but a beautiful young woman. "The French doctor? I worked in her clinic."

"Ah yes, poor Sophie. How could I not remember you, Galaya?"

JACK HATED WALKING POINT because of the mines, but never let his men do it, always did it himself. Particularly he hated walking point at night when there was no chance of seeing a tripwire or the disturbed dirt or dead grass that might indicate where a mine was buried. But tonight he didn't mind, in the cool midnight with stars thick overhead, in the damp grass scents of early autumn, Bandit trotting silently ahead, the trail slinking down to a little stream gurgling under a stepping-stone bridge, the other men spaced behind him. As a kid he'd made up a poem once, about a bridge over a stream in a small child's dream.

That night, he was seven maybe, he lay in bed saying the poem and watching the stars slide across the windows. When he recited it next morning his father said *where'd you steal that?*

At night now the Soviets usually didn't patrol. In the three months since Loxley's death Wahid's men had won back part of the Panjshir; nowhere now could the Soviet helicopters or MiGs fly without fear; every time they neared the earth a *Strela* waited to knock them down.

Still at the back of his mind a haunting worry... Could imagination warn him of danger? Could time reverse: could he see his future and be allowed to change it?

He'd done what he came to do. But that didn't matter. What *did* matter? What if he'd become a soldier only to finish what his father had begun? Was that *him*?

Wars would never end: each grew out of those before it. His foot splashed and he shook it quickly so the water didn't soak it. *If you take the wrong path*, the Koran says, God *will surely punish you.*

Bandit growled, blocked the trail. Jack tried to wave the others down but they kept coming. He grabbed Husseini, whispered, "You're supposed to watch me!"

"At night there's nothing –" Husseini started to say in a loud voice.

"Shut *up*!"

Aktoub and McPhee came up. "Somebody coming!" Jack said. They ran back the trail and McPhee and Jack deployed the men in the willows with a field of fire down the trail to the stepping-stone bridge.

"Tell them," McPhee called, "no shooting till we know who it is."

"If they're up here at night," Aktoub said, "they're enemy."

"If there's too many," Husseini panted, "we should let them pass –"

A distant rustle, scuff of sandal on rock, the low steady breathing of men coming fast. "Hekmatyar's men," Aktoub hissed. "I *smell* them."

"Let them pass!"

"They're infidel-sucking scum, camel's offal, enemies of God –"

"We must kill them fast," Husseini said. "Before they can shoot."

"I said *don't shoot*!"

In a spat of green fire Husseini opened up, the shadows diving off the trail, their muzzle flashes and tracers snapping back. A man screamed, a hot spike smashed through Jack's shoulder, crushed the air from his lungs.

He lay choking face down in mud. Guns boomed and chattered. He rolled over and with his left hand tried to cover the soaking horrible hole in his right shoulder. A man stood over him, glint of bayonet flashing down as Bandit leaped roaring – a pistol shot and yelp.

Bullets snapped like wasps. The pain was awful. The firing slowed, stopped. *I'm dying*, Jack realized. *After all this...*

McPhee's voice was calm and measured but Jack couldn't understand. His shoulder was crushed, afire. McPhee lifted him. "Sling your good arm around my shoulder and run!"

"Morphine!"

"Gave you some."

"Where's Bandit?"

"Go!"

Everything grew sharp, starlight on the trail, blood pouring down his chest, the squeaking of a man's sandals as he ran past. Every step drove pain into his shoulder, sucked strength from his thighs and calves. The trail switchbacked up into a cold rain that froze on his face. "Over the top now," McPhee panted. "Down there a van. Take you Kabul."

"Where's Bandit?" Time passed. "Morphine!" he begged.

Hours of jolting agony, whistle of wind through the van's bullet-pocked window, incessant squeal of an axle, the shudder of a clutch plate each time the driver changed gear. Day became night that became day then night again. He lost Bandit then found him then lost him again, the soft fragrant fur, the rasp of a wet tongue on his cheek. McPhee's rough constant voice, the hand on his forehead or lifting up his head to adjust the tarp beneath.

"Bandit?" he asked, surprised at the awful pain in his throat.

McPhee drove the needle home. "Soon no more English. Pashto only. You're just another raghead with a bullet in him. An Afghani regular with the Russians, shot by *mujihadeen*. Aktoub's gonna stay with you. *Remember*: you've been shot by *mujihadeen*. Pick a name, an Afghani name.

Somebody you know from your village."

There *was* somebody. "Ahmad."

Thirst blazed down his throat into his lungs and stomach, down the arteries of his legs and arms, seethed up into his mouth till every breath baked his swollen lips and drove the superheated blood through his brain like lava. Again and again McPhee raised Jack's head to the jiggling canteen. "Stay with us, Jack. *Stay* with us."

"Where are we?"

"Kabul. Ebnecina hospital. Aktoub will check on you every day. I'll be in a safe house by the hospital. Soon as you're out we head to Peshawar."

Going home. Jack eased into a welling sense of being protected and cared for. Good tough dependable McPhee. He clasped McPhee's hand. "Need to find my dog."

"He died. Saving your ass."

WHITE GLARE, WHITE WALLS, stinging odors, hushed racing voices and flickering bulbs. He floated down a river smooth and silent, a gurney wheeled into a small room smelling of chemicals. Clack of X-ray plates then hushed voices sucked down into a vacuum of silence.

A woman's voice, weary and full of pain. Speaking Pashto but not a native. "For a week," she said. Another voice – Aktoub's – arguing.

"If you move him," she said, "he'll die."

Her voice turned away; another voice answered in the same tongue and he realized it was Russian. His joy switched to terror. *I'm Ahmad from Edeni. Shot by mujihadeen.*

Sooner or later you get payback. *Save me*, he begged her. *I'll love you forever.*

SOPHIE WATCHED THE DYING MAN on the operating table. It wasn't the bullet-shattered shoulder that would kill him but the septicemia. "How many days since he was shot?" she'd asked the Afghani irregular who'd brought him, but the man had just shrugged, "I wasn't there... Maybe three days? It was the *mujihadeen* who shot him."

She adjusted the floodlight over the table to shine on the wound. What did it matter who shot who? They were all assassins. They *all* deserved to die.

She was dead too but still went through the motions. You forced yourself to take a breath each time you noticed you had stopped. Every time you were alone the tears poured down your face like lost children and choked your throat till you were so worn of crying you hardly did it any more in public. Your chest was crushed; the world hummed around you, electric and false, but you couldn't find a place it wouldn't reach you.

"Hook him up," she told the nurse, "antibiotics, fluids, get him under so I can irrigate and debride the wound..."

"If he's going to die, Doctor..."

She couldn't take it another minute. Yes, a minute she could. But not another hour. Not to help this man. How many had *he* killed? Why save them when they'll only kill more?

"You'll do the anesthesia?" the nurse asked anxiously.

A clatter of stretchers being brought into the next room, a man moaning. If she could just make it through the next hour. The next day. "Nemerov's not here?"

"You're the only one tonight."

Every single thing reminded her of Leo's death. Every moment. That he was not here anymore. Would *never* be here.

The dying man's face was drained of blood. Septic shock, acute infection. Supposedly he was on the Russian side. But there were no allegiances in this horrible country. Who was to say *this man* hadn't killed Leo? She bit back a sob. *I will not cry any more in front of people.*

He wasn't going to make it. The infection too advanced, no primary treatment, the filth, bullet fragments, and dead tissue in the wound. She didn't have the drugs to fight it. But he'd been strong and healthy, she could see that, more muscular and taller than most Afghanis, a hill man probably. Beard not as dark as most, such deep blue eyes.

Unlike most Afghanis his biceps and triceps were thick and corded like those of weightlifters back home. With a number twelve scalpel she pulled out a piece of cloth the bullet had punched through the bone. It was the typical arcing trajectory of a boat-tailed AK bullet through human flesh. By habit she described the wound as she worked. "Clavicle shattered lateral third, glenoid cavity and scapular fractures, coracoclavicular ligament not salvageable... sepsis... we'll need to set him up with IV penicillin..."

"But if he's not going to live?" the nurse said. "When we need the medicines?"

With the back of her wrist Sophie adjusted her mask, took a breath to steady herself. "Go check on the new ones."

The wounded man's skin where the sun hadn't touched it was paler than any Afghani's. Bright teeth, no cavities, two silver fillings. Well done. Modern.

The nurse came back. "Three wounded, one critical. Two dead."

"Call Captain Alexov – this man's not Afghani," Sophie started to say, then stopped. To Hell with him. He'd soon die and get dropped in a hole, she didn't care.

Owe You

THE LIGHT NEARED, pale yellow, orange in its center, flickered away. It's not true, he realized, that when you die there's a bright tunnel. No, the light comes and goes.

Pain. Did that mean he was alive?

The light neared. "Who are you?" a woman said in English.

Who am I?

"Just now you spoke English," she said. "We *heard* you."

"Please," he said in Pashto. "Help me."

"Who are you?" she said in Dari.

Ahmad from Edeni. Shot by mujihadeen. Someone had told him that, but in English. He could not think the words in Dari. "Who are you?" she said, a different language.

Duki – was that the word? No, there was something wrong with that. "Help me," he said again in Pashto.

A distant knocking. Loud banging. Hard heels coming. "*Spetsnaz!*" the woman whispered.

Spetsnaz? He felt fear, not knowing why.

A loud voice, nasty and deep. Rustle of uniforms and

clink of weapons. "You can't come in here!" the woman yelled.

"We come where we want. Who's he?"

Silence. "An Afghani irregular," she said.

"How do you know?"

"The man who brought him –"

"We're looking for a *duki*. He could be the one!"

The gurney shuddered as a hand snatched back the sheet. Jack felt cold, afraid. "Stop that!" the woman said. "He's dying. Two Russians were with the ones who brought him."

"You – *you're* not Russian!"

"My husband was Russian. He was killed last month."

"Yeah, right."

"Go ask General Volnev. Now get out of here."

Silence. The sheet up to his chest. He opened his eyes. She was young and thin. He realized with sudden terror that she had spoken Russian. "Please water," he said in Pashto.

"Soon," she answered, "you're going to have to tell me who you are."

AHMAD WATCHED THE PURPLE Kabul sky and wished for rain. If this drought kept on there'd be no water for people to drink or cook with or to put out the fires the bombs and shells made. Everything so dry that even the mud and dung houses burned when tracers hit them.

It was not even September but in the orchards the withered fruit had fallen from the trees. The wheat had come up only an inch and died. The farmers were turning their goats into the fields where they stepped on mines or died of hunger or the farmers ate them first.

"Remember when the rains were good?" Galaya said. "Everyone had fat animals and tall wheat? I wore blue jeans like American girls. We went to movies. Now if you don't wear a veil they throw acid in your face."

"We had a parliament," he remembered. "A democratic constitution. Schools and teachers, a university, professors..."

"I've washed all the little girls with the last of the bath water. The little boys are yours. The water's filthy."

"But it's wet. It washes some dirt away."

"And deposits more."

He smiled. "I forget how much worse life was before you –"

She reached out. Her hand was slim and cool and tense. He felt an electric shock up his back into his head. So this's it, he thought. This's how you know.

JACK LISTENED TO THE HOMELY sounds of Kabul through the window above his hospital bed – women calling children, storekeepers yelling their wares, a donkey's bray, a rattle of trucks. A loudspeaker screeched, roared static, then a muezzin's aggrieved chant. He was back in the world and everything was wonderful.

His upper right arm was wrapped against his ribs, the forearm across his chest. With his good left arm he reached out for the tin cup of water beside the bed, drained it. The motion hurt his wounded shoulder but it was a good pain. How had she saved him? Who was she?

I know who I am. *Ahmad from Edeni. Shot by mujihadeen.* McPhee said so.

A distant whine became a howl. He cringed as a shell whined down. An instant of pure silence then the air sucked in and the bed shook and plaster sifted down from the ceiling. After a few moments the sounds of the city picked up again as if nothing had happened.

He looked up at the IV. Had to get out of here. Where was McPhee?

When he woke again she was there. "Where am I?" he

said in Pashto.

"You're not Afghani," she said, also in Pashto. "Who are you?"

"Are you Russian?" he said in Pashto.

"French. And you?"

He thought of Husseini. But if he said he was Algerian she'd speak to him in French and catch him that way. "From Saudi Arabia. I came to Afghanistan –"

"To fight the Russians?"

He sensed danger. "I'm fighting nobody. A journalist."

"We'll send a messenger to your embassy then. For them to come get you. And pay your bill..."

He reached out his left hand. "You saved me. Why?"

Noises on the stairs. He sat up. He had no gun, nothing. She ran into the corridor.

Three young men in beards and turbans burst in, dirty and hard-faced, eyes red with opium, carrying AKs. Then another, gray-bearded, pistol in his hand.

She followed them back in. "Please!"

"Silence, woman!" The older man turned on Jack. "Who's this?"

"A Saudi journalist. His embassy's coming to get him. Please leave!"

"He's a Soviet spy. Shoot them both." He stepped out the door and his steps receded down the corridor.

One of the three men gave the doctor a carious smile. "Or we sell her. *Think*, how much money –"

"Warriors of God," said a fat one with a white eye, "have no need for money."

The one with bad teeth glanced at the doctor. Another who limped pointed his head – *outside*. "We fuck *her* and shoot *him*," bad teeth said. "Then we sell her."

"Too much noise, shooting inside," said the fat one. "Hurts my ears."

More shells came drifting down softly like rain then ear-crushing explosions. "Our Muslim brothers from the north," said bad teeth. "Shelling us."

"That's Soviet 155s," the doctor said. "Now get out!"

"I won't go out in this," the fat one said, "just to shoot them."

Bad teeth cocked his AK at her. "We shoot them here."

"It'll hurt my ears," the fat one said.

"Dangerous out there," said the one who limped. "I agree, we shoot them here."

"You're with Hekmatyar," she said.

"And so?"

"When he finds out you've bothered me he'll kill you."

"He loves us," the fat one said.

"Last week I saved his brother's life. In Jalalabad. He's sworn to protect me."

"I didn't know he had a brother..."

"His brother Abdullah – you doubt me?"

"We were told there was a foreigner here," bad teeth said. "One of the ones who killed some of our men last week, in the Kowkcheh."

"I'm Saudi," Jack said. "We bring guns to Hekmatyar. We too are warriors of God –"

"Tell Hekmatyar I've saved a true believer," she called after them. "Praise God!"

When they were gone she yanked his IV. "You're not Saudi."

He took a deep breath. "You saved me," he said in French, "*Vous avez sauvé ma vie.*"

She stared at him an instant, grabbed his hand and pulled him up. "That's bad French. *Vous m'avez sauvez la vie.*"

He stood. "It's true you saved his brother?"

"*Whose* brother?"

"Hekmatyar."

"That pig. I've never met his brother." She gripped his good arm, her slim body hard against him as she walked him down the dirty corridor toward a patch of daylight. "I'm taking you to a friend in Kabul. Where you'll be safe till you get stronger."

He made himself walk faster. "When they come back they'll kill you too!"

"I'm leaving soon. To work in a refugee camp on the border. Hurry!"

"You've saved me." Jack gasped with pain on the steps. "I owe you."

"Save someone else. Then we'll be even."

Langley

I'LL GET KILLED, she thought, leading him out the door down a long street of battered buildings. She tightened her black veil round her hair and face. *He could be ISI, Spetsnaz even.*

Even weak and injured he gave off a sense of physical power, emotional solidity. Who *was* he? "You have to walk alone," she told him. "I can't touch you in public."

"Go away," he muttered, breathing hard, not looking at her. "You're going to get killed."

"Turn right there, at the bottom of the hill. Hurry! Faster!" She waved at a passing jeep but it picked up speed. "Bastards," she hissed.

"Where you taking me?"

"Like I said, to a friend. You'll be safe there. Whoever the Hell you are."

IT WAS A DARK DIRTY part of Kabul stinking of charred buildings and broken sewers. She hustled him up a reeking path to a low rambling building. Dusk was falling. He reeled on his feet, nauseous with pain. She banged on the door. "Hey!" she called softly. "It's me."

A slim man came to the door, poorly shaven, a thin graying beard, black spaces between his teeth, his hair receding, narrow glasses down his sharp nose. "It *is* you!" he smiled. "Our guardian angel! Quick, inside!"

It was a narrow entry lit by a smoky candle. Jack stared at him. The doctor took the man's hand and nodded at Jack. "Can you keep him a few days?"

Ahmad from Edeni, Jack realized. Warm happiness filled him. "Ahmad!"

The man turned. He jumped. "*Jyek!*"

She stepped back. "You know him?"

"Of course!" Ahmad laughed, dark eyes gleaming. "Why are you here, *Jyek*, for Heaven's sake? What's happened to you?"

How could he lie? "Like I told her – I'm a journalist."

"You said you were Saudi!" she snapped.

"If I'd said I was American they'd have killed me."

Ahmad squeezed Jack's hand. "Bloody palm to blood palm. Blood brothers."

HE WOKE TO the hubbub of singing children, a woman's voice repeating something, small feet running, a snatch of girlish laughter. Ahmad and the doctor were gone, dusk fading into night outside the empty windows.

He lay on a straw mattress, a horse blanket over him, in a sort of small storeroom, clay urns along one side, a bead curtain across the door. A young woman pushed aside the curtain and dipped a plastic bucket in an urn. "Oh!" She yanked her veil across her face when she saw he was awake. She backed out letting the curtain fall.

Ahmad came in and held Jack's hand. "You've slept for a night and day." He touched Jack's forehead. "Your fever's gone."

"Is this a school?"

"An orphanage. The schools are all closed. I run it with Galaya, the girl you just saw."

"Is she your wife?"

"Heavens no – don't say such things."

Jack sat up. "They find me they'll shoot you."

Ahmad smiled. "Why are you really here, *Jyek*?"

"To fight the Soviets... You know that."

Ahmad nodded. "Wahid told me. I didn't believe him."

"I saw Edeni."

"He said the Soviets did it?" Ahmad was silent, shook his head. "It was Hekmatyar, your American ally. Wahid knows that –"

Jack lay back, exhausted. "Got to get out of here."

"Your friend Aktoub came today; he found where you were from the French doctor. And tomorrow he's coming to take you over the hills to Pakistan."

Jack raised up on his left arm. It didn't seem possible that he might finally be going home. Or that he would make it. "The French doctor, what is her name?"

Ahmad looked surprised, hesitant. "Sophie Dassault."

"When you see her please tell her thank you. And that I will save somebody else."

"Who?"

"Just tell her. She'll understand."

DULLES WAS COLD and dank. Jack's plane out of Rawalpindi had been delayed in Frankfurt and now it was after midnight DC time. In the airport's hollow corridors he felt nervous, exposed. The air tasted disinfected. Bizarre signs advertised coffee, *Time*, bourbon and Winstons.

A white-haired black man pushed a broom along a hallway. A newspaper page, "*New Hopes for Middle East Peace*," scuttled down the escalator. Somewhere a radio was playing a haunting melody about *Sultans of Swing*. I've never heard that, he thought. *How long have I been gone?*

He took the airport bus downtown and found a hotel on Eleventh Street. The desk clerk looked Pakistani but when Jack spoke to him in Pashto the man did not answer.

He slept with the Makarov under his pillow and awoke at noon nauseous, shoulder aching horribly. Traffic rattled the windows. The carpet stank of deodorizer and mildew. From a corner a television watched him. He yanked its cord and faced it to the wall but still it listened, waited.

The faucet water reeked of chemicals, the soap of artificial fragrance. The shower was intolerable, pelting his shoulder with tainted water, his soles sticking to the tiles.

The sidewalks were thronged with well-dressed people. Women wore sleek revealing clothes and stepped clear of him. In a store window he saw a skinny beardless man who gave him back the finger, then laughed the moment he did.

LANGLEY'S vast echoing spaces felt spooky. "Why the hell'd you come in commercial?" Timothy Cormac said. "We had a seat lined up –"

"Sit all night with my back against the wall? No thanks."

"Hey I hear our doctors in Islamabad saved you, that you've made a great recovery."

"It was my dog, the one you were afraid of, who saved me. And the French doctor in Kabul. Three times she saved my life. And that Afghanistani Aktoub and Owen McPhee getting me out of Afghanistan to Pakistan –"

"Speaking of Afghanistan," Timothy watched him with dark-circled eyes, "we're working with the Saudis. GID –"

Jack glanced round the vinyl-paneled room, wondering where the pickups were. "Who?"

"Saudi Intelligence. It's run by this neat prince, Turki al-Faisal. Son of the former King. Hey, he's a close friend of George Bush, *and* he went to Georgetown. He's got this new guy, a rich Saudi with connections, going to help us in Afghanistan."

"I thought they all spent their money on Parisian models and cocaine."

"We're going to put *our* money where our mouth is with this new guy. Osama bin Laden." Timothy slid his tongue back and forth under his gums. "That's his name."

Sticky teeth, Jack remembered. "I think we should stop this war."

Timothy chuckled. "What a strange idea. We want to send you back –"

"Afghanistan? You *crazy*? Everybody's gunning for me – the Russians, Massoud. Even Hekmatyar's got a ransom out on me." Jack tried to settle into his seat but his shoulder wouldn't take it. "This war is hideous."

"It's got momentum now, Jack. We've got them on the run."

"Anyway I'm getting out of this game. Didn't McPhee tell you?"

"We've sent Owen to El Salvador." Timothy paused. "How's your Arabic?"

"Why?"

"Ever been to Beirut?"

"A few times. In the good old days."

Timothy eyed him brightly. "You want coffee?"

"My best friend's in Beirut."

"What, some raghead?" The yellow teeth again. "Just joking."

"A Marine. Been friends since we were kids."

"There's a guy you should meet –"

"I've met lots of guys lately. Most of them wanted to kill me."

"He's one of us." Timothy picked up an inside line and

hit five numbers. "Bernie? Come on up. I want you to meet our new man in Beirut."

Jack shook his head. "I didn't say that."

Balding and slope-shouldered, Bernie Rykoff had a soft wet handshake. "Bernie's the new head of our Middle East desk," Timothy said. "PhD from Stanford. In Middle East affairs."

"Had a few of those myself." Jack said in Arabic, turning to Rykoff. "How well do you speak the tongue?"

Bernie shrugged. "Never really had time to learn," he said in English.

"Then *how* can you separate garbage from truth – how do you *know* anything?"

"You're a field man, Jack," Timothy said. "Bernie's DI. You know the drill."

"What counts is how you put it all together," Bernie said.

"After Islamic Jihad bombed our Beirut Embassy in April," Timothy said, "State wanted to pull out of Lebanon. *We* didn't want to, Defense didn't –"

"How do you *know* it was Islamic Jihad?" Jack asked.

"That's why we need a presence there," Bernie said.

"Hey Jack," Timothy said, "what if you went into Beirut as a journalist, spent a few weeks? A chance to see your friend, relax, get to know the place?"

"My friend's due home next month, wife's going to have a baby. Anyway, don't journalists there keep getting shot?"

"You'll have cover. And backup. It's just a few weeks."

It no longer mattered, Jack reminded himself, how much he disliked Timothy. For his rotund flabbiness and portly pink smile, the way he said "Hey" to intro something he wanted you to buy. That he'd never heard a bullet fired in hatred but seemed more than ready to send others into danger.

The shoulder pain was intense. *Hey buddy*, he asked

Bandit, *tell me what you think.*

Tell them get fucked, Bandit said.

"Get fucked," Jack said.

"Now Jack don't act like that."

Bite him, Bandit said.

"I can't," Jack said.

"Why not?" Timothy said.

"I wasn't talking to you."

Bernie looked around. "Then who…"

"I'm going home to Maine," Jack said, "till this damn shoulder gets better."

"Don't take too long," Timothy smiled. "We might find somebody else."

"Please do."

Timothy shook his head as if Jack had made a very stupid decision. "See the paymaster on the way out."

The paymaster was downstairs in a windowless room. "You've earned twelve thousand seven hundred twenty-seven dollars," she said. "After taxes, Social Security, that's a nine thousand eight fifty and seventy-seven cents. You'll get a check for that and a plane ticket home. But we have no liability for what happened to you."

"Oh yeah?" Jack said. "But I do."

On the flight from DC to Portland he drifted in and out of sleep, drank gin on the rocks and stared out the window at the strange, peaceful landscape unrolling below.

It didn't seem possible, Afghanistan. Though every thud of pain from his shoulder proved it real. And every time he drifted off it was the face of the French doctor hovering over him, haloed in white light. Like an angel.

Cobbossee Woods

H E HITCHED FROM Portland Airport to Winthrop and called his mother from the pay phone at Mister Market. It rang and rang and he felt sharp disappointment. Then it was snatched up. "Yes?" his mother's sharp voice. "Now who's this?"

"It's me."

"*You*! Oh my *good*ness! Where *are* you?"

"In Winthrop. I'm on leave, wanted to call first, not give you a shock –"

He walked through rustling leaves down old familiar streets tangy with oak smoke to the white farmhouse on the shore of Lake Maranacook. "What, you ring the doorbell now?" she laughed, wrapping him in her arms.

"Jesus, Ma!" he yelled in pain.

"Oh my God – what's happened to you?"

"Those old dislocations from football were getting worse. The Army docs fixed it."

With his duffel over his good shoulder he stepped into the woodstove-warm kitchen with its checkered linoleum and the maple table and the four oak chairs his father had made. He dropped the duffle in a corner, the Makarov inside it clunking.

"All this time you can't even write? To your poor old widowed mother? Who's been pining away in your absence? What a terrible son you are!"

He laughed. "You know the drill, Mom –"

She held his face in both palms. "I was going to make soft-boiled eggs on toast and correct quizzes and do a lesson plan and read some dull book, and instead now I've got *you*!"

"I can stay a while? Or did you rent out my room?"

She laughed with joy. "There's baked beans left over and I'll make liver and onions, we'll get some color back in your cheeks, you look like you just ate Mrs. Randolph's cat."

He sat at the maple table, weary, happy and alive. "So how've *you* been?"

"Fine!" She sat opposite him, elbows on the table. "*Great*, actually. It's a good class this year, some super kids, no bad eggs... The car needed a new oil pump and Mr. Jansen did it but wouldn't charge me. Johnnie Dillon's doing the plowing this year –"

"How you feeling?"

"Fine," she shrugged. "Tell me about this shoulder –"

"You had much snow?"

"Two storms so far. Leaves were magnificent." She went to the sink, shook out a glass and took Canadian whiskey and sweet vermouth and bitters from the cupboard and Maraschino cherries from the refrigerator. "I'm going to have another Manhattan. I always have one before dinner but this is a celebration so I'm going to have two!"

"You're a wild one –"

"Doctor Liscombe said I should. *Marie*, he said, *you be sure you have your Manhattan every day –*"

"He's a good doctor."

She took an ice tray from the freezer compartment and cracked five cubes into her glass. "Want one?"

He got a glass from the cupboard and dropped in some ice. "I'll have it straight."

They tapped glasses and he drank deep, luxuriating in the heat of whiskey in his throat. "You look like your father," she said. "It's like sitting across from him, the way we did, having a Manhattan or two before dinner."

The years vanished, he was a boy coming into the kitchen for dinner shaking snow off his clothes, the smell of potatoes baking and hamburgers in the frying pan, radiators clanking, his dog leaving fat wet prints across the linoleum. "Sit on your bed, Thor," his mother would say, and the dog stepped into his willow bed with the red cushion, turned round, flopped down and uttered a groan as if no dog in history had ever had to endure such a life.

"So," his father reached out to squeeze his arm, "what's new?"

"Up on Cobbossee ridge a hawk or owl got a rabbit, yesterday or last night. The deer have yarded up already in the hemlocks south of Upper Narrows..." Jack unlaced his boots and turned them upside down on the radiator. "What's new?"

His mother young then, slender-faced, dark-haired – *it's the black Irish in me* – "Your father's got to go away a while."

Now Jack glanced through the frosted windows at the October night. "Early winter."

"Night of the first snow Toby Lemieux spun out his cruiser and hit a hydrant and there was water everywhere and then it froze. The boys at the fire station were real pleased."

"Serves him right."

"Chief Mullin's going to take the repairs out of his pay." She sloshed her ice cubes round to pull out the cherry by the stem and ate it. "Damn that was good." She clasped his hands. "My God what joy to see you!"

He poured the beans into an iron frying pan and set it on to warm, cut two onions and simmered them in butter, drinking his whiskey and turning the onions as they talked, then laid the liver on the onions and turned up the heat on the beans. She cut some bread and put it in the pewter bread dish one of his father's First Cav buddies had given him that said *Give Us This Day Our Daily Bread*. "Russian rye," she said. "I put molasses in it and a little coffee. Makes it real dark."

They ate dinner and drank more whiskey that in his weariness made his head spin. *I'd forgotten*, he realized, *what it's like to be loved.*

When he went up to his boyhood room it seemed smaller, the bed under the pine-paneled dormer too short and narrow. He fell asleep but woke then couldn't sleep, sat on the bed staring through the frost-etched window at the village in bare-branched dancing streetlight shadows under its pale sheet of snow, and it seemed unwise to trust this peace, the house made of wood that would never stop a bullet and the yards with no cover and open fields of fire everywhere. Finally he took his pillow and blankets and dozed in the bullet-proof safety of the cast iron bathtub, with the Makarov on safety across his chest.

Next morning he drove his old Camaro one-handed down the Monmouth road past the farm where once he'd picked apples for school money. He walked the ridge between Cobbossee and Upper Narrows in thin snow scattered with red maple leaves. There were raccoon and rabbit tracks and the wandering prints of deer. A great horned owl watched him sleepily from its hole in a dead spruce; he thought of all the little creatures it hunted, how they lived in constant fear. *But I'm safe here.*

Toby Lemieux stopped his cruiser on Main Street as Jack

was crossing. "Shit," he snickered, "we send you to West Point, and all you do is sit in Guam listening to the radio?" He spit disparagingly. "Christ when I do that here at least I'm catching speeders."

"*You* didn't send me to West Point, Toby. You sent me to jail."

"You deserved it, too. Jerry can still barely walk."

"He's lucky he's alive." Jack turned away.

While his mother corrected geography exams he sat in the den watching the Patriots beat the Chargers. "Real men don't watch sports," he said as they sat down to pork chops and potatoes and cornmeal muffins. "Better if everyone was out playing sports than sitting in Barcaloungers watching TV."

She laughed. "Most guys around here they'd get a myocardial infarction."

"Because they're out of shape." He grinned thinking of a raggedy old Afghani *mullah* hitching up his pants to go deep for a long one.

"What's this – you don't say grace anymore?"

"Got out of the habit."

"Even if you don't believe in God, it's good to be thankful for food when so many people don't have any."

He saw Afghanistan's barebacked hills, the children in Ahmad's orphanage, their thin faces under wispy hair. "Sometimes I forget."

"By the way, I saw Susie Franklin this afternoon. That man left her with a baby and no child support – I told her what do you expect from somebody from Lewiston?"

"She made her bed. Let her lie in it."

"She's gone through a hard time. It'd be nice you called her."

"I told her goodbye long ago."

"So you only think for yourself now? The Army's

149

changed you."

"Look what it did to Dad." He winced at what he'd said, wanted to take it back.

"It's okay," her voice thick. "It's true."

He thought of her imprisoned by winter in this house. "You should've married again."

"I never met another man I wanted to."

For a while he said nothing, then pushed back from the table. "In the morning I'm going by Cole's, see his folks."

"Barb's living with them now. She's still taking vet classes full time though the baby's due any day. Imagine him a Marine – just yesterday you two were throwing apples at each other in the orchard."

Jack grinned at the memory of two scrawny boys like Indians hunting each other down. "If he was here we still would be." He glanced down at the place in the corner where Thor's bed had been.

"It's out in the barn," his mother said, following his gaze. "You'll get another dog someday. You'll need that bed then."

"I had one," he said, turned away.

"What, in Guam?"

"Yeah," his voice thick. He wanted to tell her all, losing Gus, Loxley, all the people he'd killed, Bandit dying to save him, the shoulder screaming with pain as if the bullet had just hit.

And most of all, the pain that he could tell her nothing.

"You did right, son, what you did."

"Jerry? I should've killed him."

"And spent your life in jail. For a dog?" She made a sour face. "Sweetheart, we have to forgive."

He knew what she meant: *I had to forgive losing my husband.* "Life's a beautiful gift," she said. "A magnificent mystery. When we get all tied up in revenge we forget how

Springdale Public Library

Phone: (479) 750-8180
www.springdalelibrary.org

Checked Out Items 9/28/2017 12:52
Tonoli, Frank Anthony

Item Title	Due Date
34224402364406	10/12/2017
Assassins	
34224402556142	10/12/2017
Undoctored : why health care has failed you and how you can become smarter than your doctor	

Thank you!

beautiful it is."

"I'm tired, Mom." He carried the dishes to the sink and began to scrub them one-handed. "Still on Guam time."

IT WAS BOW SEASON FOR WHITETAILS, and next morning he took his recurve from the closet and strung it but could only draw it halfway. The shoulder pain brought tears to his eyes and he wondered could he ever use it again. He drove to Monmouth and sat on the front porch with Cole's folks till the cold drove them inside. "Got a letter from him last week," Cole's mother said. "He says the folks in Lebanon are glad to have them and the food's pretty good."

"With Cole *any* food's *always* good."

"That's true," Cole's father smiled.

"I still don't understand," she said, "why they sent them way over there –"

"Just peacekeeping," Jack answered. "To stop a civil war between Muslims and Christians. The French paratroopers are there too. And the Italians... It's a good thing."

"That's what you were doing, Jack?" Cole's father said. "Where were you, anyway?"

"Guam. Just a translator listening to Soviet communications. No big deal."

Barb came back from vet class, her belly huge as a basketball under her coat. "Hey," Jack grinned, "what'd you ever *do* to get like that –"

"You should talk!" She pushed him. "All the girls *you* enticed into the back seat of that Camaro!"

"Now Barb," Cole's mother said. "He was always going with Susie..."

"This weather," Cole's father said. "Coming on to snow."

IT'S RISK I NEED, he decided, and drove up to the White

Mountains. But with the shoulder he couldn't climb and the peaks were puny after the Hindu Kush.

Finally he called Susie Franklin and they went to Augusta to see Nick Nolte in *North Dallas Forty* and drank Shipyards in Rocker's overlooking the Kennebec River. In Afghanistan he'd often dreamed of this – a girl, a cozy bar, no one trying to kill you, a warm car to drive home in. Back then it had seemed a beautiful mirage but now felt meaningless. "I should've stuck by you, Jack."

"Nah. Thrown out of the Point, a tough guy with no job, no future –"

"That wasn't you."

"I thought it was."

"You should stay in Maine. They need teachers, Readfield needs a football coach."

"They wouldn't hire me." He watched the silky Kennebec under the newly risen moon. Waning now, the moon that many months ago had been a sliver when he'd landed in the Hindu Kush. When Gus fell, and then when Loxley...

"They'd love to have you. People forgive..."

It annoyed him, her optimism, that she felt there was something to forgive, his buried antagonism from a separation that wouldn't heal. "So you went off and married that asshole –"

"I was pregnant damn it." She too looked out at the River, her dark hair like a curtain down the side of her face. "I was getting over you."

"You could've fucking waited."

"You told me you hated me, hated everybody. You were leaving, soon as you got out."

"Yeah. And so I did."

Driving home she slid next to him, her hand inside of his thigh. He turned on the Monmouth road and then on the fire road to her trailer on Lower Narrows. Where an old farmhouse had stood now were new manufactured homes on tiny plots. A shepherd chained to a doghouse came out barking.

"I was glad you'd come home," she said, coming into his arms after the baby-sitter left. It was so easy to fall back in time, her urgent cries, the way all tension seemed to flow out of him but then built up again.

"You knew I was here?"

"Everybody knows," she said, nestling her long nakedness against him.

In Afghanistan no one had known who or where he was, but in Maine everyone already knew. It bothered him, this lack of concealment.

"You're all lean and mean." She wiped sweat from his brow. "You need meat on your bones. And that shoulder's real evil-looking."

Through the frost-stippled window the moon glittered. Out in Cobbossee Woods a great horned owl hooted. The furnace kicked in with a great thump. In the next room the baby began to cry. She rose up on one elbow. "Let's see if he quits."

Jack listened to the baby crying and the north wind under the door. Damn shoulder was hurting. No matter where he moved it didn't stop.

"I have to get him." She slipped out of bed, a pale sylph through a crack of moonlight, came back with the baby. "Can you imagine what he feels? Not knowing anything, dropped into the dark, alone in the world?"

He slept late, a lazy Sunday morning, luxuriating in the warm covers, the lessening of pain, the relaxation of being with Suze, of being known and cared about. The smell of coffee and the tang of raisin bread toast, a faint mumble of TV. It was his fault, really, they'd broken up. He could come back, teach languages, coach football, let that other stuff go.

Bandit's right. I'll tell Timothy forget about Beirut.

"Jack?" Her voice was strained. "*Jack!*"

"Take off that bathrobe and get in here."

"Look at the TV!" Tears were running down her face. "The Marines in Lebanon. That's where Cole is, right?"

He sat up, pain shooting through the shoulder. "Christ *what is it?*"

"Somebody just blew them up. Oh God they're all dead. All our Marines. Hundreds of them."

III

Lebanon

Beirut

October 1983

THROUGH THE SCRATCHED plexiglas of the Middle East Airlines 727 the whitecapped Mediterranean gleamed iridescent green. "Islamic Jihad did it," Timothy had said. "Some insane kid in a garbage truck with a thousand pounds of *plastique*."

"Then they hit the French paratroopers with another truck," Bernie added. "We don't understand..."

In his stomach the cold queasiness of fear, a prickling of little hairs along the wrist, the tense heart and weighted breath, a weakness in the limbs. They killed three hundred Marines and *paras*... How easy would *he* be to kill? Maybe he was just more afraid now, after Afghanistan, the pain-filled weeks.

The plane dropped to ten thousand. He saw the ragged Lebanese coastline and tawny hills with raw mountains behind them. At five thousand feet humid air streamed across the plexiglas. There were cars and trucks on the coast highway, farms behind rock walls. Ochre roofs, dirt roads, rock-bordered fields, orchards of broken trees, a greasy black column that at first he took for a burning tank but was just a dump on fire.

"We're sending you in on your own," Timothy had added.

"You said there was backup."

"You won't need it –"

"You don't have anybody left in Beirut, do you?"

If Islamic Jihad caught you, how would they kill you? A bullet in the back of the head, a wire garrote? Or more likely, slowly with the greatest possible pain?

The plane banked over the crushed Marine barracks, the trucks of debris, the new American flag bravely flapping. He had been making love with Susie the moment Cole had died. Now he was here to kill Cole's killers, revenge the 241 dead and 120 seriously injured Marines, the deadliest single Marine death toll since Iwo Jima. As if that would bring them back, bring Cole back. Or heal his parents' hearts. Or fix Barb's ruined life.

Kevlar-vested U.S. Marines with M-16s patrolled the airport, looking hard and angry, but he did not speak to them. The Lebanese customs inspector in a mildewed blue sweater glanced at his battered passport. "Ireland?" he said in French. "Why you come here, Mr. Flaherty?"

"Journalist."

The man flipped through the visas of France, Germany, Denmark and other innocent places, found an empty space and stamped it. "You've come to tell the world what's happening here? Go home. Nobody cares."

"TAKE THE COAST ROAD," Jack told the cab driver in French.

"The other way's safer," the driver said. "This goes too near the Palestinian camps."

"Take it anyway."

They drove along the sea past burnt-out buildings, blasted cars, donkey carts, overturned buses and shell-holed houses, around gaping cavities in the tarmac where mines had blown, past young bearded men in Palestinian head-scarves with AK-47s. A bullet-pocked blue sign said *Avenue du Général de Gaulle*. "I don't dare go further," the driver said.

"What about the Hotel St. George –"

"Blown to bits, the world's most beautiful hotel, by a bunch of gangsters. This was the Paris of the East before the Palestinians came..."

They took Avenue de Paris with clear white beaches on the left and the shattered walls of hotels and villas on the right. Then on the right a great ruin of gaping walls and concrete floors hanging down. He thought of the rotten bodies still under mashed concrete. "What was that?" he said off-handedly.

"You don't know, eh? The U.S. Embassy."

"I thought Americans were liked here? The American University, foreign aid, even the Marines came here to en-force the peace –"

The driver dropped the battered Peugeot into first gear to negotiate a shell hole in which a dead donkey lay placid as a bather in a tub. "American money goes for schools, modern ideas, for birth control that frees women from hav-ing so many babies. And peace? Do you think the madmen who plant these bombs want peace?"

The driver turned up a curving street. "Here's Rue Ken-nedy... If we could have a Kennedy now in Beirut! And there's American Hospital... Imagine, these Americans come here to cure people, so the Muslims kill them – when do Muslims ever go to help people in other countries, eh? Here's Rue Hamra – all I go. Three blocks that way, at the corner of Rue Baalbek and Nehmé Yafet, the Hotel Commodore. Where all the journalists stay, eh? Those who don't end up as guests of Hezbollah?"

At the Commodore they offered him a room on the second floor but there he was an easy target so insisted on the fifth floor where he could be shot from below only if he stood near the window. "Don't worry," the desk clerk told him. "Everything here just fine."

A lurid sun was sinking beyond the steely bay when he went down to grab a quick dinner in a sad café near the hotel. Eyes gritty, he climbed the stairs, dragged his blankets and pillow into the iron bathtub and slept fitfully, grabbing the gun each time the elevator clattered in its shaft or shots erupted in the streets below.

The first days he walked the safer streets, talking with the few shopkeepers, with Palestinian militiamen, journalists, then the deputy head of Police for West Beirut. "You remember what the Christians did," the deputy head said, "during the Crusades –"

He met with the senior French intelligence officer, Colonel Max Ricard. "President Reagan doesn't dare fight the Muslims after they kill all his Marines, so what does he do? He attacks Grenada. What a *farce*!"

"I'd like to talk to some of these fundamentalists. Find out how they think."

"Read the Koran. That's how they think."

"What about your fifty-eight dead *paras*?"

"We're governed by apologists," Ricard lit a new Gauloise from the butt of an old, "who believe any Muslim atrocity must be due to some prior injustice on our part."

Late nights he talked in the Commodore's bar with a chubby English journalist named Welkins who got drunk on Egyptian Scotch. "All these different fundamentalist groups, Flaherty," Welkins said, "– they're *all* Islamic Jihad, if you get my meaning. There's twenty brands of soap powder in the market but they all do the same thing, don't they?

"So why'd they hit the Marines?"

"You don't *know*? In August, when Reagan had the USS *New Jersey*, *Virginia* and *John Rogers* shell the hills above Beirut for days? Supposedly in retribution for the bombing of the American Embassy last April... Whole villages destroyed. And so the Marine barracks bombing was retribution for that –" He peered at Jack sideways through watery eyes. "What was your paper d'you tell me?"

"*Galway Times*."

"You must've run the story. Horrible thing, turned the whole Middle East against America. Terrorism's best friend, Reagan is."

"Maybe I should ask whoever runs Islamic Jihad about it?"

"Ismael al-Haji? You'll never find him. Nor do you want to."

A shell hit nearby, shaking the walls. Welkins cocked his head. "That one was down by the Grand Sérail, the Beaux Arts, by the sound of it." He waved a chubby finger. "Don't go near there... Shiite territory... Dangerous."

"So who *do* I talk to?"

"Any of twenty different madmen running twenty different fanatic groups. Islamic Jihad's just a front for Hezbollah, and Hezbollah's just a front for Iran... Other nutty Islamic groups are backed by the Syrians or the Saudis... When they can't kill Christians they kill each other."

"I'd like to get some stories, present their view..."

"What you're likely to *get*, my dear fellow, is kidnapped. Or out in Shatila with your throat cut. Remember your Old Testament: *The violence of Lebanon shall cover thee* –" Welkins downed his scotch, slid the glass across the bar. "Why do you suppose this crappy corner of the desert became the breeding ground for so many God-obsessed women-hating fanatics who've had such a tragic impact on the world? Christians, Muslims, Jews – all from one little cesspool?"

Jack shrugged. "Religion's a collective neurosis."

"Trouble is, we can convince ourselves of *anything*: that a biscuit from some cookie factory is the body of God, that dancing round the guts of an eviscerated goat will make it rain, or being decapitated by a 50-caliber bullet will send you straight to a paradise of willing virgins..." He sniffed. "Ah that it would – I'd be in the front lines myself."

The bar was empty, damp and chill. "Ever meet this Ismael guy?"

"Heavens no. He's up in the Beqaa Valley running his Hezbollah terrorist camps, living off Iran and Saudi and Qatari charities. Westerners can't get there. Shot twenty times before one gets halfway."

"So who wants his side reported?"

Welkins shrugged: *I've warned you. If you insist, it's not my fault.* "You could talk to Khalil Yassin. He's the good face they put on for the West."

Mektoub

FIVE THOUSAND DEAD CIVILIANS. Sitting on the creaky bed in his hotel room Jack tried to imagine all those people dying, how each felt, the piles of bodies, the sorrow and the pain. If the Marine bombing was payback for that, then who really killed Cole and the Marines?

Had Reagan truly killed the five thousand people in retribution for the Embassy bombing? But had *that* just been payback for some earlier atrocity? Did the cycle of murder just keep growing? Wasn't that what he'd learned the night he'd smoked *khief* with the teenage hooker in Rawalpindi? When he'd seen through to the core of the world?

He could go home now. He'd finished the mission, learned why the Marines had been killed. And that the head of Islamic Jihad was Ismael al-Haji. Who could be found in Baalbek.

Suze, the little trailer, the owl calling in Cobbossee Woods, the bare trees of winter, all seemed too precious and what he was doing insane, and he had to stare a moment at the bright window to keep from choking.

Cole nonchalantly tossed him the football, the neck of his jersey black with sweat. "No, you turkey, *you* go deep."

Find them. The ones who killed Cole. How could he go home till he'd done that?

HE FOUND KHALIL YASSIN in a bunker off Independence Avenue six blocks from the Green Line, the death zone separating Muslims and Christians. "You've got a bad image in the Western press." Jack waited for the staggered thuds of incoming 155s to tail off. "What if you could tell your side of the story?"

"You're not a journalist?" Yassin raised three fingers to his mouth, the sign for concupiscence. "Just a 'mouthpiece'?"

Jack glanced at the disinterested young men with their guns and grenades, the sweating gray walls, the kerosene lantern dancing on its cord to the tune of falling shells. "Was it for retribution that Islamic Jihad bombed the Marines?"

"It was very stupid what Reagan did, killing all those people, no? We *had* to punish him... And he got the lesson – pulled out right away."

"Perhaps Ismael al-Haji could give me details..."

"*Mektoub*." With a long fingernail Yassin picked between two upper front teeth. *It is written.* There is no cause and no effect, no natural law, because God creates each instant anew... "I would be insane to send you to Ismael al-Haji."

"Why?"

"He'd kill us both."

IN THE PALESTINIAN markets he bought used clothes and leather sandals, two blankets, plastic bottles of cola and orange soda, goat cheese, dates, currants, and hard bread.

At the Commodore he poured the sodas down the drain,

tore off the labels, rubbed the empty bottles on the tile floor to scratch them and filled them with tap water and two drops of iodine in each. He spread his map of Lebanon on the bed and memorized it again.

He dressed in the used clothes, holstered the Makarov under his left shoulder, wrapped the food, water, and spare clothes in the blanket roll, tied it across his other shoulder Afghani style, and followed Independence Avenue toward the Damascus road.

There was firing up ahead so he turned south toward the Hippodrome. Cars full of Palestinians raced toward the firing, shooting their guns in the air and screaming, but the people on the sidewalks paid no heed. At a crossroads he rubbed dust into his face and clothes, skirted Christian Beirut and took the Damascus road into the hills.

Before dusk he ate bread and goat cheese on the last ridge above Beirut then backtracked after dark to lie up in a deserted barn's dry hay.

As kids he and Cole had once floated a gray plastic model battleship on a pond in Cobbossee Woods and shot it with a BB gun till it sank. He'd been excited, imagining the gun crews shattered and killed, the bridge blown apart, water rushing through holes below waterline. If the *New Jersey* hadn't shelled Lebanese villages would the Marines still be alive?

Before dawn he walked north around the Syrian checkpoints. Stone villages lay in the folds of the hills and dwarf junipers marched along the crests. The *baaing* of goats and once the wooden thunk of a barley mill came up from a valley. Tiny red and yellow flowers hid in cracks in the rocks where the goats couldn't reach them.

He crossed a dirt road with recent jeep tracks and continued north, stopping often to pull thorns from his sandals. In late afternoon he drank and refilled his bottles in a pool where water spiders skittered over his hands. At dusk he came upon a ruined castle and slept under the eaves by a crossbow slot where a scimitar moon shone through.

On the third day he crossed mountains he remembered from the map as Jabal el Mnaitra. Ravens soared high above on updrafts. Towns and terraced fields lay to the west, on the Christian side, and beyond them the gauzy sea. To the east on the Muslim side the Beqaa Valley spread north and south, green in its center where irrigated by the Litani River, sere and arid in the foothills and stony on the crests.

The sun set behind Jabal al Mnaitra, glinting on farmhouse windows on the Syrian side. He came to a pool where a river rushed from a hole in the mountain through the fallen columns of a Roman temple. This, he decided, must be the river above Yammouné. He filled his bottles, added more iodine, ate the last of his bread and cheese and slept in a ruined hut, wakened several times by mice scuffling in the straw.

In the morning he found the mice had chewed through a sandal strap. It seemed a bad omen and he felt lonely and afraid. He didn't have to do this. He was going to get horribly killed.

Yammouné was a clean village with purple flowers in red clay pots and chickens scratching the dust, sheep and donkeys in pens beside the houses and children chattering on their way to school. He went into a little shop with clumps of garlic, tomatoes, onions, tangerines and lemons hanging by the door.

An old woman in black came through a bead curtain at the back. "Do you have leather?" he asked, conscious of his poor accent.

She cocked her head as if not believing what she'd heard.

He held up the sandal. "To fix this."

"Ah, you must be sore-footed." She dug into a cardboard

box and tossed some twine on the counter. He bought hard bread, cheese, and a goat sausage, and followed a path by a lake where ducks quacked and dabbled. Out on the flat-lands doves rose and fell in dizzy clouds; larks and black-birds sang from cattails along the canals. Roman columns stood over dusty villages like relics of a giant race.

As he walked he invented a life for himself. Ahmad Katswah, born in Edeni. Ahmad's mother was his, and Ahmad's father who had been killed by the Uzbeks when they stole his sheep. A year of university in Kabul, returning to teach in Edeni's schoolhouse under the yew tree. Now he spoke aloud in Arabic, trying an Afghani accent.

"That's a strange story," said a voice behind him.

He spun round. A barefoot boy with a stick in his right hand, a plastic bag in his left, something moving inside the bag. "Where'd *you* come from?" Jack said.

"Catching frogs in that ditch. What are *you* doing here?"

"Going to Baalbek to find work."

"There's no work in Baalbek since this War. Should've stayed where you were."

Jack sat on a stone to tighten the twine on his sandal. "I didn't hear you."

"Shouldn't talk to yourself. Anybody might hear."

Jack noticed Roman letters and numerals carved into the stone. *A Roman mileage marker.* "Hey," he started to say – but how would an Afghani know Latin?

"I can't believe a guy like you ever went to university," the boy said. "Look at you, all dirty and dusty! University people drive cars and wear nice clothes."

"I only did one year. I was poor."

The boy squinted up at him. "You still are."

Baalbek's Roman columns jutted up from sprawling slums as if left behind in some hasty departure. In a café two men were drinking mint tea and another with burly arms was shelling walnuts into a plastic bowl. Feeling out of place Jack asked for a tea which the burly man brought him wordlessly. He tried to understand their conversation and realized they were talking about rebuilding an engine. He shouldered his blanket roll and left, wanting to take a bus back to Beirut.

Four delta-winged Mirages passed over. Minutes later he thought he heard distant explosions. For a while he sat on the edge of the ruins. *Temple of Jupiter*, a sign said in French. Beyond it were more ruins, rows of columns like organ pipes reaching for the sky.

There were many things to think about but most of them were dangerous. That he might die here. What they'd do to him if they found him out. Like all liars, he realized, he wanted to convince himself of the safety of his lie.

He ate lamb *mishwi* for dinner in a café and slept under the stone lid of a sarcophagus, nosed by a dog whimpering with hunger.

He gave her bread and she fell on it, choking. I never felt alone, he told her, when I had Bandit. When I had Thor. She begged for more and he gave her a little, then tried to shoo her off, but she turned round three times at the foot of his sarcophagus and went to sleep.

Next morning he stopped two men in the street carrying Kalashnikovs. "Can you tell me where the fighters are?"

"Who are you?" one said. He was taller, with red hair, blue eyes and freckles.

Jack told his story. "How did you get here?" the red-haired one said.

"From Karachi, a port in Pakistan, to Mecca for the *hajj*, then Alexandria with a boat of pilgrims going home, then Beirut."

The other thumbed the rifle slung from his shoulder. "Know what this is?"

"I've killed seventeen infidels with a gun like that –"

"You have your own war. Why come fight ours?"

"It's the same enemy. And because we're backwards in our fighting we may not win. I've been sent to learn your ways."

"Our ways? We may not win either."

They took him to a hut near the ruins, blindfolded him and handed him an empty gun. "Strip and reassemble it," one said.

The blindfold pinched the bridge of his nose. He heard them taking apart his blanket roll.

The gun was an old AK-47 with a metal plate around the front of its stock and a flat metal receiver cover. Willing his fingers not to tremble he felt for the catch on the cover, shoved forward the recoil spring guide, lifted out the recoil spring and guide assembly, slid back the bolt assembly, snapped the bolt to the rear of the carrier, twisted it and shoved it forward. It was too loose, worn on the right side. *How many men*, he wondered, *has it killed?*

He slid the bolt back into the carrier, replaced the gas cylinder and twisted the bolt carrier assembly back into the receiver track. They tugged off the blindfold. "You carry no weapons?"

"A pistol here, under my arm."

They took the Makarov and made him drop his trousers to show he was circumcised. "So maybe you're a Jew?" one snickered. They took him through the alleys to a stucco house with a radio antenna in a plane tree in the courtyard. The red-haired one went inside and came out with a slender limping man. He had been wounded in the face and the scar had contorted his lips into a permanent snarl, the teeth on the left side of his mouth visible. He placed Jack's Makarov on the table between them. "I am Ismael al-Haji."

It took Jack an instant to realize the man had spoken

English. "I understand your name," Jack said in Arabic, "but not what you say."

Ismael al-Haji slid the Makarov from the holster. "You have a strange accent."

"Arabic is different from our Pashto tongue."

"Speak some of that –"

It was easy and very comfortable to drop into Pashto, telling him of the war in Afghanistan, the Soviet invaders.

"Enough. I do not understand you." Ismael thumbed the magazine catch and slid the magazine from the grip. "These are Soviet bullets?"

"Nine millimeter."

He snapped in the magazine and thumbed the safety. "Down is safe?"

Jack ignored his fear. "Up is safe. Down is fire."

Ismael nudged the safety down. "Now tell me," he said in English and pointed the gun at Jack, "why are you here?"

Fear drained him. "Why do you aim my gun at me?" Jack said in Arabic, "when I have come all this way to learn from you?"

"This is your first lesson. That we watch everyone. And if you're not true we will kill you."

With his good left hand Jack tugged open his shirt. "You see this shoulder? An infidel bullet did it. Why do you doubt me?"

"*Permission is granted unto those who take arms against the unbelievers, for they have been unjustly persecuted by them...*"

"I give you back the same Sura: *Those who have fled their country for the sake of God's true religion – on them will God bestow an excellent recompense –*"

Ismael pushed up the safety, snapped the magazine catch and piled the bullets on the table. "Where did you learn your Arabic?"

"From the Koran. And from the *mujihadeen* who come from Saudi Arabia to help us fight the infidels."

"It's for that you have the Saudi accent –"

"In Afghanistan we don't understand explosives." Jack scooped up the bullets, reloaded and holstered the Makarov. "How to blow up a truck among the infidels."

"And if you learn?"

In this Jack could speak the truth. "I'll go home and use this knowledge."

Hezbollah

"NEVER AIM," Jack said. "Look at the enemy. The bullet will hit where you're looking."

"How?" said the kid, a new recruit from the Shiite slums of Beirut.

Jack took the Israeli Galil from the kid's hands and draped a headscarf over the rear sight. Seventy yards away among the bullet-pitted Doric columns stood a cardboard man. "See that yellow stone – beside the target's foot?"

"The little one, to the right?"

"Watch it." Jack focused on the stone and fired. The stone pirouetted away.

"Praise God!" the kid said.

Jack rubbed his scarred shoulder where the recoil had punched it, handed back the Galil. *Who*, he wondered, *am I training him to kill?*

The first night he'd slept with five others in the ruins, awake most of the night for fear he'd speak English in his sleep. For several days they'd held exercises there, firearms use, the principles of urban combat, religious indoctrination. "To be a Muslim," the lead instructor, a narrow-chested man named Samir repeatedly told them, "is to kill non-Muslims. *That* is why God put you on this earth."

"Why train here?" Jack said one day, "in the middle of these old temples?"

"In this rubbish made by infidels two thousand years ago, the Israelis and Americans will not bomb us." Samir snickered. "For fear of destroying what is already ruins..."

Early next morning three of them were told to gather their things, knelt hastily for the first prayer then were blindfolded and led into the back of a panel truck. "Where are we going?" Jack asked but Ismael did not answer.

The truck jounced through Baalbek's streets then picked up speed on a paved road. The rising sun through his blindfold showed they were driving north. There was a reek of poppies. Twice vehicles passed southwards. He calmed his breathing, slowed his pulse to sixty and counted: after forty-three minutes the truck slowed; he heard other cars and trucks and the stopping and turning and voices of a town. They gained speed, swung more to the east and uphill.

This road was unpaved and rough. He kept shifting position to calm the pain in his shoulder. After eleven minutes they slowed for another town. The sun had shifted more to his right so they had turned north again. He steeled himself to think only of his fabricated memories of growing up in Afghanistan.

The driver dropped to first, the truck jerking in and out of ruts, chuffing uphill. The cool air tasted of snow and junipers. The truck shuddered downhill for seven minutes and forty seconds and squealed to a stop. The engine gave a last rattle and died.

The back doors scraped open. "Take off the blindfolds," Ismael said.

They stood in a great cirque of brown rock, in its center a *wadi* and a cluster of sharp-peaked Bedouin tents umber as the rock. Camels by the tents, scruffy chickens, young bearded men with guns. A machine gun nest on the far side of the *wadi*, and another, better camouflaged, in the cliffs. Ismael took his elbow. "Are you ready to die?"

He kept his voice steady. "Die?"

"For God? To drive a truck to the home of your enemies and destroy them?"

"Our warriors who destroyed the American Marines in Beirut..." Jack looked at the ground. "Did they come from here?"

"That's not your concern. You must simply prepare yourself to do the same."

"Despite all my fighting I'm still afraid of death."

"The very instant of death we're in *Bayit al-Ridwan*, the finest garden in Paradise, reserved for martyrs and the Prophets. That's not enough?"

"You believe in Paradise?"

"God does with us what He wants." Ismael turned, and Jack had a sense that Ismael was perhaps more adept at sending others to their deaths than facing his own.

The days were constant training for desert and mountain combat, ambushes in *wadis*, how to cover yourself in dirt and stones, ignore the scorpions and wait for the enemy. Some of it was led by trainers from Iran who spoke poor Arabic but were experts in making bombs from a variety of explosives, and who talked constantly of the need to kill Americans.

"But in Afghanistan," Jack said one night, "the Americans give us guns, ammunition, RPGs, surface-to-air missiles, information from the sky on enemy locations. They bring *mujihadeen* from other Muslim countries to join our fight. Why do we attack them here?"

"There is only one God," answered Ismael.

"And so?"

Ismael spat a pistachio shell that stuck to his lip. "Everything evolves from this truth."

"I'm a poor schoolteacher from Afghanistan. Please explain."

"That's your mask. Just as mine's this wounded face. The Koran is the only truth. Our God the only God. The Koran orders us to destroy all that is not of our God. Nothing else to say. Nothing else to think."

Two weeks Jack had been there and still they watched him, especially the Iranians. At night in the crowded Bedouin tents, in the day with other recruits, making sure he was never furthest away. Even during the five daily prayers as he bent facing Mecca with the others he was conscious of eyes on him, ears listening to the authenticity of his prayers.

"You don't use a prayer rug," Ismael said one day.

Jack watched a chicken digging itself into the dust in a vain attempt to escape its lice. "It's not the custom in our country. God made the earth we kneel on, also."

"You're not in your country now..."

He was aware of a subtle need to annoy Ismael – "change one letter in your name," he told him silently, "and it's *Israel*..." Then forced himself to think what antagonizing him would mean.

"For now we group our forces here," Ismael said one night. "To someday retake all lands where Muslims live."

"But Muslims live everywhere –"

"Precisely."

This base, Jack had decided, was near the Syrian border. To cross Syria meant hundreds of miles in any direction. But to recross the Beqaa Valley westward into the mountains to the Christian lines was only fifty miles at most.

When it came he wasn't ready for it. "Your prayers have been answered," Ismael said. "He will be here this morning."

"*Who* will be here?"

"One from your country. Another Afghani *mujihadeen*."

Jack could not steady his voice. "I must go meet him."

"I want you here till he arrives."

How had he given himself away? "I'll return to my training."

"No. Stay near me."

Now he would die. For being foolish enough to come here. For not listening to his fear. He ambled over to several men working on the engine of an old Syrian truck. They fell silent and he moved on.

Rising sun blazed down the canyon wall. The day's first breeze came up the *wadi*, too hot to breathe. His wrists would not stop shaking.

At the well he kicked aside manure where the camels had clustered, and dropped the bucket into the damp darkness. A hen clucked, announcing a new egg.

Drinking deeply he scanned the camp. Seven men moving up the canyon, rifles glinting in early sunlight. Changing of the crew on the far machine gun nest. From within a Bedouin tent a radio burst forth, fast Arabic chatter.

The Syrian truck was revving. Readying for the food run down to Labwé? Or to pick up burlap sacks of crushed poppies to trade the Syrians for guns?

Behind him Ismael and a squat bearded man were bent over a map. Jack slipped behind the Bedouin tents, picked up a Galil, ducked a hissing camel, and climbed in the passenger side of the Syrian truck. *Time to die now.*

Exhaust pulsed up through the floorboards. "No one leaves the camp," the driver said, a sallow unshaven man named Hamid whom Jack hated.

Jack slid the Galil butt-first to the floor so the muzzle pointed straight up between them. "I have to meet the new Afghani."

Hamid raised his hands to say only God would've ordained *me* to drive this fool. He tried to get the truck into

first but it wouldn't go so he slipped it into second and jerked and sputtered up the hill. Looking back Jack saw that no
one seemed to have noticed.

As if moving the gun from the gearshift he turned it over.
The fire selector was at the Hebrew character for *Safe*. He
slid his thumb down the breech and shoved it all the way
back to *Semi*.

He glanced back: no one was coming.

They drove down the hills, the Litani river valley like
a green billiard table below. Still no one behind, no dust
plume on the road ahead. He swung the Galil up, shot Hamid twice in the head and grabbed the steering wheel as
Hamid jerked sideways, blood spurting down the inside of
the door.

Hamid's sandal was jamming the accelerator. Steady-
ing the wheel Jack kicked at the foot till it slid free. The
truck puttered to a stop. Ears ringing, Jack went round
and opened Hamid's door. It was streaked with blood and
brains. He dragged Hamid into the desert, yanked off his
headscarf and wiped down the outside and inside of the
door. He moved the Galil's fire selector back to the middle, *Automatic*, and drove fast toward Labwé, the rising sun
casting his shadow far ahead of him.

Sleeping with Scorpions

"YOU'RE OUR ONLY asset who's ever seen a Hez-bollah camp." Timothy Cormac tipped ashes from his cigar. "Let alone got out alive."

Jack crossed to the motel room window and bent down a blind, the glass opaque with rain. In the three days since he'd landed in DC not a hint of sun. "And what good did it do?"

"What Timothy means," Bernie Rykoff said, "you guys on the ground, you sometimes can't see the whole picture."

"The whole picture? The day I got to Cyprus I *gave* you the location, names, troop strength – the whole *fucking* picture I risked my life for! I drew you a map that was couriered *the same night* to Langley. You had it next morning..."

"Not till afternoon, actually," Timothy said.

"You could've erased that camp! The *Independence* was right *there* in the Med. F-16's in Turkey... Instead you pissed it away. Everything I did."

Bernie spun round a chair and straddled it. "Jack, we burn fifteen million barrels of oil every day in this country. Nearly half of it's from Arab countries."

"They sell us oil and we let them kill us?"

Timothy peered disdainfully at the Day-Glo print over the motel bed, the cheap ornate lamps, the brown nylon bedspread and dirty shag rug. "You're too passionate by half, Jack."

Jack thought of Timothy's Georgetown home, the antiques, Iranian carpets, the modern abstracts, of Timothy going through life scorning some things and collecting others. "I'm glad I didn't go to Yale. At West Point, at least, they taught you to be who you are –"

Timothy smiled, unoffended. "And so they did at Yale. But as I remember you got kicked out of the Point." He smiled again. "Didn't you?"

Bernie tucked up a trouser seam. "It's natural, Jack, when you've been in danger, to be pissed at folks you think haven't supported you. Hell, I felt that way after Nam."

Under Bernie's short sleeves his biceps were skinny as his wrists. Jack couldn't see him humping sixty pounds plus weapons through the paddies. *You were a clerk somewhere.*

"Hezbollah, Islamic Salvation, Hamas," Jack said, "they're hitting us in Europe and the Middle East now, but soon they'll hit us in the States! They've got tons of opium in Lebanon and Afghanistan and billions of oil dollars from Saudi charities, all the training they need from Iran. At least let's stop heroin shipments out of the Beqaa!"

"Cut off heroin?" Bernie huffed. "Want to start a revolution in New York?"

"It pays for weapons," Timothy said. "Money Congress won't appropriate."

"These Arabs we're bringing into Afghanistan, they're *deranged* by Islam."

"Islam," Bernie said, "is a perfectly acceptable religion."

"The more you're biased, Jack," Timothy said, "the less useful you are."

He glanced at Timothy's pasty fingers, at his own hard hands. "When they're preaching that every non-Muslim must be exterminated?" He grabbed Timothy's puffy forearm, felt him withdraw. "It's like Kristallnacht, Hitler coming to power..."

"Kristallnacht was November nineteen thirty-eight." Timothy said. "Hitler came to power in thirty-three. Learn your history."

"Even *then* we could have stopped them, saved millions of lives –" Jack opened the door, walked into the rain to let it wash the DC filth out of his hair.

"You shouldn't do that," Timothy called.

"We're not endangering any enemies – we're just boys playing war." When he came dripping back inside Timothy and Bernie broke off their conversation. "You asked me to stay Inside?" Jack said. "Well, I'll make you a deal –"

"We don't *do* deals," Timothy said.

"You get together a high-level meeting – the President's office, State, Defense... Let me present these issues to them. See what they say..."

"There's so much you don't know, Jack. *Can't* know. That's going to impede your reaching people like that. Getting them to carry the ball for you."

Why, Jack wondered, were the people who used football metaphors the ones who'd never played a down? "Give me one shot."

He checked out of this motel room they had rented him in Reston under the name of Evan Dougherty, drove the Caprice they had rented him to Georgetown, and took a room in his own name at the Sheraton. When the rain stopped he wandered the streets. How many weeks – eight? – since he'd walked these streets with a ruined shoulder after coming back from the Hindu Kush? After *she'd* saved him and Bandit was dead? When Cole was still alive... And he'd found

Cole's killers but *they* weren't going to kill them.

He tried to imagine the lives of other people he saw – loud-talking smart-suited young men, nylon-legged girls in Burberrys hurrying home for dinner and affectionate sex, older men in town for conventions clustering on the sidewalks like lost ducks.

All these bars and restaurants full of people trying to have fun. Did they all live half-lives, not intense and aware like you did on the edge?

He ate Cajun food and drank too much tequila and ended up in a bar with a band named Slinky Pete, beside a dimpled girl who kept putting out her cigarette and lighting another.

"Why don't you just *do* it?" he said.

"What, quit? What would I look forward to?"

After all the tequila it was a mistake to drink Black Russians but he kept at it. Her name was Lindy and she was a secretary at the Department of Agriculture. "What do you do?" he said, trying to keep his voice steady.

"I type crop replacement forms."

"Crop replacement forms?"

"When a farmer gets paid to not grow a crop he has to send us information on how many acres he didn't plant, what he would've planted, that kind..."

"*Not* to grow a crop?"

She looked at him. "Agricultural subsidies. We pay billions of dollars to farmers not to grow stuff. Each one has to be typed up. I'm one of the ones –"

Maybe he couldn't understand because he was drunk. He thought of the hardpan scrabble of the Beqaa hills, the flinty bedrock of the Panjshir, of farmers whose children died of hunger. "You don't go insane?"

"What do *you* do?" she challenged him back.

"Wish I knew," he laughed, feeling good from the Black

Russians. "Journalist."

"*The Post*?"

He shook his head. A mistake, for the room kept going round. "Up in Maine."

"Really? What're you here for?"

"Conference." The music was too loud. "Paper manufacturers, that kind of stuff."

"Oh." She lit another Vantage. He imagined the insides of her lungs dripping tar.

When they danced he could feel her little pubis rub his thigh,

> *All through the shadows they come and they go*
> *With only one thing in common*
> *They've got the fire down below*

Someday she'll be married with kids, he thought, and all this long gone behind her.

She had a roommate but snuck him into her own bedroom. Her mouth tasted of gin and ashes. "Want some hash?" she said after they made love, taking out a little plastic bag.

He thought of the teenage hooker with her opium pipe in Rawalpindi, the opium camels crossing the Hindu Kush and the missiles coming back the other way, the blasted alleys of Beirut, the poppies tossing in the wind across the Litani lowlands.

But the *khief* he'd smoked had shown him an inner world, the connectedness of all things and all people – was that what everyone was seeking? And failing to find?

THEY MET IN A SIXTH floor room at Langley, no windows. A rubicund Middle East specialist from State, a gangling NSA man, an eager crewcut fellow with glasses from President Reagan's national security group, a bejowled

Defense Intelligence General with a tall square forehead and lots of ribbons, Bernie, and Timothy.

"You've seen my memo," Timothy said, "on what Jack's done. His introduction of heat-seeking missiles into Afghanistan led to the destruction of over thirty Soviet aircraft and substantial losses of men and matériel. He's united the northern *mujihadeen* against the Soviets, though he was seriously wounded in the process."

"Bravo!" said the President's man.

"And I've mentioned," Timothy added, "what he's done more recently in Lebanon. Hence our discussion today..." He turned to Jack. "You have twenty minutes."

"Taking out that Soviet major –" the General said. "Good job."

"What concerns me today," Jack said, "is not Afghanistan or Lebanon but the growth of Islamic fundamentalism everywhere. And how our country is at risk –"

He spoke without a break, trying to cover Hezbollah and other Islamic militants from their roots in the forties, the growth of Arab fanaticism in the sixties leading to the joint Arab attacks on Israel during the 1967 Six Days' War, the bitterness of that defeat, and the decision to focus not on more dangerous military actions but on easier attacks on civilians.

They sat silent, the State man toying with his coffee cup, the General rock-still, Bernie doodling with a silver pencil down the edge of a yellow pad. *Do they already know all this?*

"And now by tricking Iraq into a war with Iran," he continued, "one that's cost millions of casualties and impoverishing both nations, the weapons we're giving Saddam – even *nerve gas* –" he looked at the President's man – "the false satellite data that got him into it – we're creating generations of hatred."

"We had to pay the Iranians back," the NSA man said, "for the Embassy takeover."

"But *that* takeover was caused by *our* overthrowing their government in fifty-four."

"They're all just terrorists," the General interrupted.

"You can't run a terrorist organization without money. They get it from us in Afghanistan, from drugs in both Afghanistan and Lebanon, and from Saudi Arabia, Qatar and other oil sheikdoms via the Wahhabi charities."

"Keep the Saudis out of this," the President's man said. "Vice President Bush – our former *Director*, mind you – has been their butt boy for years..."

"Politics," State interrupted, "means succeeding at the possible."

"Five minutes more, Jack," Timothy said.

He took a breath. "One day coming into an Afghani village I heard awful screaming. I was afraid one of our fighters had been burned by napalm. I ran to the hut where the screams came from... Inside were ten, twelve Arab *mujihadeen*. Guys we'd imported from Saudi, Algeria. They had something tied to the wall – were flaying a side of beef, a sheep maybe. But it was bright red, writhing." He fought to keep his voice steady. "It was a Russian prisoner. They were skinning him alive."

He looked round the silent room. "'What are you doing?' I yelled at them. 'It doesn't matter,' one of them said to me. 'He's an infidel –'"

"What'd you do, Jack?" Bernie said finally.

"The Russian was just a kid, a draftee. His eyes out of that skinned sinewed face looked up at me in horror. I shot him in the head."

"Jesus Christ," the NSA man shook his head. "Holy shit."

"These," Jack said, "are the people we will face."

"Jack," Timothy said softly, "we all respect what you've been through. But you can't extrapolate from the behavior of one individual – okay, a few individuals – to the belief set of an entire religion composed of many nationalities, hundreds of ethnic groups."

"We're at war with the Soviet Union," the General said. "In war, soldiers die."

"In Afghanistan there's a story," Jack said, "of a man who puts a scorpion in his brother's bed so he can inherit the farm. The brother dies and he takes over the farm. But the scorpion has nested in the brother's bed, and he wakes to find them crawling all over him, stinging him to death."

Bernie quit doodling. "This Ayatollah Khomeini in Iran, he's published a book on how good Muslims should live. In it he deals with sexual abstinence. Says that if a man is horny it's okay to fuck a chicken. But then he asks, well, what of the chicken? Can it be eaten?"

"Puts a whole new spin on oral sex," the NSA man observed.

Bernie held up his silver pencil. "And the answer is *yes*! Although you may not feed it to your own family, you can to someone else's." He grinned. "I swear it's true."

"Feeding it to your own family," the President's man said, "wouldn't that be *incest*?"

"So the answer," the NSA man laughed, "is chicken soup?"

Jack stared them down. "*Their* answer is for *us* to be dead."

"I don't think you've proven that," said State. "We need to show the Muslims some understanding, work *with* them to resolve their issues. Not bomb their camps for God's sake. Don't forget, Hezbollah's doing a lot of good in the Beirut slums, keeping kids out of crime, that sort of thing."

"*That*, I might say," Timothy put in, "is the dominant

Agency view."

"Because you have no assets in the field," Jack said. "Because you don't *know*."

"Since Vietnam," the General said, "the American people don't want casualties."

"Two hundred fifty-four Marines and sixty-three people in our Embassy dead, another thousand injured, many maimed for life... *Those* aren't casualties?"

"You saw what happened last time the crude supply constricted, in seventy-eight?" Bernie said. "The barrel price went out of sight and drove us into a recession. That's how Reagan beat Carter."

"And now Reagan's up for reelection," the President's man said. "So we can't risk *any* hitch in the economy."

"Even if we win in Afghanistan," Jack said, "we're creating a permanent civil war among rival clans. Before we came all they had were knives and muzzle-loaders. Now they have the best murder tools we can provide."

"Not nukes," the General said. "They don't have nukes."

"What will you do," Jack stood, wanting to strangle him, beat them all into awareness, "when they do?"

Sawtooths

"I WANTED YOU to see your grandson," Sophie said. "I've named him Leo. For his father."

"We hoped you'd come," Leo's mother held the baby in the crook of her arm, away from her body as if he'd break. "But I was so afraid to see him." She gave him back and arranged the blanket on her lap. "So. How was your flight?"

"Fine. It was fine." Sophie felt she had to say more. "Paris to Leningrad, it's direct."

The baby kept crying, hunching his body into every scream. "His ears," Sophie smiled. "Babies can't get rid of –" she couldn't think of the Russian word for 'equalize' – "the pressure." She pinched his little nose shut but this just made him scream louder. She unbuttoned her blouse but he twisted his head away and kept screaming.

Leo's mother followed with her eyes as Sophie walked up and down the crowded room rocking the baby. Through the rust-streaked window Sophie caught glimpses of another concrete building ten feet away, other windows filthily reflecting the late afternoon sun. The window was part way open but that did not disperse the heat inside.

"My husband will be back soon." Leo's mother sat still in her chair, under the wool blanket. "He'll be pleased to see the baby."

Sophie looked round. "Have you always lived here?"

"When Leo... When Leo was little we lived in the country, out east. Ekaterinburg. Later we were lucky to get this place."

"Your husband – where does he work?"

"He's retired now. Military pension, though for a while he kept working, in a truck factory... the Kamaz trucks – do you know them?"

"They had them in Af... They had them in Afghanistan."

"In Paris you don't have them?"

"No, we have our own trucks."

The baby was quieting and Sophie sat. The chair was too soft; she would never get out. "We have a saying," Leo's mother said. "Maybe you know it, such good Russian as you speak. The heart which hardens itself to sorrow hardens also to joy."

"It's the same heart," Sophie said, "that feels both."

"But it's not true." Leo's mother raised her voice. "Sorrow wipes out joy. Joy doesn't exist. Not any longer."

Clasping the baby to her Sophie took her hand. "Everything passes," she said lamely.

Leo's mother looked up. "It passes for you already, this sorrow?"

"No." Sophie closed her eyes, took a breath. "I don't think it ever will."

The old woman seemed mollified. "Why did he go there! *Why?*"

"Leo loved what he did. Then we met. And he didn't want to do it anymore."

"Without you," the old woman said ruefully, "maybe he

wouldn't have died."

"I hope that's not true." *But maybe it is.*

"I shouldn't have said that... Sometimes my heart aches so I can't breathe." She massaged arthritic knuckles. "We have some of his things – toys he had as a boy, a few clothes, a yellow and blue soccer ball... Maybe you should take them, for little Leo..."

"No, you keep them." Sophie wiped her own tear from the baby's face. "I do my work, but I'm living inside a shell. It's been a year now... but it doesn't go away."

A gaunt man came in, white-haired with ragged stubble. He took her in his arms. "So, daughter, you've come to see your Russian family."

Sophie fought her tears but they streamed onto his shoulder. She felt the old man's ribs against her breast, his narrow spine against her arm. The baby began to cry. "Achh what a voice! A true Cossack." He held the baby high. "Aren't you, little Leo Gregoriev?"

Leo's father sat beside his wife, took her hand. "Our son..." He paused, gathering his breath. "He wrote many things about you. How brave you are, working in the operating rooms with the bombs going off, the children you've saved."

"I've lost too many."

"And now?"

"Now I work in a hospital in Paris. Emergency Room. And take care of little Leo."

"You should come here and work. Such good Russian as you speak. We have the best doctors in the world... Except, of course, the French."

Sophie smiled. "I learned Russian because I fell in love with Leo. I would've learned anything – Sanskrit, Chinese – to be with him." *This is crazy*, she thought. *I've got to stop.* "I speak to little Leo in Russian. With my bad accent. But at least he'll grow up learning it. There's a Russian school in Paris. I'll send him there, part time. When he's older." She got up, opened her suitcase and took out several packages. "I didn't know what to bring..."

"You brought our grandson, child..."

She gave them the packages, a cashmere sweater for Leo's mother, a leather jacket for his father, French cheeses, a bottle of Armagnac.

"So many people lost their sons in Afghanistan," Leo's father said. "You could say we're lucky... At least we have this little boy."

"In our war against the Nazis," Leo's mother said, "every family lost its sons, its fathers... Why do we humans keep doing this?"

"Katerina's fixed a lovely dinner," he said. "There were beets today. Do you like beets? And we've fixed up our bedroom for you and the baby. We'll sleep out here."

Through the half-open window came forlorn laughter from the alley. *I have to get out of here*, Sophie thought. *I'm a doctor – why am I so afraid of pain?*

JACK WAITED TILL THE WATER in the blue enamel pot began to boil then poured in a handful of coffee. He opened the lid on the woodstove and brushed the grounds off his hands into the fire. He shoved the pot back over the flames.

When it had boiled for a while he poured some into the blue enamel mug that went with the pot. He took the green bottle of Jack Daniels from under the table and dumped in a judicious bit. That cooled the coffee enough to drink right it away.

This, he raised the cup to the dawn-tinged Sawtooth peaks beyond the cobwebbed window, *this* is the life. Here in Idaho, Afghanistan and Beirut were months away. Some nights he didn't even dream much of Loxley, Gus, all of it.

The girl from Salmon had left a purple sock by the foot of the bed. To be sure she was gone he went outside and found the tracks of her pickup tailing down the pasture and out the gate. He noticed his coffee cup was empty and went inside and filled up again, pouring in a double shot of Jack.

He hadn't done yesterday's dishes but wouldn't do them now. The mice had left little turds in the sink but so what – they had to eat too. Imagine what it was like before the white man came. Mice had the run of the place.

A fly was buzzing against the window. "Don't be silly," he told it, "you can't get out that way." He put a beer glass over the fly and slid a sheet of paper under the glass, opened the screen door with his elbow and held the glass up. The fly lingered a moment on the rim then flew away.

The fly had had no way of understanding glass, something there yet not there, invisible but impenetrable. *But aren't I the same, beating myself against a barrier I can't see?*

The fly should have searched for a crack in the logs, an open door. Instead it had persisted at what didn't work, *because it expected it to work.*

And why didn't he turn from what he couldn't see and kept colliding with, what he expected to work but didn't, what caused pain and imprisoned him? Would he continue doing this till he died?

He crossed the pasture and shoved his head into the creek, drank his fill and let it sluice his eyes and wash through his hair. At the corral the appaloosa mare nickered and came bobbing over, stuck her head across the jack fence and whuffed at him. He went into the barn and came back with a battered aluminum bucket half-filled with oats and let her bury her nose in it. "And you, my pretty," he said, "you can't see *your* barriers either – that with one shoulder you could push over this fence and be free –"

She didn't answer and the roan gelding named Big Red came over shuddering the sleep off his ribs and licking his hairy chops. Jack refilled the bucket and tipped it toward him but the mare bared her teeth and Big Red swung his head aside. "Be a bitch," he told her, "see what you get." He shoved her head away and let the gelding snuffle down into the bucket, Jack pushing the mare's head back each time she neared.

Once in Afghanistan they'd come into a deserted village where in an empty manger a starving little girl was chained by her ankle to a post, pleading up at him with frightened hostile eyes. "Don't worry," Wahid had said, "she was left for the hyenas – there isn't enough food for girls."

When Jack climbed into the goat manger and shot the chain off her ankle she didn't flinch. He fed her barley and chunks of dried lamb, everything he had, carried her all night on his shoulders, his sheepskin coat wrapped round her shivering frame, her bony fingers wrapped in his hair, to the next village and gave them five hundred *afghanis* to feed and shelter her. "They'll keep your money," Wahid sneered, "not her." And two months later when they'd passed through the village the girl was not there. "Oh, we sent her to Taloqan," the villagers said, "to Doctors Without Borders."

"There's no Doctors Without Borders there," he'd answered.

"People in Taloqan, they took her..."

You have to stop this. He walked back to the cabin and took the half-full Jack Daniels bottle onto the porch, picked up the 30.30 Winchester lever-action and blew the bottle off the rail. He sat in the rocking chair on the porch and shot out the windows and mirror of the old Chevy pickup rusting in the grass by the barn, the horses watching him nervously from the far side of the corral. On the road a quarter mile away there were glass insulators on the telephone poles and he shot at them missing till his bullets were gone.

He went into the cabin, tipped the gun against the wall, put on running shoes, shorts and a t-shirt and started to run up the pasture but that made him sick so he walked up the steep rocky canyon of the trout creek till the firs thinned into pines and some of the sickness of the whiskey sweated out of him.

The sun was high. Far below were the pasture and two horses and tiny cabin and the truck tracks curving through the pasture to the dirt road that led twenty-three miles to Salmon.

Long ago Colonel Ackerman had said every dead man would come back to keep him company. How could he get free of them?

Keep running. Go somewhere new?

Wasn't that what he was doing, running into one invisible wall after another?

He was the one who'd killed them. He was the one who volunteered for Afghanistan. How could he escape what he couldn't see in himself?

Pipeline

I T HAD RAINED three straight weeks in Paris.

Sophie hated the gray skies, the nasty wind from the battlefields of the Somme aching her bones with all their dead. The Seine snaked its bitter chill through the city, its icy mist chased by the wind down the wide boulevards and narrow alleys.

La Pitié-Salpétrière Hospital took up a vast chunk of Paris behind the Austerlitz train station in the Thirteenth Arrondissement, a neighborhood of minimum wage laborers, low-income office workers, Arab and Asian immigrants, and students too poor to live nearer the Sorbonne. It was a dismal quarter far from the monuments and tourist stops, its stripped bicycles chained to the leafless sycamores, the dog shit on the sidewalks, the mean cafés where unshaven men clustered at dented zinc bars, the pollution-stained empty churches, the little groceries selling wine in cardboard liters and kabobs and day-old pastries, the reeking *tabacs* where ill-dressed people came out of the cold to buy cigarettes to kill themselves and lottery tickets for a hopeless shot at a better life.

Ever since AIDS appeared all the doctors wore latex gloves when working on the maimed souls the ambulances deposited so steadily at La Pitié-Salpétrière's Emergency ward, yet she always felt blood beneath her fingernails. After every patient and at the end of her shift leaning over the sink in the prep room to scrub under her nails with a brush and anti-bacterial cleanser. But the sensation never left.

It bothered her now as she waited at Boulevard St. Michel for the light to turn green. She dug her fingernails under each other but couldn't banish it.

The light turned green. She stuck her head out the car window to see round the bus ahead, ducked back in as a scooter snarled past. The bus belched a black cloud, inched forward and stopped. The light turned red.

She beat her palms on the wheel, snapped on the radio and shut it off. But now with all the subway bombings everyone was driving and it took two hours to cross Paris. She should have gone on foot, but walking four miles from the hospital to pick up Leo at school then back to the apartment still took longer than driving.

The light turned green but now cars blocked the crossing. The bus edged forward. She gunned her Renault round its back bumper, between jaywalkers and through the intersection and down the ramp onto Quai Voltaire along the Seine.

If these Muslim bombings continued Paris would be unlivable. No neurosis, no paranoid schizophrenia, could excuse what these bombers did to totally innocent people.

The traffic picked up, her tires trundling faster over the cobbles. The Eiffel Tower loomed ahead and she smiled up at it. Late sun cascaded through sycamores on Avenue de la Bourdonnais. Leo was waiting in his blue school smock and cap among the other children. "I made a flower today," he said, holding up a crayon drawing. "I made a castle, too, but

Mademoiselle LaCaille said to finish it tomorrow."

"I left the hospital early," Sophie said. "But the traffic... look what time it is!"

"Why are they doing this?" Mademoiselle LaCaille said. "What did we do to them?" She knelt for Leo to kiss her on both cheeks. "Okay my little soldier, see you tomorrow."

Sophie drove up La Bourdonnais and left onto St. Dominique. There were no parking places. She drove round the block twice, gave up and parked on the sidewalk. "We'll have to move the car," she said, "before it gets towed."

They walked around the corner to the open-air market, Leo skipping and swinging her hand. "What shall we have for dinner, my little cabbage?" she said.

"Hot dogs."

"We had those last night." There was a line at the butcher's so she inspected fruits and vegetables. "Do you want strawberries or peaches?"

"Peaches."

There was no line at the next butcher's. "We'll have sausages, no?" She followed him slowly up the stairs to their third floor apartment and kicked the door shut behind them. There were eighteen messages on the phone. *Screw them*, she told herself.

"You have to put up my picture," Leo said.

She taped it to the refrigerator, turned on the French fryer and dumped the new lettuce into the sink. "Did you fix any people today?" he said.

She tried to remember. A kaleidoscope of emergencies, frantic calls, suffering patients and impatient nurses. "A few."

He raised his arms for her to pull off his smock. "I'm going to watch TV."

"In a few minutes you can help with the salad." From the living room came the blare of the television, followed by a click-click as Leo rotated the dial looking for cartoons. She opened a bottle of Mâcon red, went out on the terrace, wiped the day's pollution off the table and sat down to watch the sun sink into the orange clouds.

The wine was light and fruity, reminiscent of the sun-soaked Burgundy hills. But she couldn't relax. It was the eighteen messages. If one of them was a patient in trouble...

"There's no cartoons," Leo said. "Somebody blew up the *Métro* – is that real?"

She knelt down to face him. "Maybe it is, *chou-chou*."

"How could they do that?"

"Maybe their parents didn't love them, maybe..."

"You love me, don't you, *Maman*?"

She buried her nose in his neck. "What do you think?"

"And Papa loved me too, before he died?"

She kissed him. "More than anything else in the world."

As he walked away she thought of Sisyphus, of this little boy with a great weight on his shoulders. *I can't do that to him.* She went back on the terrace but the sun had set.

"*Merde*!" she yelled. "The car!"

When she reached the corner a woman with a baby carriage was standing where the car had been. "Did you see them tow a car," Sophie gasped, "a green Renault?"

"They screwed it up good, too," a man said, "getting it off the sidewalk."

"They think they can do anything," the woman said.

"But if everyone parked on the sidewalk," the man said, "where would people walk?"

Seven hundred francs for the towing, three-fifty for the ticket. She climbed the stairs slowly. This was life, and when you got tired of fighting you died. You put your life into your children so they could grow up and put their lives into theirs. She spent her days sewing up people and her nights getting ready for the next day. Was there more?

Leo sat on his bedroom floor lost in a castle book. She rinsed the lettuce and spun it, sliced the potatoes, put the sausages in a pan, washed a tomato, mixed olive oil, garlic, and tarragon vinegar, dropped the potatoes into the fryer, refilled her glass and called the police. After ten minutes on hold she hung up and called Leo for dinner.

"You didn't let me help make the salad," he said.

The food made everything better, and having her little boy to talk to, with his brown cowlick, solemn face and deep eyes, the way already at three he measured everything, just like a man. I mustn't depend on him, she thought. He's got to grow up just like any kid, free of guilt and adult worries. "It was okay," he said, "the car?"

"Bastards towed it."

"Oh." He thought for a moment. "Now what will we do?"

She caressed his cowlick. "In the morning we'll walk to school. We'll stop at a café for pastries and hot chocolate. Then I'll get the car."

"What about the hospital?"

"I'll just have to come in late." But tomorrow she was lead trauma surgeon from eight a.m. – and if someone came in badly hurt... She'd have to get the car later... There *had* to be more to life than this.

JACK WATCHED THE WAVE RISE as it neared shore. The crest turned green and feathered at the top when the wind caught its edge. As it surged he lifted up and leaned with the surfboard into the curl. It was the perfect instant and he stood sliding down the slope of the wave and rode the pipeline till it finally cascaded down on him in a thunder of foam and no longer free and weightless he sank back into the sea.

Before sunset the swell began to ease. Seated on the

board that rose and fell with the waves, his legs dangling in the cool deep, he watched the sun sink toward the horizon. It pleased him that these waves had traveled from China all the way across the Pacific, that this was the first point where they'd touch land, and from this unknown corner of Tuamotu they'd continue unabated to Antarctica.

As the sun touched the horizon it was blocked by a huge wave darker than the sea. He leapt to his feet on the board to make sure – the board sinking – and yes, another great black back surged above the waves and slid beneath them. Whales.

They passed twenty yards away, blocking the sun. One whale's spray wet his face and lingered like smoke in the sunset.

He rode a last wave toward shore, lit a fire of palm fronds and driftwood in a ring of lava rocks, opened a warm beer and cooked the rockfish he'd caught that afternoon. Behind the beach mynahs and doves were calling in the palms and monkey pod trees.

He could see the curve of the earth in the wide span of the sea. The stars grew thick and sharp, the breeze softened. He felt a moment's loneliness to be so far from his own kind.

If he were on another planet, in another universe, would that be far enough? He glanced up at the myriad stars, tried to imagine all the humans living their complicated lives all over the earth. Somewhere was there someone he could know, could love? And who'd love him too?

The whales stayed with him like a mystical, ancient and unifying force, greater than he, than human life, the heart-beat of the universe.

They were together. They're not alone.

IV

Paris

Perfect Strangers

September 1986

"IT'S ABOUT TIME you called us back," Timothy said. "You know we've been trying to reach you."

Jack glanced up from the phone booth. No one was near him on the sidewalk. A pickup clattered past dragging its tailpipe. In a shop window a stuffed grizzly bear snarled at him. "So I heard."

"It's been over a year. You're supposed to stay in touch."

"What you want?"

"I checked your bank account in Maine. You're down to your last three hundred twenty-seven bucks."

"I might have other income."

"You don't. But I'm offering you some." There was a moment's silence as Timothy checked the call tracer. "What the bloody Hell are you doing in *Fair*banks?"

"Hanging out with wolves and feeding mosquitoes. What you want?"

"The French police think some of your boys are bombing the Paris *Métro*. Mitterrand's on Reagan's ass and Reagan doesn't like it."

"I don't have any *boys*."

"*La Police Nationale* thinks you do."

"I don't know anybody at *La Police Nationale*."

"Yes you do. Some guy named Richards..." The phone buzzed as Timothy shuffled papers. "No, here it is – *Reecard*, Colonel Max *Reecard*. Says he knew you in Beirut."

"Your accent's horrible, Timothy."

"How soon can you get down here?"

"What are you paying?"

"More than you're getting now. We need deniability. You're the one to do it."

Jack hung up. Amazing how life changed when you least expected. Maybe in Paris there'd be fewer mosquitoes.

THE MÉTRO CAR WAS TWISTED and charred. Its walls had blown outward and the floor was gone. It smelled of seared metal, charred rubber and something evilly metallic. Dried blood coated the distended ceiling and lay in an ugly brown spray over a Galeries Lafayette poster of a pretty girl twirling in a black dress.

"How can anyone do this," Jack said, "to perfect strangers?"

"Easy." Max Ricard lit a Gauloise. "Just leave your five kilos of *plastique* in a shopping bag under your seat and get out. Five minutes later, the infidels are in Hell for the crime of not being Muslim. And you're a step closer to Paradise." Ricard took a puff. "What do you suppose is the link between the 'Islamic Army of Salvation' who blew up this subway car, and the Algerians you trained in Afghanistan?"

Jack glanced round the echoing Métro depot. "Why would there be?"

"Some of these guys boast to other Muslims that they were *mujihadeen* in Afghanistan. How many Russians they killed, the missiles they used to shoot down Soviet planes..."

He watched Jack. "They say they'll do the same here."

"Why would *mujihadeen* do this? Why not Abu Nidal – they bombed the Rome and Vienna airports last Christmas? Or Shiite Amal or Islamic Jihad? This detonator's the kind they teach in Hezbollah camps..."

"You'd know about that," Ricard grinned over his cigarette. "Wouldn't you?"

"... and they've been hijacking American planes, killing Americans too! TWA 847, the *Achille Lauro*, TWA 840, our soldiers in Germany... last week that Pan Am plane in Pakistan –"

"As you know, Algeria's in a civil war. The fundamentalists want to make it a true Islamic state – *Sharia*, Islamic law, all that. And we have five million Algerians in France."

"You were crazy to let them in."

"Our beloved president said we have to let in the families of those already here." Ricard waved his cigarette. "Turns out, every Arab in the world is related..."

"But you're military – why are *you* on this?"

"Got pulled out of Beirut and transferred back to DST, where I started out –"

"DST?"

"*La Direction de la Surveillance du Territoire*. The part of *La Police Nationale* that deals with terrorism... I run agents inside Muslim groups, tracking people..." Ricard pulled a piece of paper from his breast pocket. "This'll jog your memory."

Jack glanced at the name scrawled in Arabic script, handed it back, took a breath of cold air, a cloying fragrance of blood. "Who is it?"

"Don't give me that shit."

Jack looked at the name again. "Never heard of him."

"Two of our assets inside Muslim groups were told, separately, that *he* set this bomb. That he got off one stop before the explosion. I'm *sure* you know him."

Jack shook his head. "Sorry."

Ricard raised his eyebrows. "Let's try it this way: if you *were* to have known him, who might he be? If, as they say, he fought in Afghanistan?"

"It was probably through Pakistani intelligence – ISI. Have you asked them?"

"Go fuck yourself."

"You've got millions of illegal Arabs in the slums around Paris, Lyon, Marseille, all your cities. How are you going to find him?"

"According to our agents he was last seen at a mosque in Sartrouville. Trouble is, no one knows what he looks like. That's why I wanted *you* to tell me."

ON THE MÉTRO back to his apartment near the Panthéon Jack looked for packages under seats, studied every person for an awkward move, a flicker of fear. In a tunnel he glimpsed a dangerous man reflected in the window across the aisle then realized it was he.

Walking uphill from Cluny he scanned the cafés, watched every Arab passing on the sidewalk. Most of them, he told himself, were law-abiding, some even happy to be here.

He went into a café near the Panthéon and downstairs to the men's room. There was one man in the stall, no one in the women's. When the man left, Jack dropped a fifty-centime piece in the phone and called Timothy collect. "It's one of our guys."

"No, Jack. Even if it is it isn't."

"So what do you want me to do?"

Timothy thought a moment. "Lead them astray."

"People are getting killed here. By a guy *we* trained."

"Can they tie him to us?"

"*I* trained him, Timothy. A squirrelly little Algerian

named Hassan Husseini. I taught him to fire the SA-7s that we helped Wahid trade opium for."

"You're dreaming, Jack. Making this up –"

"He shot a wounded prisoner once, a Russian major. Now I think of it, he's the reason my dog died. And why I got wounded."

"No one has time for your private memories, Jack. This guy does not exist."

FOR DAYS AND NIGHTS he rode the Métro watching everyone, every package, looking for Husseini. There were plainclothes cops riding it, too; after a while several noticed him.

"Where you going tonight?" one asked, a pretty young woman with a short haircut and slender muscular arms and an MAB 9mm in a hip holster under her silk Cardin jacket. She checked his papers, saw he was an American student at the Sorbonne and waved him off.

In the DST offices on rue Nélaton in the 15th Arrondissement he studied photos of Islamic fundamentalist leaders in France, told Ricard in all honesty he'd never seen them.

He met a few of the beautiful women who crowded this gorgeous city but none he dared get close to, realized he felt lonelier here than alone in the Pacific or in the wilds of Alaska. Would there ever be someone?

Loneliness is just a state of mind.

Repair the evil you've done. Find Husseini.

RAIN SLANTED ACROSS the café window. He had finished a simple dinner and a bottle of wine, a little drunk and in a mood to be straight with himself.

Wanting to defend his country he'd helped create Husseini the killer – do we always create the opposite of what we seek? Facing too much death had set him outside life, a loner locked in his habits of concealment and distrust, *of not being who he seemed.*

The bartender wiping out a glass, a waitress laughing at a customer's joke, a grizzled old man reading *Le Monde*, two lovers staring over wine into each other's eyes, a family eating ice cream – these people weren't going to kill him, this wasn't the Beqaa or the Hindu Kush.

The French doctor had saved him in Afghanistan, but for what? He saw her strained face, her angelic beauty in which sorrow seemed so inexplicably mired. She'd known Ahmad. How? Where was she now?

Surrounded by whales at sunset in Tuamotu a year ago he'd felt awed and humbled by their ancient beauty, felt they'd changed him. But he was still the same.

I owe you, he'd told her. *Save someone else, she'd answered. Then we'll be even.*

A song was playing – *In my life, I've loved you more* – over the hiss of the espresso machine and clatter of conversation. Tears came to his eyes unbidden. Casually he asked for more wine.

Doctors Without Borders. Their head office in Paris could tell him how to find her.

If he caught Husseini before he killed again, would that be saving someone?

SARTROUVILLE LAY in a great oxbow of the Seine twenty minutes northwest of Paris. Once a farming town, it had become like many Parisian suburbs a site for installing thousands of North African immigrants. In place of orchards and farms now rose vast concrete *cités* – welfare towers and grim streets of dismembered cars, windblown trash and graffiti-spattered walls. Places the French cops, tough as they were, were told not to go.

The once-beautiful high-speed subway was like its destination: graffiti across the walls and ceilings, the high-tech seats slashed by knives and burned by cigarette lighters. "If *we* can't be happy," the destroyers seemed to say, "no one will be."

The mosque was eight blocks from the station through streets of silent men and veiled, downcast women with their arms full of children. The front of a former department store, its windows boarded and covered with posters in Arabic script, it was a low room with a linoleum floor.

The *mullah*, squat and one-eyed, strode back and forth at the end of the room where a sales counter had been shoved against the wall. He spoke fast in a North African dialect that was hard to follow, spitting out sections of the Koran with commentary between them.

"The Holy Book tells us to *strike back* against evildoers and perfidy!" he roared. "And listen ye, this is a country of infidels! Because they do not believe, God confounds them. And because God confounds them, they do not see the cause. The Koran tells us, *the cause is their own infidelity to God*!"

He faced them, hands upraised. "There is crime in this country – because of *their* evil ways, but they blame *us*!"

He coughed, spit in the corner. "And listen ye, there shall be great *destruction* in this country – because, as the Koran teaches, *God will bring down destruction on evildoers*!"

Back and forth he strutted in Day-Glo slippers and wrinkled robe, pounding a fist into a palm, head tilted back, beard wagging. Jack focused on his own dirty fingers splayed on the rug to keep from laughing. But as he glanced round it was clear the others were inflamed by it. "You're all here on welfare!" he wanted to yell. "You get free medical care and free schools and free apartments! If you don't like it, go back where the Hell you came from!"

After the service he approached some young men arguing in North African accents. One grabbed him. "What you want?"

"I am from far away. Afghanistan, where we wage *jihad* against infidels."

"I don't know this place."

"We're a Muslim republic attacked by the Soviets. Near China."

The young man called the others over. "I've heard of that," one said.

"Because he's a teacher," another explained.

"Please excuse my poor speaking," Jack said. "Though the Koran is written in Arabic, in Afghanistan we speak another tongue. My little Arabic I learned from an Algerian freedom fighter who came from Paris."

"Yes, some Algerians have gone there," the teacher said.

"I have been sent to find him, to ask him to send us others," Jack said. "He told me of this mosque. Do you know him, his name is Hassan Husseini?"

"Don't say that name," the teacher said.

"Why? It's a name to be proud of. He's a brave fighter, has killed many infidels."

"He's changed it."

Jack waited a moment, as if puzzled. "How will I find him then?"

"Where do you stay?"

"In Paris, with *fedayeen* from Beirut."

"How do we find you?"

Jack looked around the tawdry room. "I can come back. Tomorrow night."

"If we hear of him who had that name," the teacher said, "who wishes to see him?"

"Tell him Wahid al-Din. Eagle of the Hindu Kush."

I Can't Save You

IF HE CALLED HER he'd have to explain why he'd been in Afghanistan. But he couldn't tell her. Anyway she probably wasn't even in France. Certainly not in Paris. Why would she care about somebody she'd saved four years ago?

Doctors Without Borders was in the phone book. A man answered on the first ring. "I was a correspondent in Kabul," Jack said. "I met one of your doctors there, a woman, in September eighty-three –"

"That would be Sophie Dassault – the only one who stayed that long in Kabul. After the others got killed."

"Is she still there?"

"She's a trauma surgeon at La Pitié Hospital. On our board of directors too. Why are you asking?"

Half an hour later he arrived at the Hospital's Admitting window. "Is Dr. Dassault here?"

The woman glanced up at him, the clock. "She's in the operating suite. Won't be out till her shift ends at five. What's your name?" she said as he turned away.

All day he rode the Métro looking for Husseini. *If we could read the secret history of our enemies*, Longfellow had said, *we would find in each person's story enough suffering and sorrow there to disarm all hostilities.* But he'd kill Husseini now, no matter his secret sufferings and sorrows.

Hadn't he too had sufferings and sorrows – fatherless at ten, a heartbroken benumbed mother, the years of poverty, the long Maine winters, the determination to work and work and work and rise above it, getting into West Point then losing it all? Hadn't he too been made heartless by pain?

The trouble with thinking, Bandit said, *is it gets you nowhere.*

At 16:30 he was leaning against the fender of a parked car watching people leave the hospital. At 17:10 a slender woman in a white raincoat came out and walked purposefully across the lot, a briefcase slung over her shoulder.

"Please wait!" he called in Pashto.

She turned on him, eyes wide. "*What* did you say?" she answered in French.

It was *she*: the slender incised cheeks, the wide eyes, the auburn hair cut short now, not long like it'd been... He saw her face as it had looked down at him under the white light... *I can't save you,* she'd said.

Her fingers round the briefcase strap were long and slender. A ring – no, not the wedding finger. Under the white raincoat a blue and red scarf. "You're a doctor," he said in Pashto.

"Yes," she said reluctantly in Pashto.

"Kabul hospital four years ago. You saved me."

Her mouth opened. "Three times," he said, "you saved me."

She stepped back. "I have to go now."

"You saved me from a bullet in the shoulder. Then from the *Spetsnaz* –"

He saw her eyes widen at the word. "– then from Hekmatyar's men."

Doubt hardened her face. "You're not Afghani. You have an American accent. Who are you?"

"I told you I was a journalist... I got shot. You took me to Ahmad's –"

She edged away. "Please," he said. "I need to talk to you."

"I have to pick up my son. I'm glad I was able to help you. Goodbye."

"Wait!" he begged, aware of people watching.

"Please go. Before I call the guards."

THE MOSQUE in Sartrouville was nearly empty, a few men filing in for evening prayers. Jack edged along the back, watching for Husseini. What would he do if he saw him? Follow him, tell Ricard? He hadn't thought this through.

Too obsessed with Sophie. Yes, just to say her name. *Sophie.*

When your head isn't where you are, that's how you get killed. He forced himself to watch the growing throng of dissatisfied men, listen to their rancorous prayers, the *slip-slap* of the mullah's feet as he pranced back and forth in his Day-Glo slippers.

"I have to pick up my son," she'd said. She was married?

The prayers ended. Husseini wasn't there. Jack edged past the young men, his back to them, and out the door. A light rain was falling.

She didn't want to see him. He'd made a fool of himself. Like some pimply buck-toothed fifteen year-old at a school dance, terrified of girls.

He took the RER back to Paris, a vague discomfort in his chest. She would never like someone like him.

She hadn't wanted to talk about Afghanistan. To speak Pashto.

Afghanistan a cascade of memories: snow and wind,

dusty heat, McPhee's grin and Loxley's laugh, filthy villages under the crushing sky, the kindness of an old woman and the curse of a dying man, the fear before combat and the sorrow after.

He found her in the phone book, 51 rue St. Dominique, under her own name. That didn't mean anything: she could be married, living with someone. If he called her, what then? If he waited outside her building it would be like stalking her. She'd call the cops.

19:55. He could still call her. Not too late.

Who are you? she'd asked. What could he say?

SHE ANSWERED on the second ring. The phone slippery in his hand he tried to speak casually, conscious of his accent, telling himself *Don't lie.* "I need to ask you some questions, about my shoulder –"

"I don't remember anything about you. Anyway I don't have office hours."

"You told me to save someone else's life, then we'd be even..."

"*I* told you that?"

The phone was cutting in and out; he could barely hear. "I haven't been able to save anyone's life, so I still owe you. Can I invite you to dinner?"

"Heavens no. I don't have time."

"Just coffee then –"

"*Why* are you bothering me?" She halted. "When did America have journalists in Afghanistan?"

A motion behind him made him spin round – a meekish little man waiting for the phone. "I was freelancing." *Don't lie.* "When did *you* come back?" he said, switching the subject, aware how lame it sounded.

"I had to leave too – you Americans made Afghanistan too dangerous for everybody."

Behind Jack the little man cleared his throat. Jack glared at him. "It's not my fault." *Oh yes it is.* "I tried to help, tell the truth." His words sounded hollow, disgusting him.

"I don't want to think about Afghanistan –"

"Just one coffee. You can give me Ahmad's latest news. After that, if you don't want, I'll never bother you again."

"I haven't seen or heard from him."

The little man tugged Jack's sleeve. "Excuse me."

"Just a minute!" Jack shoved the hand away.

"What did you say?" she said.

"Somebody here, wants to use the phone."

"Goodbye, then."

"Wait! I'm still a journalist, doing on story on Doctors Without Borders. I need to interview you."

"There's others you can talk to."

"It's because you were in Afghanistan. And to talk about Ahmad. Tomorrow after work, I'll meet you at the café on the corner of St. Dominique and Bosquet – five thirty?"

She hesitated. "I'll only have a few minutes..."

He hung up and turned on the little man. "Couldn't you wait a minute?"

"My wife's gone into labor." The little man reached in his pocket, came up empty. "Do you have a franc?"

THE CAFÉ WAS JAMMED. Sophie watched the lithe muscular American with the deep blue eyes and golden hair. When you've saved someone's life does it bond you to him? She didn't want to be bonded, certainly not to this man. Too physical, really. Too dangerous.

Says he wouldn't be alive without me... An unnatural thought. The Cinzano clock on the wall said 17:35. *Pick up Leo,* she reminded herself, *by six.*

In Afghanistan she'd never heard of American journalists. He didn't look the part, not with those strongly tendoned forearms, those sternomastoids in his neck, the thick deltoids...

"Do you remember how they came in, those Hekmatyar guys," he said in Pashto, "all stoned on *khief*?"

"Stop speaking *that*! Someone'll think we're terrorists."

"*You're* speaking it." His voice was deep yet gentle, that funny American accent.

"I can barely remember it." Her own voice seemed thin by comparison; she cleared her throat. "Damn language all tied up with death and misery."

"You said you were leaving, four years ago. That they were going to kill you too."

"You remember what I said, way back then?" She watched his hands twirl his beer glass. No ring on his finger. "They killed every woman who wouldn't wear a veil, any woman with a profession. Even Doctors Without Borders, they were killing us..."

The waiter elbowed to their table. "Another *demi*?"

She raised her hand. "Got to go."

He took her hand, an amazing forward gesture. "Four years I've wanted to find you. Don't go – this's the best day of my life."

She pulled her hand away. "It's bad luck saying that –"

"Most of the kids were beautiful," he said. "If you saved them young."

She watched the sharp curve of his mouth – *was that pain*? "What kids?"

"Before I was a journalist –"

Behind her the hiss of an espresso machine. "Yes?"

"Nothing." He shrugged. "Always liked kids."

"Have any?"

He shook his head. "What I most want to do, really, is have kids. My dad died when I was young..."

"How?"

"Vietnam."

"*Merde*." She nodded at the waiter. "Yes I'll have another *demi*." Glanced at the clock. 17:50. "No!" she waved at the waiter. "Got to go."

He stood, an amazing fluid motion like a dancer. "I'll go with you." She shook her head. He put a twenty-franc bill on the table. It stuck in a circle of wet beer.

He took her arm as they walked toward Avenue de la Bourdonnais. She wanted to shake off his hand but didn't. *When we get to the school I'll say goodbye*, she decided. *Poor man, alone in Paris.*

This thought made her like him more. *He's very kind*, she told herself. They walked past a flower store and he let go her arm and dashed inside. She kept going.

A minute later he caught up, handed her a huge bunch of white roses. She pushed him off. "Are you crazy? I can't take them. I don't even *know* you."

"You saved my life!" He took her arm again, annoying and impertinent. Were all Americans like this?

She waited on the curb for the light to change. "I barely remember you."

They walked in silence along the sidewalk under the sycamores. "Maybe that's better," he said.

"What?"

"That you don't remember me."

She went into the school to get Leo and when they got out he was still there, holding her roses. "Hey," he said, kneeling down to Leo, "you like it in *there*?"

Leo looked shocked. No one had *ever* asked him that. He reached for her hand. "No."

She tugged Leo's hand. "Say goodbye."

"Do you like dogs?" he asked Leo.

Leo looked up at her: *What's going on here?* "I don't know."

"I used to have one. Want to know his name?"

Leo shrugged. "Yes?"

"Bandit," the American said. "That's Russian, don't know it in French."

"The same," she said without thinking.

"*Govaritse po-russki*?" he said quickly.

She felt a stab of pain. "*Da.*"

"We can speak Russian, then," he said. "Sorry," he said to Leo in French.

"*Toje panimao*," Leo said. *I also understand.* "I go to Russian school. Twice a week."

"You and I, then," the American said to Leo in Russian, "we'll just speak Russian. I need the practice."

"I really *have* to go." She started to walk away with Leo.

The American caught up to her. "You haven't told me how you knew Ahmad."

She glared at him. "Nor have you told me."

He shrugged. "So what about our dinner?"

Say no, she told herself. *But that's impolite.* "No..."

"Why did you save me?"

"It's my job."

"I mean from the *Spetsnaz*. From Hekmatyar? Why'd you risk taking me to Ahmad?" He knelt down to Leo. "Hey buddy, tell your Mom please say yes –"

"*Maman*!" Leo stared accusingly up at her.

"Okay," she sighed, "just this once. Come to our place Friday night?"

She walked on quickly into the fading light. "*Spetsnaz*," Leo said, dragging behind. "That's Russian –"

Furious with herself she bit away tears. "Hurry!" she yanked his hand. "We're late."

"Late? For where?"

"Can't you remember *anything*?" The tears blurred her eyes. "The dry cleaning – we have to pick it up!"

Who Are You?

A SIMPLE MEAL, steaks and salad and *baguette*, a burgundy from her *cave*. With the dessert of yellow apples and Roquefort they drank the Graves Jack brought. "We're supposed to drink white Bordeaux with Roquefort," she said. "It's the new thing."

Jack smiled across at Leo sitting atop two telephone books on his chair. "I'm not much for new things."

His muscular roughness made her wrists feel weak. She imagined making love with him, dismissed the thought: after this dinner she wouldn't see him again. "What did you mean the other night," she said, "that it's better I don't remember you?"

"What did Ahmad tell you? About me?"

"I never saw him again. I had to leave, was pregnant with Leo..." She bit at her lower lip. "I dreamt all last night about Afghanistan."

"What happened there – your husband?"

She sat back. "I don't want to talk about it."

He took her hand, again that lithe forward motion. "I'm sorry – I'm bringing that back into your life, aren't I?"

She pulled her hand away. "Why did you try to find me?"

"When you looked down at me on the operating table it was like I was in the hands of God or something..." He shook his head as if to say *I can't explain it.*

She laughed. "I'm hardly the hand of God –"

"Yeah, the Muslims when they blow people up say it's the hand of God... All this time, since then, you've been in my mind... Like the rest of my life would have been a failure if I hadn't found you."

The thought made her shiver. She *could* make love with him, just this once. Would he go away then? How long had it been? She felt her pelvis throb. She ran two fingertips up the inside of his forearm, the tendons like steel. "You mustn't let other people be so important in your life..."

"What else is there?"

Leo got down. "I'm going to watch cartoons."

"Okay," she told him. "I'll be in soon to see what you're watching."

"He's barely three and a half," Jack said. "He's not watching naked girls. Not yet."

There it was: sex on the table between them, the gilded gorgeous snake. She reached for his dish; he held her wrist. "I'll clean up." He stood and pulled her to him; she was a wisp of paper, a reed, her body catching fire as she tried to show him nothing.

When he kissed her it was soft at first, just the gentle touch of lips on lips. She pulled back. "Leo will see –"

"He's watching cartoons."

She felt him hard against her. *Oh God what will I do?* She pushed away, sat down.

"Hey, let's not stop now."

"Who the Hell *are* you?"

Taken aback, he sat. "What are *you* hiding?"

"How could *I* hide anything?"

"What's inside you. What you feel –"

"Who are you to tell me what I feel?"

"You're still dying for Afghanistan? It's over."

"For whom?"

He glanced beyond her terrace to the rooftops and church towers of the Seventh Arrondissement, thought furiously of Hassan Husseini somewhere out there festering. The wine glass snapped in his hand. "Oh shit! I'm sorry."

"Idiot, you've cut your hand!"

"Thank Heavens there's a doctor near!"

"Stop joking. It's really bleeding."

He went into the kitchen and wrapped his hand in a paper towel. "It's your fault."

"Let me see it! Acch, you need stitches."

"I wanted to make love with you not argue, for Chrissake!"

"I hope you bleed to death."

He went back out and sat on the terrace, saw his roses in a crystal vase on the sideboard. "I'm so overwhelmed by you I don't know how to act."

"Just be yourself."

He smiled. "Who's that?"

"The person you've always wanted to be."

Leo came out, glanced at him stolidly. "What happened to your hand?"

"Your Mom stuck me with that wine glass."

"*Maman*!"

She laughed. "I did not!"

"There's no cartoons."

"TV's not good for you anyway," Jack said.

"Who are you," Sophie fumed, "to tell him what's good?"

"He's right, *Maman*."

"When I want *your* opinion, young man, I'll ask!"

Leo eyed the setting sun. "We should go to the park."

"I have to put some stitches in him first." She went into the bedroom and came out with a medkit. "I'll give you a shot of painkiller first."

"Just stitch it. Leo wants to go."

"I should do a lobotomy."

He pulled her against him. "I want you naked."

She glanced after Leo, who had gone to get his coat. "Don't *say* things like that –"

Chestnut leaves rustled underfoot in the aisles of the Champ de Mars. Leo ran on ahead scattering the pigeons. "Sorry I'm so edgy," she said. "It was a horrible day. We were short-handed, heart attacks, two suicide attempts, three car wrecks..."

He thought of the shredded guts in the *Métro*. "I wouldn't want to do what you do."

"I don't even know what you do."

"Most of the time I help politicians make up stories to defend themselves, or translate their boasts about things they haven't done."

They walked along silently for a while. "Your shoulder, how did it happen?"

He told her about the stepping-stone bridge across the stream, the sudden ambush, how Bandit saved his life. "I was just traveling with this bunch of *mujihadeen*. Doing a story on them. They were ambushed by Hekmatyar's men."

"*What* bunch of *mujihadeen*?"

"Some guys with Ahmad's brother, Wahid al-Din."

"Leo's father was trying to arrange a peace through Ahmad. That's when he died."

"*Maman*!" Leo held up chestnuts that had fallen off the trees. "Can we cook them?"

"Of course." She put them in her pocket. "Go find more."

"How did he die?" Jack said.

Behind her the Eiffel Tower soared brightly into the

darkening sky. She took a breath. "You're not who you say you are."

"Nobody is. Does it matter?"

"To me it does."

"These subway bombings, they bother you?"

"I asked, *who are you?*"

For a long time he said nothing, then shook his head.

"Then I don't want to know you." She ran ahead, snatched Leo's hand and trotted him quickly out of the park. For a moment Jack went after her, then sat on a bench and stared unseeing at the Tower.

A young couple came up to him speaking Japanese, motioned with a camera.

He took a picture of them smiling toothily in front of the Tower, gave them back the camera and walked into the night.

Losing Sophie was like a fork in the road and he'd taken the bad one.

Husseini was out there. Find him.

Chocolate Raspberry

AT 18:30 FRIDAY Jack slipped into the back of the Sartrouville Mosque among the old men. A checkered Palestinian scarf across his face, he scanned the crowd for Husseini.

Kneeling he pulled his hand from a cockroach squashed into the worn prayer rug. "Only *we* are God's people!" chanted the *mullah*. "*God's* sword to vanquish *His* enemies!"

"Thou art dog shit," Jack said in Pashto, then thought of Bandit. "No," he said, "thou art pig shit. The veritable shit of swine!"

Men blocked his view. Then Husseini was standing in the corner talking to the *mullah*. Jack tried to move toward the door but there were too many people. *Without my beard maybe he won't recognize me. But they'll have told him; he'll be looking for Wahid.*

I still haven't thought this through. He adjusted the Makarov under his arm. But he couldn't shoot Husseini here, not with all these people. The young men he'd met, the teacher – they'd be here somewhere.

Best to wait outside. When Husseini left he'd follow him. See where he lived. Or take him in an alley. Jack reminded himself of Bandit, the night on the stepping-stone bridge. The blood-pasted *Métro* car.

He sidestepped toward the door. "Praise God!" the *mullah* called.

"I give Thee thanks," chanted the man beside him, "for my beautiful family, for our food, for this good day..."

He reached the street, the night air cool and safe. Men were trickling out. The *mullah* had put a tape on the loudspeaker. Husseini stood near him, his beaded cap sparkling in the streetlight. Jack slid back into the shadows.

"There you are!" a voice behind him made Jack spin round reaching for the Makarov. The teacher. And four of his friends.

"He's here!" the teacher said to Jack. "Your leader from the *mujihadeen*."

"Leader?" Jack slid off the safety.

"The man you called Husseini! Come, I'll bring you to him."

"I can't," Jack whispered.

"Can't?" the teacher asked, confused.

"It isn't *safe*! Could be agents here. The *DST*..."

"It's safe or he wouldn't be here." They walked him toward Husseini. "Master!" the teacher called. "He's here! The Eagle of the Hindu Kush!"

Husseini glanced round, saw them, saw Jack. "*Aaaah!*" he screamed and ran.

Jack sprinted after him. Husseini ducked left at the corner. As Jack cut the corner four huge shapes smashed into him and pinned him on the ground. His ribs felt crushed; he couldn't swing his fists, couldn't breathe. "Help!" he gasped in Arabic. "Help me!"

"Want help?" One of them kicked him in the stomach.

"How's that?"

"He's got a gun!" one yelled in French.

Steel whacked his forehead. Pain exploded down his skull into his chest, and he reached out to fight back but was sinking, no air, feared he was dying, face down in the gutter. *Fight back*, he told himself, tried to lurch upward but many hands held him down. *Fight back.*

They cuffed him, dragged him to a car and threw him in the rear, pinned between two of them, the others in the front. "Brothers!" he said in Arabic, "what are you doing?"

One laughed. "We're not your brother, you fucking sand nigger," he said in French. "You're going to jail."

"THIS IS LIKE FISHING!" Ricard exhaled. "I think I'm pulling up a trout but what I get is an old shoe. A bag of shit."

Jack held a hand over his eyes to cut the glare. "I want their *names*. The guys that did this to me. Tell them I'm going to kill them. Slowly, one by one."

"When you ran, you idiot, they thought you were Husseini. Remember, we don't know what he looks like. You're lucky my men treated you so well. Sometimes people die before they even *get* to jail..." Ricard pulled up a stool and sat opposite Jack. "You lied to me."

"What'd you expect?" Jack tested a tooth. "I don't work for you."

"You could've given me a hint, something I could go on."

"Piss off. You have Husseini, now let me go."

"No we don't."

Jack shook his head. The pain was horrible. "You *don't*?"

"He got away. You spooked him."

"*Merde!*" Jack dropped his face in his hands. "*Merde merde merde!*"

"I'll drive you home. You should take a shower – you

smell like shit."

In Ricard's Citroën Jack clasped his head trying to soften the bumps. "I *couldn't* tell you, you know that –"

"I know that."

"So I tried to kill him on my own."

"How does that help us, you idiot? We need to talk to him. *Then* we kill him."

"I'm quitting. Going back to the States, find a real job."

"A shame."

"Yeah." Jack looked out at Notre Dame, the gleaming Seine and the turrets of the Concièrgerie. "I love it here."

"Never fear," Ricard said. "She'll come to love you."

"Who?"

"Your little doctor."

"She's taller than you, you devious Frenchman. Hey, how do you know –"

Driving one-handed Ricard lit a Gauloise. "What you need to worry about is, is there anything I *don't* know?"

"Bastard, you've been following me."

"We were waiting for you to bring us to Husseini."

"It's finished, Ricard. I don't talk to you anymore."

"I have a solution to your problem –"

Jack gripped his head as the car thundered over the cobbles. "Christ, which one?"

"Your pretty doctor. Why don't you tell her you're working for us?"

"What you want in return?"

Ricard turned up rue St. Jacques toward the Panthéon. "For the moment, nothing."

"I won't lie to her." *But I do.*

"You lied to me."

"I don't have the hots for you."

Ricard waved away smoke. "I *do* have that effect on people."

"WHAT HAPPENED to your face?" Leo said.

Jack crouched beside him on the sidewalk. "Got in a fight."

"You lose?"

"Sort of." Jack glanced down the Avenue, at the teacher standing over the children. "When's your Mom coming?"

"Any time. She has a green Renault."

"I need your help."

Leo cocked his head. "What for?"

"Your Mom's mad because I won't tell her what I do. I can't – it's a secret."

Leo nodded. "Your face looks terrible."

"You like ice cream?"

"Mom doesn't let me have much."

"Want some now?"

Leo glanced down the Avenue, at the teacher. "Mademoiselle LaCaille won't let me go with anyone but Mom."

"We'll tell her I'm your Mom's friend, that we're going across the street there, to that café, and she's to tell your Mom when she comes –"

"What kind of ice cream?"

"What kind you like?"

"They have chocolate raspberry?"

"If they don't I'll make them get some."

SOPHIE LOOKED FOR LEO next to Mademoiselle LaCaille but he wasn't there. She parked at the bus stop and hopped out. "Where is he?"

"Right there," Mademoiselle LaCaille pointed. "In the café with your friend. They said for you to come over when you got here."

"Friend? *What* friend?"

"That gorgeous guy with the American accent –"

Sophie stared furiously at the café. "I'll *kill* him."

Mademoiselle LaCaille watched her charge toward the café. "If you don't want him," she called, "*I'll* take him!"

Sophie's hand itched for a weapon. She would hit him with a chair. A table. Who *was* he, taking over her son? He could've been a child molester and that silly woman let him walk off with Leo.

A car screeched to a stop as she ran across the street against the light. "Idiot woman!" the driver yelled; she gave him the finger.

Leo looked up at her, glanced at Jack. "Hi Mom!"

She fought the urge to yank him by the hair. "Come with me!"

"I'm not done with my ice cream –"

"Calm down," Jack said. "Leo and I have been practicing Russian." He slid his chair around the table, making room for her. "Sit down."

"Leo come with me."

"Mom!"

Jack stood, again that fast sinuous motion. "You're making a fool of yourself. Sit down and have a beer. Or go away and don't come back till we're done with our ice cream."

How could he talk like this? The waiter pulled over a chair for her. "Madame desires?" She felt the world sliding away, sat down.

"You should try this chocolate raspberry, Mom," Leo said. "It's fantastic!"

Sea of Souls

I'T'S JUST LUST, she told herself, her body welded perfectly to his, feeling him all up and down inside her, it's just our bodies trying to make new ones before we die... *It's only biology you damned fool stop loving it.*

I'll stop after this. Just this one time then he'll go away –

The world exploded, spread out forever. Her body was slick with sweat, damp and full, all up and down inside her a joyous pleasure. It's the most important thing we do, she realized. What keeps us alive. And I'd forgotten...

They lay panting in each other's arms like children. Light spread across the bed like milk. He kissed down her belly, down between her thighs. She came again, a hot tidal wave up the back of her neck washing her in a sea of aching lustful peace.

Finally she lay curled in his arms, her back to his, as in the warm protection of a stone wall. *How have I lived without this? Who is he?*

She woke after midnight as he came into her again, her back against his chest, his hands strong and hard clasping her hips, and for a long time they lay together like this, barely moving, and though the feel of him inside her was new it became familiar, something she'd always needed.

At first light she wanted to wake him just to talk, to have him pay attention to her, a feeling both jealous and maternal. He woke and threw an arm across her breasts, feeling her nipples. "These scars on your shoulder," she said, "don't look like my work –"

"American doctors redid them. It was prettier before..."

Gently she touched them. "You have to go soon. Before Leo wakes."

"Can I see you tonight?"

Oh God no. This wasn't supposed to keep going. She imagined the evening alone. "I'm getting off late –"

"I'll call you."

From the window she saw him cross the streets where the lights were flickering out, and in an instant he'd vanished in the shadows.

SHE HAD NEVER KNOWN anything like this, wanting him terribly and being so terribly afraid. She'd gone to work expecting to be exhausted by a night without sleep but instead felt powerful and enlivened all day, as if her strength was far deeper than she'd ever known. He'd come the next night with wine and more roses and a book about Indians for Leo. Walking to the Champs de Mars he'd swung Leo up on his shoulders. Leo had ridden there happily, and she'd noted a gleam of victory in his eyes – no longer was he a boy without a man to care for him.

They'd made love again all night and the next night and the one after, and *it's like a drug*, she thought, *I'm becoming obsessed. It has to stop.* But it didn't stop and she didn't want it to.

When she thought of Leo's father now it was with total love but a growing distance, as if he'd stayed near her until she found someone, and now that she no longer needed him he was drifting away into the sea of souls. She wasn't remembering *him*, she realized, but rather the short episodes of her brief life with him that she'd seen over and over in her memory so that *they*, and not *he*, had become her memory of him.

Jack had asked her once or twice about him and she'd said *I don't want to talk about it*, but sooner or later wouldn't he want to know? Someday maybe she could tell him.

That weekend they drove the green Renault to Normandy and left Leo with her parents in Le Petit Andely. They wandered up and down the Brittany coast, eating *coquilles St. Jacques* with *Muscadet sur Lie* in St. Malo, the surf pounding on the beach all night outside the hotel room where hour after hour they came together and slept and woke and came together again.

This is more than I can understand, she thought. *What if it ends?*

16:40 IN PARIS was 10:40 in DC. Jack should have called Timothy over an hour ago. Should have called yesterday, last Friday. But he didn't want to think of Timothy, DC, Home Office, any of that.

In an hour he had to pick up Leo. What he wanted to do now was sit in a café with a Kronenbourg and read the *Herald Trib*.

The greatest joy in life, Genghis Khan said, is killing your enemies then screwing their women. How untrue, he thought – violence just leads to more violence, pain to more pain. *All you need to be happy is love someone who loves you.*

Slowly he was letting her into his past... had told her *please never come up behind me. Never touch me on the back if I don't know you're there. Don't ever wake me...* But those horrors were fading too.

Someday maybe he'd be whole again.

He turned off Avenue Bosquet into his favorite café, nodded to the barman and went downstairs to the telephone. Call the bastard and get it over with.

Timothy was in a meeting, his secretary said. "I'll call again tomorrow," Jack said.

"He'll be out in twenty minutes. He's been waiting to hear from you. Call then."

He drank his Kronenbourg and scanned the paper. High school kids were playing *We Will Rock You* on the jukebox and drinking beer, the boys and girls kissing. He frowned at them, then laughed at himself. He was already becoming an old fart.

"Where've you been?" Timothy said when Jack called back. "The rule is you call nine a.m. Monday, Wednesday, Friday."

"I've been in the field, hunting people who aren't there. Sometimes there's no phone." He told Timothy about Sartrouville Mosque, Husseini.

"What the bloody Hell you *chase* him for?"

"I couldn't tell Ricard, so I had to kill Husseini. Before he killed anybody else."

"I told you, France is a *denied* location! Where's your brain?"

"Ricard's guys thought I was Husseini. They beat me up and put me in jail. Ricard got me out."

"He should have left you there. *Damn.* So now he knows?"

"So now he knows."

"Bloody Hell!" The scrambler buzzed as Timothy cogitated. "So we have to admit it about Husseini. We'll have to discover it, going through the files –"

"Too late for that. Anyway a couple of days later they

grabbed three other guys who were with him, talked to them till one said Husseini's gone back to Algeria, someplace called Knetra in the Sahara. They killed those guys and dumped them in the Med."

"You've really screwed up –"

"Lying always leads to screwups."

"I'm going to pull you out, send you to Guatemala, Rhodesia, some dreadful place."

"I'm staying here."

"You work for *me*. You go where, and when, *I* want."

"I worked for Home Office. But I'm quitting." Jack checked the time. 17:50. "Got to run!" He hung up, feeling lightheaded and nervous, as if he'd cut some inviolate link.

He picked Leo up and they went shopping for dinner. "Not spaghetti again," Leo said.

"Okay, buddy, fish then."

He set brown rice on to boil, soaked the fresh bonito in lime and garlic, made a salad of spinach leaves and onions, and set the table on the terrace. When Sophie got home at 19:30 he kissed her, wanting to make love right there against the door but Leo was in the next room watching cartoons. So he held her gently and kneaded her neck till it loosened and she went into the bedroom and changed and came out and poured the Tavel.

"I'm so tired of people hurting themselves," she said. "And each other."

"Maybe you need a change?"

She laughed. "I should be a vet. Animals, at least, are innocent."

He thought of Barb, Cole's fiancée, if now she was a vet somewhere, if she'd married. *He won't be like Cole.* He pushed the memory away.

Sophie rested her head on his shoulder. "And you, my brave warrior, what did you do today?"

"I dropped your son off at school and picked him up. That's the best part."

"He loves that. Every morning he asks if you're going to take him –"

"He goes to school too much. Tomorrow why don't I take him to the zoo? Or over to Rue St. Denis to check out the hookers?"

"You do that." She kissed his neck. "And see where it gets you."

When the rice was nearly done he put the bonito on the grill and they ate the salad while the fish was cooking. They read Leo a story and put him to bed and sat on the twilit terrace with a bottle of Sancerre, the peak of the Eiffel Tower gleaming over the rooftops. "They made that Tower just to be beautiful," she said. "To celebrate what humans can do."

He reached for the bottle. "The two in New York are better."

She pinched him. "Why does everything American always have to be better?"

A jet went over twinkling against the sable sky. He imagined the passengers inside gathering their things, readying to land. "And how ingeniously beautiful that plane is... to think that in just a few thousand years we've traveled all the way from Paleolithic caves to the moon –"

She ran her stockinged toes along the inside of his thigh. "This weekend we could travel all the way from Paris to Normandy again... I told my folks we might come."

He sat forward. "That's why they hate us so much –"

"My parents? They hardly *know* you."

"No, the Muslims. Stamping out joy and choking their world on *Sharia*. Like American Christians stamping out sex and evolution. *We* create beauty and life, and *they* hate music, sex, art, freedom, everything but their forlorn imaginary God..."

"We're not thinking about all that. We're thinking about us, remember?"

"You can give up the past?"

"I'm trying –"

He was diving into a deep quarry, he realized, with no way out. "I wish I'd known Leo's father."

"You do, in a way. You know Leo. But already he's a little like you."

"In high school I had a girlfriend whose father'd died in Vietnam. Her mother remarried, some guy she'd refused long before. I always wondered how he felt, knowing he wasn't her first choice."

"This is *now*. You *are* my first choice. I'm crazy about you."

"To us, then. To giving up the past."

"And living just for us."

"And Leo."

"And Leo. Is he asleep?"

"I think so."

"Let's go to bed."

"And leave the wine?"

She cradled the bottle between her breasts. "It's coming with us."

TWO WEEKS LATER TIMOTHY called on Sophie's home phone. "How'd you find this number?" Jack said.

"Your pal *Reecard* –"

"He's not my pal."

"I have a solution to your problem."

"I don't have a problem."

"You're down to your last *centime*."

"You have no idea what I've got."

"Please, listen to my little story: After the oil embargo in seventy-three, we realized we had to counterbalance OPEC. To keep an eye on crude reserves, production, refining, shipping, that kind of thing... You listening?"

"This's your money –"

"So we and some of our oil-consuming allies created the International Energy Agency, as part of the Organization for Economic Cooperation and Development."

"Timothy, I don't give a shit about oil. Goodbye."

The phone rang again. "You're making me feel like a whore here."

"You said it –"

"Jack, there's a knife at our throats. Without oil, we wouldn't have given a damn about Iran in seventy-nine, or what the Soviets did in Afghanistan... These days all wars are about oil." His voice softened. "Your Dad died because we thought there was a lot of oil in the South China Sea."

Jack's eyes stung. "Fuck you."

"We need you back Inside. There's a job at IEA. They're located right there in Paris. With your Arabic and Russian... Pashto's close to Persian, I'm told."

"Sort of." Jack felt himself being drawn in, tried to stop. "What of it?"

There was a moment's silence, just the clicking and buzzing of the scrambler. "We *need* you, Jack. Your *country* needs you." Timothy paused. "You can make good money. And stay right there in Paris."

Payback

FIVE MORNINGS a week at 08:10 he walked Leo to school then continued down Avenue La Bourdonnais past the Eiffel Tower, crossed the Iéna Bridge over the Seine, took Rue de Passy uphill through the Sixteenth and reached his office at IEA before nine.

His office had wide oak floors and tall windows with a view of tall trees and wide lawns. He hung the camelhair coat Sophie had bought him behind the door, went down the hall to the espresso machine saying good morning and shaking hands, and made a double. He started to put in sugar but stopped. Amazing how he was putting on weight.

By noon he'd read all the newspapers and business journals in French or Arabic, had clipped anything of relevance to U.S. energy policy or operations, or having any potential effect on U.S. oil companies, had written a translation and commentary and faxed it to HO.

Lunch was usually with an executive of one of the French oil companies, Elf or Total, or with an under-minister across the Seine, or sometimes a Saudi or Kuwaiti prince who had come to Paris to buy sex with Chanel models and pretend he was working in the oil business.

Afternoons were for crude and product analyses, meet-ings on world oil policy, what OPEC's next move might be and how to deflect it. At six he put on the camelhair coat and departed, just another French businessman going home.

But still sometimes the streets and sidewalks of Paris, the shops and cafés, felt unreal. The hours on the telephone made his shoulder ache; the muscles tightened over the ru-ined bone, and month after month the pain grew.

One night he dreamt he and Husseini were fighting in the gutter outside Sartrouville Mosque. Husseini's face neared, filthy teeth grinning with exertion; he kissed Jack's cheek with hairy lips. Jack sat up. Sophie breathing softly beside him was not Husseini.

"What is it?" Her voice shocked him. When you were being kissed by Husseini in the gutter, could you be sure you weren't imagining this too?

"Can't sleep."

"What you did, darling – I know we can't speak about it, but it will go away. Over time it will go away."

He stretched out beside her. "Look what you've been through."

"I always feared it was coming. You didn't. And I've got Leo."

I've got the Russian major. And the Russian kid by the APC, the old woman shot by mistake, Hamid from the fed-ayeen camp in the Beqaa, all the others. These are my chil-dren. "I've got you," he said.

She slid against him. "And I've got you."

But you had someone else before. "Why won't you tell me what happened, with Leo's father?"

"Why won't you *listen*? There's no *reason* to talk about it!"

"It's like you're hiding something –"

After a moment she faced him. "He was a Russian officer... We were getting married soon as his tour was up. In two months."

He lay with hands behind his head imagining Leo's father, thinking of the boy's oval face, the oriental hint to his dark eyes. "What did he do?"

"What do soldiers always do? Kill each other. We're *not* going to discuss it."

He watched her face. *This* life, with her, seemed realer now. Could he make the other go away, what had happened to them both in Afghanistan?

He caressed the inside of her forearm, imagined telling her about Sin City, the Hindu Kush, the dead Russians, Beirut, the Beqaa. The brown blood on the *Métro* walls, Husseini in the Sartrouville Mosque.

He wouldn't think about all that. And slowly, over time, it would go away. Till his life with her, this regular job at IEA, became what he was.

But who was Leo's father? Why wouldn't she tell?

"Afghanistan," she said. "You were bringing arms to the *mujihadeen*, weren't you?"

"I can't tell you that." He smelled the disinfectant and severed limbs in the Kabul hospital, felt the agony in his shoulder as he lay on the gurney. He heard her speaking Pashto from another room, "*If you move him he'll die.*"

Let it go. But it itched at him, not knowing. "Why didn't you get married?"

She sighed, got up on one elbow. "The *mujihadeen* in the eastern Panjshir agreed to peace talks. Leo was the senior Russian official in the convoy. It was a trap. They were all killed." She said nothing, then, "He was executed. By those assassins."

Jack looked into the dark core of the universe. "When? When was this?"

"June eighty-three." She sat up, brushed hair from her

242

face. "Later the *mujihadeen* said it was retribution for some destroyed villages, but Leo had never destroyed anything. It was Hekmatyar, that American pawn, who'd done that."

He saw the major's pained, angry face against the bloody snow. And in the darkness the pale face of the woman he loved. What horrible irony, what maleficent fate, what grinning Devil who ran life, had arranged this?

He got up, stubbed his toe on a bed leg. "All this talk. I'm like the Spartan boy with the fox gnawing his guts."

"That's because he's hiding it."

"He can't reveal it. He's not allowed to have it." He slipped into his shirt and jeans and sat in the living room.

Shadows lay across the floor like blood. Guns were going off inside his head. He had to tell her. He couldn't tell her. It would break her heart all over again. But if he didn't tell her, how, every day, could he face Leo? Face her?

If Husseini hadn't bombed the Paris *Métro*, Jack would never have been sent to Paris. If *we* hadn't trained Husseini, he never would have bombed it. If *we* hadn't decided to bleed the Soviets in Afghanistan, Jack would never have been sent there either, never have been wounded, never known *her*, never have been responsible for the death of the Russian major.

If Husseini hadn't fired stupidly on the stepping-stone bridge, Jack wouldn't have been wounded, *she* wouldn't have saved him... If Timothy hadn't wanted deniability, Jack would never have been sent to Paris, and found *her*.

If he hadn't asked they could have lived their lives together and never known.

He didn't have to tell her. She'd never know, and over the years would forget the Russian major dying in the snow, his last words spat into your face, "Fuck you and your children. May they never have children."

Payback. You always get it, sooner or later. Whether he

told her or not she was gone.

SOPHIE FORCED HERSELF awake. Was it a dream that she and Jack had been talking? No, it had happened, he'd gone into the living room. *He's fine*, she decided, nestling down in the warmth, pushing at the pillow to get it just right under her head.

But it was unlike him to be out there so long. So many hidden facets to him. Even though there were parts of him she didn't understand, all of him was loving and warm, caring without interfering, watching over Leo like his own son.

She'd loved Leo's father, too, but not the same. The first time making love with him in that little armored car – there'd been passion and impossibility, the way love springs so easily out of war. But this love with Jack was more lasting, built on everyday rhythms between people who can be who they are.

Leo had been coarse and thick-fisted, brilliant, unconventional and purely Slavic. Faithful and kind. Jack was more mercurial, withdrawn one moment and affectionate the next, with you one moment and unreachable the next. Just as there was not an ounce of extra weight on him, as if he'd trimmed his life down to only the essential.

And if they did have children Jack would be a wonderful father. Maybe they *would* – this had gone on for months now, always growing, always stronger. What if they got married?

She really should make sure he was okay. She slid back the covers.

He was sitting in the darkness looking out the window. She sat on the sofa beside him, cuddled up to him and slipped one hand between his arm and chest. "What is it?"

"Trying to figure things out." *Don't say it now*, he told himself. *Maybe later. Just have this last night.*

But later when he told her she'd know that he'd known now and hadn't said.

The corded thickness of his biceps under her hand excited her. *He's so loving and kind*, she thought, and that made her want him too. She leaned closer, liking the feel of her breast against his shoulder. He jerked away.

"Whatever's bothering you," she said, "we can work it out..."

He took a breath. "Leo's father –"

"C'mon, honey, I said I didn't want to talk about it –"

Don't tell her now, he told himself. "I was there when he died." He swallowed. "I was with the ones who killed him."

"What!" she choked, couldn't speak, jumped back. "*What?*"

"I didn't know it was a peace convoy – I didn't want him killed..." He looked out the window at the darkness.

She hit him on the temple hard with the heel of her hand, sending shock waves of pain up her arm, hit him again, it was like hitting a steel wall, he hardly seemed to notice. "You bastard," she screamed, "you *knew*. Bastard!"

"I didn't know, Sophie. If I had I never would've plagued you."

She hit him again and again until calmly he took her wrists and held them. "I've never loved anyone like you. I wouldn't do anything to hurt you –"

"But you *did*, Oh how you hurt me. Hurt little Leo, who will never have a father! You Bastard! *Why?*" She yanked her hands free and slapped his face.

He took her wrists again. "You're going to hurt yourself."

She sat there, hands stinging, staring down at her knees. "I knew you were poison. Why didn't I listen?"

He went to the window. "Maybe it *had* to be like this."

"I'm taking Leo to my folks and going somewhere, anywhere."

"I can take care of Leo."

"You get *away* from him –"

She bent over weeping; he put his hand on her shoulder. "I didn't mean to let him die. I didn't know any of this. Not till tonight."

She looked up at him, her tear-streaked face glistening in the dim fluorescence through the window. "If you hadn't kept asking – we never would've known –"

She took a breath. "But you had to keep asking! Didn't you?"

HE TOOK A FURNISHED place in Rue du Passy close to IEA, a fourth floor walkup with three windows on a paved *cour* where a lone oak bled tan leaves on the cobbles. *This* is who I am, he told himself. *This had to be.*

What they taught you in Sin City: *Learn to never need what you might lose.*

Just like an amputation you get phantom pain. She's not there anymore but still she hurts you.

Next week he asked for Friday off, and late Thursday took the TGV to Marseille. In the men's room he changed into an old *djellabah* and put his other clothes in a locker. With a blanket roll over one shoulder he walked down to the ship terminal and bought a third class ticket to Algiers.

Sahara

THE BOAT LEFT AT MIDNIGHT. The third class passengers slept in huddled masses on the deck, using their arms for pillows. When the wind shifted and spray came on the deck they went to the other side, stepping on each other and arguing in the dark.

Algiers at dawn spread across the hills like a vast gray melanoma. It felt alien to walk the sidewalks jostling the ragged barefoot men, avoiding the women in black robes and veils, to cross the streets jammed with double-parked cars, thunderous buses and stinking trucks. Radios blared the insistent rant of *mullahs*; the air reeked of garbage, exhaust and sewers. Everyone seemed to notice him.

The bus to Ghardaia gasped up the *corniche* and over the first ridges of the Jebel Atlas. Streams ran through willow copses, orchards and olive groves. Many villages were bombed or burned. Others were deserted, no sheep or goats in the fields, the grass long and the fruit trees withered.

He slid open the window to let in hot dry wind. When he got back to Paris he'd tell Ricard what he'd done and be finished with it all, go somewhere else. If he got back to Paris.

If he hadn't told her he wouldn't be here. He'd see her every day, sleep with her every night. Wake with her naked beside him, hold hands in the market.

Ghardaia was a town of gray cement houses with narrow windows. A seething wind from the south blew red dust and trash in circles. Clothes hung over walls and chickens pecked at camel dung. A few palm trees drooped fronds under a withering sky.

He thought of the battle in the Hindu Kush when Husseini had hid in the rocks firing blindly, of Husseini's constant nasal remonstrances from the Koran, his unending jibes about the West – "Feeling lonely? Miss your shopping malls, your loose women?"

Husseini grinning when Jack had caught him torturing the Russian prisoner.

He reached Knetra at dusk, the air sere, the earth still hot. Goats bleated and roosters crowed; smoke hung in the street. After dark he skirted the village, flinching at a camel that thundered off. He dozed in a *wadi*, twice wakened by cobras coiling against him, drawn to his warmth. He sat up the rest of the night but no more snakes came. The sun rose fat and dull ochre above basalt cliffs.

With his cloak wrapped across his face like a Bedouin he walked the streets but did not see Husseini. He sat near the well but that seemed too busy so he picked a shady side street where he could watch the central square and the low, blue-painted mosque.

He watched all day but never saw Husseini, feared he wasn't there, that he was going to have to ask. Then in late afternoon an old gray Peugeot truck clattered into the square with three men standing in the back holding AKs. In the passenger seat was Husseini.

The truck juddered to a halt in front of the mosque. People gathered round it; others came squinting from their squat little houses.

Husseini climbed up into the back, held up his hands. He wore a dusty *djellabah* and the same Muslim skullcap with blue and red sequins. In the desert wind it was hard to hear, but Husseini seemed to be exhorting them, pointing at the young men, his own heart, the mosque behind him, the sky.

He talked for a long time. A few young men got in the back of the truck. Husseini fired a salvo and some of the people cheered. He got down and climbed back into the cab and the truck drove off slowly with the young men clinging to the back.

Jack followed the truck tracks up a *wadi* to the southeast. After about a mile they crossed a dune to three rundown tile-roofed huts inside a yard fenced with thorn branches. The truck and a donkey stood in the courtyard. In the shade of one hut a man walked back and forth holding a book and lecturing the young men who had left town on the back of the truck.

Beyond the courtyard and a line of dead fruit trees was a whitewashed shed that seemed an outhouse. Jack slipped back up the *wadi* and waited for night.

Sophie would be on her way home now with Leo through the lovely Paris evening. Talking about what to have for dinner.

A half moon cleared the eastern peaks, shadowing the orchard. A veiled woman came from one of the huts, went into the outhouse and left. Another woman came out with three children and made them go in one by one.

Jack felt evil and alone. Maybe Husseini wasn't going back to France, wouldn't bomb another subway. Maybe he'd just stay here, be a local celebrity.

Sophie would be reading Leo a story in bed now.

When darkness fell Jack moved from the *wadi* up behind the outhouse.

A man came out of one of the other huts and went into the outhouse and sat for a long time grunting and talking to himself. He left and one by one the lights in the three huts died. Jack edged closer till he could see into the yard. Beads rattled, and a man in a pale *djellabah* came toward the outhouse. Moonlight sparkled off the sequins in his cap.

Jack waited till Husseini had gone into the outhouse and shut the door. His heart thundered; his arms trembled. He could not quiet his breath.

The wooden door was hinged on the right. Jack waited in moon shadow behind it. He heard Husseini dip his fingers in a tin of water to wash himself, readjust his *djellabah*, snuffle and spit into the hole. The door squeaked open. Husseini stepped outside. Jack yanked up his head and drove his knife into his throat.

Husseini grabbed at the knife, twisted away, smashed his elbows backwards into Jack's ribs, kicked at his shins, gasping and gurgling. He stopped jerking and hung still.

Blood coated Jack's hands and sleeves, the ground, the front of Husseini's *djellabah*. Jack dragged him into the desert, ran back to the outhouse, grabbed up handfuls of bloody sand and threw them in the scrub. With an olive branch he swept the sand clear, walking backwards toward Husseini's body and brushing away his tracks and the two ruts made by Husseini's heels.

He circled the village paralleling the Ghardaia road, watching in the moonlight for snakes that had crawled out to enjoy the day's last heat. A few miles from Knetra he began to run along the road. His sandals kept falling off so he removed them and ran barefoot, the pavement warm under his soles.

He caught the early bus Sunday morning back to Algiers, took the night boat to Marseille, and was in his office by noon on Monday. "Sorry," he told his boss, a big rumpled ex-Purdue lineman named Anders. "I had the flu or something. Sick as a dog all weekend."

"It's been going around," Anders said.

Lionheart

WHEN SOPHIE WALKED TO HER CAR next week in the hospital parking lot a wiry gray-haired man in a cheap suit stood against it smoking. She scanned the parking lot but could see no guards. She started to back away.

"Don't worry, Madame Dassault." He reached into his coat and held out an ID. "*Police Nationale*. Colonel Max Ricard. We need to talk."

"I'll pay that parking ticket," she said nervously. "I promise."

He had a large sunny laugh for such a small man. "That's not why I'm here, my dear Doctor. Call it personal business on my part – it's about your American."

That bastard. What's he done now? "I don't *have* any American!"

"No games." He tossed his cigarette. "That's my profession, not yours."

"You shouldn't smoke those."

"I came by to tell you he's a brave man who's done great service to France. At the risk of his life."

"What's he done?"

He nodded at her car. "No need to drive to work any longer. The *Metro*'s safe."

She felt dizzy. He began to walk away, turned back. "Let's keep this little chat," he smiled, "between us French?"

THE DOOR BUZZER SNARLED and Jack spun out of his chair grabbing the Makarov and backed against the wall five feet from the door expecting bullets to blast through it. The buzzer buzzed again and after a few seconds her voice said, "It's me."

She was skinnier, more angular, her hair cut short. "I don't want to live without you."

"I'm living just fine without *you*." He swung a hand at the room "Go out every night." *Soon I'll go somewhere and die.* His body melted toward her. "You can't live *with* me."

She reached out making him think of a ladder up the side of a ship and she unable to reach it, drowning in a frozen sea. "You didn't *mean* to let him die," she said. "Just because I loved him doesn't mean I can't love you too –"

The Russian major gut-shot in the red snow pointed to his heart. "I have no explanation," Jack said. "That will ever clear me."

"I want you." She drifted against him. "Leo wants you."

"We can't live for him." He caressed her hair. "I don't understand, Sophie, why you love me."

"I must be drawn to killers. I keep thinking I can change you."

"Even I can't seem to do that."

"The only thing I ask is you quit that job. That you don't hurt people anymore."

"That's all I want, too." Joy coursed through him. "All I've ever wanted is you."

WINTER NIGHT FOG slid into Kabul, a stone wall on Ahmad's right fading into nothing, the far murmur of footsteps soft as the pads of leopards. He gripped the two water buckets tighter, their icy handles biting into his palms, tried to hurry but that spilled water so he slowed, picking his way carefully through rocks and rubble.

He put down the buckets, opened the back door of the orphanage, carried them in and lifted them one at a time onto the kerosene-barrel stove. Heat stung his fingers; holding his hands to the flames he fancied he could see through them he'd grown so thin.

"Wonderful!" Galaya said. "You found water!"

His hand dropped on hers.

"We shouldn't touch." She squeezed his hand. "If those Taliban see –"

"I love every instant you're near, the sound of your voice, when you sing to the children, giving them lessons, sitting with a sick one, how the sorrow and suffering never get you down. Why won't you marry me?"

"We *promised* not to speak of this!"

"Tell me *why*!"

She glanced away. "You'll rue the day I told you –"

"Whatever it is, *tell me*!"

"Before I came here... before the clinic was destroyed and the French doctor went home, Taliban did things to me. I can't marry you."

The sky had crushed his chest. Was the whole purpose of life pain, and love created only to intensify the pain? "It makes no difference."

"Don't be *blind*!" She turned on him. "Of course it does!"

"We can live as if we're married, all our lives."

"That's insane. If the Taliban finds out?"

"Who's to tell them? Except you or me?"

"IT'S FUCKING HILARIOUS you're getting married," Owen McPhee said. "*You*, of all the hard-assed loners..."

"No choice," Jack grunted. "Sophie told me to."

"Can't imagine why she'd want you." McPhee bent down for a stone on the gravel path along the Seine and skated it across the River's dark surface.

Jack slowed his pace to compensate for McPhee's limp, thinking *it was wrong asking him to be here. Showing him he's alone and I'm not.* "That broken leg still bother you? Or are you just being a pussy?"

"Long airplane rides stiffen it. All the way from El Salvador – Christ what a trip." He scanned the rippling, light-flashing river, the ancient houses of Le Petit Andely. "But it's beautiful here."

"You should get out, Owen. Home Office warps us; we can't be or say who we are; anyone any time can take us down..."

"Know what the new thing is down there?"

"El Salvador? I don't want to."

"*Escoger un Niño* – Choose a Kid. Our military dictatorship sends their soldiers into the countryside at night to yank some family out of their hut, tell the father pick one kid to be executed, right there, or the whole family dies."

Jack said nothing, walking along the misty quay, the old houses and River beside him. "When we joined up we wanted to do good, remember?"

"Can you imagine? Standing there in the darkness, soldiers and lights all around, and they tell you pick one of your kids to be shot, or they shoot you all? Supposed to deter leftist uprisings. People who earn a dollar a day working for an American banana company..."

"You have to quit, do anything else..."

"You aren't marrying Sophie, Jack. You're already married to Home Office. We all are. Like Loxley used to sing,

255

You can check out any time you like. But you can never leave."

"I *am* out of it. Fuck the Crusade."

McPhee limped along. "First time I got married was in Vegas, some fake stucco chapel. Turned out the marriage was fake too. You're getting married in this beautiful medieval church, so maybe you'll just stay the old-fashioned fart you always were."

Jack looked upriver to the Norman steeple, a lance pointed at the sky. "Richard the Lionheart built it when he returned after the Third Crusade, along with that castle up on the hill that he patterned on the five-sided towers he'd besieged in the Holy Land."

"Hilarious they call it that."

"At the Point I studied all Richard's battles. He was a tactical genius. But by pulling out when they could've won the Crusaders left a vacuum that got filled by Islamic hardliners who drove the Muslims into the dark ages they've been in ever since. Now we've done the same in Afghanistan..."

"How you got thrown out of the Point – why'd you try to kill that guy?"

"In Maine? I just beat him up. He's still alive."

"You got three months in jail."

"He poisoned my dog."

McPhee shook his head: *no end to human evil.* "After this," he nodded at the ancient houses leaning over the black River, "New York is gonna seem weird."

"New York's always weird. But it's where I need to be in the oil business. And the emergency room work here was driving Sophie crazy. Amazingly, Doctors Without Borders decided to open a New York office and asked her to run it."

They walked a while in silence. "When *you* getting married again?" Jack said.

"Marriage is like a hand grenade... Sooner or later it goes off and anyone near gets wasted. Being your best man is dangerous enough for me."

"If there's a God, we must be a source of unending hilarity... Imagine, all he had to do was set up two kinds of us, male and female, and he could keep us preoccupied forever, craving and not getting along with each other..."

"Or killing each other in his name –" McPhee halted, on the balls of his feet. "Bush is bringing in all his cronies from when he ran Home Office. Half of them don't know shit and the rest are plain evil."

"So who's getting payback for Lockerbie?"

"Everybody knows the Libyans did it but that the Iranians ordered it to get us back for nailing their Airbus. Bush won't punish them; he's going to hassle Qaddafi."

"Doesn't help the people who died. Or those who love them."

"Word is the Russkies are pulling out of Afghanistan. Any day now."

Jack watched the river. "I just want to be married, have kids, live a normal life."

"Guys like you and me, Jack, we ain't meant to live a normal life."

"HELP ME TAKE IT OFF," Galaya said, "this horrid thing!" She squeezed the *burkha* up and over her head. "In the market I nearly fainted."

Ahmad slid it from her and dropped it on the floor. Underneath she wore a gauzy purple gown slippery in his fingers. "On the outside," he whispered, "we must seem to be the most Taliban of all."

"But *here* we don't have to..." She shook her hair from side to side, freeing it. "Tonight we're going to feed the kids, *then* you and me. And drink wine."

"*Wine?*" he laughed. "What a strange thought!"

"I found some. In the ruins of the old Soviet press office."

He held her to him, kissing her neck. "You're not supposed to go there."

"Who's going to tell? Our orphans?"

He kissed down her pear-like breasts, the tender nipples, could smell her sex. "If the word got out –"

"The Taliban can't see *inside* us, can they?" She reached down for him. "But you, *you* can feel inside me. Can't you?"

"I can *taste* you, *feel* you, *smell* you... It drives me crazy, loving you."

"We *must* be careful. If I get pregnant the Taliban will kill me."

V

Desert Storm

Saddam

April 1990

"WE CAN AFFORD IT," Sophie said. "And since we have to live in New York..."

Jack paced the huge empty loft, dust on his shoes. It was true – in the two years since they'd been in New York he'd made enough money; she was making a good wage too. He peered through a window at the traffic and wet umbrellas on Christopher Street five stories below. Dead flies hung in a spider web across a corner of the glass. "It'll cost thousands to fix up."

"There isn't much to do, really," Mrs. Gopkind said. "That's the *nice* thing about a loft – you put the dividing walls up *any*where you want... you can say, *here's* the bedroom and *there's* the living room and –"

"We need three bedrooms," Sophie said. "We've got a son and baby daughter, and want more kids."

"Two thousand square feet," Mrs. Gopkind waved a pink-gloved hand at the cobwebbed ceiling, splintery beams, broken panes and rotten windows. "If it's an inch."

"Eighteen-sixty," Jack said. "I just measured it."

"*Any*way," Mrs. Gopkind said, "it'll be a dream to fix up. Not *that* expensive, either."

"I worked construction, summers in high school. I know how much it costs."

"So you'll know *just* how to do it," Mrs. Gopkind said agreeably. They left her fiddling with her keys and went round the corner to the White Horse. "You're being such a *pain*, darling," Sophie said.

"We should be putting all the money back into the business, not into *this*."

"Okay." She slid her Guinness glass in wet circles on the table. "We'll just keep living where we are... The trash chute by the kitchen window, the elevator by the bedroom wall, those marvelous cooking smells... And the language lessons one gets just sticking one's head into the hallway. Particularly late at night..."

"You win." He kissed the palm of her hand. "I'm so lucky to have you."

"YOU KNOW ME," the voice on the phone said, "but don't say my name."

For a moment Jack couldn't place it. "Hey! Where are you?"

"In town. Have to see you."

"It's been months... How are you?"

"Tonight, midnight. Washington Square, Fifth Avenue. By the Arch."

Feeling vaguely immoral as if planning some assignation, Jack watched Sophie take off her bra and panties and slide into bed. "Going out," he said. "Take a walk."

She scanned him over her reading glasses. "This is new."

"I always used to walk at night, when I can't sleep."

"There's lots of things you used to do you don't do any more."

McPhee was parked by the Arch in a white Taurus with Florida plates. "Why can't you be like a regular person?" Jack said as he slid into the passenger seat. "Call up a few days ahead, come for dinner, all that?"

"Regular stuff's finished, Jack. We're going to war."

Reflexively Jack scanned the empty street, the dark buildings, the yellow streetlights, all of it suddenly sinister again. "Timothy sent me," McPhee said. "Said do whatever it takes."

"I'm not going back Inside."

"Remember what *we* did? Drove the Soviets out of Afghanistan."

"Yeah, and now the country's ruined. This new group – Taliban? Means *student* in Pashto. Killing for God."

"*Listen to me*, Jack! Now the Berlin Wall's down we're gonna do the same thing to the rest of the Soviet empire... *Already* we're starting on the Middle East."

"Starting on?"

"Who were the Soviet allies in the Middle East?"

"Syria, Iraq, Yemen, sometimes Egypt."

"Only one produces any oil."

"Iraq? Nearly four million barrels a day. World's second largest reserves. So what?"

"And the world's lowest field development costs. The Rumaila and Kirkuk fields alone are almost forty billion barrels. Wouldn't it be nice to *own* that oil?"

"It'd take thousands of casualties to root out Saddam – for Chrissake he's our creation –"

"We make 'em, we break 'em."

"I wonder what must go on in Saddam's head. At first he's just some local thug. Then Iraq's new Prime Minister – what was his name – way back in –"

"Abd al-Karim Qasim," McPhee said. "In '59."

"Because Qasim won't sell us Iraq's oil fields, we hire

this thug Saddam to kill him... and even though Saddam fails to kill him, we soon overthrow him and put Saddam in his place... That was a Mobil, Bechtel and BP deal..." Jack paused, trying to remember. "Then we gave Saddam the list of all the people we wanted dead – all the educated elite, the scientists, doctors, professors, lawyers, all the Agency's usual suspects..."

McPhee huffed, looked away, knocked his West Point ring on the steering wheel, the old Point expression *Don't argue, do what I say*. "Bush wants the crude price to go up. Remember, the Saudis own him."

"You don't have a pretext."

"We will. We need you back Inside, Jack. With your Arabic, your knowledge of these people, their refineries, and now with your position in the oil business..."

"*What* pretext?"

"Remember your *Art of War*: *To defeat your enemy, first make him arrogant*? What if we're reminding Saddam how Kuwait was part of Iraq before the Brits grabbed it in World War One? Get him dwelling on Mesopotamia, the empires of Sumer, Assyria, Babylonia?"

"He'd know we're planning something."

"So suppose then our Ambassador tells him we don't intervene in regional disputes? That if he takes over Kuwait that could level the balance with the Saudis? And then we entice his Republican Guard into the Kuwaiti desert and nail them from the air?"

Jack watched a slim man walk a white poodle cross Ninth Street. "For years he's been our ally –"

"I was at Halabja two days after he gassed five thousand people."

"With hydrogen cyanide *we* gave him."

"Doesn't matter. Saddam's *evil*."

"So are all the oil rulers we've set up in these countries.

So are *we*." Jack noticed his exhausted reflection in the windshield, couldn't see past it. "This is insane... Anyway, it'd take you months to mobilize."

"There's going to be a big fuss in press conferences about how dangerous he is."

"Crude prices will go crazy. You could fuck up the economy of the entire fucking world."

"You should start buying crude long, Jack. You can make real money."

Jack looked away. Had it all come down to this? All their determination and love of country, all the deaths and shattered lives? Had it all been for money? "Please, Owen, you should try to stop this..."

"Too late. The big guys are already buying in – Exxon, Shell, Texaco... Do you know how many billions even *four months* of high crude prices will add to their bottom line? Shit, of course you do..." He grinned. "Timothy's begging for you."

Jack watched him. "Remember why you and I joined up? And Sean and Gus?"

"Sure," McPhee made a self-deprecating smile. "To *pertect* the free *wurld*," he mimicked.

"The colonels in Argentina? Pinochet in Chile? El Salvador? The *contras*?"

McPhee drummed fingers on the steering wheel. "Oil's getting short and we have to get what's left. *And* we need Middle East bases. This war does both."

"Bases for what?"

"For later: Iran, Saudi." Shadows of the streetlight cut across McPhee's face, a white-black mask. "We have to protect our way of life or they'll take it from us. Freedom, openness, imagination – brilliance, commitment –"

Jack wondered for an instant what his life might have been if he'd never returned to the Death Mountains with the *Strelas*. Never lost Loxley. Never killed Sophie's lover. Never been shot in the shoulder, lost Bandit. Never met *her*.

"It's a sin, what you're doing."

"Religion's written by the winners, Jack."

"There will be no winners..."

"All this's between you'n me, baby." McPhee jabbed him. "But remember – I was first to tell you."

Climbing the stairs to his Christopher Street loft Jack wondered what McPhee had meant.

The first to tell Jack that he'd end up back Inside?

Or that the United States would soon be at war with Iraq?

Need to Know

"**I** HAVE SURPRISING NEWS," Suley said.

Wahid grunted. "You often think you do."

"Last week in Kabul I went by the orphanage where that spineless fool Ahmad kept me. He hasn't obeyed the edict. Hasn't sent all the boys to the *madrasah*. Even worse."

Suley liked to stretch out his stories, make himself important, the little popinjay. Wahid motioned for him to leave. "I'm thinking of more important things. Battles, changes in the law. People must be controlled to create a perfect Islamic republic."

"I saw a woman there... Your brother's living with a whore."

Wahid said nothing. Then, "You should not have told me."

"The truth should always be told. Whatever filthy secrets, perversions, the Devil's dealings people do –"

"How did you learn this?"

"Long ago I killed three Pashtùn in a cellar. I told you this when I first came to you. They were holding a woman and doing it to her. One left his rifle on the stairs. I killed them. And now, when I was checking the orphanage... it's the same woman."

"It can't be. That Ahmad would take..."

Suley leaned back, his eyes narrow under deep lids. "Suppose it were known that the Eagle of the Hindu Kush has a whoremonger for a brother? What would that make *you*?"

After Suley left Wahid sat thinking. The desert people long ago told how Kâbil and Hâbil, Cain and Abel, each had a twin sister, and God told Adam to order each to marry the other's twin sister. This Kâbil would not do, wanting his own sister because she was more beautiful. "So you each make an offering to God," Adam said, "let Him decide."

Kâbil offered God a sheaf of his worst corn, while Hâbil the little ass-kisser gave up his fattest lamb. God's fire came down in a tornado from Heaven and consumed the fat lamb, but didn't touch the corn of Kâbil. Kâbil turned with righteous anger on his brother saying, "You have shamed me. I will slay you."

Hâbil the spineless fool taunted Kâbil, "God only accepts the offerings of the pious. Even if you raise your hand to slay me I won't raise mine at you, for I fear only God."

So the Devil showed Kâbil how to kill Hâbil, by crushing the head of a lapwing between two stones. But once Hâbil was dead Kâbil stupidly felt guilty, for a long time carried the stinking corpse of his brother on his back. Till God sent down a raven to kill another raven and scratch with his claws a hole in the earth to bury it, showing Kâbil how to bury Hâbil. And the children of Kâbil inherited the earth.

If God hadn't wanted this, how could it have happened?

AFTER HIS FATHER DIED Jack had taken an evening paper route that paid ten dollars a week toward the family's expenses. The first February the snow was so deep he delivered the *Kennebec Journal* to second story windows, a scarf over his face to cut the minus-thirty cold.

After he delivered the last paper to an old farmhouse at the end of an empty road he had a choice. It was dark, the wind fitful in the trees. The safe way was back down the long road under the stars, then north till he got to the road going home. The short way was to cut behind the farmhouse barn, down a deep gully and up the other side and through the forest and across a field to the road going home. It was lonely and dark, and Death waited there. And he made himself do it, night after night.

Now in New York he did the same thing, walked the most dangerous streets late at night, right hand on the combat knife in his coat pocket – waiting for what?

"Something's eating you," Sophie said. "You're going back to how you were."

He tried so hard to not be aggressive, yet the more he tried the more she accused him. He woke at night reaching for a knife or gun that wasn't there. One night a man walking ahead of them spit on the sidewalk and Jack slammed him against the wall so hard his head cracked. "You want a dirty place to live? Go back where you came."

"I can't stand it any longer," Sophie said when he caught up to her. "You're going to kill somebody."

He wanted to fall on his pinstriped knees on the filthy sidewalk. "I try not to."

"It's like rabies. Once bitten, you can't shake it, you need to bite people."

"I wasn't always that way. It's something I learned."

"When?"

"I don't know. Trying to avenge my father's death?"

"So who killed him?"

"Some Vietnamese."

"What about the men in Washington who sent him?

Who created a horrendous war out of nothing?" She went on alone into the darkness.

He stayed behind her till she was safely home then wandered the streets, walking off his anger.

At a noise behind him he dropped into a fighting crouch but it was only a rat scurrying for a drainpipe. It reminded him of something – what?

Rawalpindi. Bandit dropping a dead female rat at his feet. The little ones that starved.

You never realized how alone you'd been till you had a dog. An ally. True to the death.

Am I only good for killing?

Why was he so angry? He'd been taught, taught himself, to be that way: *You're never safe, you never will be.* Hezbollah, the Palestinians, Hekmatyar, the Spetsnaz... *Never need anything you might have to do without.*

The man who killed his dog. The men who killed his father. He wanted to fall weeping on the sidewalk, fought it off.

Vengeance is the poisoned meat you feed your enemies. But that you must then eat yourself. *Who said that?*

He found himself far downtown, looking up at his offices in the North Tower. *Why am I this way? When other people have created magnificent things like that?*

Windows on the World

"THEY'RE TOO YOUNG!" Galaya screamed. "*Please* don't take them!"

"Veil yourself," yelled the bearded man, "before I kill you."

"My husband's out seeking food, he'll be right back –"

Their flashlights tossing shadows across the huddled children, the Taliban snatched the ones they wanted, skinny boys in flimsy underwear knock-kneed and squinting in the darting light, hands across their groins.

The truck outside gunned its engine. Where, she wondered frantically, do they find fuel? The Taliban were hustling the boys into their clothes, saying, "C'mon, you're going to be a man" and "You're old enough now, this is what it's like," and she grabbed one kid as they went by the kitchen and shoved him down behind the stove, from where he looked up at her with astonished fearful eyes.

"Keep still!" she hissed. It was Yusef, their kid for years, who last year she'd saved from typhus. A Taliban came through the kitchen curtain and yanked Yusef up by his hair, the boy trooping wordless across the kitchen with this man's fist in his hair. "I'll teach you to hide like a woman!"

She sat crying in the middle of the kitchen floor. A little girl tugged the hair back from her face, repeating to her, "It goes away, it stops," another purposefully jostling twigs into the fire, a third digging cupfuls of rice from a burlap bag into a pot and pouring water over them.

"What happened?" Ahmad whispered when he came in.

"They took all the boys over ten. *Madrasah*." She turned away from the pain in his eyes. "If we could find a bus? Drive it across the desert to Peshawar with the rest of the kids?"

"A bus? They've all been used for troops."

"A truck then. Put the kids in back –"

"Even if we did, Pakistan has closed the border." His body felt powerless, his mind numb. The Taliban would return, maybe in five minutes, a day. He went outside, aching to turn back, grab Galaya's hand and run, leave the kids –

Oppress not the orphan, the Koran said. But when had he done so?

He walked purposefully through the darkness. At night the Taliban shot at any sound. In these rubbled alleys the mines so hard to see. With a screech something burst underfoot – *cat*. He caught his breath. *Go ahead of me*, he begged it. *Set off the mines.*

A green muzzle flashed and a bullet smacked beside his head spattering brick. He dove among broken walls and squirmed head-down along the shadows, tearing elbows and knees, halted gasping then ran at a crouch along a battered wall past the Haji Yaqub mosque to the old bus depot where the Taliban trucks were parked.

Quieting his breath he waited outside the wall till he heard a guard walking back and forth mumbling a Sura. Then he crawled silently as he could along the wall into the depot.

There was only one way to drive a truck out – through the front entrance where the guard patrolled. The last truck in the first row was a canvas-backed troop transport, far enough away that the guard might not hear him. He could see the guard now on the far side by the wall, a moment's rosy glow against his young face, rifle slung loosely off his shoulder.

After a while the guard stopped pacing and sat against the column on one side of the entrance, his features occasionally lit as he sucked on his *khief* pipe. Ahmad tugged a brick from the edge of a shell hole. When he reached the entrance the guard was still sitting with the rifle across his lap. Ahmad moved closer.

How do you do this? He smashed the brick down on the young man's head. The brick shattered; the guard grunted and leaped forward, fell on his face. Ahmad grabbed the rifle and drove the butt down on the young man's head; with a clatter the magazine fell off and he tried to shove it on but it wouldn't fit. He dragged the young man into the shadows and clutching the gun and magazine ran to the truck.

Now how do you do it? In an American movie once he'd seen them reach under the dashboard and cut some wires and put them together and the engine started. He ran to the wall and scuffed along it till there was a tinkle of glass, picked up a piece and ran back to the truck.

The Taliban could already be at the orphanage, have Galaya. He yanked at the wires, sawed through three and joined them but nothing happened. He found another wire under the dash and cut it, kept linking them in different ways till suddenly the truck lurched forward, banged, and died. He touched them again and the engine caught and he drove fast out the gate.

The street was black. He drove slowly, no lights. The truck gasped and died. He sat a moment in the dark fighting back tears, tried it again but it would not catch. Risking a match he glanced at the gauges. The fuel gauge showed empty. There was an empty twenty-liter fuel can and a piece of plastic hose in the passenger footwell. He grabbed them and ran back to the depot. The guard was gone.

He ran to the last truck, could not find the gas cap. *There* – under the bed of the truck. He slid in the hose and sucked on it till the diesel fuel came gushing into his mouth, spit it out and turned the hose into the can. When his own tank was full and he had an extra full fuel can in the cab he drove slowly back to the orphanage.

He and Galaya ran from room to room waking the children, shuffling them in blankets into the truck. Two-twenty a.m. With luck they could be in Pakistan by dawn.

The truck's one headlight jiggled on the bumps and cast a sallow jerky glow over the road and the barren huts and rocky fields along it. Twice jeeps came the other way but no one stopped them. "Light another one," he said.

"Three left," Galaya said. The match snapped in her hand, but in its brief glimmer he'd seen the gauge was under a quarter full. He'd put in the extra twenty-liter fuel can in Jalalabad; this was all they had. And going uphill used it faster.

On the upslopes the truck popped out of gear so he held the gearshift with one hand and steered with the other. Through the spiderweb bullet hole in the windshield he watched the sky lighten. The engine died; he coasted over the top of a knoll and on the downhill it caught again. On the next uphill it stopped.

The stars were paling. With Ahmad leading and Galaya in the rear they walked single file up the road and reached the border as a tiny yellow sun edged over the white peaks.

The Taliban guards by the crossing gate sat by a fire of plastic bottles and chunks of tire. "Show us your departure permit," one said.

"We're from Charikar," Ahmad said. "No one gave us a permit."

The guard adjusted his AK. "Go back to Charikar and get one."

Ahmad glanced behind them. "The kids can't walk that far."

"God will protect them." The guard lowered the AK. "Go."

"Please," Galaya said through the mouth grill of her *burkha*, "let them through."

"Don't speak, woman." The guard turned his back, knelt to the fire.

"I could be your sister."

He tossed his head, waving her off. "I'm taking the children through," she said. "Shoot us if you like. If you think God wants that."

"*Wait!*" Ahmad cried, but she bent under the crossing gate, beckoned the children. She held the gate part way up as one by one they ducked under and walked up the road. Fearing a bullet between his shoulders Ahmad followed the last child into Pakistan.

Safe. Ahead a sea of tents, rickety tables of merchants selling rice and barley, trinkets and guns. Tears ran down Ahmad's face. "Let's find the children food," Galaya said.

By evening the children were bedded in two large tents, their bellies full of barley. He and Galaya lay side by side. He found her hand. "Tomorrow I'll talk to Doctors Without Borders. Maybe meet someone who knows our friend the doctor."

He heard a rustling, one of the children settling in no doubt. A hard hand gripped his mouth, a blade at his throat. "Silence," the voice whispered.

Galaya whimpered once. The hands yanked him up and

twisted a sash over his mouth. In the semidarkness someone raised a knife in front of him. "Make one tiny noise," he said, "and the woman dies."

One on either side they hustled him between the silent tents on which the moon gleamed softly, down the hill past the embers of cooking fires, the quick steps of Galaya and two others behind them. One went ahead to bend down the barbed wire, standing on it with his rifle pointed at them as they crossed back over it into Afghanistan.

"A HUNDRED MILLION," McPhee took a handful of peanuts off the black glass table between them, "is what they say you could've made off the Gulf War."

"Buying crude long?" Jack shook his head. "I told you back then the idea was sick."

McPhee got comfortable in his leather armchair, glanced out the glass wall at the first headlights on the streets 110 stories below. "Clinton's signed a new Directive, to kill Bin Laden. In Home Office it's Ackerman's."

"Why just Bin Laden? There's a hundred million wannabe Islamic terrorists out there. Another hundred million Wahhabis, God knows how many other crazies."

"*That's* why *I'm* here."

"Clinton *knows* Bin Laden was ours?"

"Not yet. And he doesn't know the Bush thing."

"The Bush thing?"

"Protecting Bin Laden."

"Goddamit maybe *I* should tell him." Jack finished his Lagavullan, signaled for another. The day had begun with Leo's complaining about school, Sarah arguing with Sophie, then three cancelled crude contracts, staff infighting, a sick secretary, and a tanker caught in a storm off Spain and two days late for delivery to Esso's Fawley refinery in England. "What do you want from me?"

"Ackerman asks can you visit Wahid, try to learn where Bin Laden is."

"What for? We won't hit him. We don't ever do what we say, do we? Remember in the Gulf War how Bush incited all the Nassiriyah Shiites to rebel against Saddam, then let him chopper them to death? Thousands of them? Then how we incited the Kurds... and let Saddam bomb the shit out of *them* –"

"That was Bush. The Saudis told him they didn't want Iraq to be a democracy, make them look bad."

"I've never told you about this – still can't. But imagine a situation where we've been hit by terrorists, like in Lebanon. Lose lots of people. And one of our guys goes in and finds the terrorists' base. Tells Home Office *the next day*. And Home Office does nothing..." He shook his head. "And now you want me to intercede again? With Wahid?"

"You heard what happened? With Saddam?"

"I'm outside the loop. Where I want to be."

"We recruited a bunch of his top officers, to take over when we do a coup d'état. They all had phones, direct lines to Home Office."

"That was stupid."

"Turns out Saddam's intel guys have been studying all our coups, and figured us out. They arrested, tortured and executed the whole bunch. Then one of Saddam's intel guys calls Home Office on one of those phones, says "All your men are dead. Pack up and go home.""

"That is awful. Like when we fed the Shiites and the Peshmergas to him."

"Every war has its expendables. Christ, you know that."

"Every time we kill people for some strategic reason we're assassins."

"Churchill and Coventry?" McPhee watched a wisp of fog flit past the glass wall. "Ever count all the people you *know* you've killed? I've killed at least sixty, maybe a hundred, if you include probables." McPhee chewed his lip. "It's why we crash and burn, guys like us. The drugs and booze, the shitty lives on weird little islands –"

"I haven't crashed and burned."

Wearily McPhee shook his head. "I hope you never do."

Beyond the glass the fog shifted and folded about itself, reflecting and shimmering. McPhee glanced up. "Jesus! Is this building *moving*?"

"Supposed to. Bends with the wind."

"Spooky." McPhee raised a finger. "You know about the Saddams?"

"Him and his sons? So what?"

"I mean S-A-D-M – *Special Atomic Demolition Munitions*. The Soviets' friendly backpack nukes."

"We've got the same damn things. The Davy Crocket, the W-54 – one man can carry it in a suitcase, in the trunk of a car, leave it somewhere and blow up a whole city."

"The Soviets still have a shitload. And a lot of them have vanished."

Jack sat back pinching the bridge of his nose. "What about it?"

"Bin Laden has some."

"You're not going to get me back Inside, Owen. Not for anything."

"There are things our country *asks* us to do –"

"Like they taught us in Sin City: *Some orders are immoral to obey.*"

"Yeah? Which ones?"

"The ones that do unnecessary harm."

"That's a nice idea. *Necessary harm.*" McPhee tapped his ring on the table edge. "Clinton and Gore aren't like Bush. They want Bin Laden."

"We'd just let him go..." Jack finished his whiskey. "Every day I thank God for my wife and kids. Every meal I thank God that I'm alive to eat it."

"You got a great family. You and Sophie are so close... Maybe I'm jealous?" McPhee chuckled to cut the seriousness of what he'd said. "Not that *I* believe in marriage." He stood. "Speaking of Sophie, here she is!"

She dropped her raincoat on a chair, hugged McPhee, kissed Jack and sat with her hand over his. "What I don't understand," McPhee said to her, "is what you *see* in this guy –"

She ordered a Guinness. "He's not who he seems."

McPhee drained his glass. "And Doctors Without Borders?"

"Growing fast. Seems to be no end to suffering in the world..."

"Horrible, the way the world is," McPhee said agreeably.

"Most of it caused by wars."

"Too bad it's foggy," Jack said. "No matter how many times I come here I still get blown away by the view."

"Windows on the World," McPhee said amicably. "We're high enough to see half the damn way round it."

"What people don't say," she said, "is how beautiful these towers are. Imagine building two whole cities in the air. When two thousand years ago we lived in caves."

"It's politically correct," Jack said, "to put them down."

"When people feel safe," McPhee said, "they get arrogant and stupid."

Sophie gave him a hard look. "We're back to the Military Theory of Evolution, I see."

"Yes, Maam," McPhee smiled at her. "Show me a better one."

For a moment the fog cleared and they could rooftops far below, tiny little boxes. "*Those*," Jack said, "are the tops of other skyscrapers."

"There's a French guy *climbs* buildings like this," McPhee said. "With no rope."

"Just being out there and looking down," Sophie shivered, "would kill me."

The First Stone

OUT OF THE DARKNESS the telephone screamed. Jack grabbed and it clattered on the floor and he scrabbled round for it and pulled it up. He glanced at the bedside clock. *3:17.*

"Jack," the voice said, "it's Levi."

"Levi what the fuck?" He switched on a light. "What're you calling at this..."

"You'll know soon enough, but I'd rather you heard it from me."

"For Chrissake *what*?"

"Al-Qaeda just blew up our embassies in Nairobi and Dar es Salaam. I got the news twenty minutes ago."

"Oh Jesus. How many killed?"

"Hundreds in Nairobi. Thousands wounded. In Dar es Salaam we're not sure yet."

"Oh sweet Jesus here we go again. What kind of bomb?"

"Truck bomb."

"Can't you guys *ever* learn?"

"Owen was there..."

"McPhee? *Oh Christ no*! Where? What's happened to

him? *Tell me!*"

"I'm sorry, Jack."

"You bastards." Tears were running down the inside of his throat. "You bastards!"

"We think there's an Afghani connection. I'd like you to meet me over there soon as possible. We don't have anyone else who knows the background, speaks the language."

"You telling me it was our *mujihadeen*?"

Ackerman was silent a moment. "People linked to Bin Laden."

Jack glanced at Sophie, who had sat up watching him. "I'll try to catch the Concorde to London, then BA to Nairobi..."

"No. I'll have a Gulfstream pick you up at La Guardia. He'll have to refuel in Rabat. You can be in Kenya tonight. How soon can you leave?"

Jack checked the clock: *03:21*. I'll be at LaGuardia by four-thirty."

"Oh dear God poor Owen," Sophie sat beside him wiping away tears, one arm round his shoulder. "It never stops, does it? It never *never* stops."

"I have to go back *in* for a while. I have to find out who did this."

She looked away, biting a finger. "It won't bring Owen back." She cleared her throat. "You have two children..."

"If we don't stop these bastards now –"

She stood, suddenly old. "I'll help you pack."

AHMAD KNELT BLINDFOLDED, wrists bound behind him. There seemed to be seven of them in a semicircle before him, Wahid in their middle. A kerosene lantern hissed overhead, its light slipping through a crack in the top of his blindfold.

"You understand," Wahid said, "I can't intercede."

"We thank you," a *mullah* said. "We share the sorrow you must feel to have such a brother. We appreciate the strength it takes, the purity of heart, to bring this to us."

"Sadly, my brother would not let the young men go to the *madrasah*. He stole food and medicine our people needed, sold them and kept the money. Even when I gave him generously from my own meek resources he spent it not on the children but on himself."

"You *never* gave me money, brother. I swear by God!"

Someone kicked Ahmad. "Don't take God's name!"

"And he forced those poor orphans," Wahid continued, "on whom he preyed because they had no family to defend them – to go into the streets and beg and steal!"

"This is all lies," Ahmad said. "I know I can't reach you. You've gone too far."

"And worse," Wahid said, "he took into his house a teacher."

"She cleaned the kitchen! She has no part in this –"

"Who twisted the minds of these defenseless girls by forcing them to *read and write*!"

"Forbidden to teach girls," a new voice said. The senior *mullah*, he who declared the sentence. "Everyone knows this."

"Even worse," Wahid said patiently, "this woman is a whore."

The room was silent. "She was raped years ago," Ahmad said. "By *your* men."

"You calumniate us all," the senior *mullah* said mildly.

"When the girls got old enough," Wahid said, "she sold them, night after night, in the back streets of Shari Kuhna..."

"She's done nothing," Ahmad said. "I am the cause of all."

"She must be punished equally," Wahid said. "*She* took my brother down to Hell."

"The Devil snares men's hearts," the senior *mullah* said, "with women's eyes."

They led him blindfolded and bound into the Soccer Stadium. He kept tripping as they hit him with rifles to make him go faster. "The blindfold," he said, "please remove it."

"You're better off not seeing," one of the soldiers whispered, "what's to come."

"Ahmad!" Galaya said.

"Dearest! Where are you?"

"I can't see. I'm tied here, to a pole."

"I love you, dearest love –"

Hard metal smashed his mouth. "Don't talk that way!" a man's voice said.

The crowd grew silent. "Because he was my brother," Wahid called out, "I shall cast the first stone."

DOWNTOWN NAIROBI BLAZED with lights. The Gulfstream pilot banked over the Embassy, the shattered hull of a great building, another flattened beside it, the cranes and masses of people picking over the still-burning ruins under the arc lights.

Jack met Ackerman in the basement security room of the station chief's villa in the suburbs north of Nairobi. "Why were there no Marine guards?" Jack yelled.

"It was a moderate-threat location," the station chief said. "We had Kenyan guards."

Jack stared at him. "You stupid fuck."

"We'd been tracking some of these people." Ackerman sat heavily. "But they left Kenya. One even moved to Texas. We thought we'd scared them off."

"You don't *scare off* these guys," Jack shouted at him. "You *kill* them. *When* are you going to listen? When are you going to *kill* Bin Laden?"

"I didn't fly you over here to take shots at me," Ackerman rubbed his stump, turned to the station chief. "Clarence can you excuse us a few minutes?"

The station chief shut the door. Jack listened to his feet climbing the stairs.

"We've had a plan to hit Bin Laden in Afghanistan," Ackerman said. "Clinton wants it. But Timothy and the other top guys in HO won't back it. The Republicans are all over Clinton for this bimbo thing – he doesn't have the power anymore."

Jack paced, wanting to punch Ackerman, the wall. "So why was Owen *here*?"

"Doing a round of the African embassies, checking security. He was furious about the Kenyan guards. Wanted Marines."

A week later Jack flew back to New York. The Kenyans had arrested several Muslims who'd fought in Afghanistan, low-level gofers. The top guys had vanished, and HO had no idea how to find them.

Not long ago in Windows on the World McPhee had asked Jack to find Wahid, help get Bin Laden. *What if we'd got him? Would that have saved McPhee?*

McPhee in Afghanistan hobbling broken-legged through the snow after Jack and Loxley had rescued him, then saving Jack after the battle of the stepping-stone bridge, then taking him from Ebnecina Hospital to Pakistan, after Sophie had saved him from the Spetsnaz and Hekmatyar's fanatics. At Jack's wedding telling him about El Salvador, then in the white Taurus in Washington Square saying that soon the United States would start a war with Iraq.

"I'm lucky to have a friend like you," Jack had said once. "For when the bullets start flying."

"The bullets are always flying, man," McPhee had answered. "That's the point."

Intel

"THE TALIBAN NEED US." Timothy opened a desk drawer and took out a cigar box. "And we need them."

"You asked me down here to say that?" Jack said. "We need them *dead*."

"That's not operative anymore. Not since Bush got here."

"They shelter Bin Laden and we shelter them? While Bin Laden attacks us?"

"Think Machiavelli, Jack. The world isn't always what we want." Timothy took out a cigar. "You and Wahid al-Din, you're still close?"

"Never were."

From a drawer Timothy took out little gold scissors and cut off the cigar tip. "Just getting a little background." He lit the cigar.

"Strange," Jack said, "it's against the law to import those, but you have them."

"Once we knock over Cuba these'll be available to everyone..."

"Once *we* knock over Cuba? When do *you* lead the

troops up the beach?"

"Same old Jack." Timothy tipped ash into a silver sal-
ver. "Wahid's now in a leadership position in the Taliban.
They have friends here – Kissinger, friends of George Bush.
The story is that the Taliban are good for Afghanistan, that
Bin Laden's okay, we misunderstand him." Timothy waited,
puffed the cigar. "And now that Bush is in, hitting Bin Lad-
en's off the table."

"I remember being here in Langley a few years ago, a
meeting with you and Bernie, with State, NSA – that's what
Reagan was saying about Hezbollah."

Timothy poured Oban into two glasses. "What we *need*,
Jack – given your prominence in the oil business – is your
help with these pipelines we want to run across Afghanistan."

Jack set his glass untouched on a side table. "My help
with the *Taliban?*"

"We're not asking for full-time: we know you're a busy
man. Company to run. Fine wife and son, fine little daughter. How old, you say?"

"I didn't say. Leo's sixteen, Sarah's seven."

Timothy nodded as if he already knew. "Offices in the
World Trade Center, mansion on Fire Island... Done well for
yourself."

Jack glanced round at the huge office, the Isfahan carpets, the neoimpressionists on the walls, the French antiques. "And Home Office has done well by you..."

"That's the secret," Timothy grinned over his cigar, "is
it not?"

"The secret is that the Taliban's protecting Bin Laden.
And that you're one of the guys who doesn't dare to go in
and get him."

"Jack, it's a new millennium. The oil and gas in Kazakhstan, Turkmenistan, and Uzbekistan may be more than *all*

the Middle East – you know that. Unocal wants to build these two pipelines across Afghanistan to keep that oil and gas from passing through Russia or Iran. The gas to Pakistan, the crude to us. Otherwise we have to invade Iraq again, run the pipelines that way, down to Basra..."

"The Taliban are pathological –"

"So was Arafat! Think how many people he's blown up. Now he's got a Nobel Peace Prize for Christ's sake!"

"He's still a murderer. The Peace Prize is a joke – even Kissinger has one!" Jack leaned forward. "If we don't get Bin Laden, far worse things are going to happen. To Hell with Bush – we have to show resolution, strength, justice – or in the Arab mind we're doomed as easy targets –"

"Speaking of Kissinger, he's lobbying for the Taliban now, pushing State to recognize them as Afghanistan's legitimate government so they don't get put on the list of terrorist nations, and so Unocal can get World Bank funding for their pipelines. They've got some ex-diplomats and Congressmen on their side. Speaking of Republicans, Jack, you could help *us*, we could help *you* –" He smiled "– and if you want a piece of these pipelines..."

"I don't want a piece of your goddamn pipelines. And when Bin Laden hits a couple of airliners, or sets off suitcase bombs in US cities, SADMs? Or germ warfare? What then?"

"Get *real*, Jack."

"How many Soviet suitcase bombs are unaccounted for? Out of a hundred thirty-two we *know* were made, eighty-four are missing. That's eighty-four missing one-kiloton bombs that a man can carry on his back and set off anywhere he wants. Each one will take down a whole center city, contaminate it for millennia! And *you* don't think there's a problem?"

"You know that after seven or eight years the plutonium degrades –"

"That's when they're *more* fucking dangerous. And what if they've been recharged? They can go another decade and still be used! And the Palestinians and Chechnayans may already have some – and you don't think there's a *problem*?"

"President Bush is on top of this. He *wants* these pipelines. He feels, and Cheney and Rumsfeld agree, it's safe to work with the Taliban."

Jack set his glass on Timothy's desk. "You tell Kissinger to shove his Taliban pipelines up his Machiavellian ass."

"I'll be sure to tell him that." Timothy said sarcastically as he snuffed his Cuban cigar. "Levi wants to see you on the way out."

"WE'VE GOT NEW INTEL," Ackerman said, "something big's coming down."

"Not according to Timothy," Jack said. "What kind of big?"

"An attack. Here. We're not sure what kind. We've told President Bush it's an emergency, we just don't know what it is. Not yet."

"I thought he was in Texas. His six-week vacation..."

"Christ, he's been on vacation since he got in the White House. Anyway, I flew our Al-Qaeda team down to Crawford last month, laid it on the table."

"What kind of attack, Levi?"

"A multiple hijacking, that's what we think. We want heightened security on all passenger flights, but Bush won't do it."

"Won't *do* it?"

Ackerman shrugged. "He blew us off and went fishing."

JACK CAUGHT the evening shuttle back to Newark. Ackerman's Intel was more than upsetting... Timothy sucking up to the Taliban, Kissinger backing them at State, Bush protecting Bin Laden. How had things got so upside down?

He shaded the window with his palm trying to see the stars, remembering them thick as shattered crystal above the Panjshir heights, in the Sawtooths, in Tuamotu where the whales swam, high over the Alaska tundra. But all he could see was the arc lights of freeways and bridges, cities and suburbs overlapping in blazing spider webs. A whole system that would break down without oil.

To change the world you needed power. But you didn't get power without evil. So to change the world you had to be evil. But if you were evil you liked the world the way it was.

The middle-aged elegant woman next to him in First Class glanced across at his copy of the *Washington Post*. "I can't *believe* they'd do that," she said.

He turned from the window. "Do what?"

"France – look at that story – they're forbidding Muslim girls to wear the veil."

He glanced down at the paper. The only good news he'd seen all week.

"Don't they believe in freedom of religious expression?" she said.

He felt unutterably weary. "They've also forbidden the Muslim practice of genitally mutilating girls – you know about that?"

She looked at him primly. "I don't believe so."

"They cut off the clitoris and often the labia too. So the woman has no interest in sex. And if she doesn't submit to her husband she gets beaten and thrown in the street. Or killed."

She huffed, not believing him. He wanted desperately to make her understand, this well-meaning woman who had never been beaten for not wearing a veil or for speaking in the presence of men. "The French have always outlawed all religious manifestations in school," he said. "The crucifix, the skull cap, veils – any of that crap."

"I still think it's wrong." She turned away.

He felt depressed beyond measure. How do you defend a society that doesn't see the dangers you're protecting it from, sentimentally attached to what it believes is its own liberality and good-heartedness?

The standard dilemma for warriors throughout time. Maybe you're supposed to just ignore the society you're fighting for, just do your job. *But that's not my job any more.*

In the taxi from Newark Airport into Manhattan he felt better, seeing the city's incised diamond canyons, home and workplace of millions on a tiny isle, the most extraordinary single human achievement on earth. And his two beloved towers rising high above it, nexus of the world.

Fire Island

"**H**ERE COMES THE SUN," Jack hummed as he carried his double espresso onto the rooftop te race outside their bedroom and set his cup be- side Sophie's on the glass table. He kissed the top of her head, inhaling the fresh scent of her hair, smiled round at the soaring blue sky and the roofs of other buildings turning golden in the sunrise, stretched luxuriously and sat beside her, tugged aside her hair to kiss her cheek, slid a hand into the folds of her white terrycloth bathrobe and up her thigh.

"Stop that!" She slapped at him absent-mindedly, read- ing the *Times*.

He slid it higher. "I'll never stop this."

"Can you believe this story?" Sophie shook the paper fiercely. "This crazy terrorist he hijacks a plane in nineteen seventy-one and now, *thirty years later*, they find him! Liv- ing in plain sight in Mount Vernon! Under his own name! Don't they even *try* to track them down, these people?" She shoved his hand away.

"That's domestic, Honey. The Feebies." He sipped his coffee, strong, bitter and delightful, glanced over her shoulder at the paper. *Violence in the Middle East*, a headline noted, *Despite Plans to Talk*.

"It never changes," she nodded. "That headline."

He slid his hand up her thigh again. "Tha's why I don' pay it *no* 'tention no more," a mimicked Southern accent.

She grabbed his hand, nibbled his lip, flicked her tongue at his. "The kids'll be up in a moment –"

"Honey it's been *so* long –"

"Don't be silly... We have years and years to do it."

He glanced up. "Look at this sky! A magnificent day!"

She laughed. "You nut!"

He crossed to the edge of the terrace and looked down into Christopher Street, the people and cars small and busy below. As always his gut recoiled at the height, his mind imagining the fall, the scrabbling at brick, the awful smash of concrete. But if he hated heights why did he live in a penthouse and work atop an office tower?

He went inside to the head of the stairs, called "Leo!", grabbed a battered Wilson football from his bedside table. "Leo!"

Leo clattered down the stairs, running shoes untied, eighteen, long-haired, unshaven. "Re*lax*, will you?"

"Don't be too long," Sophie called. "I want to leave by eight."

He went back and kissed her, carried away by the sweet taste of her lips and their solid feel on his. "You have to help me, Doctor... my little guy may not make it till tonight."

She glanced past his shoulder: Leo had gone. She slipped a hand down and squeezed him gently. "Getting to be such a big boy already. But I think he'll be fine..."

The ache for her kept rising inside him. "Let's go back to bed, for just a minute..."

"I want to too, Darling, but there isn't time –"

She was right, but still... Passion was supposed to cool

after years together, wasn't it? But theirs never had, not from the first days in Paris, nor had his loving her diminished since the first time he'd looked up from the bloody hospital bed in Kabul into her green eyes – she'd been the angel of desire to him then, and still was... In how many ways had she saved his life? He kissed her again, not wanting to stop. "We'll make up for it tonight."

He and Leo jogged west on Christopher Street past Greenwich then downtown. Leo pushed ahead then slowed for him as they broke west toward the River then south on the jogging path along the highway, flipping the football back and forth. "I told Mrs. Gravitch I wouldn't be in to-day," Leo called, "that I'd give her my report Monday."

"You tell her why..." Jack panted, already winded, "you aren't going... field trip?"

"I said we go to France every summer so why do I need to see the Cloisters again?" Leo chattered on about how silly to dismantle abbeys in Europe only to rebuild them on the Hudson, and do you suppose the surf will be up at Fire Island this afternoon so he could use the boogie board, and after a while Jack just listened as they jogged, too winded to talk.

At Battery Park they took turns running and passing, Leo gunning them fast and flat, Jack lobbing them, favoring his bad shoulder. Leo yanked one down and trotted back to him.

Jack pump-faked. "Go deep!"

"What *is* this?" Leo reached for the ball. "*You* go deep."

He smiled at this tough gentle kid he loved so much. "*I'm* not the one who wants to make wide receiver at the Point! *You* go deep!"

They turned uptown, the World Trade Center on their right. Jack counted down 12 floors from the top of the North Tower to his office, imagined the sun pouring in, the computers humming sleepily and waiting for his people to bring them to life.

When they got home Sarah was eating Raisin Bran with sliced banana, watching the Today Show and listening to K-ROCK. "Television rots your brain," Jack said.

"Daddy stop fussing," she said through a spoonful. "It's current events – we're 'sposed to know what's happening in the world."

"And that music! All they think they need any more is a tattoo and a guitar."

"Don't say 'any more', Daddy. It dates you."

Sweetheart, I *am* dated... First date I ever had with your mother, time stood still..."

"No more puns. You promised –"

He made another espresso and sat beside her. "Yuck," she said. "You should take a shower."

"You don't have current events today. You're coming with Mother and me to the office so she can take you to the dentist at eleven. Then we're going to Fire Island."

"I *won't* wear braces. I'd rather have buck teeth. You have buck teeth, Daddy, sort of."

"I do *not*!"

"– and *you* never wore braces. Mommy has little teeth and mine are going to be like hers."

"How do you know?"

"Because we're both girls, silly."

Sophie came in fluffing her shower-damp hair out, still in the white terrycloth. "Someone called from the Saudi Oil Ministry while you were gone. Wants you to meet some deputy minister, first thing, at the Plaza. Name's by the phone."

"What the Hell for? You tell him I was busy?"

"The secretary said it was very important –"

"*Whose* secretary?"

"Dammit go look on my note!"

"Mother!" Sarah pointed at them. "Stop arguing! You too, Daddy."

7:22 on the kitchen clock. "Nearly three-thirty in the afternoon in Riyadh." Jack chuckled. "Someone's working late."

Karim al-Saleh, the note said. *Plaza 9:00.* "Who is this guy?"

"He wants to meet you before the markets open." Sophie snapped off the television.

"*Moth*er!" Sarah protested.

"You know the Ministry," Sophie said, ignoring her. "All nephews of some sheik or other. With his four wives and twenty concubines taking up God knows how many rooms at the Plaza he's got to pretend to be doing something."

"No, he's got some deal going on the side, sold some crude short, wants to burn it in the market. I'm not going."

"Jack!" Sophie slapped the orange juice pitcher on the table. "This is what you *do*, remember? You *deal* with these assholes."

"They're not assholes," he grinned. "They're President Bush's close friends."

"I'm leaving." Sarah got up. "You two are insupportable."

Sophie giggled. Jack grabbed Sarah, tickling her ribs. "That's French, not English, sweetheart." He looked at Sophie over Sarah's head. "So I see this Saudi for half an hour... If he's Feisal's guy what can it hurt? Then I meet you three at the office –"

"Can I go with you, Daddy?" Sarah wriggled free, arms round his neck. "I *won't* go to the orthodontist. Daddy *please*?"

For an instant he wavered. Just her presence in the taxi uptown would be a joy. How she saw so much he never did or had forgotten how to see. How she *inhaled* life. But bringing her to the Plaza made no sense, and to an Arab would be an offense. "You go with Mother, darling."

With a dissatisfied, alien feeling he showered and dressed, a plain blue shirt, a hand-tailored Paris pinstripe rather than the regular bespoke suits from London, a crimson tie – red is the color of aggression, and with the Saudis it was always good to be subtly incursive.

He should relax; life wasn't always war... And he wasn't who he'd been; the world was safe now. And to have this lovely family – so much happiness – how had he deserved it?

SOPHIE rinsed off the bowls and put them in the dishwasher. "Brush your teeth good," she called to Sarah who stalked off tossing her hair. The dishwasher wasn't full but Sophie ran it anyway, thinking *we won't be here tonight.*

How lovely having a weekday in Fire Island, nobody there, to sit on the porch and watch the surf roll in. At night in bed, Jack close as her own skin. Another month and it'd be too cold at night to leave the windows open and you'd barely hear the ocean any more.

She ran the hair dryer one last time, angry at the few gray strands in the brush. Everyone gets old. Everyone dies. Her father in his white sweater vest, his white moustache, in his rocker on the porch in Normandy. "You've got a wonderful husband, Sophie. You've got Leo and Sarah. And think of all the lives you've saved. Of what you've already done with your life. It's time to make peace with what you've got."

"IT'S STUPID getting braces," Sarah said over the roar of the incoming subway. "My teeth aren't even grown up yet. Who *knows* what they'll be like?"

"What a mutant," Leo said. "*I* didn't have to have braces."

Sophie dug three tokens from her purse. Never enough time, she thought. You think you're catching up but more new things keep cascading down.

The subway clatter drowned Sarah's retort. *Downtown Investment Bubbles*, yelled a headline of the *Post* in a man's hands. *Data Processors – Double Your Income!* an ad on the side of the subway car promised.

The North Tower elevator was packed; she had to squeeze the kids in beside her. "It was great food," a woman was saying, "but the place was *so* loud."

"My boss just had a baby," a man said. "Today's her first day back."

The elevator raced up the shaft. Everyone fell silent. A bell bonged and the top floor numbers lit. When it slowed Sophie felt lightheaded. She thought of the long dark hole dropping back down. *That's silly*, she reminded herself. *It's safe.*

Eight-thirty and already the office was full. *Jack has such good people.* "You want to stay out here with Patrick?" she said to the kids, "or come in Dad's office?"

"I'm going to work on Daddy's computer," Sarah said.

Leo sprawled on the office couch poking his Game Boy. Sophie sat at Jack's desk, glanced away from the papers stacked across it. Strange how this paper had made its way high up inside this tower, paper with the power to make or lose money, that could change lives.

"What's 'adolescence'?" Sarah held out printed pages. "I got this off the internet."

It was a monograph from the Harvard School of Dentistry, *Jaw Patterns Not Set Till Early Adolescence.* "Much early retainer work may not be necessary," it said.

"Do braces give you headaches?" Sarah held up *Maxillary Anomalies Resulting from Inappropriate Orthodontic Procedures.* "Jaw and headache pain, as well as bite abnormalities," said a boldface box, "may be due to premature or invalid installations."

"I'm printing out nine others!" she added.

Sophie laughed, leaning back in the chair. "Darling don't ever become a lawyer."

"Okay, Mom – you give up?"

Sophie sighed. "I'll call Dr. Schwarz's office and cancel. Till your Dad and I can –"

"That plane! What's it *doing*?"

A jetliner too low. Coming between the buildings. Curving on one wing coming crazily closer and closer then hit with a brain-crushing roar and the building exploded knocking her down in shuddering raging fire and smoke. She couldn't find Leo, tried to stop Sarah's screaming then realized it was her own, dragged her from the caverned floor, people and desks and chunks of concrete tumbling into flames. "*Leo!*"

The ceiling kept falling. Sophie couldn't see or breathe the boiling black smoke and flaming kerosene, couldn't hear through screaming metal. Hair on fire she crawled with Sarah to where the window had been, air howling in, then the backwash almost blew them out. "*Leo!*"

Sarah pointed at the hole. Her skirt caught fire; Sophie rolled on it and it stuck to her, flaming. They stumbled through a shattered wall, the air unbreathable, staggered tripping over cords and cables, chairs, a body, bookcases, piles of paper, feeling for the door. It was shut but the wall was half-gone and they squeezed into the corridor. A woman grabbed them yelling "*This way!*" and shoved them along the corridor to stairs where flames seethed up.

"Stay here!" Sophie ran back into the office. "*Leo!*" With a screech of metal the ceiling thundered down into the floors below. She ran back to the stairwell and grabbed Sarah, holding her breath against the blazing air.

These steps coiled down into hellish fire. Sophie fell and

Sarah landed on her, got up and kept going down. "Go, Mom, hurry!"

Stair by stair Sophie felt the way, tripping on rubble and smoldering bodies. The stairs below crumbled into flames. They ran up three flights, felt blindly along the corridor through blazing smoke to the next stairwell but it was burning. The next stairwell and corner of the building were gone, nothing beneath it. Sophie saw blue sky and far below the tops of skyscrapers.

The building shuddered. People were caught along an edge with no floor behind them. A man caught fire and jumped. She found the fourth stairwell and they ran down it past corpses and rubble and blazing debris, the melting concrete slippery. It was hard to go down against the tornado of fiery wind howling up the stairs. Her wrist hurt terribly and she realized it was broken. Ninety floors to go.

The building yawed, tipping. *Eighty more floors.* "Hurry!" Sarah yelled.

Voices came from below. "Go back up!" A husky man, face and hair burnt. "Stairs gone," he gasped. "Go up!"

"There's nothing up there!"

"The roof! Helicopters!" They ran up through the searing air that would not let them breathe. Sarah fell; the man grabbed her and they ran higher, over burning bodies and rubble.

He fell across the stairs. Sophie tried to pull him up. He pushed her away. She grabbed Sarah and kept climbing, the fire screeching like a hurricane.

Daylight now above the smoke. Ten more to go. Nine. A helicopter, that sound? The last stairs, the shattered door, people crying, calling. "Once they get the fire out," a man said, "we can go down."

"We made it," Sarah wailed. "Oh God Leo."

Terror of falling off the edge, the building swaying. The

roof of people waiting, kneeling praying begging watching. Talking on cell phones, weeping, holding each other. A man alone by the edge looking out over the city.

"Where's the helicopters?" Sophie asked a woman with broken glasses.

"Not yet," the woman coughed.

"We're safe now Mom," Sarah begged, "aren't we?"

The building yawed. Through seething heat the gray-blue horizon danced, the perfect blue sky, the glistening city far below.

Helicopters please save us.

THERE WAS NO ONE at the Plaza named Karim al-Saleh. "He must be here," Jack said to the desk clerk. "He just called me. I mean his secretary did."

The clerk made a show of glancing down the computer screen. "Look under A," Jack said. He felt nervous, edgy, tried to hide it. "Or under S."

From the Plaza's front steps he called the Pierre and the Waldorf Towers, annoyed at Sophie because maybe the secretary in Riyadh had said another hotel. But Sophie never got things wrong. And no, there was no one staying at either hotel under that name.

In the Koran, he remembered, Saleh was the messenger God sent the infidels, telling them to believe. And when they did not God brought down upon them a great catastrophe. His Nokia buzzed: Sophie. "This guy's not here –" he started to say crossly.

"A plane hit us!" she screamed, "everything's on fire, I'm on the roof with Sarah –"

The phone died.

HE RACED DOWNTOWN in a taxi, kept calling Sophie but there was no signal. Flashing police cars blocked

Broadway. "Drive on the sidewalk!" he yelled at the driver but it was jammed with screaming people so he leaped out and ran through them, gasping and choking, falling and running, torn and bleeding, in the wail of fire engines, scream of sirens and crash of the flames so high above, pieces of building thundering down, a dead man, necktie over his shoulder, two firemen holding up another, a running woman smashed by a chunk of wall, a police car howling through rubble past a blazing fire engine, firemen and cops running towards the Towers, bodies flattened in pools of blood.

The ground shook, tilted. From above came a gnashing of concrete and steel, wailing wind and fire and the day turned black. Someone shoved him down concrete stairs. The earth thundered, smashed him sideways into a wall, knocked him the other way off the stairs onto a concrete floor.

Choking, deafened, blinded, his arm broken, Jack scrambled over mounds of concrete and twisted steel into what had been a street. White debris hissed down like snow.

A mountain of roaring darkness where the tower had been. People staggered through blazing streets past crushed fire engines and burning cars.

A room of voices crying and screaming and yelling orders. He could not breathe, went outside, couldn't breathe.

He circled the rubble past half-blinded weeping stragglers, medics and cops. "Sophie!" he screamed, "Sarah! Leo!" till his burnt voice was a hiss. He saw Sophie lying in the street half-crushed under a concrete slab but it was another woman with bulging eyes.

He glimpsed them in the distance and ran but it was a blonde woman with a little boy over her shoulder. From a shattered store window he snatched cardboard but could not find a pen so rubbed at his torn arm and wrote their names in blood and carried the cardboard through the streets stopping everyone, but saw no one from his office, no one he knew.

The Nokia still didn't work. He grabbed a ride with an ambulance to West Houston Street and ran home but the apartment was empty. He left a note inside and another on the door saying he'd be back at four. He ran back downtown, pushing away helping hands, cops, crazy people with cameras. "No list yet," a fireman said. Tears and sweat streaked the dirt down his face. "Lots of people got out. Keep looking."

Medics tried to take him. Cops warned him away but he kept going. Cameramen shoved him, strangers pushed microphones in his face and yelled questions.

A cop grabbed his shirt. "You can't go there." She was tall and tough, covered with dirt and blood. A badge on her breast said *Sharpshooter*.

"My family. I have to find them."

"Go to the rescue centers."

"They're not there."

She looked behind her toward the smoking mountains. "Give it time." She steered him back up the street and let him go. "Go home, maybe they're there."

"You need help," a doctor said. "Your arm's broken. Your head's bleeding badly."

A blonde woman grabbed him. "Do you know Bill Hinthorn?" She shook his broken arm. "Have you seen him?" She turned away, grabbed someone else.

When he got home there'd be a message. They'd be there, Sophie weeping and holding him, Leo acting tough, Sarah in his arms. When the plane hit they'd already left for the dentist. But she wouldn't have left till ten, and the plane had hit the North Tower before nine. Maybe they took the morning off, decided to stop somewhere.

Sophie never wasted time like that.

BY NIGHT HE KNEW THEY WERE DEAD. Each time he reached out in his heart they weren't there. He'd been to all the hospitals, read all the lists. He'd called Sophie's parents and his mother and the families of his employees. No one from his office had been found.

For the first two nights he searched, never giving up, going home twice a night to check, each time telling himself maybe they'd be there, weeping in hopeless pain each time he found the apartment empty.

Without the tiniest hope he kept at it for five days. Wandered the streets with a sign, begging for news. One afternoon he found himself before a little church, entered and knelt down between the hard wooden pews in the choking white dust but the only message that came is *they are not alive*.

On the sixth day he had the arm set in a cast and went to Fire Island. He couldn't sleep in their bed, either here or on Christopher Street, couldn't go into Leo's or Sarah's room.

There was no end to pain. Now and forever there would be no end.

Payback. You always get it, sooner or later. In the living room the mantel clock struck nine, the sound a spike into his heart.

The only thing that conquers all is death.

He walked the beach all night and sat looking out to sea. The surf rose hissing up the sand, receded. *All is flux* it said, gaining and losing, gathering and dispersion.

Somewhere across that cold deep were the men who had done this.

And he had helped spawn them.

Sun Tzu

SEVEN DAYS AFTER 9/11 Jack sent three obituaries to *The Times*,

Sophie Craig, thirty-nine, lover of all that is wise and beautiful. Suddenly September 11 in the World Trade Center

Leo Craig, seventeen, a young warrior with his whole life before him. Suddenly September 11 in the World Trade Center

Sarah Craig, eight, future astrophysicist, lover of the unknown. Suddenly September 11 in the World Trade Center,

and drove to DC. It was a cool blue afternoon. His heart was dead, his mouth tasted of metal. The cities, towns, farms, fields and forests, the endless black highways and swarming cars and trucks were artificial, estranged and vulnerable.

It made no difference to wish it had been he. It made no difference trying not to think.

There was nothing but revenge.

But he had helped to cause this. How do you take vengeance on yourself?

AT LANGLEY the mood was bleak. Secretaries moved quietly with bowed resolute faces. The air had a still, cold taste, like the grave.

"We want you with *us*," Levi Ackerman said. "Not on your own."

"Or *we* could kill you," Timothy grimaced yellow teeth. "By mistake."

Jack glanced round Timothy's expansive seventh floor office, the English hunting prints on the walls, the photos of Timothy dressed in camo standing with generals, with Bush and Cheney. "*We* created Al-Qaeda," Jack said. "Then made ourselves their victims."

"That story won't sell, not any longer." Timothy swung his feet off his desk. "When you've been attacked it's time for patriotism. Not self-examination."

"Nearly all those nineteen hijackers were Saudis, the people GW Bush and his father work for. The backers of GW's crappy fake oil company, Harken Energy."

"Jack, you're talking about the President of the United States. Have a little respect –"

"I don't respect crooks. I don't respect liars. I don't respect cowards."

Ackerman patted Jack's knee. "We were crushed. All of us –"

"Yes," Timothy opened a cigar box and selected one, "we're all heartbroken."

"You piece of shit, you don't have a heart to break. And you're both guilty; we all are. Find Al-Qaeda."

Ackerman gripped his stump as if it pained him. "There's a hundred million Wahhabis and other rabid Muslims out there. There's a billion Muslims who listen to them. Their hatred of America, of anything modern, their vileness about women – spewed from mosques, radio stations, newspapers

– how many casualties will it take to root them out?"

"So we stop buying their goddamn oil. Till they change."

Timothy took out a box of wooden matches. "C'mon, Jack, you're an oil man."

"Most of my people are dead. I told my lawyers sell the assets and give the money to their families. I'm going back to Afghanistan. Either with you or on my own."

"Anybody not with us," Timothy lit his cigar, "is against us."

"The opening phase is going to be SF," Ackerman said. "Out of Tampa. Tommy Franks has decided. Sadly, we're in the back seat. *We're* the ones being blamed. Even though we kept begging them to do something, *we're* taking the hit."

"You guys fucked up. You keep fucking up but nothing ever changes."

"So find Wahid," Timothy said. "And bring him over."

"You'll be assigned to a twelve-man SF team," Ackerman said. "As a resource."

Timothy blew out smoke. "Who knows the lingo."

"Our strategy's evolved," Levi said. "We're no longer on a blind battlefield. The JFC has moved to technology warfare – satellites, sensors, linked forces –"

Jack shook his head. "It takes *people* to kill people."

"Transformation," Timothy Cormac said. "That's what it's called."

"I NEED TO KNOW WHO CALLED ME," Jack said as he and Ackerman walked the sad corridor to the elevators and down to Ackerman's office. "That morning just before the planes hit, whoever sent me on a wild-goose chase to the Plaza to meet this Karim Al-Saleh –"

Ackerman punched in his code and clicked the door shut behind them. He sat down wearily, nodded at another chair across the table. "To save you?"

"Someone Inside? Someone *you* know?"

"Bullshit!" Ackerman glared at him. "Christ, if you'd stayed Inside you'd be running this Afghanistan thing now."

"What for? We used them as cannon fodder against the Soviets. When their country was ruined and a million people dead we walked away like we'd never been there."

"Big countries always use little countries to fight their wars, Christ, you know that." Ackerman stared at him bleakly out of sleepless red eyes. "Forty-two times we warned the President. *Forty-two times*! Even the Principals ignored us. Now they're blaming us, calling for intelligence reform."

"Intelligence. Such a stupid word."

Ackerman slapped a folder down on the table. "How long do I put you in for?"

"I want Timothy to admit it. What he's done wrong."

"You're dreaming. He's going to *use* this. He's going to come out on top."

"How many times did I beg him –"

"Timothy does what GW tells him."

"GW belongs to the Saudis. So does his father."

"How do you think Bush senior got to be Director?" Ackerman waved his hand at the building, the Agency. "We all know that."

"He let that plane full of Saudis out of the country one day after 9/11, when everything else was grounded... There were Saudi terrorists and Al-Qaeda on that plane."

"It's not just his special relationship with the Saudis –"

"The Wahhabis."

"– it's the pipeline deal, too. Bush won't do anything to piss off the Taliban."

"I guess it doesn't matter anymore what you do. Just what you say."

"You know where Bush *was* the afternoon after it happened?" Ackerman snickered, "when they got him out of

310

DC? Cowering in a STRATTON basement at Offutt Air Force Base in Omaha. Practically catatonic."

FROM THE TERRACE OF HIS VILLA overlooking Jorm, Wahid watched the dawn and contemplated the genius of God. Had the Koran not predicted this – *Wherever ye be, death shall overtake you, though you be in lofty towers*? Now who would not believe?

But the infidels had also been warned in other ways. Why had they not listened? *If God is mighty and wise, what is His plan*? He beckoned to a boy waiting in the shadows. "Come, little one, rub my neck."

The boy was tall and slender as a young willow, the mascara round his eyes darkening them to pools of black light. His lacy fingers slid down Wahid's neck.

Yet the infidels refused it when the Koran was revealed to them: *How many cities have we destroyed, whose inhabitants lived in ease and plenty? But the Lord did not destroy those cities until he had sent unto their capital an apostle, to rehearse our signs unto them.*

So they had burned, these infidels in their infidel towers. And would burn in Hellfire, never dying, in agony till the end of time. *For God is mighty and wise.*

Holy War, the infidels destroyed and Islam to sweep the world. A Taliban for every country. A *madrasah* for every boy. All over the world.

The infidels had been warned. Why had they not listened? Did they not care?

He tilted his neck to let the boy reach deeper, felt a little shiver of belonging to God, of God filling his body. How often he'd looked forward to Paradise. Terraced gardens, scented trees and voluptuous flowers. Cool streams over mossy rocks into pools where naked boys cavort, velvet water veiling and revealing their golden bodies.

He kissed the sleek skin between the boy's slender fingers. Most men were slaves because they accepted everything they were told without question. The Koran did say that lusting after other men is perversity and abomination, but that referred to the impure bestial copulations of camel herders and the sad conflicted hungers of drunks. God made all men to love each other's bodies, or why would woman be made so ugly, impure, and stupid?

He drew the boy closer. A device for making children, woman. He had a moment's distasteful memory of his mother. Could she have survived, had he tried to save her?

The Koran could not dwell on man's righteous desire for other men, for then all men would desert their wives for each other, and the duty of making children would be forgotten. But he who'd never stooped to consort with women, he was free of the Koran's dictum. As were the boys he took, for were they not too young to marry?

The sky had grown orange, the last stars fading like coals in a fire. Soon the Holy War would come, and like an eagle he would soar over it, high as the sun, the earth renewed by God's purifying fire.

RAWALPINDI WAS EVEN DIRTIER, smellier and more crowded than Jack remembered. There were jeeps and trucks of Americans and Brits everywhere, taxis of journalists and international relief staffers, Pakistani soldiers looking truculent in their ragtag uniforms. Every time a truck of Afghani irregulars growled by he watched them but recognized none.

Bernie Rykoff was there, having worked his PhD in Middle East Affairs to a top Pentagon post, with a belly now, soft and venal. He had a crewcut and spoke in clipped sentences. "Glad you're back." He flipped a chair round and sat astride it.

"Your wise men in Langley didn't know shit. Did they, Bernie?"

"We're flying you up to K2 and choppering you and nine SF and SAS guys into Jorm, north of Edeni. As far as we can tell, Wahid's camp is about twenty klicks from there."

"Don't try to sound military, Bernie."

"When you find Wahid, like Timothy said, you bring him over. Not dead. Alive." Bernie tried to look stern. "He's gonna play a big part in our new Afghanistan."

"IF WE DO FIND HIM," Sergeant Corwin said, "We're going to cut off his balls. Without them he can't get into Heaven. Well he *can*, but all those virgins won't do him any good."

"I hear he's not that way," Walcott the SAS man said. "That he prefers boys."

"Well he won't be able to diddle the boys either," Corwin said.

Walcott ignored him. "Apparently in Heaven their peckers still work. Or why would they blow themselves up? Unless they could get put back together?"

Corwin adjusted his rifle. "Jack knows but he ain't saying. Ain't that true, Chief?"

"When you were here before, Chief," Engle said, "were these people crazy like this?"

"I was here before the Taliban –" He thought about it. "But yeah, they've always been crazy –"

"But *we* tricked the Soviets into invading, right?" Corwin said. "Walcott here, this dumb Brit, doesn't believe me."

"We stirred up the Afghanis with fundamentalism to open a front on the Soviets' *soft Muslim underbelly*, as we called it. Then we started Stars Wars so they had to spend billions gearing up for that. Then we drove down the crude price their economy depended on."

"Classic Sun Tzu," Corwin said. "Force your enemy to prepare for attack in all places. So he can be strong in none."

"Then once the Wall came down and they asked us for help we screwed them over with Harvard economists," Engle laughed, "and now they're really broke."

"Remember what else Sun Tzu said." Jack halted in the low doorway. *"There is no instance of a country having benefited from prolonged warfare."*

Stars filled the sky like shattered glass. He could see the dark outpost walls, beyond them the shadowed village, a bare tree, the starlit valley and black mountains high above it.

He went silently down to the forward LP. "All well?"

"Nothing lately but an owl, Sir," Ray whispered. "Grabbed a rat in that field."

"Amazing, these NVDs. We started to get them when I was here, but the Russians had better ones." Through Jack's NVD the valley popped into lurid greenish yellow, the low mud houses wavering, the mountains arrested in motion. "Guy out there," he said, "taking a leak."

"That's his second one, since I came on."

"Keep an eye on him, but don't let him distract you from something else."

"Yes Sir."

"Sorry. You young guys don't need my advice."

"We're lucky to have you, Sir. I always wanted to meet you. Sorry it's in these circumstances. . . From your perspective," he added after a few minutes, "how are things?"

"When I was with the *mujihadeen* I never knew these guys we're with now. They're northerners, not the same tribe or language as the Taliban. It'll be hard getting them to take on the Taliban, when they've already been beaten by them..."

"I don't trust them."

"I don't either. That's why we keep our own watch."

"I'd die to avenge your family, Chief. And all the others. We all would."

"That's the trouble with war, everybody dies avenging someone else."

Through the NVDs Jack watched the mountains. "When I found my village destroyed, I blamed the Russians. Then later I found out it wasn't the Russians who destroyed it, but Afghanis working for us. I still blamed the Russians because they'd invaded. But in a way we pulled them in, just like we did a decade later with the Iraqis in Kuwait. So who do I blame?"

"You don't think this's right, Sir, hitting the Taliban?"

"Of course it us. But we can't stop there. We have to deal with every fundamentalist Muslim in the world. They're close to getting nuclear weapons, germ warfare. We have to kill the worst ones and intimidate the rest. Still the question is, who's responsible?"

"Beats me, Sir. I'm just here to kill the bastards."

Taliban

FOR DAYS THE BOMBS had fallen. Their thunder kept knocking Wahid down and split his head. The earth leaped and shuddered like a wounded beast. When he stood blood ran from his nose and ears and the earth tilted up to meet him.

Every time they regrouped new bombs came silently out of the sky, terrorizing the survivors with their blasts.

How had this happened so fast? Only weeks ago God had punished the infidels; now everywhere explosions rained down on the Taliban. In the Soviet War the bombs had come from MiGs, easy to see and hide from, but these bombs came from nowhere, from Heaven itself.

How could the infidels have these bombs when the Taliban were God's chosen? And now the infidels had even turned the Northern tribes, fellow Muslims, against the Taliban. Why would God allow that? Why had God made *him*, poor Wahid, endure this?

Was God doing this to test his faith?

He could barely see the praying men in the dust and smoke, the glisten of rifles with which they dreamed they could fight back against the bombs.

The thunder eased as the bombs moved eastward and Wahid crouched weeping and begging the bombs to kill the others and leave him be.

"Praying again?" Suley's voice.

Despite the gloom Wahid could see how Suley's eyes glistened. "You've been smoking *khief* again – you think they smoke *khief* in Paradise?"

"In Paradise there's no need for *khief*."

"You know, do you?"

Suley took his hand. "When my parents died you showed me favor. These things you wanted from me, I did them in thanks. When I fought bravely it was to show you I could."

Wahid stood. Dizziness sickened him. "Now the bombing's stopped, the enemy will come." He climbed over shattered boulders into the dawn that stank of explosions, seared rock and death. Another bomb could come, he thought, wanting to crawl back into the bunker. But death sat in there, waiting and smiling like an unwanted guest.

"Brothers!" he called, his voice hollow in his ears. From outside came a distant crack of rifles. "We are not *snakes* or *toads*. We are not *women*!" He looked for his gun, could not find it. "Our warriors *destroyed* the Devil's towers in the Devil's country of *evil!* Now the Devil is angry and we must fight him! Fear not, for God stands beside us with *His* rifle, and God shall not lose."

"We've lost this fight," a man called. "Let's go home, protect our families."

"That's true," said another. "They won't kill us if we surrender."

"Of course they will!" Wahid shrieked. "Did I not get the weapons and money from them to defeat the Soviets? I know them! They'll torture you, then kill you!"

"There's supposed to be a path across the mountains,"

someone called.

"There's no passage," Wahid shouted. "I know – I herded sheep with my father in this valley. If God wanted us to run He would have made one."

The next bunker had been imploded and no one answered when they called down into its acrid darkness. A wind had sprung up that cut through his coat into his ribs. He thought of his dreams of *jihad* and brushed tears from his beard.

The valley began to fill with light. His ears had cleared and he could hear the steady grumble of trucks. There was no understanding God, he decided as he watched how quickly the trucks came, and behind them hordes of fighters, northerners who had betrayed their Muslim brothers and would burn in Hell forever.

A huge blast knocked him down spouting a great column of dirt and rocks across the slope below them. His ears screamed with pain. He saw the trucks and running fighters had neared, and terror gripped his heart.

"Brothers!" he called, "Fear not to die for God!" He waved and the men ran yelling toward the trucks. As Suley ran past Wahid grabbed him. "Don't go down there!"

"You just said –" Suley gasped.

"That's for the others. Let *them* taste death. *You* go with me."

"They'll be at God's side," Suley spat. "In Paradise."

"The people need you. You shouldn't be wasted here." Wahid ducked as another plane passed. "There's a passage up there, through the cliffs. *Come!* – God wills it!"

FROM THE CAB OF THE FIRST TRUCK Jack watched the bombs explode against the mountain. "God is great!" the driver yelled, "See how He kills them!"

Jack glanced back at Corwin and Walcott gripping the

truck's bed among *mujihadeen*. Fifty yards back, Ray and Engle followed in a battered Hyundai pickup with a wild-eyed driver.

They pulled up a quarter mile from the mountain. Taliban were running downhill through smoke and dust, firing wildly. Ray focused the SOFLAM on them as Engle got on the satellite radio and an F-18 dropped another laser-guided 1,000-pound bomb and the hill seemed to implode, whitened, blurred as the whole mountain shook and a spiral of rocks and dirt tore upward and bodies and shredded clothes and splintered rocks tumbled across the hillside. A northern chief named Abdulla radioed Jack. "The ones who are alive ask to negotiate."

"How many?"

"Forty, they say. Plus twenty wounded."

"Wahid?"

"Gone. One of my men says there's a passage, out the other side."

"*Gone!*" Jack screamed at him. "Goddammit why didn't you guys cut it off?"

"These Taliban may not know it. And in any case that's not how we do it, here."

"How *do* you do it, here?"

"We leave the enemy some room, if we have beaten him. Then if ever in the future *we* are beaten, our enemy will perhaps not destroy us either."

"That way nobody ever wins," Ray said. "So they can always keep fighting."

The prisoners were a surly bunch, stunned and disoriented. "Where's Wahid?" Jack yelled at one with a head wound bandaged by a scarf. The man jumped, surprised to hear him speak Pashto. "You want to go home," Jack said, "or to prison in America?"

"You're feeling proud to have won this battle?" the man

sneered. "It's not because you're a good fighter. Not because you're brave. Only because you have planes and bombs."

"And because God wasn't on your side –"

The man's fist came round and the knife dug a streak of hot pain across Jack's chest. Afghani soldiers pulled them apart, kicking the man and smashing rifle butts down on him.

Jack fell holding his chest. Blood spurted but when he breathed in it didn't bubble and the pain didn't feel *inside* his ribs. *Idiot!*

"It caught in a rib," Ray said, cutting away Jack's shirt. "Hey stop killing that guy!" he yelled at the Afghanis. He probed the wound for bone splinters, applied a pressure bandage and stood wiping his hands on his pants. "Abdulla," he yelled, "I *told* you do a full search on these prisoners! Search them *again*! Jack goddammit translate for me!"

"These bandages are too tight." Jack stood carefully. "Have to go up the mountain, cut off Wahid."

"Fuck that. We're gonna chopper you down to Bagram, get you stitched up. There's three Taliban criticals to go down with you. Corwin'll be there, help you ask questions."

"Bring me the guy who knifed me."

"So he can try again?"

They brought the man, beaten and bloody, held up by two *mujihadeen*, his black eyes blazing at Jack. "I'm sorry they beat you," Jack said.

The man did not answer. "It takes courage, what you did," Jack said. "And it's true, without the planes and bombs we would not have won." He turned to the *mujihadeen*. "Keep this man here. I want to talk to him when I get back."

AT BAGRAM THERE WAS NO SPACE so they took the prisoners to Kabul's Ebnecina Hospital. Walking hunched-over to hold in the wound, Jack limped after Corwin down a corridor.

Something was hideously familiar. As if he'd died here and now come back to die again. The jaundiced halls, the scarred linoleum, the dirty windows, rusty pipes and peeled walls came back just like it had been before.

Sophie bent over him talking to herself in French, "He's not Afghani, this one, despite the beard, God the clavicle's shattered – how the hell can I splint that?"

She'd saved him three times, taken him to Ahmad. He'd told her he'd love her forever.

Sophie please come back. God how I love you. Please let's start again from here.

I wish I'd never torn apart your life.

IN THE CHOPPER back to Jorm he couldn't sleep, the floor clattering its loose rivets, rotor blades thundering, pain no matter how he lay. For three nights now he hadn't slept, felt horribly nauseous and dizzy, wanted to die.

If years ago Sophie hadn't saved his life in Kabul, she and Leo would be alive now and Sarah never would have existed. How could Sarah, so full of life, have never been?

If they'd stayed in Paris? If he'd never told her about killing Leo?

If *he* hadn't helped train the people who killed them?

He tried to stand; the gunner glanced at him. Through the door he saw the coal-black hills, the pilots' faces underlit by the green instruments, their beetle-helmeted heads. What alien breed *was* this spreading across the universe, deadly and uncaring?

Stenciled on the fuselage wall in faded Cyrillic, *Load Ammunition This Side*, and handwritten in Arabic over it, fading too, from the Twenty-first Sura: *How many cities have we overthrown because they were ungodly?*

He saw Wahid coming up from the river in Edeni, beard

glistening.

Nothing's more dangerous, they said in Sin City, *than an enemy who's insane.*

Slowly the towers fell in their cauldron of smoke.

He ached with fatigue yet each time he slid toward sleep, Sophie and the kids were running downstairs as the building crushed them, or waiting on the roof for the choppers till the building dropped away beneath them, or falling a hundred stories in an elevator. Or dying slowly, days and nights, beneath the rubble.

"No one's alive!" He sat up. Inside the dark chopper he could see Corwin and two other SF guys sleeping, the gunner leaning on his gun. "Bad dream," Jack said.

"This is the place for it," the gunner answered.

IN THE CP at Jorm a metal Russian ammo box sat beside his cot.

"Don't open it," Corwin said.

"Fifteen-year-old ammo," Jack said. "All they have, most of these guys." He flipped the top open. "Oh Jesus."

"What?" Ray said. "*What!*"

Matted black hair, a head. Jack kicked the box over, the head rolled out. The man who had stabbed him, the man he'd saved to start a new Afghanistan.

Ray took the box and head outside and threw them down the hill. "We ain't never gonna help these people." He wiped his hands in the sand.

SAND HAILED HIS TENT all night as Jack lay there awake. Bandit came and licked his face and nuzzled him. "You're shivering, Chief," Ray said as they drank *chai*, waiting for dawn.

"Wahid – he's in a cave."

"Relax, Chief." Ray refilled Jack's cup. "You're not going anywhere."

"I just remembered it. The only other person who knew about it was his brother."

"So where's this brother?"

"Wahid had him stoned to death."

Ray sighed. "This fuckin country."

"It's in the hills above Edeni." Jack stood. "We can be there tonight."

"Could we chopper in?"

"He'd hear us. Better by foot."

Ray drained his cup. "You don't see it as retribution, do you, what happened to your family? For something you'd done?"

"For something I didn't do."

"That's crap." Ray put down his cup. "I'll call up the line, see what they say."

"Even without you guys I'm going."

THE FORTY MILES TO EDENI took all day, their trucks weaving round carts of refugees, lines of people, burnt-out vehicles and bomb craters. Jack crouched in the cab, trying to protect his aching arm and bandaged chest. *This is Hell, and I keep coming back to it.*

No refugees were coming down the Little Kowkcheh trail from Edeni, the snake-head buttress above the canyon as evil and ugly as it was eighteen years before when he'd joined forces with Wahid, and four years before that when he'd come up the canyon the first time.

The sun had retreated up the east canyon wall and Edeni's overgrown ruins lay in shadow. He went ahead with Engle through the caved-in houses. No one was there but the rats that rustled ahead as if clearing the way. Engle dropped back to wave the others in.

Outside the school walls a new yew was growing from

the roots of the old. "This's where I taught," Jack said.

"It's a goatfuck," Ray said, "this place."

"Too narrow," Engle said. "From above open fields of fire on both sides."

Emboldened by the dusk the cliffs seemed buttresses of a cathedral. "Let's make like we're setting up here," Jack said. "Then after dark take the trail to the top and RON up there."

Ray glanced up. "How far?"

"Two-three miles. Three thousand feet."

"Fine. I want to stay high."

"I don't trust these Tajiks."

"So we leave them here," Ray said. "Find Wahid on our own."

In the dying light Jack climbed to the rubble where once he had lived in the fellowship and warmth of a stone-age village. Then down the path whose cobbles still showed randomly through the dirt and grass grew in scrofulous patches. One of the Tajik scouts was defecating against a wall and it made Jack angry. He tried to find the threshold into the courtyard where Ahmad's mother had made barley gruel each morning. She'd been Wahid's mother too.

He couldn't find it and turned back toward the school, remembered suddenly a girl saying *If I had twenty oranges I would save them all for my family.*

Figure Eight

THEY CROSSED THE RIVER after dark and ascended the canyon, the steep path slippery with mist. They climbed fast, nobody breathing hard, Jack with just his gun and web gear, the pain of his torn chest taking his mind off the climb.

Part way up was a ledge where they stood looking down at Edeni. Long ago he had liked this place but now feared falling.

At the top he led them to a rocky knoll with clear fields of fire, where they could dig in, take turns eating, sleeping, watching. No fires, soft voices only, spread out among the rocks so almost nothing could get them.

The dark grew colder. Shivering in the rocks, chest throbbing, he waited for dawn.

Dampness fell on the back of his hand. Against his nose. He looked up. Snow. It sifted down like cinders from a far-away explosion. "This sucks." Ray pulled his poncho over his shoulders. "We're going to stand out like a nun's tit."

At first light they moved out, traveling overwatch with a twenty-yard spread, Engle on point with Jack behind him so each time the trail split he could wait and Jack would show him the way.

They crested ridge above the meadow in front of Wahid's cave just before dawn. The juniper by the cave was dead, gaunt branches against the rock. "What if no one's in there?" Corwin said.

"Can't you smell the smoke?" Ray said.

They set up with Corwin and Ray on the angles opposite the cave, an eighty-yard shot, and Engle and Jack to go around the meadow and come up each side. "He's gotta come out to piss," Ray said. "Take him then."

"Man don't piss," Engle said. "Forty years he's held it all inside."

"When the sun comes up," Ray said, "it'll be in his eyes."

Under the new snow the dead leaves and grass made no sound. Jack slipped through the scrub near the cliff. His breathing was loud and he stopped to calm it. He couldn't see Corwin across the meadow among the rocks, nor Ray further down, nor Engle coming up this side to meet him.

A bird twittered. He checked the meadow, the far side, the hill above, could smell the cat-urine odor of the dead juniper ahead. "If they roll out a grenade," Corwin had said, "it'll get anyone near the entrance –"

"Remember," Ray said, "you can't kill him."

"Question is," Engle had said, "how many guys in there with him?"

"Just one, the prisoners said. A younger guy."

"Unless there was already more."

Ten feet from the cave Jack stopped again to scan the meadow, listening for sounds. Another bird called, echoing off the cliff, Mars setting like a tiny ingot.

He tried to remember inside the cave. A tunnel you squirmed through for thirty yards into an anteroom where you couldn't stand and then a larger inverted bowl of a chamber with a fire pit at the far wall.

Engle came up to ten feet on the other side. *Hear anything?* he hand-signaled.

Jack shook his head. Engle scanned the meadow, the far side, the hill above. *I'll listen here*, he motioned. *You move back to cover.*

Jack took off his web gear, boots, and helmet, racked the Makarov and crept to the cave. *What are you doing*, Engle mouthed, waving him back.

Jack slipped into the cave and waited for his eyes to adjust. Every hiss of cloth echoed. He slid forward one elbow, the other, holding the Makarov before him. His breath thundered off the rock. *Anything fired in here will hit you.*

At the last bend in the tunnel the wood smoke smell grew stronger. He waited for a long time but heard nothing. He inched forward and looked into the chamber.

Red coals in the fire pit, fresh-cut wood beside it, a blackened pot, blankets.

Nobody.

"HE'LL COME OUT SOON," Suley said. "Then shoot him."

"I'm tasting this," Wahid whispered. "For years I've wanted it, and now..."

"See – he's coming out! *Fire!*"

Wahid peered through the brush between two rocks. Down in the meadow one American crouched beside the cave as another slid from it. *Jyek*'s dark hair, lithe ruggedness. Wahid nestled the front bead on Jack's chest and touched the trigger. "Fire!" Suley hissed.

"Quiet! Be ready for the two we can't see under the hill here, when I shoot."

"You're afraid!"

Wahid raised his finger from the trigger. "The two below

us are a danger. We should let all four pass by in front, as they leave. It will be easy to hit them then."

"I remember when he was my teacher."

"His dwelling shall be Hell, and an unhappy journey shall it be thither."

THEY CROSSED THE MEADOW in fire team file, twenty-yard spread, Corwin on point, Jack second.

If Wahid wasn't here he could be anywhere. Kabul, Paktia with Pashtùns, across the border in Pakistan, Kashmir. In Saudi where no one could touch him. That evil and horrible place where women are completely enslaved, can't go out without a male family member, have to keep covered from head to toe lest a man see their flesh and be tempted into evil. Where for a woman to uncover her face could get her quickly decapitated by the *mutaween*, the religious police.

Suddenly he felt Leo's little hand in his, like one day years ago walking up Fifth Avenue to F.A.O Schwarz. "Papa," Leo said, "remember in Sin City?"

"Hey," Jack looked down at him, "I never told you about that."

"Colonel Ackerman, he always said..."

"I never told you about him –"

"When making a withdrawal, sometimes to do the Figure Eight?"

"True, even when not expecting contact. Because you're never safe as you think. But how ..?"

"The Figure Eight?" Leo tugged his hand. "Show me!"

His hand was empty. The cliffs above cast down a frigid light. "Corwin!" he yelled, "Figure Eight!"

Any man could call it, in the line or whatever. If he saw something. Felt something. Silly here but what the Hell. Jack followed Corbin east then north again, then east, then south.

There, on the snow. The imprint of a sandaled foot.

He waved the others down. A goatherd maybe. But why no goat tracks? Snow freshly compressed, angled. Someone just ahead.

"YOU SHOULD HAVE SHOT HIM!" Suley hissed. Now we've lost them!"

"Don't speak like that!" Wahid felt the urge to smash Suley's face. "Little sparrow," he said. "Imagine, that's what I used to call you."

"I never was your sparrow."

"Leave now. I'll stay to cover you. We can meet tomorrow in Edeni."

"You'd stay here? For me?"

"Of course. I'll get away too. Don't worry."

"You must!" Suley held him. "I'm sorry, what I just said."

Wahid smoothed the hairs on Suley's wrist. "We'll always be together."

Suley stood. "After my parents died...You were my father... everything."

"Go. I'll protect you."

He waited till the sound of Suley's sandals vanished then scrambled away. After he'd gone perhaps fifty yards came the staccato rip of rifles, voices yelling. Ducking low, sandals slithering on snow, Wahid ran for the knoll on the ridge.

"WOULDN'T DROP HIS GUN," Corwin said.

Jack watched life drain from the young man's eyes. "It's not Wahid."

"Who then?"

"Looks familiar."

"After a while," Engle said, "they *all* look familiar."

"Fire team wedge," Ray called, "twenty yard spread. I'll stay on those tracks, Corwin and Engle on my left, Jack on my right. Remember, we can't kill Wahid."

They went up through the new snow, Jack thinking how Leo's words had saved him. Ahead were the sandal prints of one person. "Tracks," he called. "One set, northeast at two o'clock. I'm checking them out."

These tracks were a man moving fast, and beside them the marks of a rifle butt used as a cane, no, the fool was shoving it muzzle-down into the muddy snow in his haste to get away. Jack ran after him over the ridge, no cover now, not caring.

"Jack!" Ray yelled. "Don't kill him!"

Wahid saw him, scrambled for the cliff edge. He had nowhere to go and turned aiming at Jack. The gun didn't fire; Jack walked up to him and slapped it away. Wahid stepped back, his foot slid over the ledge and he fell, grabbed the grassy edge. "*Please*, Jyek, *please* – I can help you –"

The huge deep canyon sucked Jack's breath away. He thought of Gus dropping through cold darkness, Loxley slipping from the cliff, Sophie and Leo and Sarah in the falling tower.

"You and I, blood brothers," Wahid begged. "*Please* – I'll tell you about Bin Laden –"

With the muzzle Jack pried Wahid's left hand off the ledge. "*Where* is he?"

"Running to Pakistan. *Help!*" Wahid grabbed the muzzle with both hands, his weight skidding Jack toward the edge. "I'll take you –"

Jack dug his heels into the ledge. "You stoned Ahmad to death."

"God makes us do mad things –"

"God's no excuse." Jack slid the rifle sling down his arm. "Anybody can use that."

Ray ran up behind them. "Jack!" Ray yelled. "We *need* him!"

"*Help*!" Wahid called to Ray. "Help me!"

"Goddammit Jack!" Ray reached past him and yanked Wahid up. With his other hand he pulled Jack back. "Let's cuff this bastard and take him down to Jorm."

The new sun had dimmed, Jack saw, a blizzard coming. "I'm done with killing."

"Crap." Ray threw Wahid down and zip-cuffed him. "The killing's just begun."

"I'LL JAIL YOU for this!" Brigadier General Clyde Szymanski yelled. "Your mission was *find* Wahid, not terrify him." Szymanski chomped his cigar stub. *Like a baby's pacifier*, Jack thought. These book generals had watched too many Patton movies, not fought any wars. They thought all you had to do was chew a cigar and act tough.

"So you bring him in hog-tied like a goddamn PW!" Szymanski waved his arms, "and Chrissake what'd you threaten him for?"

Jack waited for two F-18s to thunder over. "To find out where Bin Laden is."

"BL's *my* AO, not yours." Szymanski spit cigar juice into a metal wastebasket. "You better pray Wahid stays healthy and happy. Cause if he don't, *you* go down with him."

"Looking for a second star, are you?" Jack yanked out a chair and sat. "With just a few hundred SF guys we've taken half of Afghanistan, and now Kabul. When the Soviets couldn't do it with a million men in ten years. More than your regular Army could with ten divisions."

Szymanski ignored him. "Wahid's a senior warlord, a guy we can depend on."

"He's going to traffic opium and build Islamic fundamentalism behind your back!"

"Shit!" Szymanski snickered. "My job's winning, not babysitting."

"We can *force* cultural change. Like MacArthur in Japan."

"You heard President Bush. We're not into nation building. The White House says we stick with this Wahid guy."

"When I first knew Wahid he used to shit in the river then go downstream to drink."

"We're gonna have a little council with these Afghans. A whatta they call it, *durga*?"

"*Jirga*. They're for show. Anything important's worked out before."

Szymanski stabbed his cigar at Jack. "*You* can translate."

Jack nodded at a bullet hole in Szymanski's window. "Who's shooting at you?"

Szymanski followed his gaze. "That? That was before my time."

"Wow!" Jack stopped at the door. "Close, huh?"

ONE BY ONE they filed into the circular room. Clan leaders, warlords, opium shippers, the *mullahs* and tribal chiefs who two weeks earlier had fought beside the Taliban. The air was seedy with *chai*, moth-eaten rugs, ashes, spices, and a toxic damp as if the floor had soaked up some of the blood saturating the soil of Afghanistan.

In a new orange-pink robe Wahid trotted in late and sat regally among them. He glanced steadily round, caught Jack's eye and gave a slight smile.

They were all dressed in turbans or headscarves, long cloaks or pajama-like trousers, all bearded. Men in their thirties to seventies, many veterans of the *jihad* against the Soviets and the civil wars that followed. Some wanted peace. And some wanted more war.

"Good group," Timothy said.

"They were losing," Jack said. "So they've jumped on the horse that's winning."

"Tell 'em we're here to discuss the new Afghanistan," Szymanski said, "decide who gets what."

"Friends," Jack said in Pashto, "when the Taliban came seven years ago they promised to unite the country, bring back the King, and heal the bitterness and separation of war."

They watched him, many hostile, some leaning back, sarcastic. "Instead," he continued, "they united the world against you. Brought in foreigners, people from Saudi Arabia who professed to love Afghanistan but have used you for their own ends –"

"You Americans did the same," a Pashtùn chief said.

Szymanski leaned toward Jack. "What the Hell you sayin?"

"Osama's a true believer," a *mullah* said.

Jack turned on him. "Does a true believer bring down destruction on his friends?"

"You Americans were not the same?" the Pashtùn said.

"Keep it short, Jack," Timothy whispered.

"But if God loved Osama," another *mullah* said, "He wouldn't have done this."

"Dammit Jack what're they sayin?" Szymanski snapped. "Tell them our war's not with them Talibans. That we need strong folks to run this place."

"And an interim government," Timothy said, "run by someone not openly Taliban."

"Like this Hamid Karzai guy," Szymanski said.

"Afghanistan is desert and mountains and a few narrow valleys," the second *mullah* said. "We can't grow food for all our people. We must buy it. And for money we must grow opium."

"We can send you food," Jack told him. "For many years to come."

"That's slavery. We want to be independent. And we

have just one thing to sell."

"Tell them," Szymanski interjected, "America doesn't give a damn what Afghanistan does with its opium. We gotta *pretend* we care, but we won't get in your way."

"In return for?"

"Al-Qaeda."

"That's not so easy." Wahid looked round. "It's a big thing to give away."

"The Eagle of the Hindu Kush is right," the first *mullah* said.

"To give up Al-Qaeda," Wahid raised a single finger, the way Jack had seen Bin Laden do in videos, "there is one other little thing –"

"Tell them they can pick the government posts, the Ministries," Timothy whispered.

"*What* other little thing?" Jack asked Wahid.

"I personally must lead the search for Bin Laden. With Zaman Ghamsharik and Hazret Ali. In return for ten million dollars."

"You piece of shit," Jack said in Pashto. "Last week you were begging me for your life."

"It doesn't matter what you think," Wahid continued in Pashto. "This General of the impossible name, and this other old man – Timothay? From now on I deal only with them." He turned to Timothy, speaking English, "Because my beloved brother was teacher, for honor to his memory I like to be Minister to Education."

Lieutenant Colonel Szymanski checked his watch. "Works for me."

"He'll use it to set up *madrasahs*," Jack said.

"What the Hell's that?"

"It'll warp this whole country. All over again."

"Enough talk," Szymanski stood. "I've got a war to win."

"Special Forces has already won it for you," Jack said. "But it looks like you plan to lose it again."

Tora Bora

B IN LADEN'S NEARNESS was a pestilential odor, the smell of a dead rat that infects a whole house.

But it seemed to Jack that what Szymanski and Timothy had said was insane. Why let Wahid, Ghamsharik and Ali take over the hunt for Bin Laden when they were his Taliban allies, his "Muslim brothers"? Was he, Jack, missing something? An agenda he didn't know?

Somewhere a rooster was crowing. Gray December dawn was slinking like a jackal between the hovels and battered buildings of Jalalabad. *MON 12-10*, his watch said. *06:4326*. As he watched it the *26* was *27*, then *28*, soon *35*, then *50*, and as it hit *60* changed to *06:4400* and the little seconds started climbing again. It seemed life was running out, with no gain.

No matter what he'd get Al-Qaeda. Bin Laden. With the United States or without it.

THE JALALABAD ROAD south to the junction of the Pachir-Gandemak roads was clogged with old Soviet Army trucks and Toyota pickups full of Afghani irregulars. Snow lay over the Spin Gar Mountains like new linen. To the east above the Tora Bora foothills the Pakistan border peaks were a white-capped wall, above them 15,600-foot Sikaram blazing in the sun.

"We've got Rangers in reserve," Jack said, "why don't we use them to cut off any retreat?" For a while the truck made too much noise to talk, so he scanned the mountains, looking for places where the Taliban might escape through the snow to Pakistan.

"According to Szymanski," Corwin said, "the Pakis are putting troops on the other side of the ridge." He pointed at Sikaram. "They're supposed to interdict escape."

"The Pakis?" Jack laughed. "The Taliban's butthole buddies?" He lined up the GPS coordinates on the map. "There's a road, looks like a gravel road – all the way from this village up ahead – what's its name, Pachir? – from there across the border to Parachinar in Pakistan. What's to stop them getting out that way?"

Corwin glanced up at the mountains. "Deep snow."

"I don't understand it," Jack said. "Why let the Afghanis take over?"

"We'll be there, painting the caves," Corwin said finally. "Maybe our Afghanis'll get the job done."

"If you were AQ, what would you do?"

"Pull out, slide into Pakistan."

"Doesn't Tampa know that?"

"Tommy Franks does what he's told."

BOMBS BURST BLACKLY over the Tora Bora hills. The air smarted with cordite, burnt soil, and pine resin. They took positions with another SF team on a rocky ridge. Tora Bora rose above them across a steep valley with a dry streambed.

"We've been hitting them since yesterday," the other SF

team's XO yelled over the rifle fire and crunch of high explosives. "Every time we let up they come out, spray some munitions and run back in. They've got a Zeus up there somewhere but we can't see it."

A bullet barked off the rock by Jack's head and sang away. "Random shit," the XO yelled, "but wise to keep your head down."

Jack crawled forward to a warrant officer with a designator and a spotting scope sitting half-down on its tripod. "What you seeing?"

"So much dust," the warrant officer said, "can't see shit," timing his words and keeping his mouth open between the bomb bursts. "Got two F-18s and a B-52 on deck."

Jack lay flat to look through the scope. It brought the inferno up close, the boiling dirt and smoke in which great dark chunks were falling back to earth. Slowly he eased the scope back and forth, seeking human movement among the blazing pines and crumbling slope, catching glimpses of hillside as the fire and smoke blew this way and that.

"I caught the entrance to something, people running out," Jack said. "Something burning."

The warrant officer glanced through the scope. "I'll light it up." He called in the designation. "F-18 incoming," he said. "Little present from Allah."

Through the scope Jack could see people running in and out of the battered cave mouth, a few working their way uphill, then a great flash of white sucked them up into a blazing tornado spewing mountainside and trees and people and when it ceased the cave mouth was gone, the people, just the smoking hillside like the slope of a volcano.

"We keep this up," the warrant officer said, "Allah's gonna run outta virgins."

WHEN THE OTHER TEAM was pulled back to

Pachir, Jack stayed with Ray's team on the ridge. The bombing had eased, just the occasional passage of a Spectre gunship lighting up the night. At dark all Hazret Ali's mujahedin had vanished down the mountain and the SF team was alone. After midnight the dust and smoke cleared and stars blazed across the darkness. Jack dozed among the rocks next to Engle, who lay with his NVD scope and an M-40 sniper rifle waiting for the survivors to leave their holes in the mistaken assumption they couldn't be seen in darkness.

Every time Engle's sniper rifle roared, Jack jumped in his half-sleep, cradled his head in the rocks and tried to not think of the human life that had just been smashed apart. Before dawn he gave it up, sat up beside Engle in the chill wind, an MRE uneaten by his knee. Then Engle went to lie down and Jack took over the spotting scope and sniper rifle, scanning the tortured hillside, not expecting to see anything alive.

He was thinking of Bandit leading him through the blizzard in the Hindu Kush, standing over him that night on the stepping-stone bridge, when something white flitted across the scope.

He blinked, rubbed his eyes, peered again. The figure was tall, bent over, in a white headscarf that hung down the back of his black-checked robe, limping at a quick uneven pace up the trail on the far side of the dry wash, three men ahead of him and five behind. "That's *him*," Jack whispered, trying to keep the spotting scope on the fast-moving men. "Bin Laden."

It was seven hundred fifty yards, maybe seven-eighty. Jack was shaking so hard he could barely aim, the fast-moving men dancing up and down in his scope. The men passed behind an outcrop, just the top of the tall man's white headscarf floating above it. Jack locked onto the far side of the outcrop and slowly breathed out.

The first man cleared the outcrop, bending forward as the trail steepened. The second reappeared, the third. Jack took in a quick breath, slowed his pulse. The tall one cleared the outcrop. *You coward*, Jack told him, *you weakling. You killer of children*. He aimed eighteen inches ahead and three feet above him, squeezed the trigger.

The tall man dropped. The others ran to him, one raising his hands to the sky. Jack reloaded the rifle and fired at the downed man but missed. The other men pulled up the tall one's body. He fired again hitting the outcrop. The men dropped the body and ran up the trail.

He turned the scope back to the tall one's body. It hadn't moved. "I just took down a tall skinny guy," he radioed. "Might be someone we know."

Engle ran up, half-awake, bent to look through the scope. "Who'd you get?"

"Tall guy, white headscarf, bunch of guys around him..."

"Corwin! Ray!" Engle yelled. "Get up here!"

With the others spread out on the ridge to cover him Jack ran downslope across the dry wash up the steep other side, trying not to hope, thinking he'd never seen an Afghani this tall and this man had been wearing Arab clothes.

The man lay on his back, a huge bloody hole in his side, one arm smashed and twisted, his blood pooling down the trail. Curly thick black-gray hair, silvery running shoes. Jack knelt and turned him over. The top of his body turned while the lower part did not.

A face locked in agony. A broken tooth, nose smashed by his fall, sunken cheeks, the foam of lung blood down the corner of a wide thin mouth. *Not an Arab. Not Bin Laden.*

Jack stood, dizzy. Around him the still-dark crags of Tora Bora rose blistered and smoky toward the Spin Gar peaks.

The Twin Towers fell in their aureoles of flame and smoke.

"Negative," he radioed and went back downslope between the boulders and pines along the dry wash. He saw the gravel in the wash, the lichen on the boulders on the bank, a twisted willow stalk and bent grasses, and yet he saw nothing, was aware of seeing everything and nothing.

A dead old man lay up the hill. He had killed him. What had brought the old man to this place? Whom had he been trying to protect, or what injustice had he been trying to right?

Hearing the gravel crunch of the slope beneath his boots, winded from the climb but barely noticing it, he wondered why in his own life vengeance always took priority. The idea of justice. When someone or something is wronged you have to fix it. Vengeance nothing but a means to effect justice. But like life itself, the question of wrong was becoming such a mystery he could not comprehend it.

He crested the rise to Corwin and Engle holding their rifles on three Afghanis with hands on their heads. "They came in like this, no weapons," Corwin said. "Can you talk to them?"

"Cuff them first."

He sat on a rock catching his breath as the three men were flex-cuffed. Across the valley he could see the white spot of the dead man's headscarf.

The first Afghani was tall and slender, long-faced with a thin jaw. He flinched when Jack spoke Pashto, scanned him curiously. "We're not Taliban."

"Where's Osama?"

Again the man started, surprised. "You don't know?"

"Tell me what *you* know."

"Five days he's gone – up this trail over the ridge to Pakistan."

"You lie." Jack stepped back. "I'm sending you to Kabul prison –"

"It's true, Lord! It's true! Haji Ghamsharik and Wahid al-Din and the others helped Al-Qaeda escape Tora Bora."

"*How*!"

"They took mule trains and many trucks. It was going on for days, this escape. From Lalpur they took the Khyber Pass to Pakistan. The American planes never stopped them."

Jack stood on the rocky barren ridge with the December wind in his face, looking out on the far sawtooth peaks, as if this blue icy world was here to rend us, shred us, leave us for the gods. "Drive them to Jalalabad and drop them off."

"We're supposed to bring them in, Jack."

"They're just dumb shits got caught up in this. Like we did."

Ray sat on a rock, wiping grime, sweat, and gunpowder off his face. "Where's fucking Bin Laden?"

"Escaped." Jack felt weary beyond any exhaustion he'd ever felt. "We paid the Afghanis ten million bucks to help us get Al-Qaeda, and they led them to Pakistan instead."

VI

Baghdad

Casablanca

January 2003

A WOMAN'S VOICE drove him from a dream of the raw hills of Pakistan where Osama Bin Laden had escaped. A crisp peremptory British voice. He rolled over on his blankets and clamped his hands over his ears.

The voice neared, cheery and self-assured, Sergeant Weiss answering in monotone, "He doesn't normally talk to people –"

"He'll *want* to talk to me."

"Jack!" Sergeant Weiss stood in the doorway, blocking the light. "This reporter here to see you. Says you'll want to talk –"

"I'm not here," he whispered.

"Oh yes you are!" she called. "I can hear you." She came in and sat on his trunk, tugging up the knees of her camo pants and pulling her cap off her black coiling hair.

He sat up, scratched at his whiskers, his breath sour. "What you want?"

"Isabelle Palmeiri from *The Independent*." She shook

his hand with strong cool fingers. "I'm assigned to SAS command and a couple of them said come see you about Tora Bora –"

He noticed a fly buzzing at the single window, trying to get out to die in Jalalabad's frigid daylight. "I wasn't there."

"Oh yes you were." She glanced at Sergeant Weiss.

"You can go, Sergeant," Jack said.

She flashed Jack a smile. "So, why'd you let Bin Laden get away?"

He stared down at the dirt, counted three breaths. "That's idiotic."

"Come *on*, it's all over the *base*! The order came all the way down from Tommy Franks, didn't it? But *why?*"

He wanted to stand and scratch his balls – anything to drive her out. But she sat there calm and self-contained as he shuffled outside to piss in the back yard, tucked himself together, and came back in. "Lady you got the wrong guy."

"Listen, I *know* why you're here. And *why* you want Bin Laden. I'm sorry but I do. What I *don't* understand is why you'd take part in this disgusting roadshow – *The Tora Bora Traveling Circus of Ex-Taliban Double-Crossers and Media Patsies* – staged by no other than US Central Command... And a few insignificant Brits of course."

He sat on his bunk. "Go away."

She gripped his knee. "Not till you tell me *why* –"

He noticed how the amber dawn splashed across her face, how her fiery voice lit the room, her smooth fast questions that were never off the mark and never let go, as if it was her right to be answered fully and honestly and any failure to do so a breach of faith. "Go away."

She circled back to her first questions like a wolf that has run the herd and now returns to the weakest animal. "So why did Centcom let Hazret Ali, Wahid al-Din, and Ghamsharik make the final attack on Al-Qaeda?"

"To let the Afghanis take the lead? Show they'd rejected Al-Qaeda?"

"But they'd been Taliban *allies*! And why were there only two Special Forces units in the whole area, and they were – excuse me, *you* were – held back and only did the painting?"

His tongue was thick and tasted awful. He noticed his coffee cup sitting in a new coat of dust on the ammo crate beside his bunk. "I have to catch a flight to DC."

She resettled herself on his trunk. "I've had a chat with all your mates –"

"I don't have any mates."

Her eyes appraised him. "You did though, didn't you? Have a mate –"

"That's nothing to do with this."

"I'm sorry but it's the *nub*: you're here to kill Bin Laden. So why are you covering up Tora Bora? Doesn't it *matter* why we gave him and a thousand Al-Qaeda a free ticket out of Armageddon? When we had them pinned down? Don't *you* need to know?"

He whacked his boots together upside down to shake out scorpions, and slid them on. "And what's all this talk," she added, "about Bush wanting to invade Iraq?"

He bent to lace a boot, grunted with the pain in his chest. "Nobody's that stupid."

She stood. "If *you* were a Brit, and maybe you'd lost someone in 9/11, or lost a soldier here – wouldn't *you* want to know?"

He started shaking sand out of his clothes and throwing them into his duffle. She stopped at the door. "If I didn't know better," she said, "I'd mistake you for a lifer –"

He listened to her soft footfalls fade. *Bitch. Acting like she knows what's right.* As if there were an innate moral good that is universally understood and all actions should be measured against it.

He stood, weary with sleepless days and nights, old injuries and new wounds, old and new sorrows, the nausea of bad water and worse food. He wanted to kneel on the floor and become innocent again but there was no way, so he shouldered his duffel and walked across the courtyard to the jeep waiting to take him to Kabul.

She seemed to want Bin Laden as much as he did. Why?

LANGLEY'S LAWNS WERE GRAY with frost, its attentive guards, trim walls and echoing corridors all making him feel even more hopeless.

At Langley you got ahead Inside by making the right friends Outside. If you stayed close to Congressional Intelligence Committee members and fed them the right stuff and produced critical situation reports with the conclusions they wanted, you got ahead. But if you spoke the inconvenient truth you ended up in Rangoon or some godawful hole in Africa.

The Agency had split between those who were trying to make a better America and a better world, and those who were trying to get ahead. And those who were looking out for Number One came out Number One, while the country lost.

He rode with Ackerman in an unmarked Crown Vic to the White House. "Casablanca," Ackerman called it: his little game. "Since long before 9/11," Ackerman said, "even in Transition, all Bush has wanted is to invade Iraq. We're going to take sixty percent of Iraq's crude, the Brits twenty. Spain, Italy, and Poland all get their piece. We've offered France seven percent but they want nothing to do with it."

"They're right."

"Wolfowitz and some other top guys want to hit Saudi first, the southern fields. But Bush won't do anything against the Saudis."

They went through three sets of security to a wide office in the Executive Wing walled with modern art, Iranian rugs on the hardwood floor. "Our boy's sure come up in the world," Ackerman said.

"You always said he would."

Timothy entered with files under his arm. "Gentlemen! How *lovely* to see you!"

"Jack's just in from Kabul," Ackerman said. "What's up?"

"Bin Laden." Timothy slung his feet up on his desk. "We think he's in Baghdad."

"Last year he *was* in Tora Bora," Jack said. "But you let him get away."

"Always sounded to me like some South Pacific atoll, that place," Timothy said mildly. "Hey, no proof he was there."

"You had intercepts," Jack said. "Recorded his voice. You *know* he was there."

"So maybe, like General Franks says, he was killed in the bombing?" Timothy caught himself. "But that's unlikely, for now we think he's in Iraq."

"Why would he be there? He hates Saddam, considers him not religious enough. And Saddam wouldn't dare piss us off."

Timothy's nostrils flared. "There's a lot you don't understand."

"Like when I came back from Lebanon with the coordinates for the Hezbollah camp, and I couldn't understand why you didn't hit it?"

"This reminds me of a bad marriage. Always digging up the past." Timothy's face showed new signs of age: chicken feet at the corners of his eyes, dark pouches under the lids, dewlaps of skin beneath the chin. "We've got on-the-ground intel," he said, "Bin Laden's in Baghdad."

"I want to see it," Jack said.

"Can't. Because we need you to go there, and if you're compromised –"

"*Go* there?"

"As a former Afghani *mujihadeen*, to link up with Al-Qaeda, try to join Bin Laden –"

"Timothy," Jack laughed, "are you absolutely fucking *nuts*?"

Timothy smiled primly as if complimented. "And we know Saddam's working on nukes, germ agents, weapons of mass destruction. We have Intel from the Kurds, Chalabi..."

"They'll any lie to split up Iraq and take what they can get. Then they'll start killing each other again –"

Timothy looked at him curiously. "Those Soviet backpack nukes you've been so hot and bothered about? Apparently some are in Iraq – just another reason we need you to go there. Nobody else on our side has the languages, the experience. Christ, you've even done parachute drops with –"

"W-54s? We destroyed all ours, long ago."

"The Soviets didn't – what if Saddam gives them to Al-Qaeda?"

THERE WAS NO ONE in the dark rain at the Vietnam Memorial. *Why do I come here*, Jack asked his father. *You're* not here, your body's rotted somewhere in the Vietnam mud. He thought of Johnson, Rusk, McNamara – their hunger that millions die for *their* ambition, *their* fear.

What he hated was less them than something deep in the heart of man that had made Washington: the warheads in their silos, the Depleted Uranium bullets, the Sioux and Cheyenne prairies drenched in Indian blood, the rockets' red glare with their ten thousand bomblets each, the surprised blond Russian kid beside the tank, Leo and the thirty thousand Russian dead, all this murder in God's name, back through time.

The long black tombstone snaked ahead of him, its names glistening in the rain of tears of all the loved and loving ones these men had left behind, the orphaned sons and daughters, the widowed wives and weeping parents, the broken-hearted brothers and sisters. Of the hundred billion tears of Indochina darkening its dark earth.

What is exalted, the stone revealed, is evil. And the inalienable rights of man were just one more cover-up for raping, burning, stealing, and dismemberment.

WMDs

HE FLEW TO TAMPA for five days of briefings, and to learn how to locate each of his planned sources in Iraq.

He was not pleased to find Brigadier General Szymanski in Tampa among the other book generals with pounds of tin on their chests. "You happy?" Jack said, "with Wahid's success at Tora Bora?"

"Hey we can't hit a home run every time. We're beatin terrarism, control most of Afghanistan – what more you want?"

Jack laughed. "Anybody with smart bombs can kill a bunch of farmers."

Szymanski's little eyes narrowed. "You think *you* can't be touched? Because we need you, your languages – how you fit in with ragheads... Christ, you're half raghead yourself."

I could kill you, Jack thought, *with one move of my hand*. "Sometimes I get so disgusted by people like you. By what I'm sworn to defend."

FROM TAMPA he flew a military transport to Incirlik Air Base in Turkey, took a bus from Adana to Diyarbakir, then another to Simak near the Iraqi border. It was warm for February, and he sweated in his pleated coat, his five-day stubble itchy and unfamiliar.

It was like leaving Beirut for the Beqaa, dressed in local clothes, dirty and unshaven, his target a man who had killed many Americans. Or like leaving France for the Sahara, looking for a man who blew up people in the subway.

This time he carried no gun, only a Soviet Army combat knife strapped to his leg, the kind any Afghani *mujihadeen* might have. As in Lebanon he had no papers but a worn Afghanistan passport in the name of Ahmad al-Din, the photo a cheap Third World black-and-white taken at Langley.

A timeworn Mercedes taxi took him two hours to Habur. That night he crossed the Iraqi border with a Kurdish man and woman and their three children on two mules heading to a village north of Zakhu. The man carried an old Mauser 98 and had a leather sack of bullets tied to his waist. Jack stayed two hundred yards behind them.

They walked all night, the stars thick and deep. As he walked Jack went over in his mind the contacts he would make: Ibrahim the refinery manager, Professor Younous the atomic physicist, Colonel Nureddin Sama, and Imam Ghali. A sliver of moon rose like a red knife over the eastern hills then climbed cold and white into the sky.

After dawn they reached the outskirts of Zakhu. He paid five hundred dinars for a ride in the back of a truck to Mosul, and from there took the night bus to Baghdad.

The clock on the Baghdad bus station wall said one thirty-seven, but when he looked a while later it had not changed. The room was full of people, the linoleum littered with paper tissues and scraps of food. A man beside Jack peeling a tangerine offered him a chunk. It was an insult to refuse but he did so anyway.

When the darkness outside the grimy windows began to fade Jack crossed the road into a maze of streets he had memorized in Tampa, coming out on a wide boulevard.

There was the smell of bread and fried food and strange spices on the air, the early clatter of cars and buses; the streetlights erratically flickered and died. He walked forty minutes north then turned west into a residential neighborhood with palm trees down the center of the road.

It was the eleventh house on the left, white and low under a tile roof, in gardens of pink and white bougainvillea. He climbed the gate and sat on the lawn by the back door.

Soon the house was stirring. Lights came on in the kitchen. A face looked out the window and a woman came and yelled at him. "No beggars here! Go away!"

"I am here to prune the trees," he said. "Please tell the master."

"Nothing I tell the master. He doesn't need to hear about you. Go!"

"I am here to prune the trees. Please tell the master."

A few minutes later a man came out. "This is not a good time," he said in English.

"It's the only time. Where do I meet you?"

"Walk on the far side of the boulevard toward Daura. I'll pick you up in twenty minutes. A silver Toyota. *Now go!*" he said loudly in Arabic. "Before I call the police."

Jack was a mile down the boulevard when the silver Toyota pulled over. "Who are you?" the man snapped. "Why did you come?"

"Things are happening fast, Ibrahim. I'm here to locate backpack nukes, chemical and biological munitions – weapons of mass destruction they're calling them."

"Don't *joke*! We can't even make polyurethanes now. There isn't enough food, steel, look at this road – we're not even making asphalt! How can we make weapons?"

"You've got feedstock –"

"At Daura we're down to forty thousand barrels a day. No cracker catalyst, naphtha, a thousand other things we need for basic life. Where's your Intel? Your satellites can look under our beds, can see what every general has for dinner, what page of *Harry Potter* Saddam finished last night – don't tell me you don't know we're going back to the Stone Age!"

"Your refinery's a perfect place to make chemical weapons. Thousands of miles of pipelines, crude towers, reformers, hydrocrackers, huge steel tanks, laboratories, underground storage... That's why the Israelis bombed you in '81 – remember..."

"You think I don't know if someone is making weapons in my refinery?"

Jack watched the tawdry storefronts, dusty palms, noisy vehicles and discolored concrete buildings flit by. "So what do people think?"

"Most Shiites and Kurds would like Saddam gone. But then they say what would come after? We're not even a real country – we were cobbled together by the British. Without a strong dictator we'd explode. We know what happened to Yugoslavia – you bring in a little freedom and people use it to cut each other's throats."

Ibrahim's cell phone buzzed and he answered it driving one-handed. "Cut the run," he said in Arabic. "Stop the number two crude line. Yes, shut down the vacuum unit." He closed the phone and turned to Jack, still driving one-handed. "Every day a new pipeline break."

"Watch that bus!"

"Our pipes are corroding, too much clay in the soil. You think in Iraq we can make new steel pipe? All we can make anymore is babies."

"Who would know about small nuclear weapons, old Soviet stuff?"

"Are you crazy? Saddam wouldn't dare..."

"Bin Laden, Al-Qaeda? They here?"

Ibrahim pulled over. "There's more chance Bin Laden's in New Jersey."

Jack opened the door. "I'll tell the President."

"Please do. So if he wants he can bomb New Jersey. It's a Democratic state, no?"

AT A MARKET he bought jeans, a blue dress shirt, and sports jacket, changed, walked to the University Physics building and up to the third floor, and knocked at the second office on the right.

"He's not there," called out a teenager in a Baltimore Orioles jacket, Walkman plugs in his ears, coming down the corridor with an armload of books.

"When's he back?" Jack asked.

The young man tugged out an earplug. "Say what?"

"When's Professor Younous back?"

"Maybe ten-thirty. You a teacher?"

Music blasted from the earplugs. *Pearl Jam*, Jack thought, *My son Leo used to play that... No, that's not who I am – I'm Afghani. And Leo's dead. And he wasn't my son.* "No."

"You know string theory?"

Jack couldn't understand the term in Arabic. "It's a mathematical model," the young man said, "for understanding the universe." He looked Jack over. "Where you from?"

"Afghanistan."

"Uggh – for that your accent. Poor man, to be there with all those religious nuts."

When he returned at ten-thirty Professor Younous was there, tall and angular in a wrinkled gray suit. "I come at the request of Ibn Khani," Jack said.

Younous looked surprised then scared. He reached for the phone among the papers piled on his desk but drew away his hand. "Perhaps we'd better look at your problem."

They walked wordlessly across the half-deserted campus. It seemed an impoverished version of an American urban state college. "The UN's been here many times," Younous said. "IAEA's sampled every possible site, every factory and old barracks. We're no closer to making nuclear weapons than Bermuda."

"I'm told that once there was a program and you refused to work on it."

"Any scientist who works on weapons is an assassin."

"What about those Soviet suitcase bombs?"

"Bush talks about us having them? We can't even fix our sewers. The man's insane."

"Al-Qaeda's working on a bomb –"

"Not in Iraq. Pakistan has the Bomb, and it's been home to Al-Qaeda and Bin Laden for years. So why do you keep looking in Iraq?"

HE TOOK THE NIGHT BUS to Ramadi. There were not enough seats; he had to stand till Al Habbaniyah. An old woman beside him was eating dates from a paper bag; their smell made him nauseous.

During the night Sophie came to him. They didn't talk, everything was understood, just the dear clasp of her hand and she was gone.

Next morning in Ramadi he called the Army base from a pay phone and asked in Russian then Arabic for Colonel Nureddin Sama.

"Major Dvorak!" Sama said gloomily in Russian. "How surprising to hear from you."

"I'm here a few hours, my friend. Can I see you, for old time's sake?"

"Is it necessary? Well then... After work I walk my dog on the canal near my house, about a kilometer north of town. There's a white water tank and a goat path that goes west up to an abandoned farmhouse. If you really need to... you can meet me at the farmhouse –"

Jack spent the day checking the base perimeter, counting vehicles in and out, artillery and choppers. In late afternoon he followed the canal, stopping once or twice to throw stones into its stagnant pools the way a man with time on his hands will do.

The water tank had been painted white over its rust and the flaking paint gave it a scabrous hue. On its back had been painted *Allahu Akhbar* – God is Greatest – but the letters had weathered so all you could see was... *God .. eat.*

He sat outside against the still-warm wall. The dog came running across the crests, the man picking his way after it.

The dog was a desert greyhound, sleek and gray with a chain collar that jingled when he ran. Nureddin Sama, slender with a hawkish face, came up and sat heavily beside Jack. "It's crazy, your coming like this. You could get me shot."

"They'd torture you first."

"They'll do the same to you."

"I'm getting out. Before my friends get here."

Sama laughed coarsely. "We don't want war, don't have the ammunition, the trucks, even uniforms. Look at mine – a Colonel and my trousers are frayed."

"The White House thinks you have chemical, biological weapons –"

"Because of your embargoes the last twelve years have been hell. No food, no medicine, no parts for machinery or equipment or anything that's normal in the modern world. Don't you remember, you fools, what happened to Germany after Versailles?"

"This is not my choice, Colonel. These little Soviet tactical nukes –"

"The suitcase bombs."

"Where do you have them?"

"I've been in the Army twenty-two years. I've been at the top of the Defense Ministry, close to our President." He stared at Jack. "I can tell you we don't have them."

"You can *tell* me?"

Nureddin glanced away. "When we were young, we had such plans... Using our oil to educate our kids, build hospitals and roads, decent homes for everyone. Say what you want, our President loves Iraq. He keeps us together –"

"If we come in from Kuwait what will be your order of battle?"

"I'm not a traitor! Haven't you seen the wonders of Babylon at the British Museum? Haven't you read *Gilgamesh*? When your ancestors were chewing bones in caves we were a great empire of golden cities. We were writing books of wisdom while you were picking the lice out of your bearskins!"

"Ah, lice. I've had them in Afghanistan."

"If you want to live, don't say you're from there." Sama lit a cigarette. "After the Iranians made fools of you in seventy-nine, you showed us false satellite photos, gave us weapons and paid us billions to attack them. Two million died. Now you're using us again –"

The dog came running back to check on them. Jack patted him, thinking of Bandit. "What about Scuds?"

"Your Special Forces guys are out looking for them now – you know that."

"Why haven't you grabbed them?"

"We have nothing to hide. And if we did, Bush would use it as an excuse to invade." Sama looked at him bleakly. "Nobody here wants war – why do you?"

"You have too much oil, my friend."

"This time you won't catch us in the open. We'll fight you in the cities, in the towns, appear and disappear, small units, a few men here and there... You saw what happened to the Russians in Grozny? Our cities will kill you. You'll have no medevac, no safe streets, no way to find us, nowhere to hide. *We* don't want war. But if it comes we'll bleed you to death."

IMAM GHALI WAS HIS LAST SOURCE, a rotund little man with a white beard, bright cheeks and merry eyes. He sat cross-legged on his pillow and waited patiently till Jack had finished speaking.

"*Whosoever fighteth for the religion of God*, my son, *whether he be slain or victorious, we will surely give him a great reward* – is this not true?"

"The Fourth Sura," Jack answered. "Of course it's true. But that was not my fear."

"This war will start a long struggle the Americans are too soft and lazy to win. We will bleed them for years. They will not be safe no matter where they hide. We'll turn the world against them, strengthen and temper the heart of every faithful Muslim. Think not of years, my son, but decades. Centuries."

Dusk had fallen when Jack left the mosque. Unease was eating him as if someone were watching – were they waiting till he'd met all his sources, then planning to grab him before he met his contact? He wondered who his contact was, if they'd be at the Hotel Palestine as planned.

Afraid to take a cab, he walked across Baghdad to the Hotel, asked for the number of the Marduk suite and went up and knocked on its door. It opened suddenly, half-blinding him.

"You!" He stepped back.

"Get in, *get in*!" Isabelle Palmeiri yanked him inside and shut the door.

He stared at her. "You?"

"I couldn't tell you in Afghanistan – wasn't part of my mission."

He sat heavily on the couch, looked up at her. "And *this* is?"

"You look a mess –" She moved toward the kitchen. "You want tea, coffee?"

He followed her. "I'm supposed to download to *you*?"

"Your guys have nobody here, dearie. Have to put up with me."

"You're a pain in the ass. That day in Afghanistan what the Hell were you trying to find out?"

She turned from the sink to face him. "Why didn't you *get* Bin Laden?"

"Christ!" He clasped his head. "You think I didn't *try*? What the Hell do *you* care?"

She drew back and he was stunned by how lovely and unapproachable she seemed. "My husband died in the North Tower. I lost a mate, just like you."

Doubled

"SO YOU'RE THE ONE." He looked at her. "I took you for a journalist."

"I am. *The Independent*. I told you."

"I paid no attention. I'm sick of war."

"Which one?"

"This new one in Iraq that Bush is so hungry for. Afghanistan too." He paced the suite, the bedroom, bath, and living room with the kitchen alcove. "Let's go."

"I've run the checks. We're good here."

The chair seemed to rise up and suck him in. "For days I've been afraid of being captured. Shot. Now in the middle of Baghdad I feel half-safe."

"Until the bombs and rockets hit. Though they're not supposed to hit this hotel."

"They still have room service?"

"Comes and goes. What you want?"

"Food. Lots of it. And whiskey, best they have."

"It's a hundred quid for twelve-year-old single malt. Up to you – *we* won't pay."

She called the order down in mellifluous Arabic. He went

into the bathroom and stood in the cold shower for a long time, dressed again in the jeans and shirt and sat watching Al Jazeera till the food came. "It's going to happen, isn't it?" he said.

She handed him a glass of whiskey. "Sorry, no ice."

"How I like it." He drank the Talisker and ate the roast chicken, pumpkin soup and chocolate cake. "I better take your report down," she said, "before you pass out."

"I can stay here tonight?"

She studied him. "On the couch there."

"I didn't mean a damn thing. I'm tired of back alleys and bus seats."

"Probably was good for you." She went into the bedroom and came out with a laptop. He put the food tray outside the door and filled his glass again.

She typed as he dictated. First his interview with "A" – Ibrahim the refinery manager, then "B" – Professor Younous, then Colonel Sama, Imam Ghali, every detail memorized. Then the lack of troop movements, the absence of callups, the general mood of a nation unprepared for war.

Two hours later he had finished, the bottle nearly empty. She sat back. "A bleeding tragedy, this!" She reread the file, encrypted it, hit the hardware cipher, went out on the balcony, and sent it off into the night. Five minutes later she went out again to confirm it was received, came back in and deleted it off her hard disk.

"Spying just isn't what it used to be," he said.

"Like taking candy from children. They're so unprepared, these people."

"Suppose it won't happen?"

"We've just had the largest anti-war protests in history against it. Thirty million people marching in seventy-two different countries. Three million people in Rome, nearly two million in London and in Madrid... Never before have so many people protested a war. And it hasn't even begun yet."

"Bush said the protests don't matter. He called them a 'focus group'."

"The man's clinically homicidal. Cheney too, looking to make billions for Haliburton, the other war companies."

"The UN inspectors, led by Hans Blix, says there are no WMDs. I can guarantee they're right."

"Doesn't matter. Tony Blair has the hots for it. Bush is wetting his pants with excitement. Of course it'll happen."

"And you?"

She toyed with a black scarab on a gold chain round her neck. "I'm sticking it out. That's my job."

"Which one?"

"Both."

He stretched his back muscles. "I'm going out tomorrow, same way I came in."

"Good luck to that. They'll be watching the borders."

"So let's have some wine. Then I'm going to sleep."

"Wine? You've just had nearly a bottle of whiskey. Anyway Muslim women don't drink."

He eyed her. "You're not Muslim."

She smiled, tossed back her hair. "I've known so many Muslim women, felt so sorry for them... Can you imagine, never allowed in public, wrapped in hideous black veils?"

"A *burkha*, with just eye-holes and a little grill for your mouth..."

She shuddered. "One night in Riyadh I was invited to an all-women party, all these elegant women who spent their public lives completely covered were smoking hash and dancing naked together. It was sad, warped, crazy – I had to leave." She went to the phone. "Bordeaux?"

"Works for me."

A moment later she called to him, "They have a ninety-nine Médoc or a two thousand one Margaux."

The Margaux had still been on the vine the day his family died. "Médoc."

She sat across from him, trim and composed. "I'm sorry about your husband," he said. Her face hardened. *A mask,* he thought. *Am I like that?*

"He'd gone over from London the day before 9/11," she said. "A deal he was working on. He was an investment banker like you. Had the flu, I didn't want him to go."

"All the time when we talked... You could've told me."

"What good would that have done you? Or me?" She said nothing, then, "I buried myself in work. For weeks I couldn't sleep – every time I closed my eyes I was with him, falling inside the tower. The pain, when it crushes you – it's awful." She looked away. "Oh God, I'm sorry."

"It's okay. I go through it every day."

At a soft knock on the door he stepped into the bedroom, heard her thanking the bellboy. A queen-sized bed, her white underpants and bra tossed across it.

When he came out she was pouring the wine. "Once they made great wine here. The syrah grape is supposedly from Shiraz in Iran. Where my father came from."

"You grew up there?"

"Heavens no. My parents were journalists, got out of Teheran when the Ayatollah came in. My mother's British, so we had no problem. I was seven, grew up in London."

He grinned. "Kabul on the Thames? Londonistan?"

"It was different then. Now everybody's so full of political correctness we won't admit our capital is a breeding ground for Islamic terrorism. We Brits are always weak when we should be strong and strong when everybody expects us to keel over..."

"What would've Iran been like, if we hadn't overthrown Mossadegh?"

"Probably a peaceful, wealthy, modern nation. The France of the Middle East."

"Sometimes I wonder, do these American politicians understand? Maybe they do, and just want chaos?"

"Chaos? It's fantastic for oil prices."

He smiled at the irony. "Where'd you learn Arabic?"

"Cambridge, like everyone. Then Cairo, Yemen, lots of nasty places."

"Always MI6?"

"Journalist first. Got recruited after."

He told her about the false meeting with Karim al-Saleh, his frantic dash through the streets. The waiting. *Yes*, she watched him, *the waiting*.

"It's easy," he said, "to cauterize our pain. But what happens to *us* doesn't matter. It's what happened to *them* – your husband, Sophie, Leo, Sarah –" he could say their names now without choking. "And all the others."

She had the clearances so he told her a little about Afghanistan, training *mujihadeen* to kill Russians, how every war sows the seeds of the next. And how religion is evil because it separates and excludes, incites righteousness, condones mass murder in the guise of war.

"Vengeance is like what Churchill said about democracy," she said. "It's a lousy solution, but better than anything else."

"We learned a Longfellow saying in school... it's always stayed with me: *If we could know the secret lives of our enemies we'd see enough sorrow and suffering to disarm all hostilities*. But that's doesn't matter now. I just want to get Bin Laden, Al-Qaeda –"

She sat back. "But you *didn't*."

He felt a little drunk. "That pisses me off."

"So who gave the order to hand Tora Bora to the Afghanis?"

There she was like a wolf again, closing in. "That proves nothing," he said finally.

"Blair won't admit you let Bin Laden go. MI6 doesn't want any part of this Iraq invasion – a recipe for disaster – they tell Blair but he won't listen –"

"Your North Sea fields are running out. He wants the oil."

She eyed him. "If you guys *had* Bin Laden? What then?"

He looked around, avoiding her. How bizarre the room seemed – the blank TV, the yellow walls, the greenish drapes, the ornate lamps with their frilly shades – when they and the city around them were so soon to be destroyed. "We'd lose our pretext for invading Iraq –"

"Every night I fall asleep determined to kill that liver-lipped assassin. To make him die the death of every single person he's killed. One by one." She bit her lip. "Bush and Centcom blew it in Tora Bora. And now you're chasing this Iraq thing, letting him get further away. Making him a hero."

"*I'm* not letting him get away..." Aching to ease her pain – *or was it his?* – he pulled her close, neither resisting nor accepting, her hair against his cheek. He held her a long time as she breathed softly against him, not in desire nor consolation but in sharing whatever dim human spark their loved ones had lost. "I've been doubled," he said. "By my own country."

She smiled up at him. "Just by the ones at the top."

"Imagine, the people who believe in them, respect them. What fools we all are –"

"Cheer up – in ten million years something new may evolve, wiser and less evil."

"You don't get to the top except by standing on everyone else's head."

Finally they slept, half-sitting side by side on the sofa,

her head against the shoulder Sophie once had healed. Then on the bed, dressed, under the coverlet. At the muezzin's first wail she ordered four room service breakfasts, two for each.

At the door he reached out to touch the side of her cheek, the hard bone beneath the soft skin. "Go home. Your dying here does nobody any good."

She pulled back. "Nor does yours."

BACK IN DC there seemed no threat of war. The streets busy with people, shoppers with bags of expensive trinkets, newspapers stories about movie actor love affairs and TV shows where people get marooned in fake settings.

Survivor – they don't even know what that means.

War movies, video games of killing people... War so sickening, horrifying, breaks your heart – how, he wondered sadly, can anyone be excited by that?

An obese young woman passed him, a sweatshirt tented over her vast bulk, on it the words *No Man's Good Enough for This Girl.* Don't you understand, Jack wanted to ask her, when there's such a fatal disconnect between what you think and what is real you're headed for disaster?

"FINEST RECON I ever saw," Levi Ackerman said. "If anyone could do it you're the one."

"Rumsfeld's seen it? Powell? The other Principles?"

"Jack –" Ackerman crossed to his office window. "Timothy's got data that conflicts with yours. Sat photos, other agents' reports of WMDs."

"All he's got is the Kurds and Chalabi, who say whatever he tells them to."

"It's what the President wants to hear."

"What he said in the State of the Union – that they have tons of anthrax, sarin, and botulism – he *knows* they don't!

How many times have we *told* him! He said they have thirty thousand warheads – Christ, they can't even clean their streets! And Al-Qaeda – Bush says the Iraqis are protecting them – it's a lie! *Why?*"

Ackerman rubbed his stump. "Not mine to reason why. Or yours either."

"I'm not inventing an excuse for war."

Ackerman looked like an oncologist giving a patient bad news. "You keep a copy?"

"My report? Of course not."

"Because it didn't happen anymore. That's an order from the White House. In three days we go into Iraq. Massive force, killing everything in sight. SF already controls a quarter of the country and if we have to we'll flatten the rest."

"Iraq's an independent country – of *course* they'll fight back! But they've done us no harm! It's sick."

Ackerman sighed. "There's many ways to think of this. Sure, you can say *no war, no war no matter what* –"

"I'm not saying that."

" – or you can look at it like some people in the Administration do, as a chance to change the world." He leaned forward, earnest. "Look, we know the Muslim world has been stuck in the Middle Ages, a totalitarian Fascist theocracy with no human rights, no personal freedoms... And an insane determination to control the world..."

"War won't change that! It just plays into their hands – the West as the cause of all the problems and backwardness in the Muslim world!" Jack shook his head in frustration. "You and I have spent years fighting wars. We know no war changes anything for the good."

"World War Two? When my family was dying in Treblinka?"

"World War Two was caused by World War One –

Christ, *you* know that!"

"Suppose we knock off Saddam and install a democratic process in Iraq? Suppose we can slowly help the Muslim world evolve into freedom and democracy? Consider it a preemptive strike, against everything that threatens our future."

"You don't convince people by killing their families and friends. If we want to change the Muslim world, take some of the billions we'd spend on this war – trillions probably – and build clinics and schools and libraries and all the other things civilization means."

"That doesn't sell weapons, Jack. Anyway it's too late now, the President's decided."

"What about the Iraqi people? These poor civilians –"

"President says we're liberating them." Ackerman stared at him. "Get over it."

"Can't you *see*, what's become of us?"

"Soldiers follow orders."

"Not evil ones."

"The White House is determined. Don't get in their way."

"And all these people will *die...*" Jack stopped at the door. "Fuck you all, you miserable evil bastards. I'll find Bin Laden without you."

"Not likely. Timothy wants you back in Afghanistan, holding Wahid's hand. Building on our success there, he calls it."

MIDNIGHT IN DC WAS 08:00 IN BAGHDAD. He called the Palestine. *How strange war has become; we can chat in its midst.* Isabelle answered breathless. "I was dashing out to a Foreign Ministry press conference. They're allowing more inspectors – everything Bush asked for!"

"Get out now. Don't make me say why. Please?"

"Come *on*, Jack. Bush won't dare attack! Our chief

weapons inspector, Dr. Kelly, he's told Blair there's no WMD's. So there's no *possible* excuse –"

"Cheney and Bush are pushing this insane story that Saddam was involved in planning 9/11. They've just made it up, but Bush keeps repeating it on TV and now seventy per cent of Americans believe it."

"It can't happen, this war."

"It's going to. So go home. *Now!*"

"Don't try to order me! Got to *go*! Bye!"

He sat with the dead phone in his hand. *If she won't get out it's her fault.*

What if he flew to Baghdad, tried to convince her? Would she leave then?

Don't order me around, she'd said.

"If you want to make a call," said a recording in the phone, an annoyed woman's voice, "please hang up and try again."

He stood at the window, seeing and not noticing the city lights. *Do what you have to do, before what you want to do.*

Bin Laden could be anywhere among the hundred fifty million Pakistanis, nearly all fanatic America-hating Muslims. How easy would it be for him to hide?

And one American alone wandering the hills, not speaking the dialects – what chance would *he* have to find him?

Bring 'em On

CITIES AFIRE, bloodied bodies, crushing heat of rockets and bombs – relentless and implacable the Americans tore into Iraq. From Kabul Jack hunted the TV for news of Isabelle, even a glimpse of her face.

But all he found was TV commentators with perfect hair, the grinning generals trying to look severe before the cameras, the antiseptic films of rockets zeroing in as if this were a video game and there weren't thousands of terrified Iraqi draftees burning to death or being blown apart, thousands of frightened eager young Americans soon to be killed or crippled.

We make no judgment about this, the journalists said. We're just reporting. But isn't it exciting? Don't we feel important? For our viewers nothing's more romantic than war.

How can you feel no shame? he yelled at them. *Why do you legitimize this?*

Isabelle's cell phone didn't answer; he called the Palestine but the lines were down. BBC mentioned an unnamed *Independent* correspondent in a battle south of Ramadi and he felt a deep prickly fear and went out into the spring rain, hearing its soft susurration and trying to reach her in his mind.

All spring and early summer in Pakistan's Toba Kakhar mountains he wandered from one hardscrabble farm to the next, asking, "Have you news of Osama?"

The men inspected him with cold distance, not trusting his Afghani accent. One night in a smoky hut a young man with fierce eyes said in English, "I know who you are."

Jack said nothing. "You're going to be killed," the man said. "Osama's not here."

"I understand some English," Jack answered. "What are you saying?"

The man nodded out the door at the wind-bitten hills. "In the morning take the trail down to Qamr-ud. Go back to Afghanistan. People here intend to kill you."

"I'm looking for Osama."

"All you'll find is death."

AS THE SPRING RAINS turned to searing summer in Afghanistan the Taliban slid away to tend their opium fields and beat their women. The tribal warlords stockpiled their American weapons and dollars, and lauded democracy to the few reporters who hadn't run away to be embedded with the Americans in Iraq.

He'd heard Isabelle was still in Baghdad. *But she doesn't mean anything to me. I don't mean anything to her. My job is find Bin Laden.* He imagined a medieval knight on a hopeless quest dedicated to a woman who barely knew he existed.

Bin Laden and Al-Qaeda weren't stupid. They had the whole Muslim world to hide in.

GW had pranced across the deck of the *Abraham Lincoln* in his soldier suit taunting "Bring 'em on" at the young Iraqis huddled in the ruins of their country. He who had never heard a bullet fired in anger, had never killed anything but tame ducks in a pond, who had dodged the war that killed Jack's father. He who would never be endangered by such a boast.

And when any country is attacked, weren't those who join the aggressors called traitors, and those who defend it called patriots? Wouldn't most Iraqis want to be patriots?

The war went on, and on. In the Afghani fields once drenched in blood the red poppies danced; it was going to be a good opium year. In Kabul now were hamburger stands and bars, more whorehouses than mosques; you could buy an AK for a handful of dollars. The opium lords drove Hummers and took over people's homes and bought whatever girls or boys they wanted. The opium went out the old way, across the Hindu Kush, or in planes out of Uzbekistan, and a month later hit the streets of New York, London, Moscow and LA. "I was wrong," Wahid told Jack when they met by chance one day in Kabul. "Capitalism is a *good* thing."

15:20, a day in November, the sky grim. When the sat-phone buzzed Jack was standing in a bitter sandy wind questioning five farmers caught up in a sweep near the Pakistan border. "Morning, Levi," he said. "You're working early."

"Iraq's not going well," Ackerman said after a moment's silence. "They want you back in Baghdad, talking to people like you did before. Then to go out with some of our units, see what's going wrong. They need some ground truth, Jack."

"Who's *they*? Timothy? Rumsfeld? Powell? I only wish *they* were in a Humvee with no armor going into a firefight, instead of some poor kids from Michigan or Georgia."

"Timothy's got one. A yellow Hummer. Drives it to the White House every day."

"At least it's the right color."

Ackerman snickered, ten thousand miles away. "We're getting into quicksand in Iraq. There's no viewpoint we can trust. You're American but you speak the lingo, understand the culture... Tampa's begging us for on-the-ground shit."

"Since when do they *care* about Intel? It's their war, let them rot in it."

"They're not the ones dying, Jack. Bush doesn't care how many guys we lose, how much it costs, for him it's an ego thing. Rumsfeld, Wolfowitz, Rice – they're nuts, but *we* can't change that. The change has to come from the JCs – *they've* got to see they're being fucked over again like Vietnam, by a bunch of scumbag politicians."

"*Our* Joint Chiefs? They're finally getting to play with all their Tonka Toys. They should be happy –"

"Tenet's with us, Jack. He *knows* it's a clusterfuck."

"He backed up Powell at the UN, nodding every time that asshole lied about WMDs. When the French Foreign Minister told Powell to his face he was lying, that there were no WMD's."

"He got set up by Cheney – the Niger letter."

"Since when does the CIA *Director* get set up by an obvious fake?"

Ackerman cleared his throat, taking his time. "When your Dad died I promised myself I'd always watch over you, try to help you any way *he* would've wanted –"

"You got me into West Point. Before I fucked it up."

"*You* got you into West Point. I just let them know you were coming." Again Ackerman cleared his throat. "Could you talk to your old sources in Iraq? Then go out with some of our units, not SF but National Guard, see how the situation looks? Just a SITREP, we can really use it. We'll be reminding the Principals, the Joint Chiefs, *Here's the guy who was right before, who you ignored before, and here's what he says now* – that kind of thing."

"Fuck them." Jack shook his head as if Ackerman could see. "Fuck you too, Levi."

"Don't do it for me. Do it for those kids from Michigan or Georgia. The ones in Humvees with no armor."

FROM A SHATTERED BALCONY Jack scoped for snipers in the ruins of Najaf. Two weeks he'd been in Iraq and already knew there was no exit. Ambushes, mines, car bombs, hit and run. Vietnam again. You can slaughter them by the hundreds of thousands but they will eventually win. As Colonel Sama had said nearly a year ago: *Our cities will kill you.*

The cordite smog of automatic rifles lay thick in the air. Beyond the broken-toothed buildings bodies bobbed in the Euphrates under black-red skies. Fires from A-10 bombing runs spat up sheets of flaming air that writhed like tormented demons.

A random round wailed off the sheet metal over his head. He grunted with displeasure and crawled along the balcony to the stairwell, crablegged down to the CP.

"Can you believe this?" Colonel Eames glanced up from his laptop. "That picture of Bush at the Thanksgiving dinner last week – handing out this huge turkey to the troops? Turns out it was false. A plastic turkey."

"That fits."

"Yeah. It fits."

"After I visit the locals I'm going out with some Reserve unit. Company Commander named Mudge, Major Elwin Mudge. Heard of him?"

Still watching his computer screen, Eames shook his head.

"I'm supposed to see what kind of situations they're getting themselves into."

"That's easy. They're the ones taking the casualties these days."

MORTARS HAD HIT Ibrahim's refinery, and the crude pipeline had been blown. One of the diesel storage tanks was still burning. "We can't put it out," Ibrahim said. "Our men get shot by snipers."

He was thinner, weary black circles under his eyes. "We can't get food or pay our people. My wife's sister and her husband and two kids were shot last week because they didn't stop at a checkpoint. My son's school was blown up. Every school, hospital and museum pillaged and burned. I *told* you –"

"And I told *them*."

"Killing thousands of people, destroying whole cities and towns, you're turning the whole country against you. The whole Muslim world. My son's nineteen. Three of his schoolmates have already joined the *fedayeen*. Good middle-class kids. I keep begging him not to, but some day he will. Soon he'll be killing your Marines. Or they'll be killing him."

Jack thought of the young man in Baltimore Orioles jacket when he'd waited for Professor Younous in the Physics Building. Pearl Jam the kid was listening to. And worrying about some physics problem. "Together, Ibrahim, Americans and Iraqis," he didn't believe it but said it anyway, "we can work this out."

"I'm sorry, my friend. I can't support or defend you anymore."

HE GRABBED A RIDE with a National Guard engineering unit headed to Ramadi, guys with thick glasses and potbellies outlandish in their new desert camo. They handled their guns inexpertly and were uncomfortable in their helmets. Jack felt sorry for them and wanted to be far from them if something happened.

They crossed a wasteland of blasted mud-brick villages, shattered palms teetering over withered canals. Bullet-pummeled vehicles sprawled along the road: burnt-out cars and trucks, a semi on its back, its load of wheat spilled randomly, two contorted Humvees like moths burnt by a flame. A stench of rotten bodies, corpses chewed by dogs and ravens, a blackened car whose occupants had crawled into the ditch to die.

The men looked out, impassive, on this wreckage of a nation. "I didn't want to be here," one said. "But now people are shooting at me. I have to kill them or they kill me."

"I never seen anything like this," said a big black sergeant with a gap in his front teeth and wideset ears. "Long as I live I'm going to remember this time."

"Yeah," the first laughed. "Long as you live."

IN RAMADI he tried to reach Colonel Nureddin Sama at the base but the phones didn't work. He asked the US clerks in the commandeered office but no one knew about any Iraqi officers.

He took a patrol of three Humvees up the road to the house below the white water tank. He could see the goat track undulating over the hills toward the abandoned farm where a year ago he'd met Sama and his desert greyhound.

He pulled the cord on the gate and a bell clanged inside the house. A woman in levis and a black blouse came out, closed the door behind her and crossed the garden to the gate. Forty-five and beautiful, with tanned features, a black scarf, and wide brown eyes.

"I'd like to speak to Colonel Sama," Jack said, conscious of his accent.

"You'll have to find his grave."

"He's dead?" he blundered stupidly.

"You should know." She stared at him with hatred. "You're the ones who killed him."

HE FOUND ISABELLE in Samarra with the Black Watch near the ancient palace. "Oh *hello*," she said, coming out of a tent to shake hands as if they'd once crossed briefly and now chanced to meet again. Cupping a palm over her eyes she smiled up at him against the sun. For a moment he wondered if she'd found someone, an officer in the Black Watch, and felt embarrassed and strangely pained. She took his arm. "Let's walk."

"It's all mined. Beyond the perimeter."

"I know where." She walked on, tugging his arm. "Heard you'd come back."

"Three weeks ago. Been trying to call you."

"Oh that mobile's knackered. I'll give you my new one."

Do you have somebody here? he wanted to ask her. How crazy. *I was afraid you were in danger*, he wanted to say, but that was crazy too. "Things are getting nasty. You should go home." *I sound like a dyspeptic uncle.*

She sat on a chunk of marble column from an ancient temple. "Heavens, I was worried about *you!*"

He sat beside her on the stone, her dark hair fragrant with sun. "I tried so hard to stop this war –" Their shoulders touched and he pulled away. "Now I'm in the middle of it and don't know what to do."

"Two weeks before the invasion our Chief Weapons inspector, Dr. David Kelly, came back from a detailed inventory in Iraq and told Blair there were no WMDs."

"Lots of people on my side told Bush the same thing."

"And after he challenged Blair on the WMDs, Dr. Kelly was murdered. An amateurish job, they tried to make it look like a suicide. Took him out in the woods in Oxfordshire and force-fed him a pill and cut his wrist."

"So maybe he did kill himself?"

"No, the vein he supposedly cut wouldn't have killed him, and though there were twenty-nine empty pill packets beside him there was only one pill in his stomach."

"So who did it?"

"SIS? Your folks? Maybe Chalabi's thugs?"

"So you're in danger, from writing about it?"

"No, no, it's out now. BBC did a huge piece, then Blair's press minister accused them of treason."

Jack raised his boots one at a time and tightened the laces. "Tuesday I go out with a Reserve unit. Tour of the battlefield."

"The battlefield's become Iraq."

"There has to be a way to help them stop this."

"They don't want to stop." She watched a dust dervish spin, a desert *jinni*. "Tell me, what are *we* doing here?" She turned to him, sun in her eyes. "You and I? No excuses."

Out on the desert the wind rolled empty beer cans back and forth. "With all this kidnapping, you should go home."

"*The Independent* wants me to. MI6 doesn't. I told the paper I'm staying and filing stories whether they like it or not –"

"To Hell with MI6."

She lowered her voice. "SIS wants to make *sure* Blair knows the truth. Whether he wants to or not. That's why I'm staying. But you shouldn't waste time here. Or your life."

He drew up his knees, arms around them. "Sometimes I think it's unstoppable, some huge wrathful catastrophe. Then I think maybe it's worth one more try – these kids, they're getting all shot up for nothing."

"Fifty Iraqi civilians die for every U.S. soldier –"

"I signed on to get Bin Laden and AQ. Not this."

The low sun reddened her hair, gilding the cartridge cases strewn across the desert. "Maybe we'll never get him."

He put his hand over hers. "If we can't?"

"There'll always be *this* mess."

"We stay in Iraq much longer you'll be kidnapped and I'll be killed."

She grinned. "There's always that –"

"While I'm with this unit –" *Why am I saying this?* "– I won't be able to reach you."

She reached inside her collar and slipped the black scarab on its golden chain from her neck over his. "For three thousand years this has been with someone... watching over them. Now it can watch over you..."

"No," he said, fearing he'd be killed and the scarab lost. Dust caught in his throat; he wanted to kiss her, hold her.

"Yes," she answered, settling the gold chain round his neck. "You bring it back to me."

He didn't dare promise. "I'll keep trying to find an answer, and you keep telling them the truth. Maybe something good will happen..."

She glanced toward the far walls. "A thousand years ago this was a vast palace. Silken tents, dancing girls in see-through gowns and golden bracelets, wine and song and happy families, jealousies and intrigues and joys and sorrows... Makes me think of that story from the Babylon *Talmud*, the one O'Hara used in *Appointment in Samarra?*"

"Don't know it."

"A merchant in Baghdad sends his servant shopping. The servant comes home terrified, says he met Death in the market and she threatened him. He borrows the merchant's horse and flees to Samarra. The merchant goes to the marketplace and asks Death, *why did you threaten him?* Death says she had been merely surprised to see him, because she had an appointment with him tonight in Samarra."

"When you're fucked you're fucked." After he spoke he saw her note what he'd said. It somehow made them man and woman again. Not just allies, people who might fuck.

"I fear you won't come back," she said. "You'll go away and leave me –" She laughed to counteract this. "I mean somehow we won't meet up again –"

"I have to give you back your locket." He pulled her close, her hair soft on his cheek, and she leaned her body into him digging her nails into his neck and pulling him to her like a cat and kissed him, her lips rough on his. "God this is good," she whispered. "It's so good to touch someone. Oh God it's so good to touch you."

She pulled his hand inside her camo shirt against her small breast, the nipple hard. "When you come back I'll be here for you. Any way you want me."

Rifles fired, he pushed her down grabbing his M-4 but it was just soldiers shooting at the beer cans on the desert, spiking little pirouettes of dust.

I don't want to die, he thought. *Not after this.*

SHE WATCHED HIS CONVOY grow small against the desert, its wistful dust plume reddened by the dusk. She reached to her neck where the scarab had been and smoothed her collar, thinking of him in the Humvee's cabin scanning the darkening hills for death, her black scarab round his neck.

She hungered to send him a prayer, anything that might protect him, but if you'd stayed in this place long enough you knew prayers had no value, saved no one, prevented no harm.

On the scarab's back was a tiny image of Osiris, god of good and of sun, and his wife Isis. But Osiris gets killed, she remembered, by the god of evil and darkness.

In the line of clouds against the sunset was a camel train from centuries ago, a long line of camels heading east on the Silk Road, and in the clouds she could see each camel's nodding head, its bundle of goods piled high on its back, and for an instant she saw the whole panoply of human endeavor, the whole falseness and beauty of it, *that we could crave so much.*

"I want you to be safe," she told him. "I want you to stay safe."

The Purpose of War

THEY REACHED A VILLAGE, a bullet-splintered sign, *...ed al Fakhr*", hanging sideways where two dirt tracks merged into a rutted street between two rows of mud-brick hovels with reed shacks behind them.

"Not what the map says," Tony Decourt said.

"Nothing in this shithole," Jason Ortiz added, "is what the map says."

"Hold it," Jack said and Ortiz braked the Humvee. Tony on his radio tried to halt the others but the comms were down again so Tony jumped out and waved at them. Jack glanced back at the Humvees strung out like geese. "Two men off each of the first four trucks," he said. "We split up and go through town. Everything's fine, we call you in."

"Nothing here Sir," Ortiz said. "But desert dogs and garbage."

"And fuckin camel *sp-spi*-spiders," Brad Wiley said.

A rifle banged and Jack dove to the ground aiming

for motion but the trooper who'd fired waved his hand *no problem* and pointed to a white goat writhing on the ground coughing great gobs of blood into its whiskers. *This is where they get the word goatee,* Jack thought madly. "She moved, Sir," the trooper said.

"What if she'd been a child?" Jack said. "An old woman?"

"What if she was a bad guy?"

"Sorry, girl," Jack said, and shot the goat through the head, thinking of the family coming back tomorrow after the American sweep, an old man saying, "the Americans didn't bring us freedom. But they blew up my town and killed my family's milk goat."

Beyond the village they waited for the Humvees to catch up. "It's gross," Ortiz yelled down from his Mark 19. "There's mosques and minarets in every fuckin town. These people they're *brain*washed by religion."

Jack glanced at his watch: *18:35, Sunday – 10:35* on the East Coast, churches full of people worshipping the very things Christ forbade... Others worshipping TV football, the announcers discussing each play *as if it mattered,* with the gravity of doctors reviewing a complicated procedure. And these kids moving with him through the dusk, all they wanted to do was go back to that world.

Was that the purpose of war – to give life meaning?

War is death. *And it's death that gives life meaning.*

AT NIGHT THEY CIRCLED the Humvees like Conestogas, put out sentries and Claymores and dug sleeping holes. Jack felt out of place among these young men speaking freely about why they hated this war. "My problem with these generals?" Tony said. "They *love* war – what they've always wanted. But they most was too young for Vietnam. Never seen combat."

"They don't ha-have no ri-risk sitting in Baghdad," Brad Wiley said. "They like th-th-that."

Tony's closest friend, Brad was a sparse young man with a quick stutter, the kind of kid that back home whom Tony the cop might catch for speeding. "I don't understand *w*-war," Brad had said last night. "Like the *Ci-Civ*-Civil War? I'm from Mississippi but I don't *see* this thing about black and *whi*-white." He'd glanced at Tony. "You're black and I'm white, but you're more like a brother to me than an-an-an-any-anyone."

Tony's self-effacing smile. "Yeah you my brother too," and Jack felt a sudden warmth for him. If I do one thing in this horror show, he told himself, I'm going to bring these men home.

He tried to imagine Tony's life as a cop in Pueblo, Colorado, the little split-level home, the girl seven and boy nine, Tony's wife staying busy, waiting.

He'd fallen again, Jack realized, for war's oldest trick: a month ago he'd hadn't even known these men and now he'd die and kill for them, *anything* to get them home alive. They were no longer strangers but people with lives they wanted to live, with loved ones, fears and aspirations. Captain MacAllister, a burly cheery Santa of a man whom the men called "Mac" unless senior officers were near, was no longer just a face but now someone that Jack liked to sit with in the quiet times drinking coffee and talking books and folk music, motorcycles and trout fishing. Mac ran a Kinko's in Oregon and had joined the Guard years ago after a flood had hit part of his town, and the Guard had come in and saved it. "I joined up to help the American people," he said one night. "Not to kill people in some foreign place just to steal their oil." He tossed his coffee on the ground. "Oh for a Starbucks double espresso right now."

Protect each other: the universal soldier's rule. And on

the other side the Iraqis in their bombed-out basements trying to shield each other against the Cobras' 20 mm uranium-clad bullets, hadn't they made the same subconscious pact?

What his father had once taught him he'd relearned in Afghanistan: an officer puts his men first. But if an officer is responsible for the lives of his men, what does he do when an incompetent commander orders them unnecessarily into danger?

Which is the greater duty: to follow orders no matter how unwise, or not to put your men in harm's way without a valid cause?

ISABELLE STAYED IN HIS MIND like a lost battle. How could he care about her so much when he barely knew her? Did this horror heighten the hunger for love? Was that the purpose of war?

I'll still be here for you, she'd said, *Any way you want me.*

But by not looking out for her, wasn't he doing what he'd done with Sophie?

Isabelle wasn't Sophie. He couldn't protect everyone. His job was get Bin Laden.

But Bin Laden wasn't here. And instead of hunting him he was stuck in a Humvee in the desert trying to protect a bunch of guys who wanted to go home and watch football.

Strange how death made even the mundane seem glorious.

How could he love Isabelle when he loved Sophie?

How can you love someone who's dead?

"DEEP ABIDING FAITH is what you need," Major Elwin Mudge said. "To see the purpose in this."

"What purpose?" Jack said.

Mudge glanced at his watch. "Nine p.m."

"You mean *21:00*."

Mudge unwrapped a silver-foiled package of peanut butter cookies and began to munch them. "I mean to get the men in for prayer."

"Some are on watch. The ones on next watch are sleeping. The rest are beat."

"It's prayer that bonds us all together, gives us God's power..." Mudge squinted through dusty glasses into the darkness beyond the Humvees, and turned to his XO, a tall saturnine lieutenant named Krass. "Call the sentries in."

Jack dispersed his squad into the desert to replace the sentries Mudge had ordered in. "That man Mudge," Tony said, "he know *nothing*. He a *car* salesman."

"Motion on the perimeter!" Brad yelled. "Ten o'clock."

It moved fast, a quick shadow. "Don't fire!" Jack called.

It was a wild desert dog, yellow eyes in the moonlight. Jack walked across the sand, oblivious of mines, of snipers beyond the berms between the canals. "Come here, pup," he called. "You wouldn't eat an MRE would you? No I suppose not. Hey Bandit, what do we give this guy?"

Tell him get lost.

"He's hungry. Can't you see?"

I was hungry too. All the time in that shed.

"Before I rescued you –"

I can't believe you didn't step on a mine. First time I was ever impressed by a human.

"C'mere, pup," Jack called. "Don't listen to Bandit, he's full of shit." He knelt, the chunk of MRE Chicken Alfredo hanging from his fingers like a dead rat.

The dog dashed forward, snatched the MRE in fast teeth and darted into the night. Like the *fedayeen*, Jack thought. How we going to kill *them*? And why?

NIGHT WAS FADING. The wind died, the air cold and thin as if seeping into space. High in the west pink contrails caught the sun – a fighter group heading north. To the southeast a wide black column from a burning pipeline tilted far into the sky, twisting south toward the Gulf. A fuel convoy rumbled west, guarded front and rear by Bradleys, a Cobra flitting over them like a herd dog with cattle.

Soon the desert filled with motion: trucks kicking up orange dust, fighters streaking east, guns twinkling like Christmas lights, Cobras dropping TOW missiles, their machine guns roaring, the gray sun smeared by the smoke of explosions. Weariness weighed on him.

Human hearts had turned evil, we so easily did what normally would horrify us. In America you see a person killed by a car and for weeks you can't get it out of your head; here you see a charred Iraqi family on the roadside and you barely notice.

WHEN HE'D FIRST COME to Iraq he'd thought it could never be a trap like Vietnam. In the jungle the enemy had had perfect widespread cover. Here was just desert, rolling hills and bleak cities. But to win, he was learning, you had to destroy every city, every town, every rock in the wasteland where a man could hide.

A pair of A-10s came in dropping phosphorous bombs that bloomed into vast infernos filling the village and sky. *We're eating MREs while right in front of us people fry alive.* "We just here till the 'lection, Sir," Tony said. "President can't look bad before the 'lection. Then maybe we can go home."

"Some of you may not like being here," Major Mudge told them. "But we're only human and have to follow God's will."

"Hey wait a minute," Tony laughed. "*God* didn't will

this."

"God wants this false religion punished. If we don't do it who will?"

"One thing I've learned as a cop," Tony said, "is killin's the worst possible solution to a problem. Ain't you Christians discovered that?"

Short and stout with a bland round face, button nose and colorless hair, Mudge was an accountant for the KIA dealership in Fort Hays, Kansas, "Finest place on God's green earth."

Perhaps, Jack thought, because Mudge had spent most of his life looking out on the endless horizontality of central Kansas his soul had told him the world was flat. And thus his disdain for science: it contradicted his impression of the world. And wasn't this a normal response to a world that's changing too fast? Isn't that what Muslims did too?

Because Mudge was company commander Jack tried to not let the men see how he scorned him. Yet more and more he caught himself taunting him – "But Elwin, the dinosaurs lived sixty million years ago – how can the world be six thousand years old?"

Mudge checked his watch. "God created the world six thousand and eight years and ninety-one days ago. All those fossils, God just put them here to test our faith."

Falluja

WHEN A MARINE ATTACK on a village southeast of Ramadi got pinned down, Mudge's company was called forward to support it. From the rear Mudge sent Mac's platoon into the village. "We in the *shit* now," Tony Decourt said.

The last Iraqis had retreated into a schoolhouse and playground. Two LARs had fired thousands of Bushmaster rounds into the school and Cobras had dropped TOWs that shuddered the earth and spouted clouds of dust and concrete and flesh.

Jack crawled ahead of Mac and two of his men along a classroom wall. An A-10 came in fast and low and the school convulsed as another rocket hit. Mac bent his head and Jack wondered bizarrely was he praying for the poor souls trapped in that inferno. "Stay here!" Jack sprinted forward to a fallen tree. A rocket whacked into the classroom behind him.

"*No!*" Decourt yelled. "Who sent in that fucking locate?"

"Hold them!" Jason Ortiz was screaming into his radio. "Hold the *fucking* rockets! Hey Jack the comms are down!"

Another rocket hit the classroom wall where Mac and his men had taken cover. In the roar and blinding white flash the world congealed, came apart.

"Blue on blue!" Ortiz screamed into the radio, "*Blue on blue* you assholes!"

"*Mac!*" Jack ran through smoke and debris toward the still-falling classroom from which a trooper staggered dreamlike holding an arm in his hand and fell to his knees, blood pouring from his severed shoulder.

Another rocket howled in knocking Jack sideways into the wall and all that mattered was to stumble across this cloud of shrapnel and maybe Mac was fine, the others – but no, one had died already, without the arm – another trooper digging at the chunks of roof and walls that filled the center of the building. "Down there!" he screamed. "They're down *there!*"

Ortiz got the radio working and called off the A-10s. He came up with tears streaking his blackened cheeks and they brought in a Humvee to winch away the tons of sharp-edged concrete. Jack dug as if Sophie and the kids were under the rubble, as if *they* were expiring every second and he still might save them.

They placed the pieces of Mac and two of his men together on camo tarps, pulled the biggest chunks of concrete out of their flesh, tied them up and another Humvee from Mudge's command drove them away.

Jack sat in the blasted building with his M-4 in his hands and emptiness everywhere. Sunset lay like orange sludge across the peaks. The wind prowled, hungry and cold. Mac was everywhere, his wide cheery face with his two-days' graying beard, his reddish Santa cheeks, his burly good-natured laugh, the affectionate grip of his thick-knuckled hands, his bright eyes, his huge body that at first one might mistake for soft, the rolling walk that belied his strength, the kindness that masked a lack of fear.

Now he was dead and the wound too great to feel.

"IT'S GOD'S WILL." Mudge sat beside Jack with two MREs in his hand. "Much as it hurts, we have to realize that. That gives us comfort."

Jack stared at him. "What would you know about God's will?"

Mudge filled his mouth with cheese crackers. "Well, if God hadn't wanted them to die, they'd still be here."

"My family was murdered by people who believed in God. And just like you they were sure what they did was right."

Mudge stirred powdered chocolate in a cup of water heated by C-4. "This," he nodded his chin at the tangle of buildings and tawdry desert, "it's all going down to everlasting fire."

"Isn't that what the Air Force's trying to do?"

Mudge cleared his throat, spit. "What killed Mac and his men was an IED – there wasn't any blue on blue."

"You nuts? I saw that A-10 come in – we *all* saw it."

"I've talked with the men. We've concluded it was an IED." He gave Jack a patient look. "We don't want to aid'n comfort the enemy with crazy stories about us bombing our own men, now do we?"

"You're afraid it won't look good on your record? Is *that* it?"

"You oughtta focus on this war. On how we can win. Instead a causin problems."

"You try to cover up what happened to Mac and his guys and I will end your career. You'll never get that pension you hitched up for."

Mudge poured the dregs of his chocolate on the sand. "When Jesus returns, He'll take all of us who believe in

Him, who've lived by *His Word*, up to Heaven. And leave the rest of you behind." His feet crunched on glass as he crossed to his sleeping hole beside a Bradley.

As Jack drifted into sleep he remembered a long-ago rock crevice in Afghanistan where he'd lain up for an hour out of the snow. Even a moment's safety and peace...

He woke at dawn from dreams of lying half-crushed under concrete and of trying to rescue Mac while strange officers kept saying *He's not there, soldier, it's your imagination.*

The first fighters were flying north. Bombs shook the desert. Smoke blotted out the last stars and the macabre violet of dawn. To the north red tracers chased each other down the green pit of night. Mudge stood. "Thank you good Lord," he mumbled as he pissed, "for this new day."

ACROSS THE LAND OF MILK AND HONEY they drove, twirling a half-mile high dust plume up the plains and hills between the Tigris and Euphrates.

At moments Jack could see this land before agriculture and civilization had destroyed it: tall grass, glinting cold rivers, trout like shadows across bright stones, antelope and deer herds to the horizons, the thunder of bird chant and scented cool air. Then it shifted back to hot dusty horizons where nothing grew, and the air burned the insides of his nostrils and parched his throat.

They took a short halt on the road to Ramadi. "I keep having this dream," Tony turned aside to spit, "we going to die here."

"Everybody always thinks that." Jack listened to the uneven rattling of the Humvee's diesel. "Years ago in Afghanistan I used to all the time."

"In this dream you get pinned and I try to save you and we both get wasted. I see my blood pouring on top a this dirt –"

The Humvee's engine died. Ortiz cranked on it, revving it hard to keep it going. A *samarra*, Jack remembered, was the cloak victims of the Inquisition wore to their executions.

It didn't matter about Tony's dream. *Except for Tony.*

Mudge came up, his rifle slung upside down over one shoulder. He knelt to retrieve something, peered at it in his hand. "Look at this willya –"

A small chunk of clay with thickly compressed writing. "A cuneiform tablet," Jack said. It felt sacred in his palm. "Five thousand years old. From Ur, oldest civilization on earth. The first writing." He could almost reach the person who had made it.

"Your timing's off," Mudge smiled.

The column ahead was taking machine gun fire and they called in CAS. For an hour the town boiled under black and red smoke and phosphorent flashes, the thud of bombs and rockets shivering the earth where they waited, two miles away.

Moving in next morning they split up to check the ruined streets. As Jack paused in a courtyard he heard a bell sound, looked up to see a bamboo wind chime hanging from a wrecked trellis. Ortiz came out of the house, heavy under his vest and ammo belts, boots crunching the courtyard's painted tiles. "Clear," he said. "They're all dead."

There must be, Jack thought, some respite from this horror. In books there might be periods of violence or sorrow, but then the author would toss in some humor or joy so the reader wouldn't lose faith – *comic relief*, wasn't it called? But where, here, was the comic relief?

The wind chime rang melodically, making him think of the family that must have lived here and how familiar that sound had been.

You can check out any time you like. But how could he

leave these men?

They waited three days in the sun drinking Kool-Aid in recycled water. Other columns passed, dust so thick it coated their eyes and lungs, faces and uniforms; you could wipe it away but it came right back.

ONE AFTERNOON they scouted a town near Samarra that had been bombed before a Marine advance column had hit it – narrow streets of caved-in houses under splintered palms, the Humvees' tires crushing oranges that had been blasted from the trees.

The dust and smoke were so thick it seemed a dream where wraithlike soldiers flitted, where walls and trees slid out of the mist then vanished. In the center stood a ruined museum where a stone torso lay blackened by bullets and a disembodied marble head stared at the sky. Inside the walls a marble hand lay in a welter of glass and plaster; there were rows of shattered vases where someone had blasted all the display cases with an M-4 on auto.

Amid the crump of tank fire came the whistle of jets, and he wondered what it looked like to the pilots way up there, the smoking ground and tiny mutilated houses.

The toxic smoke made him cough. They went out through the museum across a field, boots crunching on shards, here and there a naked tree, once the body of an old man holding a rope with nothing tied to it.

They came to some berms, the sand collapsing at the edges, but there was no one and they took no fire. Returning through the museum he heard a scraping down a corridor, like a wounded soldier dragging across the floor.

It was Mudge shoving things from a display case into a camo sack. His rifle lay ten feet away. Surprised by Jack, he jumped up clasping a black marble head with a tight curling beard, strong nose, and high eyebrows. "Lifting this thing, *whew*," he mumbled. "Must weigh fifty pounds."

Three small sculptures lay next to Mudge's pack, one a perfect lion with an arrow in its chest. "These are Assyrian," Jack said. "Three thousand years old. Put the damn things back."

"It's a lie, science." Mudge peered at him intensely. "Can't you *see?*"

"I'll have you busted for pillaging. You know the force order on that."

Mudge glanced across the floor at his rifle. As Jack turned away for the first time in his life he felt fear of being shot in the back by one of his own men.

Fragged. He walked out of the museum toward the line of Humvees.

IN THE BATTLE for Falluja the bullets came from everywhere, off buildings and cars, sparking the street, rat-tatting off tanks, screams and yells through smoke, the thunder of bombs jerking the earth back and forth under his feet as he ran down an alley of bullets spattering off walls. He leaped over a woman dragging herself sideways toward a child with no head. Up front Ortiz tossed in another grenade and the shock knocked him into a wall. The alley opened into a concrete pentagon between five buildings – blackened windows and cars burnt down on their rims – a place many guys could die if he didn't do this right – and he wanted to tell the men run back up that alley, back through the smashed streets, get in the trucks to Baghdad and fly back to America.

"Rake those windows!" he yelled at Tony and Ortiz, pointed at a wall and sprinted for an archway on the far side, boots crunching concrete and glass, body armor heavy and hot, helmet slipping, everything happening slowly, plenty of time for anyone to shoot him down.

He reached the archway and spun round firing on the windows spattering splinters and concrete with Ortiz close behind him, and after him Tony running awkward and fast then like a doll yanked sideways falling against the wall, his blood graffiti down it, Ortiz calling for a Cobra and Jack jammed in another magazine and ran across the square expecting the bullet's crushing pain, *wanting it* for what he'd done to Tony, dragged Tony to the archway and sprayed the windows thinking *Fucker's gone now, heard the chopper coming*, and knelt down and saw that the bullet had cut through Tony's neck shattering the spine.

"We're in the alley on the north side," Ortiz repeated into the radio, on his hands and knees twisting the map this way and that to read it. "This square's in front of us, to the south. Hit the building on the west side, we're taking small arms from there – no wait!" He shuffled the map, "Can you see it? Ali Darfour it says, some shit –"

Something was wrong in the approaching thunder of the Cobra. "No *we're* on the west side," Jack yelled. "Call him off!" Ortiz shook his head under the bulky helmet as Jack grabbed the radio and called it off, the gunship hovering.

That night in the light of a fire of a broken dining room set he tried to write,

> *Dear Mrs. Decourt,*
>
> *I sent Tony to his death and nothing can alter that. There seems no purpose to this, but perhaps life to him was less important than what he did...*

Jason Ortiz came in shaking dust off his helmet. "What ya writin', Sir?"

"Bullshit." Jack tossed the letter on the coals.

"You oughtta email," Ortiz said. "It's faster."

Punishment of God

O N THE THIRD DAY they turned back toward Ramadi, crossing from Salahuddin province toward the Euphrates. The villages they passed had not yet been hit but seemed haunted as if everyone had already died.

How sadly strange here with Mac and Tony gone. *Dead*, he told himself. *Not gone.*

It was better not to believe in God, even if there *were* a God. For what virtue was there in following a moral code because you'd be eternally punished if you didn't? What counted was to develop your own moral code, an innate hewing to the good.

The inverse of Pascal – if there were a good and loving God, wouldn't that God be more drawn to us by our natural goodness than by any obedience to "His" handed-down laws?

At the Baghdad cutoff a mile-high wall of brown sand roared over them cutting off the sky. They shut down and waited, the men uneasily spread out on the perimeter, squinting through sand-blistered goggles at swirling phantoms.

The wind howled, screeched and pummeled their faces and knocked them down, hailing sand across the Humvees. Once the ground quivered like an earthquake.

The sandstorm thundered away, dust tornadoes and debris chasing after it. The radio screamed, "They're hit! *They're hit*, Callahan's hit!" and Jack ran back to Callahan's Humvee half-crushed, twisted and smoking, a hand sticking through the roof. "A rocket," a trooper said, a kid he didn't know. "I heard it hit, from back there –" he pointed to the next truck.

"Where from?"

The kid nodded at the desert. "Out there."

Jack walked into the desert not caring where the Iraqis were, happy to die locating them. So his men could kill them.

There were no tracks, no tire treads. Helmet tipped back, panting and sweating in the heat, lungs full of fine sand, Jack glanced back. The Humvee lay crumpled sideways, the rest of the convoy like a great worm that has suddenly been truncated.

"They couldna been this far," the kid said. "We're beyond RPG range."

"No sign anywhere."

"Never is, Sir. We're shooting at phantoms. Getting killed by phantoms."

A Bradley was dragging the Humvee off the road when they got back. "Flyboys see no one," Ortiz said. "Just sand and *wadis* for miles and miles."

The three dead soldiers were bagged and boarded and the convoy headed southwest again. The men's mood was hurting, angry.

By late afternoon the air had cleared. A red pickup truck drove toward them trailing a tuft of dust. "Bad guys!" Mudge screamed.

Jack grabbed the radio. "Maybe civilians! Turn aside! Go out on the desert!"

Mudge's Humvee rocked to a stop, the .50 cal rotating like an ugly stinger toward the approaching pickup.

"Move into the desert!" Jack yelled. "Do not engage unless he follows you."

The second and third Humvees behind Mudge pulled away from the road. The pickup neared, slowing. Its rear bed was canvas-covered.

Red tracers spat from Mudge's Humvee to the pickup, which reared up and half-spun, slowly falling on its side, shivering as the bullets blasted through it. "No!" Jack screamed into the radio. "Drive!" he yelled at Ortiz. "Drive out there!"

"I don't want to see," Ortiz said.

"Mudge!" Jack radioed. "Get out here."

"I don't take orders from you. It could be a suicide –"

Jack stopped Ortiz a hundred yards short of the pickup. He walked to it across the sand, heard a strange keening like a dying engine that became a woman's voice.

Three men sprawled in the bloody cab. Jack eased to the rear where a woman knelt on the bloody sand, bleeding from the head and chest, cradling a bloody child in her arms. A younger woman and two other children lay dead and spattered, half in and out of the truck.

Ortiz held a fist across his mouth. As Jack turned toward Mudge's Humvee, Ortiz fell to his knees and threw up.

The gun was tight in Jack's fist and he smelled blood and the bile and excrement of the dead Iraqis. "S-S-Sir!" Brad Wiley grabbed his arm. "S-S-Shit happens!"

Jack switched his weapon to his other hand. "Get back with the men."

As he walked across the desert a strange memory returned: he sat astride a surfboard rising and falling with

401

the sea, and a fine spray touched his face. He remembered, thinking to *re-member* is to make whole again, seeing so clearly before him the line of humpback whales against the setting sun.

Mudge backed away. "*What* are you doing?"

"It was a farm truck full of people."

"Could've been a technical." Mudge watched Jack's gun. "How could I know?"

"You killed them because you wanted to."

"Jack, they're Arabs."

Jack raised his gun slowly and Mudge held out his hands as if to block the bullets. The trigger was fire-hot against Jack's finger. Mudge knelt begging. "Remember, Jack, Christ loves me. What will He do if you kill me?"

That was it, the deepest reason to kill him, that he was not only evil but that *he believed his own evil to be good.* Jack jabbed the barrel into Mudge's cheek.

"Jack!" Ortiz came up. "This shit happens every day. Let's move on."

Mudge grinned at Jack. "See – Christ wouldn't let you kill me!"

Jack glanced back at the crumpled pickup. "Call a medic for the woman."

"She's gone, Sir," a trooper said. "Nothing we can do."

He wanted to walk into this desert, walk till the world's end. He feared throwing up, bit back tears, thought of Isabelle, felt her hand on his brow, the tug of her scarab on his neck.

You can't fight the world's ills. All you can do is not add to them.

He'd become a soldier because he loved America and wanted to defend it. But soldiers have to follow orders no matter what. No matter if the order's insane.

We must never give our souls to someone else, control of

our lives, our deaths.

He would go back to the Green Zone. *Like Medieval occupiers we hide behind thick walls and free-fire zones. Install ourselves in the palace of the dictator we deposed. And wonder why the people fear and hate us just like him.*

He'd make his report to HQ, Timothy, Ackerman, Szymanski, the others: *How do we get out of this?* What did the Germans think, at Stalingrad?

What would *he* have done at Stalingrad? Do you turn your back, imagine you can walk away?

If a man believes in a war his country wages but does not fight, he is a coward. But if he doesn't believe and does fight he is also a coward.

But all wars are born from previous wars. There is no good war, no good battle. The only war to end all wars will be the extinction of the human race.

An officer never leaves his men.

Maybe Isabelle would be there.

Isabelle

"THEY SAID YOU WERE DEAD!" She stumbled back in shock, laughing and crying, grabbed him so hard it hurt. "I *thought you were dead*!"

He stepped inside and locked the door, held her, inhaling her, her hair against his cheek, her arms round his ribs, her fingers gripping his back. "Who said?"

She kept kissing him saying "I thought you were dead" and he lifted her up and carried her into the room. "Don't ever go away like this again," she said, her fingernails sharp in his neck, eyes bright with happy tears.

He held her face, fingertips in her soft hair. "*Who* said?"

"That Centcom creep, that civilian."

"Timothy?"

"Him. Said I should leave, my cover's blown."

"That's crazy, why –"

She clasped herself to him as if he were a cliff and any instant she could fall. "I can't take it again, I can't take losing you."

"Hey," he cupped her face in his palms, "I was afraid *you*'d left."

"I *told* you I'd never leave while you were here."

He kissed her again, feeling guilty for her pain, loving the taste of her mouth, the feel of her lips and tongue. "Hasn't been a day I haven't thought of you. An hour."

"My world collapsed when I thought you were dead. And now I have it back." On tiptoes she clenched herself to him. "Every day I thought of you. All the time. In a press briefing they'd talk of some convoy somewhere, some fire-fight..."

He saw the crumpled pickup, the slaughtered family. "I want to be with you."

"At night I'd lie here wondering where you were, were you in danger... I told myself if you came back I'd tell you how much I want you, wouldn't pretend... And then I lost you. And now you're back –"

"But I have to go –"

"Go?"

"Afghanistan. Osama."

She pulled away. "Of course."

Jack saw Mac's robust cheery face, Tony saying *I see my blood pouring on top a this dirt.* "They've screwed us, these politicians."

"They just announced there were no WMD's."

"Who?"

"Your bloody WMD inspector. Some guy named Du-elfer. Says they aren't here."

He shook his head. "Bush and Blair, they always knew they were none."

"Fuck them. Fuck them all." She laughed at the surprise in his face. "You used that word, last time I saw you."

He remembered the Samarra wind taunting her hair, her supple tennis-player's body beneath the shapeless camo. The way she'd held his hand against her breast. He felt terror it would end.

She pulled herself against him. "All that has no meaning. I want *you*."

He caressed her hair back from her face. "I'm still Sophie's. The kids' –"

"I feel that way about Colin, then I think *it's been three years*."

"But it never goes away."

"It never will." She smiled. "So we learn how to live despite it. And live well."

He felt a sweep of gentleness, as if the planet shifted. He caressed her cheek, his calloused palm against her smooth skin.

She brushed his lips with hers and kissed his chin, nestled her mouth against his neck. "Sophie and Colin would want us to love each other. They'd want us to be happy."

She stood back and rolled up her white sweater and slid down her skirt and reached out to him. "You're so lovely," he whispered, could hardly speak.

Coming into her the world was beautiful again, hope nearly real. *You are absolved*, he thought. By this sacrament of love *You are Absolved*.

"THINGS ARE BAD," he told Ackerman, with Timothy patched in from DC.

"That's not news," Timothy said.

"We may have 'won' the battle of Falluja but we're losing the war..."

"In *your* view..." Timothy said.

"In most people's, for multiple reasons. *One*, we invaded their country and most of them hate us and will kill us if they can. *Two*, our troops are not ready for this. We have inexperienced National Guard units fighting sophisticated enemies on their home turf. *Three*, We have let loose a Pandora's box of religious and tribal hostilities with no short term solution. *Four,* These conflicts are central to their very existence and they will die for them. Most Americans by comparison barely know they exist. And *Five,* They will never give up."

"So what you're saying," Ackerman said, "is we should get out?"

"No. The harm that would result from our pulling out now is far greater than that caused by our staying until this place is at peace and can move forward, everyone working together. No more car bombs or assassinations, no more tirades. A Sunni-Shia democracy, the kind al-Sadr talks about sometimes."

"You're saying we can't leave till there's a strong central command," Timothy said.

"Yeah," Jack couldn't resist. "Like back in the days of Saddam."

"Don't always go there," Timothy answered.

Jack waited a few moments. "Yes?" Timothy finally said.

Jack waited more, then, "Why did you tell Isabelle I was dead?"

Timothy spluttered as if it was ludicrous, such a question, not worthy of response. "That's not true."

"You told her I was dead. Why?"

A long huff. "I may have mentioned the risks you faced, out there with inexperienced troops... that kind of thing. Just to prepare her, you know, if you did become a casualty... it worries me, you always sticking your neck out, I wanted to warn her..."

"Where was this, Timothy? When?"

"Some embassy dinner somewhere. The Turkish embassy maybe. Some bowl of shit we all have to go through... I'm so tired of this –"

"You told her I was dead. Did you think I was?"

"No no no, I told you. It was a warning."

"If I turn up dead, there are five little envelopes that will get opened by Special Forces and Home Office folks, explaining exactly who you are and what you've done and why you're probably behind my death."

"I would never –"

"Yes you would. But it's over now. You have me killed and you fry. Understood?"

"Jack, I –"

"Timothy," Jack could feel the hatred building, the fierce, dominating power. "Do you *understand?*"

"Yeah yah, I understand that's what you're saying."

"So we have to work together. We have to convince the next administration that we can't walk away from Iraq. It's a lovely idea full of liberal promise and good feelings, hopeful and optimistic, but we can't do it."

"Things can't get worse. And I promise you, you're wrong. I feel I can trust you with my life – the same as you can trust me with yours."

THINGS DID GET WORSE in April 2005 when the Shiite cleric and warlord Muqtada al-Sadr organized a huge peaceful demonstration in Firdous Square opposite the Hotel Palestine protesting the American occupation. "What it does," Jack told Timothy, "is erode your last pretense of authenticity. No one wants us here."

"Don't forget, we're here because *we* want to be here, not because *they* did. We don't give a sweet fuck, except in public, what *they* want."

"Firdos Square was where that staged photo was taken, you remember, of an Iraqi crowd toppling Saddam's statue? When in truth it was US troops under orders from Centcom, and the Iraqis were rounded up to complete the picture."

"Yes, exactly. It was very well done."

"We're just their next Saddam."

"We've staged elections. For the first time in half a century –"

"Not the Sunnis. It was bogus, it won't go anywhere."

"And your point is?"

"We should work with this guy al-Sadr."

"Fuck, how many of our guys has he killed?"

"He wants to do a truce and bring the Sunnis and Shiites together."

"That's a horrible idea."

"At this point it may be our only way out."

A LOVELY OCTOBER EVENING. Jack crossed Saadoun Street headed for Firdous Square and the Hotel Palestine two blocks away when a huge *Bang* knocked people to the sidewalk and blew a cloud of flame and black smoke skyward in front of the Palestine.

Isabelle. He sprinted along Saadoun toward the concrete wall outside the Hotel. *Wham* another blast tumbled him to his knees, the sidewalk quivering. He staggered up and ran through billowing smoke – this one had gone off in front of the mosque across the square… car bombs it must be, other cars streaming madly away from the blasts, honking horns, tires screaming.

A huge thundering explosion crushed his ears, his body, shuddered the earth and smashed him into the concrete wall; he tried to hold on but everything was gone.

AT THE FIRST BLAST Isabelle was standing before the bathroom mirror with one hand lifting her hair while she swept a hair dryer back and forth above it. She was thinking that Jack would be here in a few minutes and maybe it'd been a waste of time to shower because he'd probably start kissing her and she'd run her fingertips down the hard muscles of his back and in no time they'd be doing it like teenagers, on the living room floor, the couch, the squeaking bed… she couldn't get enough, didn't want to stop, nor he either, and they'd be doing it again tonight –

The *Boom* knocked her sideways into the wall. Lights flickered, the dryer died in her hand. Glass tinkled. Her ears howled. She ran to the window; below, in front of the Hotel on the edge of Firdous Square was a blazing smoking hole, a wide swath of shattered concrete and the fiery chassis of an automobile. *Wham* another blast sent her reeling backward – this one a huge column of fire across the Square, in front of the mosque, people yelling in the corridor outside the room, she should get away from the window, she knew, but couldn't… there were bodies in front of the mosque, between the dark smoke billows…

Why was that concrete truck coming this way instead of running away from the explosions? For an instant she had the crazy idea he was coming to fix the hole in the Hotel's concrete defense wall that had been blown by the first car – but no it was a big bomb that would take out the hotel just like they'd taken out the World Trade Center – the truck hesitated, rocked back and forth, small arms fire hitting it now and she should get away from the window and it crashed in on her in a violent life-shivering roar that knocked her face down on a carpet of glittering glass diamonds or maybe it was the ocean she couldn't tell or she was swimming through stars and space. She pushed to her feet, staggered to the door and opened it, the hallway full of smoke. She shut it and ran to the bathroom. The water still worked; she soaked a towel, wrapped it around her face and went into the corridor, people running, yelling, fluorescent ceiling tubes flickering, someone calling in an Asian language.

A woman staggered past with hands to her face, blood between her fingers. Isabelle grabbed her. "You're okay?"

"Got to go down, got to go down." It was a Spanish reporter, Isabelle couldn't remember her name.

"Your eyes – can you see?"

"Yes. It's cuts on my face, from the glass."

"Where's your flak jacket?"

"In my room I think. Got to go down. Before they hit us again."

They *should* go down, Isabelle thought. If there were more bombs the building might collapse. But was outside more dangerous? She yanked the woman into her room, ran to the closet, grabbed her flak jacket, slipped it up the woman's arms and shoved her back into the corridor. "What's your name, I can't remember?"

"María. María Hidalgo. We must go down –"

An Iraqi with a TV t-shirt came holding up his hands. "Everyone sit against the wall. Keep your flak jacket on. It's all under control."

"Downstairs," a reedy British voice called out, "how is it?"

"Broken glass in the lobby, lots of smoke, a few folks with cuts and bruises. That's all we know."

I saw bodies in front of the mosque, Isabelle started to say. I saw bodies. Where was Jack?

She tugged at a piece of glass sticking in her cheek. It came away with a pulse of warm blood down her face and off her chin down her breast.

Time had passed, she checked her watch. *18:02.* Where was Jack?

A BLACK-VEILED FACE peering down, deep brown eyes. She tugged at him. Her lips moved but he couldn't hear amid the screech in his ears and everywhere the scream of sirens.

"Are you hurt?" she was saying.

He couldn't remember why he was here or why she was speaking Arabic. "Who are you?"

"Can you sit? Your head is bleeding."

He sat. The air smelled of smoke. "I must go," she shook him again, glanced down the sidewalk, back to him.

He wanted to hold her hand, this person. "What *is* this?"

"A bomb. The Palestine."

He rolled to his feet. *Isabelle.* The hotel still stood, blackened up the wall, shattered windows like affronted eyes. He turned to the woman but she'd gone, a small black figure hustling away on the empty sidewalk.

He limped then ran toward the Hotel, broke through the crowded lobby and climbed the stairs. People were coming down, all yelling and calling to each other. Someone bumped his shoulder making him double over in pain.

Their door was open. She turned from the window. "Oh my God!"

He held her as if somehow that might prevent danger, death. "You're okay!" he kept saying, "You're okay?"

She pulled back. "You've got a cut over your eye, we have to stitch it. And look at your hands and knees – you've ruined a perfectly good pair of pants…"

He held her as if they could always protect each other. "I just took a shower and dried my hair," she said. "Now I'll have to do it all over again."

"Amazing no one killed."

"I saw bodies. Iraqi Police guys, somebody said they stopped the second car."

She glanced past Jack's shoulder out the blasted window. I've been in Iraq and Afghanistan five years, and this's the first time I've ever been bombed.

"I'M GOING TO KABUL," Jack said one evening coming back from the Green Zone.

"What?" She ignored the bottle of Lebanese wine he'd put on the table. "What for?"

"Wahid al-Din."

"Eagle of the Hindu Kush?" she said derisively. "What does that have..."

"I just found out he killed his own brother Ahmad. My blood brother. My best friend in Edeni."

"Who told you this?"

"A Home Office guy from Kabul. Said Wahid stoned Ahmad to death in the soccer stadium. Stoned Ahmad's wife to death too – I may have met her..."

"When?"

"When Sophie saved me from the Spetsnaz and then from Hekmatyar's guys then walked me to Ahmad's clinic – he was trying to save orphans, you know –"

She said nothing, then, "So you're going to kill Wahid?"

He unclenched his hands, looking out the window, seeing nothing.

"Get away from there!" she snapped.

"Yeah." He turned to her. "Fucking death around us, all the time. People wanting to shoot us, blow us up. We just have to realize the medium we're in. The rest is illusion." He turned back to the window, forehead against the glass. "It's deeper than sex, vengeance." In the fading light, the early evening smog of Baghdad, the F-18 vapor trails tinted blood-red by the setting sun, he got again the awful sense that this war has been going on here for ten thousand years. Would always go on.

She tugged him from the window and stepping to the side let down the blinds and shut the curtains. "Someone like Wahid, it doesn't matter if he dies, he's so evil. But what's his killing do to you?"

"It's what a blood brother is in Afghanistan. Someone who avenges you."

"If you kill Wahid, won't someone feel it's *his* duty to kill you?"

"That's what I told a SF guy, way back after 9/11. He was saying he'd do anything to avenge my family, and I said that's the trouble with war, everybody dies avenging someone else." He sat, tried to rub the weariness out of his face. "There's no way out."

She sat beside him, held him. "Find some other way to punish Wahid. That's the way out."

"He's a one-man plague. It'd be like killing Ebola."

"Please darling give up this idea of Kabul. Let Wahid stink in his own misery."

"I can't be with you, with anybody, till I do what I have to do."

"I thought I'd lost you. Now I have you. I won't lose you again."

He tousled her hair. "It's an easy trip. In and out."

She watched him steadily. "And then?"

He shrugged, feeling the impossibility of it. "Osama."

"He's probably in Saudi, where most of the 9/11 killers came from... Or Pakistan?" Her fingernails dug into him. "Give it up, Jack."

"Vengeance is the poisoned meat you feed your enemies," an old Tajik once told me, "but that you must then eat yourself."

"When? When was that?"

"Years ago. Before we killed his sons."

He felt her recoil. "What do you want," he said. "Lies?"

She stood quietly for a moment, chin up. "It's horrible, that's all."

"I'm shriven –"

"How?"

"My family paid for my sins."

"That's an awful way to look at it."

"Show me a better one." He thought sadly of McPhee in Windows on the World, when Sophie had said *We're back to the military theory of evolution* and McPhee had said *Yes, Maam. Show me a better one.*

Blood Brothers

HE CAUGHT the Aero Contractors Casa 235 from Baghdad to Kabul, surprised to find Timothy sitting up front. "What the fuck you doing here?" he said by way of greeting.

"I might ask you the same. Aren't you supposed to be in the desert?"

"Why aren't you on the torture run to Kuwait?" Jack stepped past him, heading for the back. "Isn't that more your style?"

Timothy smiled. "That plane was full."

Jack thought of Samarra. "Maybe you're going where you're supposed to be."

FEARING CAR BOMBS Isabelle walked fast through the streets in a long black robe and headscarf, her wicker shopping bag on her arm. She passed a café, wanting to sit there like you could in the old days before the invasion.

But now every parked car was death, every busy market and café, every man in a burly jacket that could hide explosives. Before Jack had come back from the dead she would not have cared, might have sat there anyway, for she'd had nothing to lose, had already lost it all, the hope that this man she barely knew but wanted so much would ever return from the desert. She'd bit down on her pain and told herself *no matter what just keep going*, life isn't supposed to be happy... you're just here to take back what you've lost.

Now vengeance seemed alien. *Of course it matters*, she told herself, *you can't let Colin's murder go unavenged. Sophie's and Leo's and Sarah's too.* Strange how she was thinking of them now as her family too... But as she'd told Jack last night you also can't let it keep you from living.

She thought of the café. How sad the invasion had stolen from these people the right to sit happy in the morning sun, to be safe, to raise their children in peace. But *she* didn't have to die here, *Jack* didn't. That didn't help these people. And there were cafés in Paris and London and Prague and Sydney. She and Jack hadn't started this war. They didn't have to pay. Not any longer.

She stopped at a butcher's to buy two mutton hocks, thinking *Jack likes lamb.* Now that they had their own kitchen she could cook whatever they wanted. She'd buy the lamb now, while it was here; he'd be right back from Kabul, they'd have it then.

In a vegetable stall she made a quick purchase of greens and cabbage from a quiet sad little man with bad teeth. *I'm sorry*, she wanted to say, *it's not my fault but I'm sorry.* But in the new Iraq it was not a woman's place to speak out, to take such a chance.

The sudden riot of bougainvillea and hibiscus over a concrete wall shocked her with its purple and orange magnificence. She thought of Jack again. Already familiar as her own skin. He'd promised he'd be careful in Kabul. The thought of making love made her shiver, this man filling her, wanting to give him joy and love.

WAHID'S PALACE spread along a slope overlooking the ruins of Kabul. The perimeter was a ten-foot wall of new concrete blocks, some stamped in red, "USAID School Reconstruction Fund", and above that rolls of concertina wire glistening in the sun. The main gate was guarded by two men with new American M-4s and by a Soviet PKS tripod-mounted machine gun dug in thirty yards back on the right.

Inside was a large main villa surrounded by dried lawns and dead hedges now being replanted. Several smaller buildings along the upslope edge appeared inhabited by the families of guards and servants. In the distance at the rear was what seemed a *madrasah*, with ranks of boys facing a teacher who paced before them.

In his Afghani clothes Jack waited in line with the others wanting to see the Eagle of the Hindu Kush.

"Why do you wish to see him?" the guard said.

"I have a debt to pay," Jack said.

"What's your name?" the guard said, using the diminutive for children and fools.

"Tell him Ahmad al-Din."

"What debt?"

"The first stone."

"WHEN THIS ALL STARTED," Wahid smiled down at Timothy, "who could have thought it would turn out so well?"

"You've done a good job bringing back the old ways." Timothy tipped ash on the floor. "*You've* done well too: the Hummers, the palace –"

"House," Wahid said.

Wahid had a cobra-shaped scar on his right cheek, Timothy noticed. Snakes, a symbol of forbidden knowledge. "Yes," Timothy added. "The *house*. The servants. The bank accounts, the boys, the new *madrasahs*..."

Wahid watched him. "It's a mistake to look too deeply into things."

"But things mustn't seem too, how can I say, *wrong* on the surface."

"Every country needs religion, to keep it together."

"Wasn't it religion that got you into all this?"

"*You* got us into all this. And now with Afghanistan and Iraq you have what you've always wanted: much oil, and military bases on both sides of Iran, which has much oil of its own. Oil's a dying thing, no? We have to grab what we can... So what matters a few million lives? A million people die a year in traffic accidents... Two million from malaria. As I used to tell your friend Jack, no one's ever innocent."

"I came to tell you, your shipments are far too big –"

"That was our deal. You agreed no limits on opium, on religious teaching... and I gave you Bin Laden at Tora Bora. It's not my fault you decided not to take him."

"As you say, let's not look too deeply into things."

Wahid settled himself more comfortably. "We continue, then, to comprehend each other."

"Long ago," Timothy said, "before Osama attacked New York, it is said there were people who warned us. People from here –"

Wahid caught a breath, waited. "We'd like to know," Timothy continued, "who they were. So we can thank them."

Wahid kept his voice steady. "I have no knowledge of this."

"Other Taliban, it's said. We would pay well, to find out."

Wahid smiled. "I am happy to ask people. To help in any way I can –"

Timothy shook his head. "We need to know, but not ask. It must not be known that we do not know." He raised his eyebrows. "But it would make it easier for us to overlook the increase in opium shipments, if we could have these names."

"In Afghanistan there are many ways of knowing. I will do my best."

"I wouldn't want our friend Jack to hear. He might misunderstand."

"He often does."

Timothy sat back. "He might have a different memory, too, of what happened at Tora Bora."

"That would be sad."

"He's here. Did you know?"

Wahid inclined his head. "No."

"Perhaps hunting Osama in Pakistan."

"I wish him luck."

"Or looking for you?"

"A shame. We're blood brothers, you know."

"I didn't."

"Happened years ago. As I said, no one's ever innocent."

"He came alone. He's staying in the usual place... Perhaps before he finds you, you should find him?"

Wahid smiled, the cobra scar contracting. "War is strange, isn't it? Sometimes our worst enemies are on our side."

Timothy stood. "Jack has enemies on all sides. We'd never even know who it was, if one of them should kill him."

The Secret

JACK WAITED TILL TIMOTHY'S armored Humvee drove away from Wahid's palace toward Bagram airport. He tried to think of reasons for Timothy's visit and found none he liked. He stepped out of the line of men waiting to see Wahid and left the palace compound.

Women in *burkhas* and men in bulky clothing thronged the street, a few cars, trucks and buses weaving through them. Diesel exhaust and the stench of burning garbage filled the air. He thought of Isabelle at dawn washing herself with a sponge from the cold water basin.

He ate dinner in a teashop and took a cheap hotel, a bed with a blanket stretched over flat springs. When the bedbugs in the blanket began to bite he lay on the floor with his coat over him, and when the bedbugs moved across the floor to him he sat in a wooden chair by the window, watching the dim lights of Kabul and thinking of the war.

What revenge would Ahmad want? Would he sorrow if his brother died? The brother who had stoned him to death in the Soccer Stadium, him and the woman he loved?

Who was she? Jack imagined her beautiful and kind,

the sort of woman Ahmad would love. Could it have been that girl Jack had seen, the night Sophie had taken him to Ahmad's?

The night so long ago in Edeni when he and Ahmad had clasped bloody palms: a blood brother always avenges his blood brother.

An officer always looks out for his men.

In the hills below glimmered the few lights of Ebnecina Hospital, where Sophie had brought him back from death.

Isabelle had come here too, like all death's pilgrims, hunting the men who'd killed her husband.

Waking beside her at dawn in her lumpy bed on the rumpled sheets he'd pulled her close again and when they made love there was nothing else on earth. *It's war that does this*, he'd thought, *no longer two but one.*

We were just a man and woman. Fucking to preserve the peace.

But the vision of her stayed with him, her in-toed quick step, her form so slim and strong that every motion seemed to spring from a steely central core.

How can someone so quickly become so much more important than you?

Do this, and he could be with her.

Don't kill him, she'd said. *Find some other way to punish him.*

There was no other way.

At 02:45 he left the hotel, moving in the shadows toward Wahid's palace. In a field where new walls were going up he found a two-by-two plywood sheet and two two-by-fours stamped with a Plum Creek Lumber logo. At the end of the compound he leaned the two-by-fours against the wall and climbed them, laid the plywood over the concertina wire, pulled up the two-by-fours and slid down them inside the wall, bringing the plywood down with him.

For fifteen minutes he watched the compound lit only by the city's dim reflection on the clouds. No one moved except one guard sleepily trudging the new gravel walks.

When the guard reached the far end Jack moved to the *madrasah* and hid the plywood and two-by-fours in the gap between the compound wall and the back wall of the *madrasah*. He waited ten minutes then crossed to the patio of Wahid's villa, and along it to the open doors of a bedroom, the sound of wet nasal snoring within. Against the inside wall to his left was a fireplace from which came the glow of coals and the odor of lemon smoke.

He drew the Makarov, stepped into the room across silky rugs to a wooden hutch against the inside wall, and waited for his vision to clear.

He saw a wide white bed and in it a small person, and a larger dark-haired man, long-bearded. The small person was not a woman, for he had short hair. The man half-turned and mumbled in his sleep. Wahid.

Silently Jack locked the patio doors, lit a candle from the coals and set it by the bed.

The boy opened his eyes, watched Jack a moment. "You're going to kill us?"

Jack nodded at Wahid. "Wake him."

The boy rolled over to Wahid. "Master! *Master*!"

Wahid woke blubbering and spitting, slapped the boy. "I told you *never* wake me!"

"Master!" the boy pointed at Jack. "He's here!"

Wahid stared in horror at Jack. "I'll have you killed –"

"Take that scarf, there, on the floor," Jack told the boy. "Tie his hands tight. If he pulls loose I'll kill you both."

With trembling hands the boy did as he was told. "Take that other scarf, there," Jack said, "and bind his eyes." He cut a curtain sash and had the boy tie Wahid's ankles and wrists to the bedposts, then motioned the boy aside. "Go sit by the fire. If you move I'll shoot you."

The boy hissed in a breath. "What are you doing?"

"This man killed his own brother, a teacher who tried to make the world a better place. Wahid is evil. Do you love evil?"

"I'm an orphan. We all are. We can't leave. He makes me do this."

"I've just seen Timothay," Wahid whimpered. "If you hurt me he'll kill you."

Keeping his gun on the boy, Jack went to the fireplace and laid an andiron on the coals. He bent over Wahid. "I want to know why."

"Why?" Wahid trembled. "Why *what*?"

Jack took the andiron from the fire. It glowed in the darkness, sending out a wall of heat. He brought it close to Wahid's cheek. "Why you cast the first stone."

"I didn't! What stone? They *made* me, the *mullahs*, would've killed me –"

"Once already I was going to kill you. Up in Kowkcheh canyon. The other American soldiers saved you."

"Please let me go. I'll be your friend..."

"I've tried to understand what Ahmad would want, what his woman would want."

"She was a lovely girl. It was such a shame."

Jack put down the andiron. It hissed against the stone floor. "Tell me about her."

"They were in love. She helped him at the orphanage. I sent what money I could..." He sniffed. "I tried to warn them. To save them."

"No!" the boy said, from the fire. "I was *there*, the orphanage. I heard Ahmad tell her that his brother would never send money!"

Jack turned. "You knew her?"

The boy nodded. "She saved me, when I was sick." He

said nothing, getting control. "She loved me. She loved us all. She and Ahmad. They loved us." He brushed angrily at his eyes. "Then the Taliban took us."

"And Ahmad?" Jack said quietly. "Do you know how it happened?"

The boy shook his head. "Many people were stoned in the Soccer Stadium. In the *madrasah* they told us we would be too, if we didn't do what they said –"

"None of this is true," Wahid said. "He hates me."

Jack turned to him. "I was going to let you go. But in this world it's not enough to do good. We must also banish evil –" He thought of killing Hassan Husseini in the Sahara, of shooting Hamid in the Beqaa, of all the others. Of Leo.

"I'll tell you a secret," Wahid spluttered. "A very bad secret. About your country."

"You have no secrets." *I have to do this.* "And you know nothing of my country."

"A secret Timothay wants to know –"

Find another way to punish him, Isabelle said. "Timothy won't save you."

"Just today he asked me. He wants very badly to know. I will tell you what I didn't tell him. If you'll let me go... Please, please don't kill me. I'll change, become a better man."

There is no other way to punish him. "You killed Ahmad."

"Timothay is asking who warned your country before Osama attacked your two towers." Wahid swallowed. "I said I didn't know. But I do."

"Warned us?"

"The Taliban warned you. Through the Saudis. They told the man who lives in the big white house. They said Osama's going to attack you –"

"You're lying again. The Taliban would never warn us."

"We're not all lunatics – we knew if Osama attacked

New York that *we* would pay. That the Taliban could be destroyed. Osama didn't care; he was using us, just like you Americans do –" Wahid swallowed, trying to say it all. "We told the Saudis and they warned their friend Bush who lives in the big white house. Why did he still let it happen?"

Jack saw Sophie and the children inside the falling tower. "Why is Timothy asking?"

"He wants their names. The ones who warned you. Because he wants to kill them."

Jack laughed. "Timothy never killed anyone."

"Others do his killing for him. Didn't you?"

Jack put the andiron by the fire. "What are you doing, Master?" the boy whispered to him.

"Where's your village?"

"Near Herat."

"If I give you money, will you go there, find a way to live?"

"How much money?"

Jack smiled. "Enough." He took the blindfold from Wahid's eyes and tied his mouth. "In the morning your men will untie you. Then you will leave Kabul and everything you own and return to Edeni. You will live in the cave in the hills and come down to the village only to beg for food. You will live alone in that cave for the rest of your life. If you don't do this I will tell Timothy that you were the one who warned us, and he will have you killed."

Wahid nodded, eyes wide with fear and relief.

"Come," Jack said to the boy. He stopped at the edge of the patio, then by the far villa wall till the guard had crunched away on his rounds. "How many kids in here?" he asked when they got to the *madrasah*.

"Twelve, Master."

"Don't call me that. Do they want to be there?"

"No, Lord."

When the guard returned Jack slipped from behind a tree, knocked him down and tied him while the boy woke the others. He laid one two-by-four on each side of the wall, climbed it, laid down the plywood as before and one by one brought the boys over. He pulled a roll of fifty-dollar bills from inside his belt and gave one to each boy. "Go to Doctors Without Borders," he said. "Tell them you come from the husband of Sophie Dassault. If you forget that name they will not help you."

He made them repeat it till he was sure some would remember, and watched them trail away in the darkness. He went down to the American compound, stepped into the bright lights beyond the guard gate, raised his hands and identified himself.

"Come in slowly," one guard called from beyond the bright lights.

"Slowly my ass. You saw me leave here yesterday morning."

"Come in slowly anyway Sir. I want to make sure it's you."

Twenty minutes later Jack slipped from his room, took a ride to Bagram in a Humvee from the motor pool and caught the first transport back to Baghdad.

SADDAM HUSSEIN had been found guilty of crimes against humanity and sentenced to hang. "For Bush, isn't that's setting a bad precedent?" an Iraqi journalist asked Jack. "For in his life, it's true, Saddam has killed several thousand Iraqis. But Bush and Cheney, they've killed several hundred thousand – shouldn't *they* be worried?"

"But remember, Jahmir, it's the winners who decide what is a war crime. It's the winners who write history."

Jahmir nodded, suddenly serious. "And that's why Bush and Cheney, they should worry."

When Jack thought of it the idea stunned him. The United States had invented the Nuremberg Principles. But never been judged by them.

Losing Iraq

MUQTADA AL-SADR was an enemy to the West but a hero to many Iraqis. He had united the Shiites of southern Baghdad and southeast Iraq into total opposition to US occupation and his Mahdi Army had fought the US to a standstill. Then, inexplicably, he ordered all his forces to cease hostilities, and reached out to "our Sunni brothers and sisters" to create a unified, democratic and peaceful Iraq.

"This guy's very dangerous," Isabelle had quipped one night as they lay beside each other in the narrow bed, "he's trying to stop the violence, bring people together, heal wounds..."

"What could be worse?" Jack snickered.

"But he's still a wacko."

"They all are – Islam means *I submit* – why denigrate yourself like that?"

"All religions are subjugation, pretending that some other force owns you."

"Until they give up the illusion that only they are right they'll never evolve into the modern world."

"They don't want to evolve into it. They want to destroy it."

"You're not being politically correct, darling. We're supposed to pretend *that* doesn't matter."

WE'RE LOSING IRAQ," he told the group assembled round the large walnut table in an Embassy conference room. "Afghanistan too. You have to decide if that matters to the future interests of the United States."

"What do *you* think?" said the Congressman from Oklahoma.

How could he explain what he thought to this "task force" of arrogant innocents whom General Szymanski, Timothy and Levi Ackerman had brought to Baghdad to find ways to shore up GW's eroding position?

"Imagine," Jack said, "you rob a bank. Maybe you got lied to, didn't realize what you were doing. But it wasn't a good idea, and great harm has resulted, to you and others. So what can you do now, to keep things from becoming worse?"

"Worse?" Melanie Harper, the President's National Security expert, snapped. "Things aren't *going* to get worse!"

"It's worse everywhere. Every month worse than the previous one. We're losing ground throughout Iraq, and in Afghanistan we've given up most of what we had." He watched them. "There is no good way out. Without a huge land war. And even that would probably lose."

He saw their faces harden as they took this in. These politicians and generals who always found ways to polish things. Unless or until it was to their advantage to destroy them. "What I am saying," he said, "is that it's too late to make things good. The harm has been done –"

"What *harm*?" the Oklahoma Senator said. He had a rolling twang he'd no doubt practiced for years, and it made him seem both comical and dangerous.

"The Iraq Study Group recommended a phased withdrawal from Iraq and opening conversations with its neighbors, Iran and Syria, seek some kind of regional solution. While I welcome any idea that might lead to peace, I doubt it will work."

"Maybe we just say we've won," the New Jersey Senator said. "And go home?"

"I'm not here to argue with you. Just to present what I know. And that is we got into something we cannot get out of. Not with honor."

"Honor!" scoffed General Szymanski. "You can always buy honor with a big defense budget."

"Even with a doubled budget, even with fifty thousand more combat troops – not that we have them – it's still likely we'll lose. Their IEDs are getting more powerful and we can't sniff them. Sunnis, Shiites, Baathists, ex-Army guys, everyone's against us. We've lost most of the countryside and now we're losing Baghdad." He stared round at them. "Even the Green Zone is collapsing, just like the fall of Saigon."

"The President doesn't want to hear that," Szymanski said.

"This isn't one of his press conferences," Ackerman said. "We can be honest."

"The President won a real mandate in his reelection." Melanie Harper stared at Jack with the dislike of political appointees for those who go into the field and bring back news they don't want to hear. "A reelection this war helped him win. And we're here to see he makes the most of it."

"Our soldiers died," Jack said, "so he could get reelected?"

"What would most of them have been doing back home? Dying in drunk driving accidents, overdosing on crystal meth? You know the kinds of recruits we get, these days." With her black eyes and smooth face Melanie seemed ageless, her wiry black hair unsilvered, her smile warming you with its false incandescence. When he'd first learned her name he'd thought *Melanoma.*

Outside the bulletproof window behind Timothy a thick morning haze covered the Green Zone. In the Red Zone beyond it the smoke of bombing runs tilted in wind-twisted columns to the south. Contrails bled rosy streaks northward across the pasty sky.

"Problem is," Ackerman said, "no one's enlisting. Or re-enlisting."

"So?" Szymanski countered. "We bring back the draft."

Timothy shook his head. "Not till after next elections. For the Republicans to keep the White House we can't piss anybody off." Timothy had grown even more flabby and flushed, Jack noticed, as if dying of something.

"In the first years after the invasion," Jack said, "we had secure provinces. Three and a half years later we have none. After the invasion some Iraqis supported us, now they all hate us. We sweep an area and they vanish; the moment we leave they're back again. While Al-Qaeda in Iraq is massacring whole villages of men, women and children. Cutting their throats one by one in front of the camera. And the longer we stay at reduced force the more casualties we take, and not one dead or maimed soldier would tell you it was worth it."

"Whose side are you *on*?" Melanie hissed.

"Do you remember 9/11?"

"Don't make an enemy out of *me*, you prick!"

"You're everybody's enemy, Melanie. That's how you get ahead." He stared furiously at the others. "We went into Afghanistan to crush Al-Qaeda and the Taliban. We had them on the run, then Bush and Cheney switched to Iraq for no reason. And now we've lost Afghanistan, goddamit, and you know it!"

"Absolutely not," Melanie said.

"All we have left is Kabul and part of the north. The Taliban controls the south, east, and west. Even if we put all our Marines into Helmand we're not going to control it. We're putting no money into reconstruction and social change..."

"How many times," Szymanski sighed, "have you been told President is'n into nation-building."

"I promise you," Timothy said, "Iraq won't be another Vietnam."

"It already is." Jack felt incurable weariness, the inability to communicate the obvious. "But don't worry – if it gets too tough you'll cut and run. Then al-Qaeda in Iraq takes over and kills the Shiites and Christians, or Iran moves in and then we have a huge oil power with nuclear weapons run by fanatic world-hating Shiites."

Timothy *tskked*. "The Iraqis'll get behind us. Anyway we're not here for them –"

"Do you remember," Jack said to Ackerman, "after 9/11, you told me how many times you and the others had told the President, the Principals, that an attack was coming? Remember how many times you told them? Forty-two times, you said. Forty-two times you warned the people responsible for the safety of our nation. You remember what they said?"

Ackerman nodded, glanced at Timothy, Melanie.

"They blew you away. GW went fishing. You said you didn't know why, you didn't understand how he could ignore this... Do you understand now?"

"Jack," Timothy said, "you're way out of line here..."

"Do you understand now? Do I have to spell it out? Or do *you* have the guts to say it?"

Szymanski stood. "I think this meeting's over."

"C'mon, Levi," Jack said. "Tell the truth for once in your life."

Ackerman cleared his throat. "I don't think you can prove it, Jack. I don't think it's something the nation wants to hear."

"Remember the words out front at Langley? *The truth shall make us free?*"

"The truth is what *we* make it." Timothy smiled. "What *we* say it is."

See You in New York

THE NEW BAGHDAD station chief, Jordan Feist, had a nervous abrupt manner like someone unsure of himself in public, a shy technocrat with long pale skinny fingers and a narrow nose. But he spoke seven Arabic dialects, including the classical in which the Koran had been written. He knew the region's history and culture, and seemed to have a deep resolve to deal with Iraq honestly and directly, and an ironic realization of what we had done and what had resulted.

"Where are we going in all this?" Jack asked him, the same question Isabelle had asked him when he'd come back from the dead.

"We've been at this war four years," Feist said. "We'd have to be nuts to think we're winning."

"Some people still do."

Feist perched his long chin on a slender hand, elbow on the table. "GW? Cheney? If a Democrat gets in next year, those guys could get brought up for war crimes."

"Never happen."

Feist poured himself another coffee and sat back down

opposite Jack. "You don't want more?" he nodded at Jack's cup.

"If your coffee is like how we're going to fight Al-Qaeda we're in deep shit."

Feist grinned. "My Dad used to take me hunting – I grew up in Idaho – and he'd put the coffee grounds in the pot the first morning and just keep adding more every morning. By the end of the two weeks you could've killed an elk with it." He glanced at the pot. "I've been here a week, so it'll be another week or so before I change it."

"I stayed in a cabin in the Sawtooths a while, few years ago, made my coffee like that."

"I know. About your being the Sawtooths, I mean." Feist tipped forward, elbows on the table. "I know a fair bit about you. You've always gone where the trouble is, never feared to do the recon and say the truth. And you've been right."

Jack shrugged. "Doesn't matter you're right if nobody listens."

"Just like here. Iraq is, in my opinion, totally fucked. But the top guys won't admit it. So all their strategies and tactics –"

"Are off target."

"That old Sun Tzu thing – if you don't know your enemy –"

Jack took a breath. "We don't. And we don't really know ourselves."

Feist leaned forward suddenly. "So why are *you* still here?"

"I keep thinking I should leave, that if Isabelle and I are going to have kids we better do it soon, that I can go back to the States or Europe or anywhere and make plenty of money and live a happy life. But Osama... Till we get Osama, maybe I can make a tiny difference in finding him, and if I'm not trying we might lose him, you know, the straw that breaks the camel's back. I owe it to Sophie and the kids. And Isabelle owes it to her husband."

Feist poured more of the thick oily coffee into his cup. "I know some amazing things about Isabelle."

"Stuff she can't tell me."

"You have no idea how brave she is."

"Yeah I do."

"And she's not even ours."

"Nor am I, completely."

Feist gave him an amused look. "Tell me."

"I'm never again doing something immoral, or bad for our country. Or the world."

For such a slender acute physique Feist had a huge barrel laugh. "Holy Christ, an ideologue. Are you becoming PC?"

Jack laughed. "Imagine your wife and kids are going to be executed by terrorists tomorrow, and you have a terrorist prisoner and know if you torture him you can find the other terrorists and save your family, would you?"

"Of course."

Jack thought of Sophie and the kids falling in the North Tower – he would've tortured as many terrorists as it took to avoid that. "We don't have the politically correct folks with us on that one."

"That's because their families have never been in danger."

IN THE DESERT time passes slowly. But when you look back you can remember little because it seems unchanging. The desert negates time, Jack decided, because it's timeless.

In three more trips to Afghanistan he'd found no leads on Osama Bin Laden. "Maybe he's dead," Isabelle said. The possibility gave him a weird letdown, as if somehow he'd failed.

"We should leave," she said. "Get out of this."

"Osama's not dead. He's in Pakistan somewhere. I can feel it."

"Bloody ISI's hiding him." She looked out the window through the walls of buildings toward the silvery slice of the Tigris. "We *must* get out of here."

"The new chief wants to see me tomorrow."

"What for?"

"Christ if I know."

"Don't do it."

"What?"

"Don't do what he asks you. Tell him we're getting out of this."

"He seems a good guy, dropped into the middle of this insane mess..."

"It's *not* your responsibility."

"Your people don't want you going either."

She exhaled. "I almost don't know where I'd go... *we'd* go..."

"As long as we can do some good, how can we leave?"

JORDAN FEIST SEEMED more confident and relaxed, having survived, politically, his first year as station chief. And he served better coffee.

"What happened to the Idaho hunting coffee?" Jack said.

"I think you were the only one who liked it."

"So what's up?"

Feist pulled his chair closer. "What do you know about Abu Bakr al-Baghdadi?"

"He's a fucking Salafist. Wants to kill us all."

"He's in Bucca."

"Oh Christ." The largest US military prison in Iraq, Fort Bucca was a breeding ground of fanaticism, where thousands of former Iraqi soldiers and other captives were radicalized by Al-Qaeda, and where to simplify operations the US had let them impose the deadliest form of Sharia on other prisoners.

"We want to keep him there forever. But it's a new Administration in Washington, and somebody very high up wants him released."

"He's insanely dangerous. They must be nuts."

"We've been asked to do a report. We're supposed to recommend release, but what if you have a good look, and say what you think?"

Jack felt a surge of admiration for Feist. "Puts you on thin ice."

Feist shrugged: *maybe.* "With a new administration you never know."

"I can't understand why they'd want to let him go –"

"We have a few files on him -- can you look at them, go down to Bucca and interrogate him, tell us what you think?"

"I want to get back to Afghanistan," Jack answered. "And find Osama."

"Maybe this piece of shit al-Baghdadi knows something that could help you."

THE FIRES OF HELL couldn't match the summer heat at Bucca. Nor could they warm you in its bitter winter. A vast corral of twenty thousand Iraqi prisoners, some here since the 2003 US invasion, most caught in the battles and sweeps since. A well-managed but dangerous POW camp on the flat desert just inland of the Gulf.

All the way down on Highway 1 he'd scanned the passing wind-scoured desert and tried to figure who at the top wanted Abu Bakr al-Baghdadi free. It would be like having a viper loose in your home. A viper that *wanted* to kill you.

Who was it?

What was the tradeoff? With whom?

A CITY OF TENTS and concrete buildings behind rolls of concertina and barbed wire, watched over by machine gun posts in guard towers, Camp Bucca was like a vast Siberian gulag transported to the desert. Thousands of prisoners dressed in orange jump suits staring across the barbed and concertina wire, or being marched, hands on head, between tall concrete walls by Army guards, or sitting in the shade of their tents under the hot white sun.

It had been a British prison called Camp Freddy left over from the 1990 Gulf War which the Brits had gladly ceded to the Americans after the 2003 invasion. The US soon filled it with captured Iraqi Army soldiers, Baathist Party members and anyone else who seemed suspicious.

As things got worse in the US occupation, more and more suspected Iraqi militants and jihadis were jailed there. After a report by US Major General Antonio Taguba described US abuses of Iraqi prisoners at Abu Ghraib, many of the most abused prisoners there were quietly transferred to Bucca and disappeared from view.

Inside the confining pressure cooker of Camp Bucca, the soldiers and jihadis began to work together. *We have a common enemy*, the jihadis said. *Let us kill our enemy and not each other.*

"You're creating a terrorism university at Bucca," Jack had told Timothy way back in 2005.

"They can be terrorists all they want," Timothy had answered. "Because we're never going to let the fuckers go."

"Someday," Jack had said, "what if we have to?"

ABU BAKR AL-BAGHDADI stood at five nine, swarthy and direct, a man so insanely sure of himself that no human voice could intervene in the dialogue he had with the Devil he took for God.

He emanated hatred like an athlete does sweat. The hatred of someone very smart and faithful to his own psychotic rules.

"Have you ever met Osama?" Jack asked him.

"Osama is a great man," Abu Bakr said. "But he made a mistake."

"What's that?"

"He tried first to kill you infidels." Abu Bakr shook his head. "First we need to clean ourselves of Shiites. Then we kill you."

"You have no idea where he is, Osama?"

"He is everywhere. He is waiting. You cannot escape him."

Four National Guardsmen had led Jack through the prison visitor center past a long row of stalls where black-cloaked women spoke through bulletproof windows to prisoners in orange jump suits. The Guardsmen unlocked a steel door to a concrete room with a steel table and two benches bolted to the floor. They returned with al-Baghdadi in ankle and wrist chains and clamped him to one bench. "You want us to stay or leave?" a Guardsman said to Jack.

"Unchain him." Jack turned to al-Baghdadi. "I'm telling them to release you," he said in Arabic.

"We're not supposed to, Sir," a Guardsman said.

"He's not going to hurt me. And wait outside."

They unlocked al-Baghdadi's wrists and feet, went out and closed the bolt.

Al-Baghdadi looked at Jack. "That was stupid," he said in English.

"What are you going to do?" Jack answered in Arabic. "Try to kill me?"

"Killing you would unfortunately make no difference."

"Yes it would. Because then they'd kill you."

"Fool, do you think I care?"

"Far more than you admit."

"So why are you here? Like the others who try to turn me?"

"What others?"

"The ones who want me out early... That's why you're here. Isn't it?"

Jack thought about this. "If we release you, what then?"

Al-Baghdadi stood suddenly and for an instant Jack tensed. "If I had a prison knife," al-Baghdadi said, "I could kill you. But I don't have a knife and I can kill many more of you if I am released. That is *what then*."

"But I'm not letting you be released."

"Then I will have you killed. I can send men to do it. Any time."

Jack felt coldness up his spine, knowing this was true. "Saying that won't help you."

Al-Baghdadi leaned forward. "You're a parasite, a virus. But soon you will go and we'll take back our country. Make it what it was, a great empire from the Atlantic to the Hindu Kush, a world power based on faith and law." He sat back. "And no matter what you do you can't stop us."

"Caliphates come and go, the Abbasids, the Ottomans. None last."

"Ours will. And like the Abbasids twelve centuries ago we will destroy anyone in our way. We will behead them, torture them, crucify them and stone them to death until they learn. When people are afraid they listen. They do what they're told."

"People love freedom, they don't want to be enslaved by ideas. People want democracy, not Sharia."

"But Sharia will dominate. Sharia will be implemented worldwide. Democracy is the opposite of Sharia and Islam. We believe Allah is the legislator. Allah makes the laws. He decides what is allowed and what is forbidden."

There was a force of will, Jack realized, that drove this man to believe he could make the world what he wanted. Like Hitler and Stalin he told himself things so intensely he totally believed them. Where religion came in, the ancient chasm between belief and knowledge. But just because you believed something didn't make it true.

"You say *I* am a killer?" al-Baghdadi huffed. "That Muslims are killers? But you, the West, have you not killed a hundred million people in two world wars? You, Americans, did you not kill twenty million Native Americans, did you not drop two nuclear bombs on Japan, kill three million Vietnamese? Have you not started oil wars across the Middle East, for nearly a century?"

"Yes, that is true."

"And you say *we* are the killers? You blame us for cutting the heads from our enemies, but did not your religions do that for centuries?"

"For us those days are finished. We are trying to build a modern world, without killing, with freedom for everyone."

"Hah!"

He questioned al-Baghdadi for another five hours but nothing changed. There was no way he should be released. But to al-Baghdadi it clearly didn't matter what Jack recommended, he knew he was going to be released.

When Jack stepped outside the hot air hit like a furnace, searing his throat and nostrils, dust stinging his eyes. How bizarre that once this place had been a wild fertile lowland of trees and grass and streams, and now a blasted desert of tents, concrete huts and sharp wire, at one side a house trailer with a huge *Subway* sign rattling in the torrid wind.

We cannot make the world, Jack thought, what we believe ourselves to be.

DO NOT RELEASE THIS MAN, he typed in bold across the top of his report, and after detailing his findings, concluded,

Although there is much pressure to release him, he represents a long-term serious risk to the interests of the United States not only in the Middle East but domestically. He is capable of shooting down civilian planes, and has the weapons sources to do it. As an IED expert, he can slaughter thousands and shake the foundations of whatever government we're trying to rebuild. I believe his group is getting millions a month from Wahhabis in Saudi, Qatar and all over the Gulf, and buying more and more sophisticated weapons. He's very adept on the internet and has, as you know, a huge following including many "compassionate" US citizens attracted to his fate. He hates the United States and the West with a passion that exceeds description. He's a miniature Guantanamo, a needle in our side we must endure because the alternative – letting him go – will be far worse.

He'd wasted his time. In return for a negotiations agreement that eventually lasted three days, Abu Bakr was delivered in a Bradley to a crowd of cheering and ululating supporters. And a week later one of the largest IEDs in the tragic history of Baghdad took out a whole Shiite block and killed 71 people.

What bothered Jack was who in the United States had wanted al-Baghdadi free.

What bothered him even more was the last thing al-Baghdadi had said when they released him.

"See you in New York."

BIN LADEN WAS STILL out there. While Jack was stuck in Iraq helping to hold together the pieces of a failed invasion. When it was Osama who had killed his family.

444

When it was Osama he'd promised himself to find.

"I can't give it up till I've killed him," he told Isabelle as they sat the kitchen table eating radishes and olives, an unusual treat.

"We may never get him. He's back in Saudi with his fellow Wahhabis, screwing his slave girls and living like a prince."

"I think he's in Pakistan." He glanced down at his clasped hands as if he were some penitent, some sinner. He thought about Abu Bakr al-Baghdadi, that we should not have let him go. Someday he'd be as hard to kill as Osama. And just as dangerous. The entire universe seemed ruined, unsolvable.

"Pakistan? They wouldn't dare. America's the only thing they've got to keep from sinking into the pit..."

"I'm beginning to think there's no difference between Paki Intelligence and Al-Qaeda... and they've got all those nuclear warheads."

"I love you darling." She glanced at the lamb ribs in the oven. "God is good: let's eat."

Assassins Gate

A FTER OBAMA took office the word came down the US would leave Iraq. But like Yugoslavia and other countries that had recently blown apart when their strong central power was gone, every hatred and religious schism soon exploded in blood.

We need at least another decade of US troops in Iraq, Jack wrote Szymanski, *before we think of leaving. Like South Korea and Germany after World War II, Iraq needs a Marshall Plan.*

If we leave sooner, everything we've done is wasted, every dead soldier – and more than a million dead Iraqis – have died for nothing.

The 2007 Surge brought us to over 170,000 American troops in Iraq while the country, if one can call it that, descended into bloody civil war. And as always it was the civilians who paid. Building the Baghdad Wall to separate Sunni from Shiite was a short-term bandage.

Shiite leaders like Muqtada al-Sadr may be talking peace but they're just strengthening their control over their regions of Iraq. Most of Baghdad is already theirs. When they decide to move against us, either alone or with Iran, they will be impossible to stop without a US commitment of far more soldiers and weapons than we have. And our enemies on the Sunni front are just as dangerous.

If these problems seem insurmountable now, they will be worse if we leave.

Why he wrote these reports he couldn't imagine. Sending the truth up the line was always a waste of time. While Washington tried to make up its mind, the recently elected Iraqi Parliament voted to have all US forces out by end December 2011. "The place will sink into chaos," Jack said to Isabelle, "and some religious nut, some strongman, will take over. It'll be a religious and every other kind of civil war."

"That's why we're getting out of here," she said.

"Not till we find Bin Laden."

GIVING THE GREEN ZONE to the Iraqis seemed like handing car keys to a five-year-old. They were clearly not strong or disciplined enough to control religious infighting and terrorism, and without continuing US troops the country would break apart.

Obama was pushing for more troop reductions, praising the success of a war he'd once called a mistake. But once we got in, Jack repeated in memos that seemed to change nothing, we have to ride it out, make sure all this blood and trillions of dollars were wasted for some purpose.

Now among the generals, diplomats and "advisors", nobody thought the invasion had been a good idea. "We got hornswoggled," General Szymanski said to Jack one afternoon in the new billion-dollar US Baghdad embassy, an entire high security city of office buildings, dormitories, shopping and residences.

"Yeah but you guys who backed the invasion are the ones who've got the stars. Not the guys who said don't do it."

"The military is politics in uniforms, you know that."

It was pointless to remind Szymanski of the needless deaths, the destruction of a fragile nation. "Humans love war," Szymanski had once said, "so it's my job to see we win."

WHEN DEFENSE Secretary Panetta landed in Baghdad offering to keep some American troops in Iraq, the refusal came not from Baghdad but the White House. And when Muqtada al-Sadr returned to Iraq from four years in Iran he promised to turn his Mahdi Army on the Americans if they didn't leave. "Al-Sadr doesn't realize," Jack told a Southern California Congressman doing a campaign video in Baghdad, "that without an American military presence the Sunnis will tear him apart."

"Hell, the Shiites and Sunnis have been killing each other since Mohammed died. Let'em go at it." The Congressman had a cheery wide grin with lots of bright teeth, a bottle tan, dyed grayish hair, and millions of corporate dollars in his Super Pac, though this trip was being paid for by the taxpayers.

"Having started this war," Jack answered, "we have to keep it from getting worse. There will be no win. Just better or worse defeats."

The Congressman scanned him for an instant and turned away, and once again Jack had the impression of being an outsider, someone who mistakenly tells the truth.

AFTER BIN LADEN was killed Jack felt a sickened, turmoiled relief, flashbacks of the nightmares of Sophie and the kids falling inside the burning tower. He wanted Bin Laden to die over and over again for every person he'd ever harmed.

Revenge. Not just Bin Laden and his insane henchmen

but also all the fanatic Saudi and Qatari oil princes who had funded him – *may they suffer hot knives tearing out their innards forever* was what the Koran suggested.

It was time to go home.

Where was home?

"Somewhere far from here," Isabelle said. "A place to follow the path with heart."

"Ever been to Patagonia?"

"OBAMA'S PEOPLE** will be in Baghdad next Thursday," Feist said.

"Good," Jack said. "Have fun with them."

"Would you be willing to –"

"No. I wouldn't be willing to. That's two days before we're leaving."

"Just an hour, Jack. Yours is a dissident view, but you often turn out right."

"They won't listen."

Feist shrugged, looked down at his desk. *That's true*, he admitted by gesture. *But please do it anyway.*

"THE PRESIDENT NEEDS** to be out of Iraq for his reelection campaign," Barbara Lawrence said. A large woman with a husky voice, she'd been a Massachusetts governor and major Obama bundler and now was assistant undersecretary of State.

"The situation on the ground won't allow it," Jack said.

Elbows on the glossy conference table, the President's military advisor General Hank Grenier looked at Jack and Feist across clasped hands. "If the United States pulls our military out of this Godforsaken place, what are the chances you guys and the Iraqis can keep the peace?"

"Are you nuts?" Jack said.

"No way *we* can keep the peace," Feist said.

Grenier nodded. "I didn't think so."

"But the President wants out," Barbara Lawrence repeated. "This is not a fact-finding mission. This is an order."

Jordan Feist let out a soft whistle. "Well you're on your own, then. We'll help where we can, but holding this country together is *not* our job."

"We all remember," she smiled, "when tearing it apart *was* your job."

THE YOUNG MAN IN THE FADED ORIOLES JACKET drove one-handed, fingering his prayer beads. His sweaty hand kept slipping off the wheel.

Traffic and carts and people in the street blocked his way. A black patch covered his right eye, making it harder to drive. He trembled, wanting to scream *Get Out of the Way!* He swung the purple taxi left toward Al Kindl Street and the 14th of July Monument, past a donkey cart of dirt-caked beets, people parting on both sides, strings of laundry overhead flickering the sun.

His foot shivered, his ankle so powerless he couldn't push the pedal nor lift the foot to touch the brake. He saw his flesh a bloody spray, his belly in red pieces on the building walls. Chunks of his bone buried in the street. Sometimes, they say, only your toes remain.

God's rough hand grasped his shoulder. *First they killed your Father, years ago in the retreat across the desert. Then Sayeed your only brother in this war –*

But if he died now what good would that do them?

Was he crazy to believe? *Did* he? At death do we wake at all? Is there truly a garden of seven pools overhung with the sweetest fruits? Slender girls with silken hair and lissome bodies?

Or are we nothing but sparks struck from a flint, ablaze for an instant then dust?

"LET'S TALK REAL," Feist told them. "Our combat deaths dropped from 960 in 2007 to 54 this year, and civilian deaths are down from a thousand a month to a hundred. But if we leave now," his cufflinks clunked the table, "in two years we'll have a higher death toll than ever before."

The President's intelligence advisor Tip Townsend had a deep baritone and a sarcastic undertone, the product of many years of saying the judicious thing. "We *all* know the real deal. That we shouldn't leave Iraq. But we're going to leave Iraq as part of the President's reelection."

"Just like Bush," Jack snapped, "who wanted the war to look good back in 2004, for *his* reelection."

"War is politics," Barbara Lawrence said.

"Iraq will fall apart," Feist said.

"Join the real world, Mr. CIA," she said. "The President decides; we do whatever he tells us."

"There's no point of having an 'intelligence' agency if you ignore what we tell you."

"We're not ignoring you," she smiled, "it just doesn't matter *what* you say."

"And we'll still be here," Feist answered. "Long after you're gone. And in three years ISIS will control half of Iraq and most of Syria. They're worse than anything we've faced yet, and you're letting them in the front door."

Jack stood. "And when GW's and Powell's senior intelligence advisors tell us that Bush and the others should be hauled before the International Court of Justice for War Crimes, we need to listen, not dismiss it like Obama's doing."

"He doesn't want to set precedent." Feist puffed out his cheeks, exhaled slowly. "You and me, Jack, all us guys, we have to go our own way."

"Christ, it's eighteen hours back to DC," General Grenier glanced at his Rolex. "Let's get a move on."

THE PURPLE TAXI BANGED across a curb as the young man drove around a water wagon. He dropped the prayer beads into his lap and banging the horn accelerated along the sidewalk, an old woman yelling, people jumping aside. *Do they know what I'm about to do? How they must envy me!*

My Beloved Son I shall guide you. Straight now, left at the corner. There it is – up ahead – the checkpoint on the right. Watch the Marines getting out of that jeep. Pointing their rifles but do not fear.

Take up the detonator. Nothing you could ever do in your past life can match the greatness of what you now do.

JACK WENT THROUGH ASSASSIN'S GATE into the fierce Baghdad heat. Four Marines behind barricades were aiming rifles at a purple taxi. It lurched forward, halted. *Can't say there's never a taxi*, he smiled, *when you want one.*

"Afternoon, Sir," the first Marine said. "We're chasing this guy off."

"Don't," Jack said. "I can use him."

"You shouldn't take a taxi out of the Zone, Sir," the second Marine said.

"Just headed to the Palestine. Anyway, life's full of things we're not supposed to do."

In the taxi the young man's fingers trembled on the detonator. Which way did he push? He realized he was begging it not to blow, tried to stop.

He looked up into the sky, saw the beauty of God's face and pushed the detonator. It skidded from his sweaty fingers onto the floor.

"I said take me to the Palestine," Jack said.

The young man spun round, shocked at his Arabic. "It's dangerous –"

"I remember you!" Jack leaned forward. "Years ago, at the University. The Physics Building... You were listening to Pearl Jam."

The young man scrabbled under the seat for the detonator. "That wasn't me."

"What happened to your eye?"

"I lost it in the *muqawama*. The resistance."

"It doesn't work, an eye for an eye. We all end up blind."

The young man found the detonator but the wire was caught under the accelerator and he didn't dare yank for fear of breaking it. "You said you were Afghani."

"You're not at the University anymore?"

"As you know it was wrecked." The young man slid the wire free. "Professor Younous was killed. In the *Invasion*."

Jack glanced from the street down at his hands, old and scarred, hanging loosely between his knees as the taxi jostled over potholes. "I didn't know Professor Younous was killed."

"An American missile, the first days..."

"It's true, *the ink of scholars is more precious than the blood of martyrs*."

"You know that saying?"

"From the Hadith. But didn't Mohammed really prefer the blood of martyrs?"

"Of course... But Mohammed isn't God."

"What is?"

"I studied physics because I hoped there'd be a single theory of the universe. Isn't that God?"

"*No misfortune happens but by the will of God*, the Koran says. But if God who turns us to evil, if we kill each other in *God's* name, how is God not the Devil?"

"God causes evil, says Sura Four. God and ourselves.

But Sura thirty-eight says it's the Devil."

"It's all nonsense. If there is a single theory of the universe, it's love."

Carefully the young man put down the detonator. "The Koran never mentions love."

Jack watched the haphazard panoply of Baghdad roll by, happy to be free of it now, the rubble and crowds, the deadly violence and sad music.

In two days he and Isabelle would be in Paris.

And a few weeks later in the Argentinian Andes. Patagonia.

"I'm very sorry Professor Younous is dead," he said. "I'm sorry everyone is dead... So many beautiful people..."

The young man nosed the taxi around a toppled building that half-covered the burnt shell of an Abrams tank, making Jack wonder if the crew had got out or had they died like so many tank crews do, in searing inferno with nothing remaining but their teeth?

"If God is all-powerful," the young man said, "why is there evil? If God is not all-powerful, then God is not God."

"There is evil because God gives us free will. To do good or not."

The young man shifted into first. "In a single theory of the universe there's no room for free will."

VII

ISIS

Quicksand

April 2014, near Esquel, Argentina

IN THE NEXT ROOM his phone beeped. He gently
slid his arm from under Isabelle's neck and slipped from
the bed.

"You getting it?" she said.

"Yeah."

"Fuck them."

"Maybe it's not them."

She turned away, silent. He padded into the next room.
A two-word message on his phone:

Check in.

Barefoot on the cold tiles he let out a long breath, stared
out the window at the pampas grass silvered by moonlight.
Took another long slow breath and let it out. Went back to
the bedroom.

"It was, wasn't it?" she said.

"Yeah."

"So what are you going to do?"

He lay down and pulled up the covers. She turned, facing him. "Jack, what *are* you going to *do*?"

Her face was pewter in the moonlight through the window. A death mask, he thought, banished it. But we're all going to die... what else is there to think about?

Up on the mountain a fox barked; another answered. "I'm not going," he said. "Whatever they want, I won't do it."

"They won't like that."

"I'll call them in the morning."

"You're supposed to call now. The minute you get the message." She turned away, slapped down the pillow under her head. "You're never going to get away from them. Are you?"

HE LAY THERE till dawn. Sometimes no matter what you did you never got free. You carried around this rucksack of your life and every year it got heavier. Every night more faces crawled out of your nightmares. Even love wasn't always enough.

In the bathroom he washed his face in cold water. Fatigue felt like ashes in his eyes. Every move of his neck and shoulders caused pain.

He didn't like how he looked in the mirror. Wearied by all he'd done and not done. Tired of war.

"God," he said aloud. "I'm so tired of it."

The mirror didn't answer, just showed the lines in his face, the worn skin, the gray hairs, the bullet-smashed shoulder and knife-scarred ribs.

He made a double espresso and called the President's man in Tampa.

"WE HAVE A SERIOUS PROBLEM," Mike Curry said.

"You always do, you guys," Jack said. "Your life is a serious problem."

"We shouldn't have pulled out."

"I told you that. Everybody who knew anything told you that."

"It was the President's campaign promise to leave Iraq."

"And look what it got you."

"This guy al-Baghdadi's come out of nowhere."

"No he hasn't. He's been building for years while you guys did photo ops and drank champagne at the White House."

"That's unfair, Jack. You know it."

"And now he's got millions of nasty motherfuckers plus all the weapons you left him."

"We need to understand the man. Get in his head."

"Have fun."

"You interrogated him twice, back at Fort Bucca. Spent seven hours with him."

"And I said we should never release him. So you released him. And a lot of other bad bastards who've been killing our guys ever since."

"President's orders. We were all going to kiss and make up."

"You're not getting me tied up in this again, Mike."

"Oh yes I am. This touches our highest level of national security. We have no choice. Nor do you. Because it turns out you're the only guy on our side who's *ever* talked to him."

"Then you are SOL."

"All we have is *two* pix of him! And the face recognition folks aren't even sure it's the same guy. We need you to go through the photo banks and see if he's there under another name. You're the only one, Jack. The only one we've got."

"Send them to me."

"You know we can't... We've set up a crisis team in the new Embassy in Baghdad, devoted only to al-Baghdadi.

Very smart, very hard, total resources. We need you there." Curry lowered his voice. "Just a month, Jack. Then you go home and we'll leave you alone."

Jack thought of mentioning Isabelle's pregnancy, to explain why he couldn't go. "What do you mean, alone?"

"If you do this, we won't ask you again. Ever. For anything."

HE MADE ANOTHER ESPRESSO and sat on a creaky cane chair on the terracotta terrace and watched the mountains turn gold with morning. A warm breeze brought odors of new grass, dew-damp soil and flowing water. The Andes so much softer, gentler than the Hindu Kush. The pampas more fertile, sunny and alive than the superheated deserts of Iraq.

Isabelle came out with her coffee and sat beside him.

"They said just a month," he said.

She looked away, at nothing. "They lie."

"And after this never again. I'll be free."

"And you believe them?"

"They worked this out between them, your guys and mine."

"I bet they know I'm pregnant."

Jack thought of her doctor at the clinic in Esquel. Of course. "I do a month in Baghdad, then we'll be free. Forever." He looked out at the golden grasslands, the white clouds. "They're creating a virtual al-Baghdadi. See how he responds. So they can develop strategy."

"The strategy should've been to never leave Iraq."

"Tell that to the President."

Though you could blame the President for leaving Iraq in 2011, in reality the president to blame was the one who invaded that poor country in 2003 on trumped-up, false Weapons of Mass Destruction charges. It amazed Jack sometimes that GW, Cheney, Powell and their other cronies were still walking around free and not in jail.

And now this President wanted to kiss and make up with the Islamic world. Who'd played the fiddle while Libya burned, Tunisia, Egypt, and now was playing the fiddle as Syria caught fire. Who had gone to Riyadh to bow down to a ruthless, bloodthirsty Saudi dictator whose country funded every Islamic terrorist organization it could find.

Guys like us, Owen McPhee had said years ago, the night before Jack and Sophie got married, before McPhee went to Nairobi and the Muslims killed him, *we're not supposed to lead normal lives.* Our job is to protect other people, so they can live a normal life. In Lebanon, Syria, Paris, anywhere. Iraq.

Trouble was, Iraq's like quicksand. The President should have known.

Once you're in you can't get out.

AND HE'D NEVER get away from Home Office, Isabelle had said. Was it really true? Would the time ever come when he'd done enough?

You could say it started because his father was a soldier. If you love your Dad, and if he's a good Dad, then *you* want to be a soldier. And if he gets killed it's even worse: now you have to avenge him. And you miss him so bad that every night, lying in bed in the dark Maine woods, you think your ten-year-old heart is going to break.

But you never tell anyone. Not even your Ma, silent, austere yet devoted amidst her own infinite grief, this indescribable harrowing of the heart.

And the two of you soldier on.

Since then, in over thirty years of war – Afghanistan against the Soviets, then Lebanon, Africa, Afghanistan again, Iraq, the other places he never thought about because he'd supposedly never been there – what purpose?

He looked out on the bright Andes, seeing every little crinkle of beech forest, the huge crests taunting in their pure whiteness. Had he made a difference?

Had he made a better world? With all the lives it cost?

Many times at the risk of his own life he'd tried to minimize that cost. And many times at the risk of his life he had protected, and even helped to save, his country.

What would have happened without him?

Who would have lived? Who would have died?

And now was he going back into this one?

Ettabe'e Allah

FROM THEIR TERRACE you could see all the way down the bluegrass river valley to the Andes foothills and then up the peaks behind them, gray-green with beech forests then stone then vertical rock and ice trailing clouds of sparkling snow.

The air was cool and the grandeur of the land extended forever. Eastward three hundred miles of grassland to the sea. To the south grassland, peaks and a thousand miles of desert to Tierra del Fuego and the Magellan Straits. To the west these vast mountains blocking off the sky, to the north more grassland and hills, then vineyards then jungle.

The house was small but fitted them perfectly. A kitchen with a fireplace and wood-fired cook stove, a square porcelain sink and cold water faucet. A living room with another fireplace, leather furniture, books in Spanish and English and a view south across the endless pampas. A bedroom with a double bed, a bathroom where you filled the tub with buckets of hot water from the kitchen cook stove. And two hours from the little mountain town of Esquel, where you could find anything any human could possibly need.

You could argue they still weren't free but for now he'd take it.

WHEN *CHECK IN* beeped on Jack's phone they'd been there eighteen months and Isabelle was four months pregnant. To Jack each day had seemed almost compensation for the bad years, that and the warm sun that melted into his injured shoulder and brought it peace. The river you could drink from, the glossy grass dancing in the wind, the blue glow of the Andes sun, this little house of adobe walls, blue shutters, bougainvillea and terracotta floor tiles was maybe what you found in heaven, if you were very lucky. Where you could find the path with heart.

And now a child. *Barefoot in the grass*, the words came to him. *Naked in the sun.*

When they'd gone to the clinic in Esquel the doctor had offered to tell them the baby's sex, but they'd both said no. "A golden child," Isabelle had said in Spanish. *Un niño eldorado.* "We don't care boy or girl."

At night however Jack kept seeing Sarah on the last day of her life, arguing about braces, Leo throwing the football so hard and straight, on his way to West Point. Then Sarah came to him one night and said, *Don't worry. Please don't sorrow.*

The night before the phone beeped they'd talked about staying. The place was rented but maybe they could buy it. Or there were so many other beautiful little haciendas in this vast and fertile junction of mountains and grasslands.

"What if we stayed here?" he'd said. "Raised the kids?"

"Kids?" She patted her belly. "There's just one."

He interlaced fingers with hers. "What if, God willing, we make more?"

FOUR HOURS LATER his phone had beeped. *Check*

in.

"No way you're going," he'd said next morning when they argued about it.

"So I'm supposed to stay here, two hours from anywhere, to get fat and pregnant while you go kill people? When I want to kill them too?"

This made him chuckle. "Honey I care about you."

"I'm going. Get over it."

He laughed, loving the set of her chin, her blazing eyes. "It's a quickie. In and out."

She patted her belly again. "How do you think I got to look like this?"

FROM ESQUEL it was two hours in a six-seat Cessna to Buenos Aires then 23 hours on Turkish Airlines through Sao Paulo to Istanbul, then another three to Baghdad. On the four a.m. armored ride from the airport the city seemed half-deserted, dirty windblown streets and skulking cars, the wind bitter and tasting of dust. The Embassy zone was lit like a space station, guards, bunkers, halogens and concrete, an armored citadel adrift in a hostile sea.

"If I'm coming back," Jack had told them, "Isabelle will be with me, and we want to find an apartment somewhere."

"We don't recommend that," they'd answered.

"It's part of the deal. We can both pass for locals... I don't want to be in a compound full of Americans if I'm trying to find an Iraqi."

"Whatever turns you on," they'd said laconically.

Jordan Feist was still station chief – no small accomplishment in this era of shifting loyalties and strategies. He seemed more constrained, even more worried than before when he met them in the conference room on the third floor of the Embassy HQ. "It's like being in a fine house on the edge of the sea, and you see the tidal wave coming, that it's going to destroy the house, destroy all you've worked for all this time." He leaned forward, hands clasped between his knees. "And you can't do a thing to change it."

"There's still talk, Panetta's for it, to bring back the troops."

"Never happen. Not while Obama's here."

"So you have to hold on," Isabelle said. "Till he's gone."

"That's three years away. By then ISIS will have the whole country. Plus most of Syria and part of Turkey."

Jack nodded. "And part of Lebanon."

"Depends on Hezbollah."

"But now he's waking up, Obama is?" Isabelle said, "about ISIS?"

"I wouldn't say he's waking up," Feist countered. "He's being told about it."

"But he okayed putting this team together," Jack said. "That's what Mike Curry told me from Tampa."

"But," Feist raised a hand, "this is independent."

"Meaning whose?"

Feist smiled. "Ours."

"What combat assets?"

"None."

"*None?*"

"We construct al-Baghdadi's profile. Interpret him, try to locate him. But everything we learn we feed to the Iraqis."

"No special units?"

"The President says no."

"So if we locate this guy, *we* can't go get him?"

"Half the Iraqi Army sides with al-Baghdadi," Isabel said.

"So we have to be very careful," Feist smiled, "who we tell. And what we tell them."

"Obama's planning what he does after leaving office." Isabelle said. "That's why he's always kissing ass with the

Hindus and Muslims. Wants to be president of the world."

"So," Jack said, "does al-Baghdadi."

THE HOTEL GOOD NEWS was not far from the Tigris and the Embassy, a six-floor concrete stack with four apartments to a floor, an antique elevator that often refused to stop at the floor you wanted, with a black metal cage door that opened and closed reluctantly, and on the ground floor a yellowish lobby with a few drooping plants, an old Sunni man sleeping at the desk and a dispirited restaurant of unreliable propriety.

But they had a bedroom, living room, kitchen and a bath with a shower that worked, good Wi-Fi and even a land line. From the bedroom and living room windows you got a glimpse of the Tigris, and here on the back streets the dangers of car bombs and missiles was less.

LIKE ALL MASS MURDERERS, al-Baghdadi was a coward. An itinerant preacher from the Samarra area, he had spread many stories of his courage but had never been in battle, said he had a doctorate in Sharia law but did not seem to understand it, told millions of people to obey him as the voice of Allah, but this was a position to which he, and not Allah, had appointed himself.

From interrogations of other terrorists they learned nearly nothing, for he was as much a mystery to his own side as to the Americans. And as Mike Curry had said, only two photos of him were in existence, and they didn't seem to be the same guy.

According to testimony from a purported childhood friend, al-Baghdadi had been a quiet and introspective child who did well in school, was able to remember even the tiniest fact, could see in his mind every page he'd read, and find therein proof for whatever he said.

According to this friend, who had unfortunately died during a 2009 Iraqi interrogation, al-Baghdadi was seven when the first Gulf War began. "Don't worry," his father had admonished his wife at the dinner table. "Saddam knows what he is doing. The Americans won't attack."

But his brother Salim had been drafted and was now on a truck somewhere heading south to face the Americans.

He had not known this till one day he'd come home from school to find his three sisters wailing, his mother weeping, his father in the garden swearing and begging. Salim was dead.

According to the friend, al-Baghdadi never recovered from this loss. Salim stayed with him, a warm hand on his insecure and worried shoulder, a comforting strong voice, *Follow your heart, little brother. Your heart knows what is best...*"

Like Salim, so many other young men did not come home from Gulf One. The years ached on, each worse than the one before. The Americans tightened their sanctions, every business was dying, his mother lost her job and his father's salary could not compete with escalating prices.

The years grew terrible. The markets half empty, fear in the streets. "We will persevere," Saddam said.

"Give up your weapons of mass destruction," the Americans said.

"We have none," Saddam said. "We can barely feed our children."

"The Americans know we have no weapons," his father said. "They will not attack us." His mother at the other end of the table, black-eyed and silent.

His eldest sister, a nursing student, died during the GW Bush invasion when a F-18 bombed the clinic where she worked. The middle one died three years later in the Bush surge. The youngest died the following year from a car bomb that killed nearly a hundred others, Shiite against Sunni or vice versa, different interpretations of the love of God.

His mother died of sorrow, and when Abu Bakr came home one day from the rudimentary school he found his father shot to death in the garden.

"Why?" he'd begged the neighbor, "who would hurt him?"

"Some Shiites came. They did it."

"Why?" he shook the man. "Why?"

WHAT WOULD I have done? Jack wondered. If this had happened to me? If I'd been the one to survive all that? With all the hatred for their killers and the guilt of a survivor – wouldn't I do anything I could to kill their killers? And who *were* their killers? Not just the faceless soldiers and inept politicians, but in al-Baghdadi's eyes the entire country of America. The Great Satan.

There should have been another way.

MANY HOURS he spent remembering and writing down every detail. How al-Baghdadi stood when he spoke, how he walked with a slight swish to his hips, his thin, pale hands – he'd been an accountant, one prisoner revealed, before the GW Bush invasion; he was a man who spent his time with paper, not guns.

Everything they learned, everything Jack could remember, went into a computer program run by an Home Office psychiatrist named Saul, a chubby, cheery guy with thick glasses and a dense silvery beard. Piece by piece, memory by memory, they recreated al-Baghdadi on Saul's computer. It was what Saul called a "reflexive profile", meaning that it would hopefully respond to stimuli and incidents as the real al-Baghdadi might.

"I want you to be al-Baghdadi," Saul told Jack one afternoon. "I will ask you questions, or challenge you, and you will answer as he would." And then Saul hypnotized him.

Afterwards Jack had no memory of what he'd said, but Saul seemed happy. "Maybe," he chuckled, "you really *are* al-Baghdadi."

The Iranians and other Shias had spread the rumor that al-Baghdadi was really a Mossad agent named Elliot Shimon, supposedly from a statement by former US intelligence researcher Edward Snowden. However Home Office, having closely studied all of Snowden's leaked data, and having had several intense "heart-to-heart" talks with its Mossad allies, decided this was pure Iranian obfuscation.

One thing was clear: al-Baghdadi understood public relations. He had taken his first names Abu Bakr from that of Mohammed's father-in-law, the first "caliph" after Mohammed, and a name with deep resonance for Sunni believers. The same Abu Bakr who had spread Islam across the Middle East on the edge of a bloody sword, who had given his six-year-old daughter in marriage to Mohammed.

Though Mohammed reportedly had waited till the little girl was seven before he consummated the marriage.

From what they learned, al-Baghdadi didn't believe that killing people would get him to Heaven; he didn't believe in Heaven and didn't care. He just loved killing.

It was said that every time he swung the sword down on another exposed human neck his loins exploded. He'd even boasted of it. And that every time he slid a well-honed blade across a human throat it spurted from him as quickly as blood from his dying victim.

What more did he need to prove these killings justified and right?

True, he'd also enjoyed shoving captive virgins down on the dirt and forcing himself inside them. Their screams, their tears and begging made it even more erotic.

After that he sold them. They were worth even more if pregnant, because Abu Bakr al-Baghdadi had had been the first to plow their field. Their new owners would boast of the child, a descendent from Abu Bakr the first caliph. Whose descendants became the Sunnis just as the descendants of Ali ibn Abi Talib became the Shiites.

But Saul's virtual al-Baghdadi turned out to be gay.

"HOLY SHIT!" Jack said. "That would explain Omar al-Shishani."

Omar was the man closest to al-Baghdadi, reportedly the only person who saw him "with a naked face" – without the mask al-Baghdadi wore even with his other associates. The same Omar who had taken his name from the deputy commander of the original Abu Bakr's bloodthirsty armies.

And from what they could tell, Omar al-Shishani was very gay.

Although homosexuality is far more common in the Muslim world than the West, due to the intense restrictions put on boy-girl contact (a male and female teenager can be arrested in many Muslim countries simply for walking on the same side of the street), it is also severely repressed. Thousands of supposedly "gay" Shias had gone to their deaths at al-Baghdadi's hands. "It's homicidal repression of the self," Saul said. "You saw it among the Nazis – Ernst Rohm and Rudolf Hess, in fact, most of the officer corps of the SA were homosexual thugs."

And like Hitler al-Baghdadi was apparently a coprophile, someone who got turned on by human feces, as indicated by his behavior when a prisoner defecated, as was normal, after being hung or decapitated.

Just as Hitler's Nazism had grown out of the intolerable poverty and despair of a defeated Germany after World War I, so had thirty-five years of war including two US invasions, the eight-year war with the Iranians that had caused additional millions of casualties, and decades of US sanctions, disabled the minds of many Iraqis, including al-Baghdadi.

Jack closed the file and shut down the computer. Sat pinching the bridge of his nose and massaging his eyes. By our continuous wars had we helped to make this Abu Bakr al-Baghdadi a mass murderer? Had the sorrow of twenty-five years of war and the loss of loved ones brutalized his mind?

Jack took a deep breath, put his hands on his knees and stood. Enough is enough.

In two days they would leave for Paris. That was all that mattered.

He'd done his best to help his country – there was nothing else he knew that Saul, Feist and the others now didn't know. Isabelle was now over five months pregnant and starting to show, and he wanted her safe and comfortable.

"*Ettabe'e Allah,*" Feist had said when Jack told him they were leaving. *Go with God.*

A Russian Airbus had just exploded over the Sinai, Feist said. "The Russians refuse to say it's a bomb."

"No plane explodes at thirty thousand feet," Jack had answered. "Except for that."

"Of course," Feist shrugged. "But Putin doesn't want to bring it out in public. Doesn't want the link with their attacks on ISIS."

"Like they say, the Russians never forgive. Never forget. At least Putin has the balls Obama doesn't."

Feist snickered. "Obama still wants to make our enemies love us."

"God laughs, some French philosopher said, long ago," Jack remembered, "at those who deplore the effects of the evils whose causes they have cherished."

"Bossuet," Max Ricard had answered. "A priest, no less."

Isabelle had left early to shop in the markets for fresh vegetables. By the time he got to the apartment she'd be there.

He wouldn't tell her about the Russian Airbus. No need.

A New Life

B UT ISABELLE WASN'T THERE when he got
back to the apartment. He felt a sharp letdown, wanting to tell her what had happened, that he was finally
free. Then realized that was silly and selfish: she was out
looking for food, would return soon. Soon they'd leave this
Godforsaken place and go home to Argentina or wherever
home was. Wherever they loved best.

This made him think of Sophie, of being so in love with
her and wanting to be free and happy with her, and how this
had led to her death and the death of their children. Because
Leo had been his too, genetically connected to him by the
death of the Russian tank captain whom she'd loved before
Jack had killed him and then found her.

He remembered Suze in her house trailer in the frigid
Maine winter, the baby crying in the next room the morning
she woke him to say his friend Cole and the other Marines
in Beirut had been killed, and like a medieval warrior he'd
left on a crusade to avenge them.

But no one can avenge anyone. Once you're dead you're
past all that. It can't bring you back to life. And if you're

the avenger you're not doing it for the victim but in hatred for what your enemy has taken from you or those you love.

It was right to go home now. He'd helped to force the Soviets from Afghanistan. Had helped find who had killed the Marines in Beirut, though Home Office hadn't listened. He'd helped destroy others who had done great harm. Had tried to stop GW's Iraq catastrophe, but again they hadn't listened. Had told them not to release al-Baghdadi, and three years later not to pull out of Iraq, but both times they hadn't listened. Now he'd had helped them track the worst in a long string of Muslim mass murderers. And this time they were listening.

This brought him back to what he so often thought about, how wars start out small, then someone gets broken-hearted because someone they care about has been killed, and rises up in fury. Hadn't he felt that fury, the white-hot anger of losing a friend and you no longer care, live or die, all you want is vengeance? To kill, to massacre those who have massacred the person you love?

All this was a long way from now. Tomorrow he and she could be on a plane to Paris and from there to Argentina and the little adobe hacienda in the shadow of the Andes.

To be free.

Free of war.

Free of pain and loss and sorrow.

Why do humans act this way?

In the kitchen he washed the few dishes – he would have undertaken the labors of Hercules gratefully just to see her smile when she came in the door, her knowing he'd done it for her, that he would always do whatever he could to show her how much he loved her.

She still wasn't here, but no need to worry. Dressed in the hijab, speaking Iraqi, she could pass for local. "We get much better veggies outside in the markets than we do in here," she'd said this morning, hands on hips to show she wasn't taking no for an answer. Spinach, she wanted spinach.

A distant blast shook the windows. Fucking Shiites and Sunnis always killing each other – couldn't they realize all you need is love? That that asshole "prophet" with his mealy-mouthed miseries about what he wanted the human race to undergo in the name of his fantasy of "God" was beyond comprehension. As the French say, *risible*.

She'd be home soon. He could see her walking through the door, wanted to sweep her in his arms, tell her how much he loved her and that they and the baby she was carrying were off tomorrow for Paris and a new life.

SHE STILL WASN'T there when he woke. He'd dozed on the couch, and the polluted gray Baghdad skies had faded to black, the smoke-tinged air cold through a bullet hole in the window. "Sophie!" he called out in half-sleep, suddenly embarrassed that he'd called Isabelle using the name of his dead wife.

Isabelle's computer was not on the side table. Why would she have taken it if she was looking for food? She hadn't mentioned an interview... had something come up? A sharp insecurity, a biting worry – where was she? He'd been here an hour – but maybe she'd left just before he came, would be back soon.

And yet.

Footsteps up the stairs but went past the door. He tucked aside a curtain to check the street where a few headlights snaked their way furtively as if endangered by the darkness, or by what hid there.

He changed into a long Iraqi shirt and jeans, clipped his gun into his shoulder holster, pulled on a black leather jacket, locked the door and went down the four flights and through the lobby past the sleepy old Sunni man at the desk and out the front door. The air had turned cold, brutal, empty, tarnished with burning plastic or rubber mixed with diesel smoke and spicy meat from the stand around the corner. He realized if she called the hotel he wouldn't be in the room to answer, so ran back upstairs. The light on the phone wasn't blinking, but maybe the light was broken or the message machine wouldn't blink anyway.

He called the front desk. "No," the old Sunni told him, "no person call."

He went downstairs again and told him he'd be outside, and to get him if someone called.

Perhaps another hour passed, a few souls hustling along the sidewalk, face down. Three ragtag Iraqi Army trucks, a dying stream of cars. Another explosion in the east, maybe Sadr City, the distant moan of sirens. What fools, to think that killing changes anything.

He was standing outside the door when the old Sunni came out bowing and gesticulating. Jack had a terrible fear something had happened, that it was Isabelle and that's why she was calling. But when he picked up the receiver it wasn't Isabel.

"Since I'm stuck in Baghdad," Timothy said, "thought I'd check to see if you're doing something special your last night in town."

Jack bit back his fear and the sallow burn in his stomach. "Staying in."

"You and your girlfriend?" Ironic, almost offensive.

Jack didn't know why, but couldn't tell him the truth. "Yeah."

"If I were you I'd be out partying. Anyway, if you change your mind there's a big do at Colonel Anders'."

"I'm not you, Timothy."

A low chuckle. "Too bad for you."

He paced the sidewalk, checking his phone. Nothing. Then nothing. Nothing.

"You didn't see her leave?" he asked the old Sunni.

The old man looked away as if remembering. Shook his head. "Never see." He had a rural accent Jack could barely understand.

"What time today you get here?" Jack said.

The old man looked up, thought a moment, pointed a spiny finger at the clock. "One hour. Yes, one hour. Unless a little after that. Perhaps one or two..."

"You never see her leave?"

The old man's head went side to side. "Not ever."

Sometimes it happened he could see the whole person. The insides, not the facade. The pulsing brain and the messages running on tiny axons back and forth, the curving esophagus, the throbbing heart and dirty lungs, the fat liver and striated muscles, the balls of shit forming their way down the intestine – he could see it all the way other people might just see a face and the camouflage of clothes.

And with this old Sunni Jack could see his brain and his interior as plainly as if dissected, the viscera, the truth. And he knew something terrible had happened to Isabelle.

HE CALLED MI6, Isabelle's local contact Simon Mahaffey. "Isabelle's gone."

"What?" Simon chuckled, "she tired of you already?"

"She's been kidnapped."

"Oh fuck."

He told Simon what he knew. Which was nothing. Isabelle's recent stories to *The Independent* hadn't been provocative, nor had she met recently with anyone unduly hated by one group or other. She hadn't been out much, she'd told him – why now? And by whom?

Simon would do everything he could. "Question is, do

we reveal this?"

"Once you tell your network then everybody knows. Then *they* get to reveal it."

"They may anyway." Simon thought a moment. "You tracking her phone?"

"I'm asking my guys."

"What's on her computer?"

"Gone."

"She mention anything lately?"

"Nothing. Simon, we need to offer big money."

"You know the new deal. No rewards –"

"What do you mean no rewards?"

"The word from the top is we don't pay ransoms any more. It just leads to more kidnappings, they say."

Jack muscled up the strength to say this: "If we don't pay, Isabelle dies."

"She may die anyway. You know the odds."

"I'm offering a reward for any information. I don't give a fuck what you say."

"Then we don't work with you anymore."

"You're saying a British citizen, a prominent journalist, has disappeared, and you're not going to do anything?"

"I didn't say that." Simon's tone gentled. "This is absolutely horrible. I want to get right on it. We'll do everything we can. Everything. But it may be wiser to wait a day or two to reveal it, see what we can learn."

"And no reward?"

Simon's unshaven chin scratched the phone. "We'll reach out to everyone we know, every contact we have. But let's wait a few days, right?"

"The old Sunni, the desk clerk, he knows something."

"You told me he wasn't there till one something, maybe two. So it happened earlier?"

"No way. When I called her at 15:50 she hadn't left yet."

"I see."

"We need the Iraqis on him. Hard."

"That won't happen."

"Or I will."

"Don't be a lone ranger, Jack, you'll only get her killed. Stay with us."

"I still don't see why."

"Tactical, Jack. Tactical. Gives us time to move on the ground."

"Don't you fuckheads dare try to rescue her."

"You're an American, don't try to tell us what to do." Simon cleared his throat. "You call your own people?"

"You were first."

"Thanks for that."

"She's your citizen. Your famous journalist. *You* have to lead. My side will be sympathetic, nothing more."

"Despite all your years."

"I've burned too many bridges. You know that."

"She was just a journalist. She never worked for us. Not in any way. That will be our position."

"I don't care."

"We'll be in touch."

Telling Simon about Isabelle's absence had made it even clearer how impossible it would be to find her. They would have to wait till her kidnappers got in touch, if they ever did.

Unless she was already dead. By the side of the road somewhere, her throat cut. In a trash heap or down by the river. In a ruined building or a cemetery for cars. Thousands of bodies out there already, waiting to be discovered.

Nothing he could do. He had to. Visions of her swirled around him. His every cell ached. The universe screamed with pain. Sorrow deep as the dark night of space overwhelmed him.

"I DON'T BELIEVE I heard you," Timothy said.

"Isabelle's been kidnapped, I said."

"Oh my Lord!"

"I need help –"

"Are you sure?" A rustle of sleeve as Timothy checked his watch. "It's not even eight o'clock – maybe she's just late or something?"

"I'm coming in."

"There's nobody here." Timothy's throat caught. "It's just me, and I'm headed back to DC in two hours."

"Nobody there?" Jack was out of breath from pacing, forgetting to breathe. "Where the fuck's Feist?"

"On his way to Qatar."

"Get him back. Who runs the networks?"

"Rickner. And *he's* over the Atlantic right now."

"Get him back too. I need to reach his people, the networks... And I need GPS on Isabelle's phone, right now."

"Don't tell me what to do, Jack. And Isabelle's *their* citizen, not ours. We have to wait till they ask."

"They're asking. Don't waste time."

"Tell them call me."

"And we have to get the word out."

"It can't come from us. Not visibly."

"Why?"

"She's not ours, like I said. *They* have to handle this."

"They're doing all they can. But we have twenty times the resources. This is *our* war, remember? They're just helping us out, giving their guys some experience. Timothy I need a list, introductions. Now."

"You could put everybody in danger, Jack. You know the rules."

"Fuck the rules."

"That's been your problem all along, Jack You've always fucked the rules. It gets tiresome. Counterproductive."

"Are you saying a long-term US military agent's next of kin may die because you guys won't help?"

"She's *not* your next of kin. That means spouse or blood relation."

"We're engaged, getting married soon as we get out of here..." The words choked in his throat, *get out of here*, their unreality now. "Rickner and Feist, get them back here."

"You're not my CO, Jack. I wish you'd remember that. We will chat with him, see what his options are."

"I want to talk to him. Now. And the other one, soon as he lands."

"Do you remember this afternoon, Jack? What you said to me?"

"I said the truth. You have a right to disagree. But I've been paid by you guys for over twenty years, done more for you than almost anyone else –"

"We'll do what we can." Timothy exhaled. "I'll call you back."

"Don't you dare leave town, you bastard."

The line was dead. Jack called him back. "Timothy if you don't help me on this..."

"Of course we will."

"I want the GPS on her phone."

"Give me," Timothy paused as if seeking a pen or paper, "the number."

"Just so you know, I'm calling *The Independent*. And going to Hassan al-Shelby."

"The Police Chief? Not yet. Her people are right: give them, give us, two days to work it out and if we don't know something we'll go outside."

"I'm offering a hundred grand. Right now."

"Don't do that either."

"And I need Feist back. Here, now. And for you to stay till we know what's going on."

Timothy sighed, a man suddenly old, a husk. "I'll call you, before I go."

"Get me the GPS, Timothy," Jack seethed, but the line was dead.

He stared at the silent phone, almost threw it at the window. But it was his umbilical cord to her; the only chance of saving her would come through this phone.

He went down to find the old man at the desk.

Retribution

"ALREADY I tell you," the old man said. "She does not come down from these stairs while I am here." "She was still here at three forty-five. I called her."

"Perhaps I was in the toilets. Perhaps then."

"When?" Jack wanted to choke his flaccid dirty neck. "*When* did you go to the toilets?"

The old man spread his hands. "For that, one doesn't look at the time…"

Jack nodded at the clock. "You must have! Don't you check to make sure no one's expected?"

"I am not from America. Here we do not live like that."

There was no choice. Jack lifted him like a straw dummy and carried him cackling through the office door into the back room and sat him in an old tilting plastic chair and shut the door behind them. "It's very simple," he said. "I give you ten minutes to tell me what happened. Every word. The truth. I can see inside you and if you lie I'll kill you."

The old man caught his breath, rubbing his throat. "They will find you."

Jack took off the old man's scarf and tightened it round

his neck. "Who? Who will find me?"

"You will kill me anyway?"

"Not if you tell. And promise Allah to be silent."

"Then *they* kill me."

"Who is *they*, you old fool? I'll get them."

A quavering snicker. "That could never happen."

Jack twisted the scarf. "So I kill you. Or you tell me *now*. Who are they?"

"They will kill," the old man fought for breath, his long fingernails at Jack's wrists, "my family."

"So will I."

"Take away the scarf. I will tell you."

The old man sat up in the rickety chair and Jack crouched before him. "They are Sunni people. You Americans have put over us this evil Shiite al-Maliki – why I do not understand, since so many of us are Sunni. So there are many young men who have survived your invasion, who have survived the troubles you unleashed on us. They want retribution."

"Against who?"

"Against you Americans who have once again destroyed our country and killed so many thousands of our people. Against the Shiites who desecrate Islam and whom you enforce upon us because you want to make friends with Iran."

"What does this have to do with Miss Palmeiri?"

"If they took her it is because she is with you. To punish you, perhaps?"

"Why? What have I done to them?"

"For that you would have to ask them."

"How do I find them?"

"You cannot. Nor can I. Perhaps they will find you."

"You told them I was here, didn't you, you old bastard."

"It is known. I did not have to say it."

Jack fell to his knees, exhausted. "Why didn't they just

kill me?"

"For that you would have to ask them."

Jack snatched a reservation form from the desk and scribbled on it. "Here's my phone number. If they come back, call me. If you lead them to me I will give you ten thousand dollars."

"They will kill me if I do this. If they do, what good is money?"

NESTS INSIDE nests. Endless skins of an onion that when you finally peel down you find was just another wrong onion. He thought of the taxi driver – not a boy any more but once a student till the Americans came. Who had lost an eye in the *muqawama*. And now was driving a taxi instead of doing physics research.

Hadn't things been better, as most Iraqis said, under Saddam? Evil as he may have been, an American executioner in the 1950s, a slaughterer of America's enemies, a ruthless ally till the 80's then suddenly an impediment in the global oil game, and thus an enemy?

And the Iraqi people who'd lived through Rumsfeld's "Shock and Awe"? So many people blasted to oblivion, their homes destroyed and children obliterated before their eyes. Everywhere shattered bodies and bloody streets. All their young men who never came home. What does it feel like to have an M-60 bullet punch through your chest?

What would *he* have done, had he been one of them?

20:55 IN BAGHDAD was not even 6 pm in London. The operator at *The Independent* was still there and passed him to a junior editor named Barbara Sachs.

"One of your reporters is in trouble. I need to talk to the Editor in Chief, the Owner –"

It took another ten minutes to find a senior editor named

Alison Krump who soon connected him to editor in chief
Lionel Hutting. "This is dreadful," Hutting said. "Horrifying. What can *we* do?"

"Think. Think how you can help. Her files –"

"She kept nothing here. All we have are her emailed ar-
ticles. We sometimes edited them, but nothing else. This isn't
an old-fashioned newspaper office full of filing cabinets."

"What about sources? You must have checked her
sources."

Hutting said nothing, then, "Her sources were vetted.
But not by us."

"You're telling me MI6 runs you? Tells you what to
say?"

"Young man I'm not telling you that at all," Hutting
huffed, "not at all. Do you have her phone? Her calls?"

"Her phone was with her."

"Your people can trace it –"

"That's my next call. And I need every reporter you
know of to spread the word we're doing a ransom."

"Who is?"

"You and me."

"While I daresay we could do something, perhaps, I
can't commit –"

"A hundred grand is what you're offering."

"Jack, I –"

"Or I'm doing a press conference about how you guys
knowingly sent her into danger."

"Journalism's a dangerous job, we all know that."

Jack's phone buzzed, an instant's hope it was Isabelle
but it was Timothy. "Feist's on his way back."

"When?"

"They turned around, soon as I called."

"How many hours?"

"Six, maybe, then it'll be three am."

"I'll meet him then."

"He'll call you. You're lucky he's coming back. Don't push it."

Jack returned to Hutting but he was gone. He called him back. "I have to discuss this with the Board," Hutting said.

"Do it now. I'll call you back. Be sure to answer."

"Don't expect miracles. Some of them may be unavailable till tomorrow."

"You have till 9 am London time. That's fifteen hours. Then I blow you wide open."

PAIN. In her skull, her arms, her back and knees. Where they had hit her, roped her, jabbed, kicked and dragged her. Her mouth torn by the rag knotted across it, her eyes driven into her skull by her rag blindfold, her wrists burning and bleeding through her bindings.

She was lying on her side on the dirt floor of a dark room. Truck engines rumbled in the distance. The arm beneath her had gone to sleep. She realized she could move, and twisted herself onto her back.

A horrible pain seared into her face ripping her cheek. A whip or something, barbed wire. "Don't move," a man said. In English.

SHE WAITED. Forced herself to breathe slowly, deeply, steadily. In, out. One, two. Up to a hundred then start again. Maybe CO_2 will dull the pain.

No it doesn't.

A thunder of jets climbing overhead. F-10s maybe. Out of Bagram? Was she still in Baghdad? How long had she been unconscious?

The van at the corner of the suddenly empty street, its doors flinging open, the men dragging her inside, she bit the hand clamped over her mouth. He swore and a huge pain hit her skull. And now this.

"Water," she whispered. A horrible pain smashed into the small of her back, the kidneys. A boot. She gagged, writhing for breath.

The whip slashed her cheek. "I said *Don't move!*"

Time passed with the slowness of a drop of water trickling across a desert. It did not pass at all. Not even one minute passed. The pain was overwhelming, more than she could stand.

Her swollen throat made it hard not to gasp. Her hands were on fire, her feet. The pain in her side and shoulder, in her kidneys and the crushed bleeding in her skull were all killing her but she did not die.

"NO TRACE of her phone," Timothy said.

He hadn't dared hope for it. "Is Feist in yet?"

"Not yet. Get some sleep, Jack. Stay near your phone."

He walked the cold dark damp streets. There were no taxis. He thought of the physics kid. He'd saved his number somewhere. Where?

The pocket of the shirt he'd worn. But he'd changed shirts.

03:10. Three hours to dawn. He went back to the Palestine. A young man with a sharp moustache was dozing at the desk. "The old man who was here," Jack said. "He was very helpful…"

"Uncle Wazir," the young man yawned. "He comes back not till Monday."

"I'm leaving but want to give him a small gift –"

"Leave it here."

Jack shrugged: *we both know it will get stolen.* "I wish to give it personally. How do I find him?"

The man yawned again, covering his mouth with the back of his wrist. He got to his feet and fumbled in a drawer, pulled out a sheet of paper and peered down at it. "Al Attar Street, number seven twenty-three."

Jack pulled the Baghdad map from his pocket. "Show me."

The young man looked at him, beady-eyed. "You are going now? At *this* hour?"

"No. In the morning." He climbed the four floors to his room, took a headlamp and the note with the cab driver's number, left the Palestine and walked the pocked, littered streets till he found a Vespa he could hot wire. Nervous of the clatter it made, he drove slowly to Al Mahdi Street where it crossed Al Attar and parked it.

Al Attar was a mix of empty warehouses, some shell-damaged, and a few broken-stuccoed apartments smelling of human habitation, cars huddled like dying animals on both sides of the road, low-hanging electric wires like vines against the dirty sky.

Number 723 was a low concrete block bungalow with a metal roof, steel window bars, and an old VW Passat parked on a dirt patch beside it.

He slipped into an empty two-story building three down from it. The door was gone, the hallway dark, broken glass and turds underfoot, a shattered window at the end, a stairway of broken treads, rats hissing as they ran out the back into an overgrown alley of broken cars. He climbed the stairs to a naked second floor room of crunching plaster and smashed furniture where he could hide and still look down on the old man's home.

05:41. An hour to daylight.

HANDS RIPPED off her blindfold and bright light burned her eyes. She blinked, closed and opened them; black shapes flitted across her sight.

Hands yanked her sideways. Black masks stared down.

Three, crouching over her with only black eyes showing through black masks. One thrust his face closer. "Keep silent. Do what we say."

She nodded. The pain in her back was more than she could take, her skull and jaw, her torn face, the agony in her wrists and feet.

He gripped her shoulder. "We are your masters. Understand?"

Again she nodded.

He slapped her. "Infidel whore."

"QATAR'S A SNAKEPIT," Jordan Feist said.

"You're back!" Jack said. "Thank God, thank you so much for coming back!"

"All these Qatari and Saudi oil sheiks funding Al-Qaeda and ISI with our money. And we can't touch them. We get to watch. And write reports. It sucks."

"Isabelle's takers haven't contacted anyone so they may not be interested in dealing." Jack swallowed, waited for the words to come. "Unless they've already killed her... So we need the reward offered fast. For a starter it's two hundred grand, from *The Independent*. Half of it's actually from me – that wipes out my savings and everything else – but it's better it all seems to come from the paper."

"We're not in that game."

"What game?"

"It's better, like Simon says, to first spread the word. That she's missing and we want her back."

"Without a reward –"

"We have a good team here. Some have teams of their own. But their lives depend on me, and probably mine on them. I can't risk, morally or strategically, any of them."

"Nobody's asking you to." Jack forced himself to slow down. "For the reward we need a callback number, anyone can leave a message, so we get the location where they're calling from."

"Home office says no financing."

"I wasn't asking you guys –"

"No, Jack, you don't understand. We can't even send out the word."

DAWN BLED across the tattered rooftops. The muezzin's first call echoed through the concrete alleys and battered buildings against an empty sky where a few rooks rose and fell on the bitter wind. The hum of traffic began as if the city were a vast, toxic beehive, a waking snake pit.

His phone throbbed. "We have some images," Feist said.

"What you got?"

"Fixed stuff." Feist cleared his throat. "We always keep an eye on the Palestine, that area. Somebody that could've been her went out the front door at four-twenty-two, turned right, crossed the street and headed for the market."

"The market." Jack fought a surge of hope. "What was she wearing?"

"Looks like a brown coat, can't tell."

"That could be her."

"Then at the corner a white van pulls over, three guys leap out and throw her inside and it drives off with her fighting all three of them. No one there seemed to see; next to a broken wall and an empty lot, parked cars on both sides blocking the view."

Jack said nothing, seeing it. "Where'd it go?"

"Out of view."

"A white van –"

"Could be a Ford, can't tell. Even one of those fucking Russian Furgons."

"You sent those images home?"

"Of course."

"When will we hear?"

"It's after hours, over there."

A red Fiat had plodded up the street and halted gasping in front of the old man's bungalow. "Wait," Jack said softly to Feist, "I have a license plate for you."

A youngish man with a full Islamic beard and a .45 holstered on his hip got out of the Fiat and entered the house. "It's a white passenger car plate, 97351," Jack said.

"Where are you?"

"723 Al Attar. Staking out the hotel clerk's house. He knows who did it."

"You're out there on your own? You're crazy."

"Our chances of saving her get worse every minute. Just ID that plate."

"You're going to end up dead, Jack. And her too."

High Noon

"**D**EATH IS THE SENTENCE for spying."

"I'm not a spy." Her mouth wouldn't work right, from having been gagged. Her teeth felt twisted, her tongue scraped and swollen.

"In almost every country in the world the sentence for spying is death." His voice coming from above her, him and two others.

"I'm a journalist," she mumbled, trying to shift position on the wooden chair they had tied her to. "Not a spy."

"Aren't they the *same*?" He had a lisp that expired on the last consonant.

"*The Independent* is independent. Objective –"

"There is no such thing as objectivity, you know that."

"Can't you please *please* loosen this cord on my wrists? Please, they are dying."

"We are all dying. Some go to Heaven, others like you go to Hell."

"What do you want of me? Get it over with." She could see Jack clearly as if he stood before her, in a future they would never have. He wore a red wool shirt, hands in jeans pockets. Silver-haired. A silvery log gate behind him against a far valley of dark firs and granite.

"We want you to tell us about your work with MI6. We will learn, as you know, one way or the other." He gripped her shoulder. "You know the rules – *You* talk, *they* pay, *you* go home."

"Then I'm dead. For there is nothing I can tell you about spying. I will tell you what I know about MI6, but that is from their media and available to anyone..." She waited for the slap but it did not come. "I can tell you about my stories but not all my sources. I can –"

It came so hard, her cheek screaming in pain, her jaw and skull thundering, blood spurting down her lips and chin onto her thigh. He grabbed her by the hair and dragged her across the floor, her tied hands scraping along concrete. "Do it here!" he said. "Use the silencer."

"Just cut her throat."

"Please, I'm not a spy, please... I'll tell you anything I know but I know nothing –"

"She's got nice tits. Feel her cunt, too. Let's do her first, then cut her throat?"

"We kill her right now. Give me the knife." He twisted her into position on her knees, a steely hand yanking back her chin. "Feel this?" he whispered, "*feel* it? It's the blade that will rip through your throat and jugular and larynx so your brain dies as you choke on your own blood... Can you *feel* it?" He slid it along her skin, a hot wire. "Answer me!"

She tried to nod, moaned through her gag. He dropped her head, knocked her down. "Stand, you! Stand!"

She tried to stand but couldn't with bound hands and ankles. He pushed her over with his boot. "You still can't remember MI6? Fine, have it your way. I sentence you to death. At noon." A rustle of cloth as he stood and checked his watch. "Yes, let's do high noon. Like in the movies."

THE BEARDED GUY came out of the old man's bungalow with an AK and cartridge belt. He tossed them in the Fiat's trunk and started the car as Jack ran to the Vespa and followed him, no headlight, a block behind.

The Fiat scuttled along Al Mahdi trailing a tail of black smoke. Half the guys in Baghdad, Jack reminded himself, carry AKs and wear sidearms. I'm chasing phantoms.

The road was filling with smoking trucks, tilting buses, scurrying cars and blaring motorbikes. The sun began to burn through the ooze of exhaust, damp fires and burning trash. A body lay at the roadside, blood- and dust-cloaked. Dead fronds drooped from the palms like hanged men; workers in dirty undershirts and rolled-up trousers were lining up at job sites; black-veiled women trotted along the roadsides. Oily water glinted in the potholes and splashed up when cars ran across them.

The Vespa stuttered, caught, jerked forward and stuttered again. A truck had moved in between Jack and the Fiat; the bike backfired, died. Coasting, he stamped on the clutch, released it and the engine caught. The red Fiat turned down an alley, picking its way carefully between potholes and avoiding a flooded oil-shiny trench that may have been a sewer.

The Vespa died. No matter what he did it wouldn't start. He tipped it against a wall and ran after the red Fiat as it turned right at the end of the alley and when Jack got there it had disappeared down a narrow long street curving left at the end. He ran several blocks each way but could not see the red Fiat down any side streets.

From a seller on the curb he bought a tin of gasoline, ran to the Vespa and drove a grid check on every street and alley, working his way farther and farther outward.

It was a wide low street with sagging wires, burnt-out cars, shell holes and shattered windows, bones of houses.

And at the cul-de-sac a white-painted car repair shop, its three bays shut by rusted metal doors, a one-window office on the left side, the red Fiat parked beside it.

Next to a white van.

"IT'S A REAL PLATE NUMBER," Feist said. "Hal-ab al-Ismaili, Baghdad Central says. A Special Forces unit captured him way back in 2007 after an IED attack. We put him in Bucca, where he hung out with all these other fucking terrorists, the Al-Qaedas and ex-Baathists, got out when we handed over Bucca to the Iraqis and all these dangerous guys got released. We've found links between him and al-Baghdadi."

"I'm moving in on this white van."

"You can't go in alone, Jack."

"What else they tell you, Baghdad Central?"

"They say leave him alone."

"Which means they're warning him, right now."

"Maybe not."

"We need to hit this place."

"On suspicion of having a white van? You know how many *white vans* there are in Baghdad? We'd have fifty thousand suspects."

"This guy with the Fiat, he's tied to the old man. The old man knew what was happening, maybe helped out."

"Still doesn't give you the right to bust in, shoot everybody. Let's put a post on it and we'll bring up some gear and see what we hear."

He hated the idea but it made sense. To listen on conversations first, because once you hit them they shut up. And everyone knows you've hit them. "I'll find somewhere and get back to you." He found another gas seller and topped up the Vespa. Back at the garage neither the red Fiat or the white van had moved.

He glanced at himself in a dusty storefront window. Just like any normal Iraqi guy, tanned skin and bristles, a worn, hard-bitten look, faded jeans and shirt, scuffed running shoes. An older guy who'd come down in the world, looking for a construction job, any job.

The street was packed dirt, tails of sand twirling away in the wind. But there was no one there, no movement among the close-packed cars. He'd stick out no matter what he looked like.

The next street was narrower and the buildings dirtier and taller, clotheslines and utility lines slung between them, battered cars crouching along both sides, people walking and kids running down the middle, one kicking an empty plastic bottle like a soccer ball before him.

The front doors of most apartment buildings were open. Many of the apartments were broken-windowed and empty. He walked purposely up one's front stairs and down a darkened dirty hall of peeling wallpaper and loose linoleum. The stairs creaked as he climbed to the third floor, where a window on the stairwell looked down on the garage.

He wondered should he find a building closer to the garage then decided to stay where he was. He climbed one more flight to the roof, which was flat and sticky and dropped straight off on all sides. He called Feist and told him where he was.

"I'll have a guy there in fifty minutes."

"Who?"

"Name's Darius. Ex-Iraqi Army elite, hates Sunnis *and* Shiites. An LP guy."

"More and more cars are showing up at the garage. We got a big meeting. I need him."

"It's an insane lead."

Jack thought of Owen McPhee years ago in the World Trade Center. "Show me a better one."

Prepare Yourself

THEY'D KILL HER in four hours. She had to face it. Live the rest of her life in four hours.

Does your brain keep working when your head's cut off? Do you know what's happened? How horribly does it hurt?

No one would save her. No one knew where she was. Jack going crazy trying to find her – all lost. Jack, all their future lives together, kids and grandkids – all lost.

How could she make it not happen?

Tell them the truth?

They'd kill her anyway.

You are going to die in four hours. *Prepare yourself.*

DARIUS was short, grizzled and rugged. He glanced around the roof carefully, then at Jack. "You alone here?"

"It's fine."

"I would not say so."

Jack nodded at Darius' backpack. "What you got?"

Darius took out a device the size of a thick cell phone. It sat on four thin legs and had a small probe he pointed toward the garage. He plugged in ear buds and set the device carefully on the roof edge, listening to it and altering the probe till he had it where he wanted. He handed one ear bud to Jack. "Bunch of guys talking. Don't seem very happy."

Jack hurriedly plugged in the ear bud. The conversation was astonishingly clear, as if he sat in the next room. "It's not our problem," a man said.

"They must make it five million," another said, older, with a harsh voice.

"She is a spy, they say. She is to be killed."

"Anyway, it is not our problem."

"They asked us, should they kill her –"

Jack felt an awful presence behind him, pulled out the ear bud. "Stand up slowly," a voice said. "Hands behind your heads."

He had not watched his back, Jack realized, and now he couldn't save her any more. He scanned the roof edge for a way down. Nothing. He glanced at Darius, who seemed sad and alone.

He'd been so caught up in finding her he'd destroyed himself. And her too. He stepped to the edge. Straight down.

"What are you doing?" the man said, pointing an AK back and forth between Jack and Darius.

"We are just waiting," Darius said, "on this roof."

Jack turned the corner and looked down again. A steel ladder bolted onto the concrete edge descended the wall into darkness. "You're going to kill me, I'd rather jump."

"Get back here!" the man yelled.

Jack leaped over the side grabbing the ladder that popped loose from the wall as he slid straight down it; he grabbed at a third floor window and squeezed through it into what seemed to be a kitchen, scrambled over a counter and waited behind the front door. The man came racing down the stairs and Jack hit him hard in the forehead with the butt of his gun, and hard again on the temple as he knocked him to the floor.

Darius came downstairs. "Thank you for this. He was going to kill me."

"Let's gag and tie him. Then we go find those guys in the garage."

"There are many –"

"Doesn't matter." Jack took the man's AK, dragged him into the apartment and tied his wrists behind him to an iron radiator. The man's head was bleeding heavily. Jack took seven bullets and a thin wallet from the man's pockets.

"You take this." Jack handed Darius his revolver and checked the AK. Full clip.

He called Simon and Feist and gave them the address. "These guys don't have her," Simon said, "but they know where she is?"

"They are in contact with the people who have her."

Simon exhaled, exhaustion and defeat. "If we go in on them we won't be able to make them talk in time to save her, in time before whoever has her moves her somewhere else –"

Or kills her, Jack reminded himself. If I don't get there first. "If we can find the phone they're using, can we trace the call?"

"Yeah maybe."

"How soon?"

"You need to go back on the roof and listen," Feist said.

"You guys don't get here fast I'm going in. Me and my friend Darius here, we'll make somebody talk."

"Hang tight," Feist said. "We'll be there."

THEY SEATED HER back in the chair and lashed her wrists and ankles to it. Someone yanked off the gag. "Say something."

Her mouth was full of pain, her tongue numb. She gagged, tried to speak. The whip ripped across her neck setting skin and muscle afire, stung more than she could believe, could bear. "Speak!" he yelled.

"Kill me. Get it over with."

"It's only ten o'clock. You still have two hours. Or more if you tell us who you talk to. What do they say? How do you send it? Who are your MI6 contacts here? Easy questions, easy to answer. To save your life."

Hands shoved her back against the chair, tugged off the blindfold. Cold light seared through her eyelids into her eyes. She shut them tighter then slowly opened them. A little room with yellow insulation on the walls, no windows, a concrete floor. Three men in tan camo and black balaclavas stared down at her. One held the whip, the others AKs. Straight before her, four feet away, on a black tripod and focused directly on her was a video camera.

The one with the whip bent to look through the camera, moved it slightly. "Now," he said, "what is your name?"

"Who are you?"

His wrist twitched; the tail of the whip slid back and forth across the concrete floor. "Tell us your name."

"Isabelle. Palmieri."

"Who are you?"

"Correspondent. *The Independent*."

"What is your real job?"

"That is my real job."

"*Why* are you lying to us? Do you think we don't know that your boss at MI6 is Simon Etheridge, that even at the so-called *Independent* they know you're a spy? And you live like a whore with that American we've just killed —"

It was like a knife. Jack please don't be dead. They're only saying this, to make me break. "Show me a photo."

"Photo?"

"Of his body. Then I believe you."

"He was shot from a distance. We do not have a body."

"Liar." She waited for the whip but its tip just lay there on the floor, twitching.

The man with the whip nodded to the others, who retied the blindfold round her eyes and gagged her. "We do not really need your information about MI6," he said. "Much better, we are going to use you as a lesson. In an hour and forty-two minutes I will hold your severed head up before this camera. We will prop your eyes open so they look into the camera, into the eyes of millions of people around the world on social media – as you call it. And we will promise the same fate to infidels worldwide, Shiites and foreigners both." He caressed the side of her face with the whip handle. "Everyone will listen."

"If you need to excrete," another said, "say so now. It's disgusting when it happens after we cut off your head."

Her body was intense, alive, nauseous, like a wire. But maybe a way to escape? Yes, she told herself. Anything is possible. "I need to."

"Filthy woman," one said as he untied her wrists and ankles and led her blindfolded from the room left down a short corridor into a stinking closet, its floor covered in feces and urine. "Shit here anywhere," he said. "They all do, before we kill them."

Liberation

I N THE KORAN liberation is freedom from non-belief. From the mind, from doubt. Giving oneself fully to Allah. Knowing that *allahu akhbar* – God is greater than any human comprehension.

So how do they think, Jack tried to imagine, these guys who took her? If anyone took her. If she's not dead.

It's their total submission to their own belief. There was no way he could reach them. No way to *imagine* them.

Al-Qaeda, the Taliban, Hezbollah, the Islamic Brotherhood, Fatah, Hamas, Boko Haram, Al-Shebaab, the endless slaughter in Syria, the vast Islamic conflict and hatred of all else.

To not value life. To hate it.

It was useless. He sat cross-legged on the on the grimy roof, hands cupped over his ears listening to the voices in the garage discussing old debts and battles, servant girls, imams and enemies.

"Another one comes," Darius said.

It was a dark-camouflaged Hummer making Jack think for an instant it was American till it stopped in the middle of the street and two men in balaclavas, tan shirts and khaki pants got out and went into the garage.

From the mike came a rumble of voices deferentially greeting the newcomers. One of the two newcomers had a loud sharp voice that seemed to humble the others even further. "As you know the Shiites are massing against us. When the Americans are gone they will rise up to kill us. Already the Shiite Prime Minister is planning this."

"We must drive them out," a voice called. "To Iran. Let them swim the Gulf."

"We must be ready."

"So what has this to do with this woman spy?"

"It has much to do. To cut her throat in front of the world will bring us much awareness. Visibility –"

"Is that a good thing?" an older man called.

"More importantly, it brings us millions of dollars from our friends in Saudi Arabia, Qatar, Yemen, all those places."

"Every time we cut a throat," the other newcomer said, "the money pours in."

"With it we buy what we need to deal with the Shiites."

"First the Shiites," someone said, "Then the whites."

"Like the old saying goes, *First Saturday, then Sunday.*" *First we kill the Jews*, it meant. *Then the Christians.*

"But cannot we get the same money," a new voice broke in, "from ransom?"

"People will pay much more for someone's death," the first newcomer said, "than their life."

"Perhaps, however, we might wait to see how much they offer?"

"The new rules they are saying in London and Washington is do not pay ransom."

"Then we must make some films showing how unfortunate she is, how she is suffering. Put them out on this internet you love so much. The money will come."

"Unfortunately she's not in a secure place... there isn't

time. Because of who she is we must assume all our enemies are looking for her. So we can't risk a transfer to a safer place."

The conversation turned to neighborhood issues, who was not living correctly and needed to be punished, what bakery was charging too much, who was to offer his daughter to whom and for what in return, which books could be read by the children when there would be schools. How to get more weapons and how to pay for them.

"If we go in," Jack told Simon and Feist, "we can get these two new guys. They know where she is."

"We'll have to kill them, Jack," Simon said.

"We can follow them," Feist said. "We'll put a drone over the garage – I'm doing that now, will let you know –"

"Hold tight, Jack," Simon said. "If the Hummer leaves can you keep up with him?"

"On the Vespa? No."

Hunched over the listening device, Darius waved to him. "Hold on, Simon," Jack said.

"They are deciding," Darius whispered.

"What? *What!*"

"To kill her."

Jack grabbed an earbud. "I thought it was agreed, no?" someone was saying.

The voices rose and fell, argumentative, declarative, sardonic, amid coughing and spitting. "For you, then," said one of the two new voices, "it is decided, yes?"

"We agree," an old man answered, "it is wiser to execute her now. For the money."

"When?"

"Now."

"It shall be done," the newcomer said.

"Film it well."

"Don't worry. We know how to do this."

"Goodbye, then," another said, "*Ma'as salaama*."

"Peace be with you all," the old man called. "Until we meet again."

THE VESPA WOULDN'T START. He tried twisting the three wires he'd cut but nothing worked. He pushed the bike, running hard, but it wouldn't catch. An old gray Peugeot was picking its way around potholes as it came toward him down the street. When it came beside him he pulled his pistol on the driver and yanked him out of the car. "Trade," he nodded at the Vespa. "Where do you live? If I can I will bring back your car."

The man gave him a tired, frightened look. "Here in this street."

Darius ran up. "I have the ears. I'm going with you."

Jack backed the Peugeot fast up the street and pulled round just as the dark camo Hummer rolled by, a black-masked face staring out the passenger window.

"We must stay back," Darius said. "Or they spot us."

The Hummer turned left onto the boulevard and began to accelerate away from them. Jack handed Darius his phone. "Call the first number. Tell him we need the drone on Karade Dakhil, the dark camo Hummer. Give him the GPS."

"If you and I go in on them," Darius said, "we have only two guns."

"If anybody goes in it's me. By myself."

"You are trying to save the person you love? Have we not had enough of sacrifices? Of course I'll go with you."

Jack wanted to cry, to break down in exhaustion. *I will not sleep*, he told her, *till I save you.*

SHE REMEMBERED way back in the early days with her father's big warm palm against her cheek, being enveloped in those strong sure arms smelling of hookah, cigars and raki. He was so kind and loving, his power so enormous... When he came into the room everyone turned with love and appreciation for this man who had done so much for everyone. When he could have gone with his family, as so many had, for relative safety in Paris, London or Los Angeles.

Dear Father was it worth it? Wouldn't it have been better to have survived somewhere in the Cotswolds or Connecticut, having each other at the end of the day, being able to look into your loving brown mischievous eyes and know I am your beloved little girl? Your tortured death in a bloody basement room by the Ayatollah's thugs, what did that make better? For us, for Persia, your beloved land?

"Hey," one of her captors said. "You are a beautiful woman, no?" He ran his hands over her breasts, down between her thighs. "Perhaps I will fuck you when you're dead."

THE HUMMER swung fast off Karade Dakhil onto a dirty ramshackle street full of wrecked cars, piled stones, broken pipes, rusting wire and broken semis, a pale discolored mosque at the far end.

Part way down on the right was a great hole where a bomb had exploded, the shop walls smashed in, a bent, burned chassis upside down along one side. "Slow down!" Darius said. "This's a dead end."

Jack pulled the Peugeot over beside the bomb hole. In a puddle at the bottom a dead dog floated.

"They've stopped!" Darius said. "See, that house! They're going in!"

Isabelle was close; he could feel her. Feel her begging him to save her. "Let's walk down the street, one on each side –"

"They'll have guards, they'll see us."

Jack called Feist. "Put Simon on too."

"I'm here," Simon said moments later.

"It's a yellow two-story house with an overhanging balcony of the northeast side of this street part way off Karade Dakhil, can't see the name but you have the locate. There's a silver Mercedes and the Hummer out front. We followed the guys here who are going to kill her."

"When?"

"Now."

"We can't get there for twenty minutes."

"That's too late."

Silence on the other end. Then Simon's voice. "Do what you have to do, Jack."

It was the ultimate admission, the final defeat: you're going to die but there's no other way. "I'll keep you posted," Jack said.

"We're trying to locate you and will be there fast as we can."

"You stay here," Jack told Darius. "They'll need you to ID the house."

A frightened smile flashed over Darius' face. "You can't get in there alone."

"Two can't either." Jack gave him a quick nod, turned and walked fast along the street edge toward the yellow two-story building with overhanging balcony.

Culling the Infidels

THEY BENT HER HEAD over the tin bucket and tugged aside her hair so her neck was clear. Fingertips ran down her vertebrae... it seemed impossibly terrifying to her that these vertebrae would in a minute be sliced by the gleaming blade they'd held up to the camera.

He yanked up her head. "Look at the camera!"

She tried to focus on the shiny black eye with the red light. That would take pictures of her dying, and after she was dead. He yanked her head higher. "Say it!"

"Say what?" her voice was a whisper, a tremor.

"Tell them *allahu akhbar.*"

"You are proof there is no God."

"See," another voice said, "that is surely reason to kill her."

"It lacks twelve minutes," the one twisting her neck said. "Till high noon."

IF HE WAS KILLED he couldn't save her. Had to get her out before he died. Get her free then cut pursuit. Kill them all.

Crouched in his thin coat with the Makarov in his hand he walked past the door under the overhanging balcony. The door was steel with bolts in the top, middle and bottom. The picture window facing on the street was barred and the blinds shut. Down the far side was a narrow piss-stinking alley with a broken birdbath, a cracked plastic bucket, old pallets and a shiny hubcap, nettles and thistles that stuck to his jacket as he reached the back corner and peered round at the rear yard of gravel and bare grass. Two windows on each floor of the back wall, both barred and curtained. He glanced up: there were no drainpipes below the second floor; those windows were barred too.

A footstep on the far corner of the building. Jack raised his gun, his back against the wall.

The toe of a shoe appeared beyond the corner, a hand, a gun muzzle's black hole, the edge of a face. Jack tightened the trigger.

"Allah – it's you!" Darius whispered, came up to Jack.

"What are you –"

"Nothing going on out there – Feist, those guys, don't need me, can locate the Hummer. What are we doing?"

"Is the roof flat?"

"Think so."

"I climb your shoulders, can reach the drainpipe up there, if it holds can climb to the roof and if it's flat there has to a door, a trapdoor, anything."

"I should go." Darius' instant smile. "You're an old man."

"I can see it. In my head, Darius. How it will happen. If we're lucky." Jack glanced up. "I'll try to get back down inside, open up this back door... Lean back against the wall here, cup your hands and I climb up, stand on your shoulders..."

The drainpipe was nine inches too high. He slid back

down Darius, ran back the side alley for the cracked plastic bucket, set it upside down against the wall. "Climb this and I can reach it."

THE CAMERA WAS ON. What will I do when they bend my neck down? Or will they cut my throat first? It was a numb fog of terror, a dumb acceptance she was about to be murdered. She remembered an old photo of a man sitting at the side of a ditch full of bodies, a German officer pointing a Luger at his head. The last Jew in Vinnitsa, the photo was. She'd always wondered why the man didn't fight. Now she knew.

Every breath was sacred, every second.

HE PULLED HIMSELF hand over hand up the drainpipe feeling it lurch and stretch with his weight, trying to go fast before it broke and gasping reached the roof edge and pulled himself over and there in the middle of the roof was the trapdoor almost as he had imagined it.

It was thick plywood with asphalt over it and down the sides. Locked from inside. He clutched it in both hands and pulled with the ferocious strength of one whose beloved is dying and it ripped loose, a piece of the rim falling inside and clattering on the stairs.

A ladder was bolted to one side of the second floor wall beneath the trapdoor. He slid through the door shutting it above him and went down the ladder to the second floor. Four rooms, one at each corner, corridors between them so you could see through the end windows the lights of Baghdad.

No sound from the four rooms. He did not dare open any doors, instead descended silently to the first floor. Here was the corridor to the triple-locked front door, and going the other way to the door at the back.

Music, in the distance. No, from below. From the basement. Like a TV intro? Somebody living there? Who?

The back door had three locks also. There was no key. He checked the windows. No way to open them.

No way to see Darius, to tell him.

He listened atop the basement stairs then started down.

THE PAIN WILL BE BRIEF because the spinal nerve gets cut before the pain has time to transfer. Unless they do it slowly like they sometimes do.

Can I ask them do it quickly? No, that will make them go slower.

There is the blade. He is holding it up in the air so the others can see, shows it lovingly to the camera. "This is what she will feel," he is saying "The last thing she will feel." And from the sound of his voice you know that under his mask he's smiling.

How could anyone be like this?

I've been a fool to think people good.

He is what we *are*.

I'm not like that. Jack isn't. My family. All our people.

I don't want to die.

Please help me God. Please help me.

When my head is being held up to the camera, my eyes pulled open, the blood from my brain filling the tin bucket, what will I see? Will I know what has happened?

Please God save me.

AT THE BOTTOM of the stairs was a basement with each room separated by a corridor. A voice coming from inside one door. A man quoting the Koran, "On the day of culling the infidels from the true believers, on that day thou shalt see the unjust in great terror!"

The door handle turned easily. The room was low and

wide. A camera on a tripod under the center light and person sitting before it.

Isabelle.

Behind her three men in balaclavas, one with a scimitar in his hand. "We seek only justice," he was saying into the camera.

A man behind the door swung an arm down on Jack's gun but he ducked and swung it into the man's face knocking him down then shot the three men in balaclavas one by one, all in less than two seconds as they were turning and raising their guns. He shot the man behind the door and slid along the back wall but could see no one else.

He ran to her and with the scimitar cut her bindings. "You," she said, "oh God *you*."

"Let's go. Fast. Fast."

She stood leaning against him. He kissed her brow, tasting the dry blood. "Let's go!"

"Why so fast?" A man said in English from the shadows behind them. "Put down the gun. No, don't try to turn, just drop the gun, kick it behind you."

Jack knelt and dropped the gun. With his heel he kicked it back toward the man. "A Makarov," the man said. "How interesting."

"Let her go," Jack said, "and I'll tell you whatever you need to know –"

"You have just murdered four young true believers. For that I will kill her first, then you."

Jack remembered knowing how it would happen, that *this* was not a part of it.

"Stand in the center," the man said. "In front of the camera. Both of you."

When the gun fired Jack shoved her aside and leaped at the man but he was already down, his head twisted up in a last cry of pain, Darius standing over him.

"Jesus," Jack said. "Jesus Christ." He pulled Isabelle to his feet hugging her. "Let's go! Go! Go!"

Darius drove while Jack called Simon and Feist. "You have her *oh my God!*" Simon screamed.

She snatched the phone. "Simon? It's me! It's me! Jack saved me. And you!" she said to Darius.

"Your man," Jack told Feist. "Your man Darius saved us."

"Get to the Embassy, the Hospital," Feist said. "Fast as you can. We'll notify the gate, have the doctors ready. Don't stop for anything."

Étoile du Monde

WAR'S ANTIDOTE, of course, is love. Yet love engenders war. He glanced at Isabelle dozing in the first class seat beside him, white cloud reflections flitting across her still-bruised face. The docs had wanted her to stay in Baghdad longer but after five days they'd grabbed a Home Office jet to Amman then this Royal Jordanian nonstop to Paris.

What had it been all about, he asked himself, this life of endless war?

Beyond the plexiglas the white clouds below the plane extended like endless fields of snow – *sastrugi*, the Japanese called them, the wind patterns in the snow. He'd loved them as a boy in Maine walking on snow-clad Cobbossee Lake, the sense of infinite mystery he could explore forever.

But had he ever succeeded at comprehending, living in, this mystery?

To do that you need to be free. Free of lies and desperation. And the best way to be free is to help each other to be free. To follow the path with heart.

Therefore teach freedom, and the world will be healed.

Each person who learned to be more free was like a prisoner set loose who would help free others too.

Isabelle stirred, took his hand. "I was dreaming we were in El Cheltén. You were crossing a stream and got your feet wet."

It made him think of Afghanistan, crossing the stepping stone bridge the night when he'd been shot in the shoulder and Bandit had been killed trying to save him. And then he'd been taken to Kabul and Sophie had saved him. And he'd killed her lover and taken her and her children to New York to die in the falling towers.

It was beyond belief.

He looked out the window. Down there somewhere below the white clouds was Greece, birthplace of western wisdom. Soon would come Rome, birthplace of the modern mind. Then Paris, étoile *du monde*.

The feedback is happiness. That's how you know you're free.

PARIS SPARKLED in late afternoon sun, the Eiffel Tower gilded under a bright blue sky, the Seine a jade serpent undulating down the middle of this magic city.

They took a taxi from CDG to the Home Office safe house on rue St. Bernard in the 11th Arrondissement. "I'm so happy to be back," he said, watching the cavalcade of stone buildings, cafés, random streets, hurrying people and busy cars flash past. "In all my life, every time I've left France I didn't want to. And every time I return I'm filled with joy. How can that be? How can anything be so special?"

"Yet you lived here with Sophie, God bless her – it doesn't give you sorrow?"

"And Leo too." The thought was like a knife in his

heart; fourteen years later he could still twist it any time he wanted.

Paris the capital of the world, étoile *du monde*, where joy and beauty came together with a deep understanding of life. Of what mattered: love, wisdom, fun, food, sex, family, history – and the great ideas that had made the western world – all wrapped up in one city.

"Tonight," she said, "where shall we go to dinner?"

He looked at her thoughtfully. "You're still a little beat up – you want to?"

She smiled, and in her smile all the beauty of their lives together was mirrored – and on top of that he'd saved her from sure death, impossibly saved her. "If we stay in the apartment," she said, "I'm going to have to eat your cooking."

There was a nice little café on rue de Charonne, he remembered, an easy walk from the apartment. "What will you have?"

She thought a moment. "Anything French would be wonderful...maybe *paté, foie gras, a salade noisettes...* then just a *steak frites*, how could anything be better than that? And for sure a *chocolat liegeois* for dessert..."

"And to drink, Madame?"

"Ah, what joy French wine, to be able to go anywhere and choose something magnificent, not expensive, just delicious, fulfilling, memorable, the deep taste of the soil of France..."

"You didn't say what kind –"

"Any *Côtes du Rhone*, just simple and beautiful."

His heart overflowed, with Isabelle, with Paris, with the joy of finally being free. Simple and beautiful. Safe.

They squeezed with their bags into the apartment building's tiny elevator and took it to the third floor.

It was simple too, the apartment, a living room, dining room and kitchen, two bedrooms, a vase of white roses on the table the Home Office staff had put there, a fresh baguette, a bottle of Saint-Émilion and a round of brie on the counter, a Saint-Véran in the refrigerator. "God bless Home Office," she said. "All the necessities of life."

While she showered he sat on the leather sofa in the living room and called his old friend Max Ricard at DGSE, La Direction Générale de la Sécurité Extérieure. "*Alors, vieux salaud*," he said, "*je suis de retour.*" Hey, you old bastard, I'm back.

"*Toi,*" Ricard said. "*Qu'est-ce que tu fous ici?*" What the fuck are you doing here?

"It's great to hear your voice. Have you stopped smoking?"

"Have you stopped fucking?"

He told Ricard briefly about Baghdad, what had happened to Isabelle, that she'd been saved and now they were out for good. "No more damn terrorists," he added.

"That's like saying no more taking a shit."

"You guys still in good shape?"

"Sure. We've got the worst president in history, a Socialist who thinks all problems with the Muslims are due to evils on our part."

"I remember you said that years ago, when the Arabs were bombing the Metro."

"It was true then too, another Socialist president blaming his own country because a group of fanatics hated us."

"Same with us. Obama won't even use the word *Islamic* no matter how many times they attack us."

"He was CIA, Obama was, back in Pakistan, between college and law school."

"We're not supposed to admit that."

"Well now France has a foreign minister who says that for young French Arabs to join ISIS is not a crime." Ricard coughed, raspy. "And an attorney general says it's understandable that young Muslims hate this country."

"Of course they do – you give them free housing, education, health care, welfare even if they're illegal immigrants. No wonder they hate you."

"The general idea is that we're responsible for everything wrong that goes on in their dysfunctional lives. They won't go to school because it offends their Islamic culture, then they're furious when they can't get a job… you know all this."

"*Plus* ça *change…*"

"Get this – I recently asked a Socialist minister, a guy close to the President, supposing a group of terrorists kidnapped your family and were going to kill them in twenty-four hours?"

"Max, that's what I've just *been* through."

"And I added, but you've captured one of the terrorists, and if you torture him he'll reveal where your family is and they'll be saved. So would you do it?"

"Of course he said yes…"

"He said no."

"He said no?" It was incomprehensible. That a man would sacrifice his own wife and children. Jack was at a loss for words.

"He said France doesn't lower its morals to save one family. So I said, supposing you could stop a terrorist plot, save hundreds of people if you just torture this one guy?"

"Don't tell me."

"He said no."

"He's saying hundreds of people must die to protect

his little PC morality?"

Ricard coughed again. "When are we ever going to be free of this?"

"Like I just said, I've done my part. *I'm* free of it."

"Of course," Ricard said mildly.

"We should get together sometime, a glass of wine somewhere? I'd like you and Isabelle to meet."

"Things are rather hot lately," Ricard said in his raspy voice. "Lots of bad static."

Jack felt himself tense. "Who from?"

"Something from Ankara, saying trouble's on the way. Your people too, some serious warnings. About some guy named Abdelhamid Abaaoud, back from Syria through Belgium."

"Can I come by, sometime, we can chat about it if you like?"

"Eight o'clock tomorrow?"

That was early; Jack had been looking forward to sleeping late. Getting slowly reacquainted with life. "I'll be there."

He killed his phone and glanced out the window at the early evening sky between the stone buildings. For Ricard to have wanted him there so quickly meant it was something bad.

But I'm out of it, he told himself. Forever. Following the path with heart.

While Isabelle took a nap he walked the nearby streets, inhaling the lovely odors of coffee and fresh bread, the early evening sidewalks filled with people headed home, beautiful women in revealing clothes, children eating pastries with one hand as they held a parent's hand in the other, teenagers chasing each other and laughing, an old man in a white raincoat smiling at them as they ran past, the ancient buildings leaning over them as if protective.

He couldn't inhale it all, see it all, feel it all – it was too much. *I'm home*, he realized, not knowing why.

Maybe he and she wouldn't go back to Argentina. Maybe stay here... raise their child in France? There was no more beautiful place on earth... Where else on earth was the joy of living more deeply celebrated, the brilliance of ideas, the passions of love and nature?

It was eight-thirty when they sat down at a table on the sidewalk in front of *La Belle Équipe*. "It's so warm tonight." She squeezed his hand. "In mid-November, to be sitting outside in Paris – can you beat it?"

To begin, he asked the beautiful blonde laughing waitress for two *kirs*, that wonderful drink of cassis and white wine, and a bowl of the little black olives from Nyon, then a bottle of rosé de Provence. "A glass of wine, a crust of bread," Isabelle smiled, "and you."

The nap had done her good; with every hour her bruises seemed to fade, her terror diminish. She had gone through pure horror at the hands of her ISIS kidnappers, had faced death at any instant. Tough as she was, he knew, the shock, terror and PTSD would be with her always.

"I'm not having any of that," she'd told him. "I'm *not* going to tolerate it."

"That's wonderful, love," he'd answered. But you don't decide *not* to suffer. You just suffer terribly and pretend you don't. As he had for so many years since Sophie and the kids had died in the blazing and collapsing North Tower.

Now it was over. Now they could heal. The baby growing inside her, the docs in Baghdad had said, was doing fine. We're going to build a new life.

"It was a movie," she said. "*La Belle Équipe*."

He glanced at the name over the door, gave her a questioning look.

"In the 1930s. Five guys out of work win the lottery. Instead of splitting the money they decide to buy a bar, fix it up and run it."

"Sounds like fun."

"Pretty soon they're not getting along, some of them bail out, the last two guys are in love with the same woman..."

"*That's* never happened before."

"So in the end one of them kills the other."

"*That's* never happened either."

"But here's what's interesting: the Socialists were running the government and didn't like the ending, so they made the producers change it to the two guys deciding that their friendship was more important than the girl... And the movie was a flop."

"Served them right," he laughed. "How you know all this?"

"I'm a journalist, remember?"

"So I'm told." He snuggled his shoulders into the warmth from the heater overhead. He glanced through the plate glass windows at the restaurant's interior of bare bricks and wood-framed mirrors, the tables of happy people eating, drinking wine, talking, expostulating, loving... "Only the French," he said, "turn pleasure into a religion."

She smiled. "What other religion should there be?"

"I called Max Ricard today, while you were sleeping," he said quietly so no one else could hear. "He's worried, expecting something to hit but they don't know where... Ankara and Home Office have both sent warnings, nobody's sure..."

"Fuck the Muslims," she said. "I'm so tired of their homicidal repressive religion."

"Probably they are too."

"Imagine, telling people they have to totally submit to the nutty rantings of some woman-hating desert-maddened murderer from the seventh century? What's wrong with their heads?"

"We've been through all that," he said. "It's over."

"Not for the poor people in Syria it's not."

"Nor anywhere else in the Middle East, for that matter." But it was GW Bush, Cheney, Powell, he wanted to remind her, Rumsfeld and all those other war criminals who'd killed a million Iraqis and five thousand Americans, and created ISIS with their evil lies about Weapons of Mass Destruction... and Bush's father before them who'd enticed the Iraqis into invading Kuwait then slaughtered them by the hundreds of thousands... All for oil, power and ego. And the most amazing thing is that they weren't in jail because of it.

"I'm done with it," he repeated. "Let somebody else take over."

"And the twenty-eight pages? You intend to forget about them?"

"If forty-six Senators from both parties can't get Obama to release them, even though he promised he would, what can we do?"

"Even if they have *incontrovertible evidence* that the Saudis planned and financed 9/11, even their ambassador to the US? And that they've been financing ISIS, the Taliban, all those insane Islamic bastards ever since?"

He remembered the dream she'd had on the airplane from Amman, of him stepping in a stream and getting his feet wet. Like years ago in the Afghanistan mountains, crossing the stepping stone bridge when he'd been shot in the shoulder and Bandit had been killed. It seemed so strange, that by being shot he'd met Sophie, whose lover he then unknowingly helped to kill, and later he and she had fallen in love in Paris and he'd raised the son of the man he'd helped to kill. And even after Sophie had known this she'd stayed with him.

And he'd taken them from Paris to New York and their deaths.

Now Isabelle and he were in Paris. Was anywhere safe?

"Yeah," he repeated. "I'm done with it."

The beautiful blonde laughing waitress brought them delicious simple food, *rillettes*, *foie gras* in salad, *steak frites* for Isabelle, *magret de canard* for him, a bottle of magnificent Gigondas – "how can anything so inexpensive," Isabelle said, "be so delicious?"

"It's France," he said. "That's the reason."

But something felt weird. Out of place. By habit he scanned the passing pedestrians – laughing couples hand in hand, an old man with a wispy beard, a little girl walking a black poodle, an ancient limping Chinese woman, a kid on a skateboard.

It bothered him, this *something*; he wished he'd brought a sidearm, but everything had seemed so peaceful. And anyway Home Office didn't want him carrying a gun in Paris. He sipped his wine, the raw ancient roots of Provence...

A black Seat slowed as it came down the street. "Isabelle!" he yelled.

Combat

AN AK BARREL out the Seat's window, an Arab face of grinning hatred, a blasting muzzle as Jack leaped across the table knocking Isabelle to the sidewalk and covered her with his body amid the hideous twanging hammer of bullets and smashing glass and screams and clatter of chairs and tables crashing and the howl of the Kalashnikov and awful whap of bullets into flesh as people tumbled crying, it couldn't be, this thing, he'd left this all behind.

But now the moans of agony, the tears, the sudden stunned silence of the newly dead.

He checked that Isabelle was safe and ran down the street after the fleeing Seat but it was gone, no man can outrun a speeding car.

The beautiful blonde laughing waitress lay on the sidewalk in a widening lake of blood, Isabelle hugging her and trying to plug the huge hole in her chest. "Hold on," Isabelle was saying to her in French, "help is coming. Hold on, darling, hold on…"

Another young woman cradling the body of a tall

black man in a blue track suit, people collapsed on their tables as if sleeping. Among the pile of toppled dead a man in a leather jacket against a wall, one leg still twitching. The silence, the shattered silence of the dead. And then the screams and anguish, of Heaven turned to Hell.

He fell on streams of blood and scrambled to her. "You're okay?"

"Fuck yes."

He ran from one victim to the next in an insane triage, who could he save and who was already gone.

There were so few to save.

AN EXPLOSION somewhere near made him run into the street reaching frantically for the gun he didn't have. It could have been anything, that dull thud, hard to locate over the rumble of traffic in nearby streets, the distant howl of police cars and ambulances, blood squelching in his shoes, the cries of the hurt and dying.

Baghdad again, the World Trade Center, Fallujah, Beirut, London, Damascus, Madrid, Tunisia, Brussels, Kabul. He had no gun and there was nothing he could do but try to help those whose lives were pumping out of them in pools of darkness.

When the police came an officer posted a few men and told him the rest couldn't stay; there was a huge attack elsewhere, Bataclan, the famous concert hall. "It's war," he said, fury in his eyes.

Jack told him who he was. "Give me a gun, I'm going with you."

"Come," the officer said, "but I don't have an extra gun."

"No worry," Jack grimaced. "DGSE will give me one

when we get there."

He rode in the back of the police car as it screamed through the streets toward Boulevard Voltaire and the Bataclan, the radio a cacophony of horrified voices, new attacks, commanders trying to understand where to direct their men, where to send ambulances, how to stop the next bloodbath before it started.

The Bataclan was a bomb scene in Baghdad. The GIGN, France's anti-terrorist commandos, had it locked down, were working their way foot by foot through a hail of bullets toward the doors.

"Glad you're here," Max Ricard said when Jack found him with a radio in one hand and a FAMAS rifle in the other.

For hours he did what he could, military first aid to the wounded, and covered the dead. Pieces of flesh lay everywhere amid exploded steel and concrete, spent cartridges, in rivers of blood. He called Isabelle; she had quit *La Belle Équipe* when there was no longer anything she could do.

He was so angry and sorrowed he couldn't breathe, reminded himself not to be furious now: be ruthless later, when it counted.

It was 04:35 when he left the blood-soaked streets outside the Bataclan and walked the aching lonely avenues back to the Home Office safe house where Isabelle had returned two hours before.

His eyes were blurred; it wasn't teargas, it was sorrow. Sorrow for the poor happy innocent people who had died this night, the hundreds handicapped for life. He hadn't cried in fourteen years – not since the night of 9/11 when he understood that Sophie, Leo and Sarah were dead. Now he couldn't stop crying; it stunned him that his body held so many tears.

France at war again, Europe too, after seventy years of peace. The entire modern world against the enemies of civilization, against ISIS and the Saudis, Qataris and other Wahhabis. But a modern world handicapped by its own "good thinkers" – those who believed, as Max Ricard had described them long ago, that all the crimes of Islam were due to evils on civilization's part. That Islam which enslaved nearly a billion women, slaughtered indiscriminately for the sin of not being Islamic, and embraced a worldview that would have sickened even a medieval European – these good thinkers who believed that this schizophrenic homicidal religion was actually tolerable and good.

Isabelle was sitting in a chair by the window watching the Paris night fade to day. He took off his bloody clothes and sat beside her, took her hand.

"How many?" she said.

"Maybe a hundred dead. Another three hundred severely wounded."

"Oh Jesus Christ."

"How many there?"

"At *La Belle Équipe*? Nineteen dead, another fifty wounded."

"Our waitress?"

"She died in my arms. Just before her husband got there."

The tears poured again from his eyes, down his cheeks and neck. He couldn't stop them. "Oh Jesus fucking Christ."

"I begged her to stay with us, stay with us. The look in her eyes..." Isabelle was crying too, trying not to choke. "When I saw she was going I told her I'd always be with her, always love her, and if there is another side I'll meet up with her there when I come…"

They sat in silence for a while. "We can't go back to Argentina," he said.

"Of course not." She squeezed his hand. "Our battle is here."

"I'm meeting Max tomorrow. We're going to build a stronger link between Home Office, the Russians and the French –"

"Obama's not going to like that."

"He'll be gone soon, thank God."

"I've talked to London. They want me here."

"Londonistan…"

"Maybe we can stop that, turn it around?"

"The Islamic State of the former Great Britain?"

"Jack, we have to do what we can."

Early day was turning the eastern sky blood red above the still-dark buildings. He thought of the hundreds of horribly injured in Paris hospitals, the frenzied doctors and nurses, the agonized families.

No way they could return to Patagonia. Life is too short and we have to do what we can to make a better world. For those who live to protect others, to protect a free way of life, to defend life itself, there is never retirement, never the option to walk away. *We can walk away when we're dead. Not till then.*

There is no greater humanity, it was clear, than to protect life. To protect liberty and justice, to fight for the good. To seek out evil and annihilate it, wherever it is found.

It didn't matter that evil is hard to define.

You know it when you see it.

He'd always sought the path with heart, the greatest

good. Risked his life so many times for peace, so that everyone could live in happiness. In peace.

But now he understood it once again: when enemies attack you, peace is a dream.

And combat is the path with heart.

THE END

The first chapter of
HOLY WAR

The best-selling novel from Mike Bond set in the wars of Lebanon and Syria, and the politics, love affairs, and arms deals behind them.

An American spy, a French commando, a Hezbollah terrorist and a Palestinian woman guerrilla all cross paths on the deadly streets and fierce deserts of the Middle East.

The Battle of Beirut is worse than Hell, an irrational maelstrom of implacable hatreds and frantic love affairs, of inconceivable terrors and moments of ecstasy, of screaming bombs, exploding shells, crashing buildings, sniper battles, and deadly ambushes. Neill, a war correspondent on a secret mission for Britain's MI6 intelligence agency, is trying to find Mohammed, a Hezbollah terrorist leader who might stop the slaughter and destruction, if only Neill can find him.

André, a French commando, is also looking for Mohammed, to kill him in revenge for the death of his brother, blown up with over 400 US Marines and French paratroopers by Hezbollah. For Rosa, a remorseless and passionate Palestinian guerrilla, Mohammed is one of the few hopes for her people, and she will give her life to protect him. And for lovely Anne-Marie, André is the only one who can save her from Hell.

Based on the author's own experiences in the battles of Lebanon, Syria and the Middle East, *Holy War* has been praised for its portrayal of war and its journalistic and political realism, and for its evocative descriptions of men and women caught in a deadly crossfire.

"One of the best reads of 2014... A fast-paced, beautifully written, heart-breaking thriller." – NETGALLEY REVIEWS

1

THE TROUBLE'S Sylvie, Yves decided. How she's never happy with what I am, what I'm doing. Wants me home.

He stretched in his army cot, twisting his back to let the muscles flex up and down his shoulder blades. Shards of sharp blue through the sandbagged window. Another lovely day in the lovely Levant. Red-golden sun through the pines, the green hill sweeping down to the sea. Incense of cedars, salty cool wind, warm earth; *promise* in the fragrant air, the buzzing insects, the gulls crying over the waves.

Off duty. Luxury of nowhere to go and nothing to do. Nowhere to go but a sandbagged perimeter and sentried corridors, maybe a quick trip to town in an armored car, the machine gun nervously scanning, the driver watching through the hot slit for an RPG, some mad kid with a Molotov. *Vive la France*, damn you, for sending us here...

He rolled out of his cot and ambled down the corridor to the WC. Why do all urinals smell like Beirut? Ask the philosophers, he decided, the ones with all the answers. Yawning, scratching his overnight whiskers and under his arms, he wandered to the officers' mess, found a dirty cup and rinsed it, clamped fresh espresso into the machine, drew up and pulled down the handle, two streams of black gold dribbling into the cup.

Makes you feel better already. He filled the cup to the brim and stood by another window, peering through chinks in the sandbagged concrete blocks at the day growing bright blue. Sylvie would still be in bed, the Paris light gray through the blinds. He imagined waking beside her, her lovely sleepy smell, the roughness of her morning voice, the smoothness of her skin.

In Normandy, Papa would already be out in his garden, watering, picking on the weeds, Mama taking fresh *brioches* out of the oven, Papa coming in with a handful of onions and leeks, taking up his coffee cup in his big fist. André on maneuvers somewhere, playing at war. Trying to get stationed back here, where there's plenty of war. But none for *La France*, for the UN Multinational Force, impartially observing the slaughter. The United fucking Nations: you want to murder each other, we'll pay to watch.

He made a second cup, loitered back to his cot and slipped into his thongs, tossed a towel over his shoulders and headed for the showers. A thunderclap cracked, the floor lurched, shivered, the thunder louder. Christ, we've been hit, he thought, dropping the cup. He raced to his cot, snatched his FAMAS, the explosion shaking the sky, men yelling now, down below.

The earth was shaking, an earthquake; he raced up the stairs to the roof, smashed into a sentry coming down. "It's the Marines," the sentry screamed. "They've been hit! A bomb!"

From the roof he couldn't see the U.S. Marines' compound to the south, just a great billowing dark cloud. He raced downstairs to the radio room. Chevenet, the communications chief, was crouched speaking English then listening to the headset as he loaded his rifle. "A truck," he said, "somebody drove up in a truck. The whole building. *The whole fucking building*!"

Yves sprinted down the corridor and down the stairs. "Battle stations!" he screamed. "*Battle stations*!" Pumping a round into the FAMAS he dashed across the lobby into the parking area. Dark smoke filled the sky. "They hit the Marines!" he yelled to the sentries at the gate. "A big truck!"

A Mercedes truck, the kind used to collect rubbish from the embattled streets of Beirut, geared down and swung into the parking lot, snapped the gate barrier and accelerated toward him. A ton of *plastique* inside it, he realized, fired from the waist exploding the windshield but the driver had ducked, the truck's grille huge in Yves' face as shot for the engine now, the distributor cap on the right side, the plugs, the fuel pump. It was too late, the truck would have them. His heart broke in frantic agony for the men inside, the men who would be trapped, crushed to death, the Paras, *fleur de la France*, his beloved brothers. The universe congealed, shrank to an atom and blew apart, reducing him to tiny chunks of blood and bone, never to be found.

CPSIA information can be obtained
at www.ICGtesting.com
Printed in the USA
LVOW11s1618040417
529578LV00003B/742/P